Let Me Lead

- How long have you wanted to write?
- Characters : how do you do it?
  Always someone you know?
  begin?

  April- Aphia then?
   - how much write?
   is true another
  Vesse - James one?

- Story
  - true / created

- Italics
- Family - true
- liberty ?
- Angel ?
- Rape ?

Let Me Lead

Kathleen Sutton

Book Design & Production
Columbus Publishing Lab
www.ColumbusPublishingLab.com

Print ISBN 978-1-63337-046-3
E-book ISBN 978-1-63337-047-0

Printed in the United States of America
1 3 5 7 9 10 8 6 4 2

Dedicated to my sweet daughter—my inspiration, my pain, my joy, my constant reminder that life is short. I miss you.

Monday, November 18

Christine O'Garra stood quietly beside her husband watching the pain pull at his shoulders, forcing his back to curve. Too proud to yield to his weakened body, he had stood for the first two hours. Now, reluctantly, he accepted a chair from their pastor then waved the back of his dismissive hand at Christine as she helped him settle. The slight twist at his mouth meant he was struggling to control his emotions, fighting back tears. In their thirty-four years of marriage, she had never seen him quite so bullheaded.

"I'm so sorry for your loss," said the next woman in line.

Seth peered up at the unknown woman as he had for the many who had come before her, had said the same thing as they shuffled past. His hand lifted briefly then dropped to his lap. The woman merely smiled at Christine, teary-eyed, before moving toward the display of photos—photos of April. "Rose White," Seth had called her, pale as snow, cameo-like.

Donavin, the best man at their long-ago wedding and Seth's work colleague over the years, stood watching from across the room. His eyes met hers and once again his thoughtful proposal was delivered to her with a slight tilt to his head. Christine leaned over and whispered, "Donavin offered to take you home an hour ago. He's still here waiting. People will understand."

She watched Seth struggle for the energy to speak.

"I'm not...leaving you...here alone." His eyes locked onto hers. In hospice for a week, yet those eyes maintained the love-filled strength she had always seen there—silent and resolute.

Christine sighed, but noticed with some relief that there really was an end to the line—thirty, maybe only twenty-five more people. A thin-voiced man bent over Seth and began a deep one-way conversation. She took that moment to leave her post, finally, to examine the photos herself. Mounds of white roses lay on the tables that held the display her sisters had made. It beautifully captured her daughter through the years: a laughing baby, a shy girl, a slender young woman.

Christine placed her finger on a photo of a twelve-year-old April and her big brother, Jesse. His nearly grown kitten, Clover, was cradled comfortably in Jesse's arms. She smiled, recalling that April had shaved the fur off the last two inches of Clover's tail soon after the photo was taken. Jesse had been absolutely furious at the sight of the naked pink tail tip flicking from side to side like a fat worm gyrating a belly dance. Christine recalled struggling to maintain a straight face while admonishing her mischievous daughter and comforting her sobbing, very sensitive son. Jesse felt everything to the core. She smiled now, still wondering how April had accomplished the feat without leaving even a scratch on the cat. She longed to be back there, face to face with her children that day, or any day, they had been together.

She peered at the photo again and poked at the cat's likeness. In a few months, it would be just old Clover and her in a very quiet house. She plucked a rose from the table, and held it to her face briefly before touching the blossom to a recent likeness of her beautiful daughter.

Her two sisters approached with the requested tissue box, interrupting her reminiscing. They had dropped everything, and traveled hundreds of miles to come. She smiled weakly at them.

"Hey, how are you holding up?" Alice asked. She too was assessing the line.

Christine nodded, but words didn't come. There was no good answer.

"The funeral director told us that April's ashes can be picked up early next week," Janice said quietly.

Christine flinched at the fleeting thought to add this to her list of errands: drop off the dry cleaning, buy stamps at the post office, pick up your daughter's ashes from the funeral home… She glanced over at Seth whose hand was being firmly held by their pastor.

"Would you take my place here for just a bit?" Christine asked. "I don't recognize anyone in the rest of the line. Just need a little break." Her sisters hugged her in turn, and Christine made her way to the bathroom, locking herself in a stall. She just stood there quietly.

The last few years had been all April. Doctors said she was too young to have fibromyalgia, but there it was—part of her, part of them all. After years of overwhelming pain, depression crept in and silently crushed her spirit, then slowly, her body. Christine and Seth had to practically drag April to the car to visit the next doctor, the next therapist, or the next outright quack who sold them a glimmer of hope. For years, they had watched their daughter die by the day. Seth would bring her a dozen roses every Friday. Near the end, white roses were the only thing that made April smile. Seth insisted she not be told about his cancer, fearing the news would put an end to her smiles altogether.

April stopped her pain Friday morning. Christine had been called out of a meeting at work to find an uneasy sheriff's deputy in the hallway. He wasn't quick enough to prevent her collapse and Christine could remember vividly the color and smell of polished linoleum, cold and smooth against her cheek. Now she stood in the bathroom of a funeral home, locked in a stall with a rose and her thoughts. Although she could still smell that floor, she couldn't recall planning this memorial service. Who had selected the music, the scripture, and the flowers that lay at the sweet photo display? When? As Christine stood pondering, two snowy rose petals released in her hand.

"I just can't believe that girl killed herself," a woman's voice said over the rush of water at the sink.

"Well, Seth and Christine always seemed nice enough, but they were too strict with those kids. Jesse finally left—didn't even come today," another retorted over the sound of towels being yanked free. "I'm not saying it's their fault, but they were always so proper, textbook perfect—always expected those kids to be perfect too."

"And Seth looks terrible. Knowing him, he probably thought he could demand the cancer leave—just make himself get healthy again. I guess Christine O'Garra is finding out life isn't perfect, not even hers, poor thing." The door outside swished open, whispered closed—leaving Christine in deafening silence.

She clutched the white head of the rose in her fist, crushed it tightly, then slowly relaxed. Petals fluttered to the floor. Christine finally emerged, washed her swollen face and made her way back to the people who had gathered to support her. It was the right thing to do.

Twenty months later…

Tuesday, July 7
Christine: Teasing Liberty

"Complaint is the largest tribute heaven receives,
and the sincerest part of our devotion."

— Jonathan Swift

Ordinarily, the shooting range target was a three-ringed circle. Today it was man-shaped, and the satisfaction Christine experienced by firing at it surprised and frightened her. The last three rounds were pulled through tears. This fierce, nearly violent, release was a foreign experience to her, a peace-loving woman who rarely allowed anger to surface. Normally, Christine had control of her thoughts, and therefore her emotions, but today her mind was poking beneath the surface pain at how little she had to show for all her years of effort. Worse, it seemed life was now nothing more than a series of replayed memories—some welcome, many painful. A scent, a touch, a sound was often enough to engulf her. This gloomy morning, however, it was emotion itself prompting memories—hurtful and bitter.

The young man in the lane beside her reminded her of Jesse. That should have brought a wistful smile, but archived angry words came to mind as she recalled Seth's burly frame towering over their nineteen-year-old who had once again dragged himself home only to shower and sleep after being out all night. She wished she could call her son, just to hear his calm, low voice. Jesse, her sensitive child with an artist's heart, had drifted during his teen years.

She adjusted her ear protection, lifted the gun, aimed and fired. She tried again to pinpoint when Jesse left. First, he left emotionally, then physically. He didn't come home one night, and not the second night, or the third. Christine pulled the trigger three times for each of those sleepless nights; the anxious pain lingered even now. The fourth day, Jesse called to tell them he was in Seattle with friends and would be back in a couple weeks. A couple weeks became a couple months. She and Seth called, left messages that weren't returned. Jesse's phone number stopped working. They had no address, no information. Months went by between his brief, unsettling phone calls—weak snatches at a fading distant relationship. Christine had last talked to Jesse five years, two months, one week ago. No amount of searching had produced even a hint of his whereabouts. Her mother's heart, however, still couldn't define him as lost—only missing. She wondered if Jesse would return if he knew Seth was gone. Sometimes, late at night, she would listen to the one brief recording she had of her son's precious voice and let her tears fall into the soft darkness. *Perhaps I will tonight*, she thought as she emptied the brass shells from the gun's chamber.

Christine slowly reloaded. The gun had become an uninvited part of her. After being diagnosed as terminal, Seth had presented this .38 revolver to her as a gift—insisting she carry it at all times and use it if need be. She avoided a commitment, but he, of course, persisted. Once she finally agreed, he visibly relaxed, knowing she never broke her promises. He had given her two more guns before he died. Guns, of all things. This morning, as each bullet was slipped into a chamber, she forced herself to acknowledge the truth: she had lived for years silently angry at her husband—never questioning his unwavering decisions, never confronting him with her feelings. A sour resentment that hadn't fully surfaced when he was alive now wove through their relationship. Even so, she missed him terribly—his laugh, heavy footsteps throughout the house, the way he held his fork midair during meals and poked it her direction to emphasize a point he had made. Christine suddenly lifted the gun and quick-fired the entire load at the dark paper man.

She imagined her guardian angel, Liberty, pacing up and down the dusty firing range, shaking his head in disapproval at how she was misusing the firearm to discharge emotions. The angel's nose flared and his molten eyes flashed her direction. A guardian angel. Christine smiled at this lingering remnant of her childhood. Her grandmother had told her that every child had an angel, assigned by God. Soon after, Grandpa Steiner had given her a Mercury dime, and told her it was really Winged Liberty. To Christine, the face on the dime looked like an angel—a man angel. So she had secretly named her angel Liberty—a majestic male angel. His proud power would do things for her that she wasn't allowed to do herself. Liberty had faded away as she aged into adulthood, but now Christine brought her angel to mind whenever she wished. Except now, she tried to think of Liberty as strong, assertive, and female. Usually, she'd forget and Liberty was male again. Male or female, the angel was a faithful friend, a constant reminder of God's presence.

"Check my target for bullet holes while you're down there, Liberty," she thought aloud.

Christine's General Conference Mennonite family would be disturbed to know she had named her angel after an iconic symbol of American values. To them, first allegiance was reserved for God, not to country or its manmade concepts and patriotic symbols. The name Liberty, however, suited her angel because although a guardian, Liberty was also Christine's symbol of freedom. Liberty was permission—permission to fight for a better future, one she alone would chart. Although she had distanced herself from the Mennonite faith after high school, she was still learning to think beyond her childhood heritage, and now beyond the sheltered life under a protective husband. An old silver dime hung from Christine's key ring as a tangible reminder of God's presence and her freedom to choose—to try new things.

"Get out of the way, Liberty." She lifted the loaded gun, and took time to steady her trembling hand. With each pull of the trigger, she stated in a firm loud voice: "I will" BANG, "love" BANG, "my" BANG, "life" BANG, she paused briefly, "and I will not live in anger." BANG. The fifth and final bullet zipped well off target and echoed against the hillside as God's voice came to her.

I'm glad to hear it, Christine.

"Then help me be at peace."

I've given you everything you need to be at peace.

"Really? Where do I begin? I've got a long list of injustices to complain about."

At least you're talking to Me. And unlike most people, you're doing it honestly.

"Sometimes I feel like I no longer have a choice."

Everyone has a choice.

"I want my life back."

You can't live with purpose by walking backward.

"I don't see anything promising on the horizon."

Horizons are My job.

"I'm tired and angry."

At least you're no longer too angry to complain.

"Well, prepare to get an earful."

I'm always prepared.

Christine unloaded the spent shells from the cylinder, laid down the gun, and leaned heavily against the wooden ledge. She had spoken her words, loudly and with force. She didn't care; no one could possibly have heard. And His words weren't audible sounds. God's messages were more like having someone else's thoughts. This wasn't something she ever told anyone. People would think she'd finally gone insane if she told them she had actual conversations with God. *I've earned the right to go insane*, she thought.

Even though she had paid fifteen dollars for an hour of shooting not thirty minutes ago, Christine was done for the day. She gathered the spent brass shells from the rough board ledge and tossed them into a nearby five-gallon bucket. They tinkled, bell-like, against one another. One escaped the bucket, skittered across the rough cement and found a retreat along the dusty edge of browned grass. She tried to determine which shell was hers among the many others left there by previous shooters. Finally, she grabbed up a handful and threw them all in the bucket.

Both her canvas bag and purse tugged at her shoulder as she struggled to gather the gun cases under her arm. Inside the modest ranger station, several men were leaning heavily on the counter in typical manly socialization posture, bantering noisily. As she entered, they turned and delivered huddled stares, closed-mouthed. None bothered to move aside.

"Hey Tom, I'm ready to sign out," Christine said as she set her burdens on the rough cement at her feet. "Gotta get back to the house and finish unpacking."

Tom pulled the registration book out from under a man's unyielding elbow, then waved the group of men aside to flop it open in front of Christine. "You get everything moved in since I saw you last week?" Tom asked.

"Oh yes. My nephews and nieces came down to help. Freezer's full, too—brought me fresh butchered lamb and a dozen quart bags of early sweet corn. The day was more like a party than a move. I'm pretty well settled." Christine paused and checked her watch to capture the exact time for the record book. "I still can't believe I start a new job Monday, starting over at my age."

"Never too late to start over," Tom said simply.

"We could sure use the rain, but it looks like it's just going to miss us," Christine said to the entire group as she left. She smiled at herself. She was getting started at a lot of things, like talking to strange men.

Dark low clouds were rolling across the tree tops to the south, threatening to push up out of the big city and invade sleepy Boone County, Indiana, as she walked to her car. She suddenly staggered sideways to step on a feather fluttering amongst the gravel. She would have been mortified to know how much the awkward motion mimicked someone slightly drunk. Christine never drank, had never even tasted beer.

She twisted her shoe to thoroughly crush the feather into the dusty stones. "You should watch where you leave those things, Liberty." No answer returned. The angel never spoke. Teasing Liberty suddenly made her feel childish, and strangely guilty. But why should she feel guilty about having a bit of silly fun by teasing a make-believe angel? Destroying a wayward feather? Christine certainly needed some fun. After all, she would be spending the rest of her day alone, likely the rest of her life.

She parked behind the detached garage of the huge brick house. The house was not new to Christine, or to anyone else in Lebanon, Indiana, having stood proudly on Meridian Street since 1912. It had always belonged to Seth's family, his boyhood home, and now it was hers. Christine paused in the backyard and imagined a nine-year-old Seth O'Garra tossing an "Andy, Andy Over" ball over the garage with neighborhood children. She could almost hear squeals of laughter and "pigtail" yelled out, but their echoes faded as she looked up at her undressed bedroom window. She needed to make and hang curtains before the end of the day.

Although the rest of the house smelled of carpet shampoo and window cleaner, the kitchen soon filled with the aroma of gun oil. Christine reloaded and holstered a revolver in her purse. Her mother's green plaid coat still lay abandoned on the seat of the fourth chair near the basement steps. Christine had no trouble locating her hammer and a heavy old hook. She positioned the hook over an existing hole at a stud beside the front door and whacked at the nail with more force than necessary. She smiled. At least she'd hit one target well today. The old hooded coat was hung where it would always be ready to serve her, patiently waiting by the front door. The huge house was unbearably hot, but it suddenly felt more like home.

After dropping the heavy hammer into the kitchen tool drawer, she sank, puddle-like, at the table. She lifted April's perfume bottle from its place on the table and applied a little to the back of her hand. The scent rushed through her. She pulled a Bible across the table where it sat unopened. The bedroom curtains needed her. She must measure and cut the fabric and the lining, sew, install the rod on the wall, and hang the curtains. It would take hours, and must be done before bedtime. The Bible regarded her for a long time before she finally reached for a tissue.

Tuesday, July 7
Jared: Dance Students

"No real gentleman will tell the naked truth in the presence of ladies."

— Mark Twain, *A Double-Barreled Detective Story*

Jared Garrison flinched at the bright jolt of lightning and the sudden clap of thunder, but all five feet, eight inches of him stood firm as wind pushed rain under the shallow overhang and onto the large glass panels that served as the exterior wall of the dance studio. He placed his finger on the glass and followed a sputtering raindrop down his reflection as the storm rumbled over northern Indianapolis. His student had cancelled, so Jared was using his time thinking—thinking about women. But he wasn't thinking about the young woman who left his apartment that morning, the way she merely shook her head and smiled when he asked if he could call her. He wasn't thinking of all the women he had met over the years like her, beautiful young women who set their own pace—fast. No, he was thinking about his students.

Over his six years as a ballroom dance instructor, Jared had taught many women—young and old, skinny and nearly obese—all beautiful women. He loved dancing with them. His students made him smile, and yet they troubled him.

Most of them were older, middle-aged white women who wistfully believed that by dancing, they would maintain their youth and desirability. Having spent the best years of their lives raising children, feeding their husbands, and cleaning their houses, they now had far too much time on their hands. These were wealthy women who were bored with redecorating, tired of book club, weary of Wednesday afternoon bridge club. Jared felt similarly, except he was bored with bars and night clubs, tired of one-time bedroom romps, weary of the furious pursuit of fun. It seemed suddenly that he spent a lot of time doing nothing—nothing meaningful, nothing lasting. He frowned at the spattered glass.

It was as if the women he taught had done some kind of math calculation and had finally realized that their investments of self-sacrifice had not paid them well. Most of the unmarried women had lost their husbands to an early and preventable death. Some divorced, thus losing their marriage, often to a younger woman. Widowed or divorced, they had been left alone with lots of money in spacious empty houses. Frustrated, lonely, angry women. He understood their feelings, felt them himself, but hid them much better than his students.

The slow raindrop under Jared's finger suddenly took an awkward turn and bumped into another. They became one, and he watched with some longing as the new drop hurried down the window, fatter and happier, without him. Like all his students, married women normally came to the dance studio alone. Jared thought about that a lot. It was strange and upsetting to hear how they had encouraged, even begged their husbands to join them for lessons, only to be ridiculed for suggesting they invest in such an "obvious waste of time and money." After years of allowing their husbands to take the lead by dutifully following them to car shows, golf courses, and sporting goods stores, these women had had enough. They realized there wasn't much time to do the things they had always wanted to do, like taking ballroom dance lessons. So, they had gathered courage, declared their resolute intent, and conquered a long suppressed desire to flip off their husbands. They entered the studio, triumphant and energized, ready to finally enjoy a little self-defined fun. Meanwhile, their sour spouses sat at home nursing Kentucky bourbon, surprised and bitter that their wives had dared to go out alone.

Jared studied the movement of his finger as it smeared a

gentle curve on the glass. His defined eyebrows pulled together as his mind wandered over his students. They were different, yes, but there was always one common characteristic—they were women. As such, each of them had been taught the importance of appearance since girlhood. The common belief that a woman of worth is beautiful motivated them to spend a lot of money to maintain their looks—thousands of dollars at salons for hair coloring, facials, manicures, body contour wraps, hair removal, and when needed, hair replacement. Memberships at fitness clubs, nutritional supplements, and surgery were all on the long list of services well worth the price to delay the inevitable. Jared knew all this, so he tried his best to show them that they were still vibrant and attractive. In his mind they were beautiful, each in a special way. No matter her age or condition, he was masterfully able to bring a woman's natural beauty to the surface.

Jared leaned against the creamy curved sofa in the lobby and spoke softly to the thin-tailed raindrop he held briefly under his finger. "Don't cry, pretty girl. Stay with me." He enunciated every word with care and precision. Although he had grown up in small town Indiana, immersed in speech patterns of the Midwest, he smiled, thinking of how the quick rushing sounds from these wealthy white women had disoriented him at first. The way they clipped off each word and rapidly moved through a thought to deliver a concise message had sounded like a foreign language. But he had listened carefully, learned to mimic them, and now, six years later, he confidently and expertly engaged in their banter. He also studied the way they held and carried themselves: erect and graceful, and with determination. He learned how they thought and knew their commonly held beliefs. He knew that other than a quick handshake, physical contact with a man, other than a spouse or close relative, was inappropriate. Touching a man was acceptable in the studio only because ballroom dancing required at least some physical contact.

Although the rain had slowed to twinkling taps on the unprotected part of the sidewalk, Jared continued staring, thinking. He found himself at the edge of the window panel. His lost finger had been tapping steadily at a sharp barb of metal at the casing, and a subtle, yet noticeable pain pulsed from his self-abused fingertip. After rubbing the ache away, he intentionally touched the barb once more before crossing his arms. He stood with his well-dressed feet set apart as his thoughts turned to a session with a typical new student. This brought a smile.

He always looked for the surprised, no, the shocked look in a new student's eyes as he strutted across the floor toward them. Clearly they had not expected a handsome young black man to be their ballroom dance instructor. They had anticipated an instructor who was fifty, even sixty years old, only marginally attractive, and most certainly white. He knew this, so he welcomed them quickly and provided them the first of many signature embraces before they could gather their thoughts to speak. Mere seconds would pass between their initial moment of astonishment and their surprise at the enjoyment of his embrace. The first hug was Jared's favorite part of being a professional ballroom dance instructor. It was wicked of him to enjoy a woman's shock and initial discomfort and their impulsive, but weak attempt to pull away, only to be held a brief moment longer—just enough time for Jared to feel them melt ever so slightly into him. They always relaxed into that unexpected forbidden pleasure, yielded to that brief moment of desire.

Jared also fully understood that any physical contact with an African American man was completely out of the question for these women. Yet, here they were in a new reality, being hugged by a young man with a bright smile, laughing eyes, and skin the color of creamy coffee. He could nearly hear their next thought: *Perhaps he's gay. Yes, he must be gay.* That would make what just happened here nearly acceptable, at least explainable. They would spend a lot of time over the next few months trying to pick up on any clues that might support this initial theory. There would be no such clues; he simply had no such interest in other men. Jared, however, was certainly very attracted to women.

Immediately following his unexpected disarming embrace, he would hold a new student's hands at arm's length and ask very predictable, ordinary questions regarding her desire to take dance lessons. Although somewhat flustered, the new student had to quickly regain composure and display the tactful poise for which the wealthy are well known.

Jared spent this time studying a new student's face—searching for the physical woman she was, thirty or forty years earlier. He would start the process by focusing on their eyes. He would visually smooth the wrinkles away from the corners of those beautiful eyes and slowly blur and firm the rest of the face until it was easy to see them as they once were. A sagging jawline or neck was more difficult to visually lift, but after a few meetings, Jared no longer noticed these imperfections. He was often surprised by how lovely they must have been when young. While they danced, he could see them and appreciate them for something they no longer were to the rest of the world:

young and beautiful. He would hold them close and move them in sensuous rhythm and, in time, beckon an inner tigress. It was hidden there, too. These were women, and Jared knew that all women, regardless of age, contain suppressed passion.

It wasn't about sex, although he had no doubt that many of his students would eagerly join him if he asked. He had never asked, however, as it was against studio policy and Jared was an employee, not an independent contractor. He liked his job and wanted to remain employed. Besides, he had no trouble finding women his own age to satisfy him. Even so, he was curious and often wondered what it would be like to be with one of these older women. There would be no fear of pregnancy, and they likely would have no desire to be in a long-term relationship. Furthermore, he was convinced that his students were of a generation and culture that held sex as merely a marital duty, a task. He doubted many of their husbands had ever sought to satisfy them, so most of them were likely virginal in the knowledge and practice of erotic pleasures. With him, they would enjoy a memory of intense sexual pleasure—one created and played out solely for the purpose of fulfilling their desires. He knew he could create at least one such memory, if allowed. When they came to dance, they only wanted a satisfying experience to enjoy and relive in their minds. A sexual encounter would be no different. But even if he could make such an offer, he was sure that some, maybe most, of his students would remain physically faithful to their husbands, regardless if the husband was living or dead.

Jared lifted his hand and poked savagely at the glass. He was angry at these men. These thankless, thoughtless fools who had a rare and wonderful thing—they had loving wives, women who had been faithful to them over their many years of marriage. Wives who loved them, gave them children, and a legacy through their grandchildren. And yet, he believed, many of these fortunate men never even considered the desires of their spouses. They failed to please their wives either in, or out, of bed. This only served to help him maintain a strong and secure list of eager students. Unlike these men, Jared thought about the needs of women a great deal. Married or unmarried, a woman was totally his while dancing.

Flirting was, in fact, part of the product Jared delivered with proficiency. A student would eventually come to expect and enjoy being treated to a brief intimate embrace, followed by his smooth expertise and professional dance instruction. Throughout each lesson, he would provide an occasional unexpected touch to her upper arm or waist, followed quickly by a professional bit of instruction. This forced her from passion to cognitive learning and back again, over and over as they danced. She would later think about these brief moments of sexual arousal. He could see each student smiling into the dark as their husband snored beside them at night.

Over the years, several students had misinterpreted his flirtatious, courteous mannerisms and had fallen for him—hard. He remembered one woman bold enough to ask him to be open about his "true" feelings for her. It was difficult to tell her that he had no feelings whatsoever for her beyond the dance floor. She had left in tears. Jared deeply regretted being part of her obvious hurt, but he was doing a job, selling a product. And she knew that, or at least she had signed the contract that made it all very clear in writing. Instructors were not allowed to spend time with students off the dance floor. There was to be no fraternization of any kind.

Jared was always very careful to follow this studio policy and took it several steps further. He tried not to be alone with a student. He never shared personal information. He didn't tell them he lived alone, that he was divorced, that he was jealous of their husbands. If he had to contact a client, he would use the studio phone or send written correspondence using the studio's address. He even parked in the back of the building so students couldn't identify his car or have an opportunity to follow him home.

Jared Garrison wasn't even his real name. After hearing the problems enamored students had caused other instructors, he had decided to use an alias when first hired. He created a name with the same initials as his real name so the work schedules would still be "J.G." It was a good choice because now his students couldn't search for his name online with any success. If they typed in "Jared Garrison dance Indianapolis," only the studio website would pop up, displaying photographs taken at dance parties and competitions. His bio merely mentioned that he had grown up in Vincennes, Indiana, with a little about his training certification and his charismatic nature. There were no other listings for Jared Garrison in Indianapolis or in Vincennes. It would appear that he didn't exist anywhere except on the dance floor.

Yet, even though he was the teacher, and they his art media, he truly enjoyed being with these women. He admired their courage. It may be fair to say that he loved them—their flabby jiggling arms, their soft yielding bellies, their giggly gentleness, and how they twinkled as they danced. He loved being with them, and he needed them to know how much, so they would continue being students, paying for lesson after lesson, month after month, year after year. Jared sighed out onto the glass; his breath fogged the reflection of the face that stared back.

He thought through the standardized steps of his job: hug students at the start of every lesson, flash a dazzling smile, provide a compliment on their appearance, blur their faces, take them by the arm and lead them onto the dance floor. During the escort, indulge in the briefest of small talk, tell them he had been thinking of them during the week, and finally ask what they had done during their time apart. It was all expertly choreographed. This disturbing realization was abruptly interrupted by Ms. Mavis Deporre, the studio owner.

"Jared, do you have your dance routine finalized for the August charity event? It's less than eight weeks away."

He snatched his finger from the window and turned to face his employer. "Nearly done. Just need Miss Lynne to keep her appointments so we can finish the details and practice."

"Well, don't just stand there daydreaming. Go download and sort music. Do something." She snapped her voice back toward her front office, "You can start by cleaning your fingerprints off that front window. Better yet..." She turned and glared at the glass panels. "Get the step ladder and clean all those panels top to bottom, inside and out. It's not raining anymore."

"Yes, ma'am," he said to her back as it violently bobbed and disappeared around the door frame. The receptionist, Donna, smiled weakly at him as he walked to the front closet to retrieve the cleaning supplies.

Tuesday, July 7
Tracy: Exodus from Vincennes

Tracy Martin's bare feet dangled over the far edge of the scratchy yellow couch, her hair flowing over the armrest like a dark waterfall. A heavy rain had rumbled through southern Indiana making her morning drive from Indianapolis tedious, and she was thinking about how nice it would be to move into her fully-furnished apartment there. But at $1,400 a month and without a job, suspicious eyebrows would be raised, questions asked. She poked at a water-filled blister of paint that clung bravely to the cement block behind her head. Twisting her face toward the yielding blister, she sliced into it with her long red fingernail and watched the release of water bleed down the pitted basement wall. The dehumidifier hummed feebly as she draped her arm over her head and searched for the indented scorch hole her father's cigarette had burnt into the upholstery years earlier. It was the largest of many scorch divots on the side of the couch, so it was easy to locate with just her fingertips.

Her mother had caught them on the couch when Tracy was thirteen—threatened to press charges if he stayed, so he left. Just disappeared. But it was still her couch. Her father had told her so, had shown her it was hers many times. The Headless Queen had tried to throw it out, but Tracy had caught her and caught her good.

At age nine, Tracy had assigned her mother the name "Headless Queen" after reading *Alice in Wonderland*. She easily transferred the image of the Queen of Hearts screaming, "Off with her head, off with her head…" to the sight of her own mother screaming, "Tracy, stop hitting Amber. Tracy, fetch me the belt. Tracy, get your ass down in that closet..." and on and on and on her mother would scream. Tracy would envision her mother dressed as the red Queen holding her own head, hot and crimson, in her arms. The HQ would shake the screeching head, cartoon-like, at Tracy. Over time, Tracy learned to return nothing to her mother—no cowering or tears, no defiant glaring—nothing.

As a teen, Tracy began openly addressing her mother as the HQ. It amused Tracy that her mother seemed to take this as a compliment. Apparently, she thought it was a term of respect. The "Head Quarters," Tracy supposed the clueless woman believed. Laughable.

But Tracy wasn't laughing at the HQ at the moment. No, she was listening to her move from room to room upstairs. Years earlier, Tracy had cut a hole in the dining room floor under the hutch so she could hear her mother's pathetic phone conversations from the solitude of the basement, from the comfort of her couch. The HQ was still very firmly attached to the land line, so the hole provided easy access to her mother's conversations with the outside world. The vacuum suddenly roared awake overhead. Tracy scowled and lit a cigarette. She'd wait.

Over the years, Tracy had heard a lot from her couch—mostly, the HQ bad-mouthing her father and making up things about Amber, her sickening half-sister. There was a time when the HQ would launch into a list of Tracy's minor infractions. Not now. Not anymore. A couple months ago, Tracy finally put the screaming-queen part of her mother to death by shoving her against the wall beside the refrigerator, and then lifting her up and holding her off the floor. Tracy had whispered what to expect the next time. Hissed into her ear. The HQ had dangled there squirming, bug-eyed, but quiet. Tracy held her there and studied her—stared into the verminous woman for a long time before providing a measured, unhurried release. The mouse slid down the wall slowly then scurried to the safety of her bedroom. Tracy had finished her sandwich in peace.

The woman was a quick learner; she had already surrendered herself to a new domestic pattern—did all the cleaning and cooking without complaint and spoke to Tracy only on command. And now, thanks to the lesson against the wall, the HQ never talked about Tracy to Aunt Nora. Tracy hadn't bothered to create a new name for her mother. The HQ was desperately boring.

As Tracy lay in the dim dampness, she realized why the HQ bored her—their roles had flipped. Her mother was small and submissive. And Tracy was no longer the child who used to grit her teeth so her mother wouldn't see any weakness during the belt-beatings, wouldn't know she was terrified of being alone in the black musty closet. Those days were long gone. Tracy was all grown up: tall and powerfully built, like her father. Except, unlike Dad, Tracy would leave only when, and if, she wanted.

She shook away the emotions of her father to review more satisfying matters, and to plan. Her business had come a long way since she started selling weed as a tenth grader. Back then, she drove the hour to Terre Haute to secure the best dope at the best price; it hadn't taken long to attract eager adult customers. Adding cocaine had increased her profits and expanded her territory to Terre Haute and now Indy. Yes, Tracy congratulated herself on her growing success in Indianapolis. Not many people her age could have broken into the market there, but Tracy provided only the highest quality cocaine to people who could pay. And she always delivered as promised, discreetly and with class. Quick, harsh retaliation for nonpayment or uppity attitude had earned her a solid reputation for no nonsense among the cartel. Her direct supplier trusted her and knew they had a strong, long-term partnership ahead.

No one would dream that a young, well-dressed woman was a high-level drug dealer. That wouldn't be "normal." Over the years, Tracy had learned the importance of appearing to be normal and now she was good at it, very good. She remained at home in Vincennes, a student, a very common community college student who started a fresh series of classes every semester with what appeared to be genuine enthusiasm, only to drop out a couple weeks later. The administrators didn't seem to mind. As long as the HQ made regular tuition payments, they fully supported Tracy's attempts to "find the right career path." But now, four bumpy years later, the "guidance" staff was weary, no longer believing. Tracy could hear it in their voices and see it in the way they suddenly found someone else to talk to when she approached. Even with paid tuition, she was close to over playing the cover. Dangerous.

Tracy scraped her fingernails up the side of her neck, behind her ear and across her scalp. She leisurely pulled her hand through her heavy dark hair and twisted the end of a strand. Although she hadn't bothered to mention it to the HQ, she had stopped attending summer classes after the first week. Now, Tracy left the house every morning with a cheery goodbye to her mother, who scampered off to work at the same time. Tracy would drive to Indianapolis, wait for her supplier, make some deliveries, and provide needed reminders to her small crew. She'd overnight in Indy on Fridays and Saturdays—the busiest nights. She was known at three Indianapolis banks by different names and always made certain to deposit less cash than would be flagged as suspicious before returning home. She liked her work, but hated the driving, the long miles. And except for the occasional fits of road rage, little excitement.

The vacuum stopped. Tracy pursed her lips tightly around her cigarette and inhaled deeply. A white stream of smoke jetted up and swirled around the helpful hole above her. She heard the phone clatter, yes, there was the dialing. The HQ was probably reaching out to her sister, Nora. Tracy didn't know much about her aunt—never seemed worth the trouble to know. From what Tracy could hear, Nora's bookstore in Indianapolis was struggling and she was having trouble keeping "good help."

Tracy lay very still and heard, "Well, Sis, I feel for you. Young people these days just don't know how to work anymore. I know a thing or two about that, let me tell you." Tracy's eyes narrowed as the careless words drifted down through the unnoticed hole. Infuriating words, but they provided a fresh idea—a delightful idea. Tracy coughed, then laughed at herself for not thinking of it sooner. She quickly rolled off the couch to avoid being heard above, crushed the glowing cigarette onto the cement floor with her bare foot. The sharp heat penetrated through her callouses as she kicked the smothered butt aside. It lay flat and lost among the others. Once in the bathroom, she settled into the familiar darkness to think, to plan.

Tracy smiled into the darkness, finished adjusting her jeans and buttoning her blouse. Her plan was complete. She had won "the game" long ago and would end it on her own terms. The HQ needed to be groomed, prepared for the idea. Tracy would inform the HQ of her decision to take life more seriously. She'd read business textbooks in the living room, maybe even apologize for being less than an ideal daughter. But, play the other end too: heap dirty clothes on the floor, leave food on the counter, forget to lock the doors at night, surf endlessly with the TV remote, fail to flush toilets. Little things. Irritating things.

Tracy would watch, and wait, and when she was certain that the HQ was worn down sufficiently, she would announce her desire to get into retail sales. Perhaps Aunt Nora could use help in her bookstore. After all, Tracy's community college training would be a great help. Working the bookstore would launch the second phase of Tracy's plan for success, her business expansion plan. Besides, Tracy was bored, bored well beyond acceptable tolerance. She was indeed very ready to leave her dumpy little hometown to take on big-city opportunities— challenging, lucrative, and of course, fun.

Friday, July 17
Christine: Welcome Home

Christine's window was the only one still shining brightly an hour after the Purdue Extension office closed. She admonished herself for not turning off her office light as she crossed the parking lot, slipped her phone back in her purse and jiggled her keys out from under her gun. Although she appreciated Donavin's call, inviting himself to her home like this was far too spontaneous. There was a dirty cereal bowl in the sink, and poor old Clover might have thrown up on the front porch again. They hadn't been face-to-face since Seth's funeral and had fallen out of touch. But here he was, living in the same community as she. Donavin Bayer—a man with relaxed calm confidence; self-assured without being arrogant. She had always admired those qualities in him. It was Donavin who introduced her and Seth to shooting sports years ago. But it wasn't until after Seth's death that she started carrying a gun. A promise made—a promise kept, except ever faithful Christine was questioning that promise now.

The sauerkraut fermenting in her detached garage was at the stage of bubbling out its dirty diaper smell, and would permeate the entire neighborhood if she opened the door. Neighbors would talk. Donavin would be horrified. So, Christine pulled up on the tree-lined street behind a little grey car. And there he was—relaxing on the steps of her front porch, holding Clover. Even though the sweet old cat loved a warm lap and any friendly set of digging fingernails behind the ears, Christine was surprised to see Clover cuddled up to a stranger.

"Hey, you must have driven like a crazy man to beat me," Christine called out as she lugged her purse and carry-all bag from the front seat. Donavin took the steps down to the street to greet her and take her bag.

"My office is only a couple blocks away, just above the all night Chinese take-out. It's okay to park on this street like this?" he asked, pointing at the grey car in front of hers.

"Sure, just not overnight. Late night Friday is trash pickup," Christine replied.

Clover hopped down the steps for his welcome home chin rub and Christine obliged. She pulled a few weeds out from under the bushes while she was bent over, then gave Donavin a sisterly hug.

"We've got to go round to the back. I still don't have a key for the front door. It's on my list of things to do this weekend."

"I haven't been here since college—forgot how big this house was," Donavin said as they walked across the side yard. He peered up at the building as they circled the back corner. "Seth's grandfather had this built, right?" Christine nodded and Donavin continued, "Those Tuscan columns at the porch are quite something. Unusual to see those on a brick Queen Anne. And I love these windows."

The tall narrow windows gleamed against the smooth yellow brick. Christine made a mental note to re-caulk them before winter.

She took Donavin on a grand tour of the house and property, everywhere except the unholy-smelling garage. He seemed especially intrigued by what lurked in her basement: the rich dark compost she was cooking for a mushroom box and a new wooden keg for making vinegar. Come fall, her niece would provide a supply of fresh pressed apple cider, a fresh "mother."

The living room created quite a stir as Donavin flopped onto an oversized leather couch. "I can't believe you still have it. I always loved this thing," he said from his comfortable position. "Always wondered where you found it."

"I didn't find that horrid thing anywhere. Seth had it custom made so he could take naps during the Cubs games. Had it made extra-long and extra-wide so he could stretch out. It was born ugly and it gets uglier every day. Nearly left it behind in West Lafayette. Fortunately, it's nearly worn out."

Donavin grinned at her from the deep soft leather. "Well, it's been good to the men in your life."

Christine was hit by a flash of grief, struck by how much Donavin reminded her of Seth lying on the man-loved couch. *It could be treated to bring out its new again.* She sighed heavily at the thought. Looking about the room, she silently admitted that she didn't like any of the furniture. Seth had picked out every piece. He had, in fact, purchased every appliance, every piece of art, every rug, even the shower curtains. He had meant each purchase as a gift of love—a gift of his time and energy, so she wouldn't have to shop.

She was revisiting her disappointment that the kitchen table had only one leaf when Donavin sat up and smiled at her. "I spent a lot of nights on this cozy monster," he said, rubbing its worn arm. Christine rolled her eyes at him as they headed for the kitchen.

Over tea and snickerdoodles, they caught up on select details of their lives. Donavin failed to mention his wife and Christine didn't bring up Seth or April—at least not directly. She did, however, share that she had ordered gemstone rings in their memory. Diamonds made from the ashes of April, made from the ashes of Seth—strange, and perhaps a bit macabre. Thankfully, Donavin seemed genuinely touched by the idea and wanted to know more, but she changed the subject quickly to his architect work. He regretted his upcoming three-month overseas project and she regretted getting involved in community advisory boards too quickly. They both agreed, however, that their work was a pleasant diversion—challenging, yet satisfying.

Donavin eyed a towel-covered bowl on the kitchen counter with curiosity. Only Christine knew of the yeasty mass that bubbled underneath. "Your house is nearly as fascinating as you are." He fingered up crumbs of cookie from his plate.

Christine's chair squawked loudly as she pushed back from the table. She returned from the far counter near the back door with a large manila envelope. It bulged and pushed at the metal clasp.

"I found these when I was unpacking and thought of you. I have an entire album, of course. These were loose extras I guess."

The old photos dumped out in a sloppy stack on the table between them. Donavin carefully selected one of the groomsmen and studied it. Christine selected one with the entire wedding party. Seth's fresh round face and Donavin's thin one smiled out at her from their distant past. Her own face captured in a bridal smile surrounded by sisters, and friends, and hope.

"Look at you. You made a very handsome best man," she said. "We were all so young, Donavin." Christine watched him nod at the photo in his hand.

"Barely legal adults, except Seth was never young," Donavin replied. "Always an old soul, even when we were in college. Fiercely serious, till he drank, that is." He glanced up and winked.

"I was only nineteen," Christine whispered as she shuffled through the photos she held.

"Christy, I remember coming here with you and Seth just after you two married. Seth's mom made a huge meal that we ate in that dining room right there," Donavin said.

They looked through the doorway into the dim darkness that was now an empty space. "Do you remember that? Still has the same light fixture in there. I remember worrying about the wiring, questioning the safety of a push button wall plate."

She nodded. "I remember. I remember a lot of things." Seth's ruddy face stared up at her through time from the photograph she held. His arm encircled her: his secretly pregnant bride in white. Christine's mother, with full knowledge, stood with a tight-lipped smile, failing to hide her disappointment— her disapproval. Her father, stern, yet compassionate.

Donavin's voice cut through her bittersweet memories. "You're not the only one cleaning and sorting out our past life together. I brought you something. A housewarming gift." He pulled a small box from his pocket. Christine opened it with care to find three small metal figures: a tiny cannon, a Scotty dog, and a little iron.

They looked at one another, sharing the distant memory of the years Seth and Donavin played their two-piece version of Monopoly nearly every Friday night. Donavin always played the Scotty dog and the top hat, and Seth the cannon and the iron. Seth had named his extra piece "The Strong Iron," a weakly veiled reference to Christine and a slight barb at her skills as a home economist. Christine turned the iron over in the palm of her hand, and took a moment to revisit their game from the distant past. She was lying in bed listening to their voices drift up the stairs as she smiled into the darkness. A slightly drunk Seth would roar out in exaggerated Irish brogue, "Get him, my Strong Iron—throw the mangy cur in jail. He owes penance for his treatment of me at Pennsylvania Station."

And Donavin would answer back, "You have your pretty

lady, Seth O'Garra. Yes, you're a lucky man, but my pup will wet your powder." Christine smiled again at the distant echoes of their boyish bantering. Donavin always slept overnight on the horrid couch, leaving behind beer cans, sticky blueberry muffin papers, bits of popcorn on the floor, and Monopoly money stuffed under the couch cushions. Christine had shared in the pleasure of their friendship as a distant observer listening from the dark bedroom. Somehow Donavin had known.

"The game board was completely worn out and these pieces were the only ones left. I thought you'd like to have them."

"Thank you. Really, you have no idea how much I appreciate these." Christine stood and arranged them on the windowsill, the iron in the middle.

She was still looking at them fondly when Donavin said, "I should let you know that I'm finally divorced. That shouldn't surprise you though, I guess."

"Oh, Donavin, I'm so sorry," she said turning to him.

"I can't believe you're really sorry, Christy. If Seth were here, he'd smack me on the back and ask what took me so long."

"Maybe so, but divorce is always hurtful, so my heart goes out to you. I've been wondering why you hadn't mentioned Julie, but didn't want to pry. I guess we both have things we need to learn how to put behind us."

She hoped he realized that she didn't want to discuss death, grief, hurt. Even so, she waited for him to raise the topics, like everyone else, and jumped when the phone rang instead.

Glancing at the incoming number, she said, "Excuse me will you? It's the jeweler." She walked into the dim dining room and then returned to the brightness of the kitchen a moment later. "The rings are ready," Christine informed. She pulled at her lower lip with her fingertips and stared at the dark phone. Donavin stood and stepped toward her.

"Would you like me to go with you to pick them up, Christy? You just told me how much you've looked forward to getting them; even so, it's got to be tough."

"That's sweet of you, but no, this is something I need to do by myself—for myself." She pressed her hands against her cheekbones. "I guess you need to head out soon, huh?" she hinted.

Donavin cocked his head and studied her a moment before delivering a quick reassuring hug.

"Yeah, I need to get going. Let me know how I can help you though, okay? You've been through a lot and I'm kind of hurting right now, too." He put his plate and cup in the sink and turned to her. "Wish I had called you earlier. I'm leaving next week for those projects in Europe. Hope to be back in three months, but it all depends on how much headway we make. It always takes longer than we think." He paused. "Can we get together when I get back? It'll be a long three months if I don't have something to look forward to."

Christine merely nodded. Donavin hugged her once again then held his hand under her chin briefly, a strangely intimate gesture. "I'll send you a postcard." His voice smiled but his eyes looked concerned as he turned to leave. She had wanted to stop seeing that look from others, but it was comforting coming from him.

She watched him walk past the back window, then she sank onto a kitchen chair and sat there, listening to his car engine start up at the front of the house. She closed her eyes and focused on the muffled purring of that motor. As she fought to capture his last parting sound, she startled at the sudden shrill song of a wren just outside the window. It hopped on the window sill chattering merrily then tilted its tiny brown head with a quick jerk before flying off. She was wasting what was left of the day listening to cars, watching birds sing.

She had delayed long enough. It was time. Although the kitchen's screen door provided the only breeze through the house, she closed the heavy back door and bolted it. She opened the drawer that held small hand tools, selected needle-nose pliers and a hammer, pulled several paper grocery bags from a closet, located a wooden cutting board and carried the strange collection to the living room at the front of the house.

"Unpack last" was emblazoned across the sides of a box there. She dug a pocketknife from her pants pocket, settled herself on the floor and sliced open the packing tape. Christine glanced to the window. The curtains were closed.

Clover, the last member of family past, meandered over and rubbed at her elbow.

"This is no place for you, old boy." Christine rubbed the odd white patch on his fuzzy black head. Just like Jesse, he loved to be held, touched. She lifted the cat and gently shooed him away.

Christine took a deep breath, slipped her hand inside and popped open the partially taped flap. Her nieces had packed the moving box with care, wrapped each breakable in newspaper. As she released each item from its shroud, she recalled the giver. She heard their words, rehearsed and hollow—a reflection of their true feelings. A yeasty resentment rose in Christine as she laid each gift one by one on the wooden floor—a small stack of books, heavy candles, ceramic angels—things, just things. She had felt obligated to keep, use, and display them in West Lafayette, felt guilty for not appreciating them. She, in fact, hated them. Not only did they remind her of loss every day, these few things reeked of heartless sympathy, shallow and insincere.

She placed an angel-decaled vase into the paper bag, and let the weight of the hammer fall. Clover dashed under the couch at the sharp shattering. Each of the four ceramic angels was destroyed in turn; their sharp wings tore at the bag before yielding into brittle bits. She pounded the candles on the cutting board until each was thoroughly pock-marked or broken. Her hammering transformed a lone piece of jewelry, a pendant necklace, into a flat useless mass. She grabbed and twisted a wooden letter opener with the pliers until it cracked and splintered. Each book was opened briefly before being laid on the cutting board where it was stabbed savagely. Deep wounds punctured the words. Entire sentences lay disemboweled. Thus, each death gift was methodically destroyed, their remains tossed back into the box.

Christine sat. A strange release, along with pricking guilt, rose within her. Although she treasured many other gifts of sympathy, she had thought about destroying these for months; dared to imagine what it would feel like to be rid of the constant reminders, never believing she'd actually do so. And now she had. Silent tears had been streaming down her face, unnoticed. Her trembling hands now reached up and cupped her wet nose, pulled across her cheeks and down her jaw. And still she sat. Clover finally squeezed out from his couch bunker and wandered under her arm where he was mindlessly stroked.

She lifted the cat and hugged him gently; his low purring

trilled loudly as he rubbed his head against her clammy hand. Christine kissed his fuzzy head, hauled herself from the floor and peered into the box of trash. She pulled out a candle that had somehow retained the readable words, *"...best things in life are the people we love, the memories we've made along life's..."* She would keep this. Just one thing. She lifted an unsteady hand to her neck before walking to the coat closet where she located a sturdy little overnight suitcase, one she had used in college. She snapped open the clasps and lifted the rigid lid. As always, the washcloth was on top. Although the familiar burgundy and green flowers were still bright, there were visible holes riddled throughout the unworn terry cloth. Christine held it near her mouth, breathed the years in and then laid it flat on the cutting board. She bent over it, spit on it, and watched as the cloth sucked at the foamy whiteness. She picked up her knife and suddenly, fiercely, stabbed it, gored at the wet spot until the cutting board peeked through the wound. She stuck her finger through the new hole then tossed the rag aside.

She lifted out the familiar folded paper, a single sheet. She kissed it, set it aside unopened, wondering if death certificates were still issued for unborn babies. It was unusual to think of the little one under her wedding dress twice in the same day. A bulging envelope appeared next—a collection of notes from both April's well-meaning, totally absurd teachers, and the most annoying of the medical "experts." Under it, the handwritten card from Seth. A few weeks after his death, she had found it stuffed between his mattress and the box spring. The pages desperately clung to one another at an old rip—once again trying to prevent her reading. Seth's heavy lettering stumbled across the page.

Dearest Christy,

I've stopped living—we both know it. I see the pain you wear. It's on your face and in the way you move and talk. It's like you're dying too.

We shared the pain of losing April, Jesse, and the first little one too. I can't stand watching you carry this alone.

I wish we had more than our thirty-four years, but the sooner I am gone, the quicker you can heal and start living again. You must find someone to be with you, someone who will protect you. You're too simple, too sweet to understand. I'll always love you.

The precious words clawed at her. *Who was he? God? To think he could just decide to die from cancer quickly because it would be best for her?* No one dies until God says it's time. And what made him think she needed protection? Was she too stupid to fend for herself? She shook her head to stop feeding the bitterness—forced herself to quickly reach the proper conclusion. *Seth loved me enough to spare me the hurt of watching him suffer a long, painful death. Rare love, real love.*

But, Seth's pocket journal lay at the bottom—page after page of carefully recorded notes: places she'd visited, dates, names of people she knew through work, church. Stuffed inside were receipts where she had shopped, lists of errands made, phone numbers and addresses she had jotted down. Yet again, she thumbed through the years wondering. *A long record of mistrust?* Her thoughts circled back, raising questions, criticism. *Stop that thinking.* Seth's note and journal made an ugly couple and she refused to think about either of them. She slapped the journal down on top of his hand-written note. Clover quick-stepped to the kitchen.

She carefully placed the battered candle at the bottom of the little suitcase, laid each item of the sorry collection on top of it and placed it back on the floor of the closet. Two sturdy plastic boxes that held what remained of the ashes of Seth and April were set on top. April's box was maroon. Seth's, dark brown. She gave the closed door a small kick. Not enough to damage the door, but a kick all the same.

You can't hide hurt, Christine. Not from Me.

"I'm not trying to hide anything from You."

Anger festers and grows in the dark. You hid it from your parents, you hid it from Seth, and you hid it from your children. You try to hide it from yourself but hurt lives through your anger every night.

"You get angry. It's not wrong to be angry."

I get angry at the sin, not at the people. You're angry at people, not sin.

"They deserve it."

Your choice, but you deserve better. I deserve better.

Christine paused at the landing to gather up a set of bed linens she had efficiently encased in one of its matching pillowcases. This freshly washed set needed to be stored at the bottom of the pile waiting in the upstairs linen closet to assure for even wear.

I love you, Christine. I loved you before you knew you even existed, I love you now, and I'll love you though eternity.

Even though her eyes watered slightly, she noticed the sheets were slightly grey. Mineral deposits. The water heater and the softener needed to be drained and flushed. Yes, although it was late, that needed to be done tonight.

Tuesday, August 11
Christine: Losing Place

"…when we finally know we are dying, and all
other sentient beings are dying with us, we start
to have a burning, almost heartbreaking sense of
the fragility and preciousness of each moment
and each being, and from this can grow a deep,
clear, limitless compassion for all beings."

— Sogyal Rinpoche

Fortunately, Christine saw the funeral procession in time
to come to a full stop at the green traffic light. Her eyes turned
to follow the sight of a woman's face pressed against the back
window of the lead car, and she lifted a sympathetic prayer
for her—this unknown sister of grief. *Cry all you need to, all
you want to.* Only days after April's death, Seth had stopped
crying—just stopped. His eyes became dull and lifeless. It was
as if he had been fighting his impending death only to keep
April alive. Try as she might, Christine, the living one, couldn't
stop death's second visit to her home. The hospice nurse came
and helped Christine fill out the record of death. The transport
driver provided proper respect, had Christine sign a form, then
zipped Seth's shell up in a bag and wheeled it away.

Once again, friends and family came and went, like appa-
ritions, well-meaning loving ghosts. Eventually, they stopped
coming and she was alone. Christine had to tell herself to walk
to the bathroom, to eat, to shower. Live, just, live. Sleep came
without being told. She would easily slip into sleep hoping it
would be forever. Eventually she would wake, lying on a damp

pillow, bones aching, still breathing. Christine found it funny to be annoyed by breathing, to feel an almost physical pain by pulling air into her body and releasing stale fragments. Pulling life in and pushing death out, over and over. Surreal movements, strangely life-like.

Last year, the month of May surprised her. How had so many weeks disappeared since Seth's death? Time had left no history on which to build, and it was early June before she not only noticed, but experienced sights, and sounds, and smells—clouds, birds singing, the smell of wet leaves pushed by the wind. Life had been moving forward all around her and she hadn't been part of any of it. Grief is like that, and Christine was intimately familiar with grief. Except, she discovered, private grief was different. No one needed her to be strong. No one leaned on her comforting words and she didn't have to hide her face in a pillow or walk the block to let her tears fall and her sobs escape. She could openly and loudly battle with her dead and distant family members, with herself, with God. She could scream, she could rant, she could wail. And so she did, often. The louder, the better.

It was at this time, God's nearly audible messages became clear. It was also when she reintroduced herself to her childhood guardian angel, Liberty. It was simply fun as a child. Now, Christine appreciated the comforting image of a powerful companion—a coping tool who readily came to mind as she daily faced her unsteady future.

She also pulled life lessons from her Mennonite childhood. She would reflect on memories of Grandpa Steiner who was fully responsible for her fondness of the strange and powerful licorice candy, Sen-Sen. Sadly, the candy was no longer produced. Fortunately, Christine had stockpiled several dozen packets of it a couple years ago, and had it vacuum-sealed and stored in a cool dry place. The smell of Sen-Sen always brought Grandfather to mind. As a child, she had spent a lot of time with her grandfather. If she, or one of her siblings, complained about having to pick vegetables in the hot sun, or herd swollen, bad-tempered sows to the furrowing house, or hike through rain to find a mud-encrusted runaway horse, he would say in low German, "Die Katze geht in den Schnee. Wenn der Schnee geht weg, die Katze geht in den Schlamm. Die Katze nur geht." Then he would catch himself, remember that his grandchildren were to speak only English and say, "The cat walks in the snow. When the snow goes away, the cat walks in the mud. The cat just walks." It wasn't until she was an adult that she discovered Grandpa Steiner had radically altered a children's song about a cat who refused to return to the harsh snowy outdoors. In the actual lyrics, that lazy cat washed its mittens and stayed inside, warm and dry. That explained her grandmother's laughter every time Grandpa talked about the ever-walking cat. To him, harshness in life was merely a test of endurance and faith. Complaining might be the natural reaction, but it wouldn't help to sit down in soggy snow or sticky mud and roll around in its ugliness. The only way to get through is to get up and walk. Just walk.

So the cat walked. After Seth's death, she walked back to her work at Purdue where co-workers once again awkwardly expressed their sympathy then quickly slipped into the safety of their cubicles. For them, thoughts of such painful things might come for a moment, maybe two, but they could easily shake the thoughts out, like a dusty rug, and move on to more pleasant things. They'd be surprised to know how sorry she felt for them. They were afraid and confused, and she couldn't blame them for feeling uncomfortable around her. It would take weeks before they would forget her hurt to the point when they wouldn't feel their emotions bump over painful awkward moments when with her.

Only, that didn't happen.

Months passed, and she continued to feel their coldness, as if she had overdrawn her sympathy account. They distanced themselves as if hardship and grief could be contagious. One tragedy too many, Christine shambled along like a lonely leper week after painful week, all the while longing to be with people who didn't know that their first logical question should be, "How can she continue after all she's been through?" Several times she nearly quit her job, stopped herself just short of walking out. Christine never quit anything.

She paused her reminiscing long enough to check the written directions to the dance studio. Fortunately, it was on the north side of Indianapolis so the drive was mostly highway. She committed to the next exit ramp and slipped into the left turn lane. She smiled, realizing she had taken an exit ramp in life as well.

She had seen the job opportunity in Seth's hometown as a sign, a chance to start fresh. Bits and pieces of her tragedies would eventually follow her, but only after people had gotten to know her, Christine O'Garra, not her past. So, although it had meant a step down in her career and a significant cut in pay, she had accepted the county-level educator position in Lebanon. It was a place where a cat could walk, skip, or dance without watchful eyes or judgment. Yet do so with care—dance within the lines.

Soon after Christine started her new job, she agreed to serve as a board member of a non-profit agency. They were desperate for one more person to volunteer as a "celebrity" in the ballroom dance competition for their November fundraiser. Sometimes God's humor was a bit much for Christine. She had asked if she could "dance" in Lebanon, and He had answered.

This would be yet one more opportunity to test her General Conference Mennonite heritage where dancing, although not strictly forbidden as in the neighboring Amish, was certainly not part of tradition. She was determined to add dancing to her toolbox of healing freedoms, along with complaining openly to God and pretending to see a large imposing angel at her side. She had even given herself permission not to make the bed every morning. These new things suited her. She was actually enjoying living "on the edge."

She parked in front of the dance studio, opened each car window a sliver to let out the heat, stowed the keys under her gun, then kissed her left finger and the two rings it held. She had broken the upper knuckle when she and ten-year-old Jesse were playfully wrestling huge hydrangea blossoms down one another's shirts. The crooked finger had never straightened. So, every day Christine kissed her knuckle for Jesse and her rings for Seth and April. "I am dancing, my loved ones. Dancing," she whispered as she entered the building.

The hot August sun flooded through the floor-to-ceiling windows. She sat with her back toward the warmth on a delicate sofa in the open air lobby while completing the student registration form. Her distracted mind and quick fingers automatically checked the box beside the word "married." She glared at her check mark. Stupid mistake, but after thirty-four years of marriage, understandable. What was she to do? Scribble it out and check "unmarried?" That would look ridiculous. She could ask for a fresh form and start over. That was silly, too. A waste of time, a waste of paper. She convinced herself it didn't matter. Who would care at a dance studio if she were married or not married?

She listed her elderly neighbor, Peter Zachman, as her emergency contact and moved on. *"Please list the names and ages of your children."* She tapped at the page. She had long ago stopped recording Jesse on such forms. And of course dead children don't count. Christine reflected on the various questions that were difficult for her to answer: "Is a woman still a virgin after being raped?" "Are you married?" "Do you have children?" She finally returned the pen to its place in her purse and returned the completed form, lies and all, to the receptionist.

Christine turned toward approaching footsteps. She caught her breath. Something about the way this person was reaching for her, his warm smile so like Jesse's, the way he tilted his head. She so wanted to hug this young man.

"Ms. O'Garra? I'm Jared Garrison and I'll be your dance instructor."

In a rare quick moment of etiquette abandoned, she stepped to him and folded him into her arms. She felt Jesse there. He pulled back and looked at her, held her hands at her fingertips and rubbed at her fingers. Jesse, yes, but this young man would be very like her lost son, her first pregnancy. His creamy brown color, his age, his height. Here was a young person she could care for, love even.

As he escorted her to the dance floor, she resolved to share only truly meaningful things with her young dance instructor. Christine hoped she wasn't being prideful in her belief that she had wisdom to share. Jared might retreat, he might dismiss her. *It doesn't matter*, she told herself; she wasn't living to be accepted or to protect herself from hurt. She would care for Jared, listen to him, and perhaps even mentor him. She and Jared needed to live with purpose—leave no regrets, nothing undone, then die wonderfully empty. First, however, they would dance.

Tuesday, August 11
Jared: She Did Not Impress

"He is a self-made man, and worships his creator."

— John Bright

Jared rolled up his second sleeve, smoothed the cuff around his arm and sighed. The charity event with Miss Lynne was still a couple weeks off, and here he was, preparing for another one. Jared understood why the dance studio owner, Mavis Deporre, donated lessons. The events showcased dance to potential customers, people who could well afford lessons, and the November event would likely generate at least three lucrative contracts. Even so, Jared tried to avoid taking on a charity student as they were self-assured, confident women, respected career-minded women. He was somewhat intimidated by them. But, they were still women and he was confident that they loved the way he made them feel—young and beautiful.

So, although reluctant, he had been assigned to instruct a woman in a series of fifteen free lessons that began today. All he knew about his new student was her name—Christine O'Garra, an unusual name. Irish, he supposed. He hung in the back of the studio when she arrived to study her unobserved. Normally, he would have stayed in the instructors' lounge to watch her on the camera monitor of the lobby, except Kyle was there on Jared's phone, filling the room with drama-filled sighs and sharp retorts to yet another soon-to-be-ex girlfriend.

Christine chatted freely with Donna, who handed her a clipboard. His new student settled onto the lobby sofa and quickly removed a pen from her oversized purse. She scribbled away. Funny, normally locating a pen in a cavernous purse such as this required substantial digging. He stared hungrily at that colorful cloth purse, pulled in a deep breath imagining its possible contents. Nothing like the smell of a woman's purse.

The registration form would provide a lot of information, but not age, so Jared made a game of guessing a woman's age at their first lesson. He would later ask probing questions to reveal how well he had predicted. The age he assigned a new student was consistently within a couple years of the truth. Poor dears, they spent so much time and money trying to conceal their age, and it did them no good. Determining Christine's age, however, was providing him a rare challenge. He quietly moved across the dance floor toward her. She was tapping the pen gently on the clipboard as if considering an answer carefully. Her skin was alarmingly fair. She had obviously avoided the sun and had likely never smoked as there were virtually no wrinkles on her face, not even around her eyes or mouth. She had dark circles under her eyes; her cheeks were variations of pink and pale. She could certainly use concealer, foundation, and mascara. Her reddish-blonde hair had no hint of grey, not even at the roots. She could be forty, forty-three. The condition of her neck reflected an older woman—likely in her late forties. Maybe even fifty.

Christine bounced up from the couch, returned the clipboard to Donna with a smile. She had a quickness that was normally reserved for women in their twenties or thirties. Jared couldn't settle on an age. She was about five foot five—shorter than Jared, fortunately. Weight sat on women differently than men, so Jared never bothered trying to guess a student's weight.

She was ready for him, so Jared noisily clip-strutted toward her, a bit upset for not settling his guess on her age.

Jared's carefully choreographed first hug wasn't delivered as usual either. Instead of the typical hesitation and tentative look from a first-time student, Christine had approached him and hugged him, not the other way around. Her enthusiasm seemed genuine. Jared pulled away and studied her closely. If designed to impress, her clothing was totally inappropriate: light grey sweatpants, a T-shirt from Belize, tired looking sneakers with frayed laces, probably white when new. No, the first impression of Christine O'Garra was far from positive. Jared pushed her overall appearance aside and focused on her eyes. Her eyes, although cupped by dark circles, were a deep grey-blue and Jared had no trouble finding beauty there.

He took up both her hands, lifted them slightly for a better look. Yes, she was likely near fifty—the age spots on the backs of her hands betrayed her face and quick movements.

There were rings on her left ring finger. Widows often continued wearing wedding rings. Rings meant nothing, but the registration form would let him know if she was married.

"So, Ms. O'Garra," Jared said, as he held both of her hands and stared into her eyes. He felt at her fingertips and noticed that the end of her left ring finger was bent like Gran's. He caressed it gently as he spoke. "I understand we'll be dancing together at an important event in November. Have you ever taken dance lessons?"

"My husband suggested we give dancing a try once; we took one lesson years ago. I doubt if you'll have much to build on from that experience. I wasn't very good."

Yes, she was married. She, and her husband, likely supported the charity with handsome financial donations. Except, this woman didn't own decent athletic shoes. Maybe they gave time, not money. Poor people have lots of time. Gran would say she was poor as a church mouse. Jared tilted his head slightly and tried to blur out the darkness from under her eyes. She touched a small bumpy scar on the side of her neck—a row of tiny raised pearls, likely from a surgery.

"Actually, Ms. O'Garra, if someone comes in and claims they already know how to dance, it can make my job a lot more difficult. I find it much easier to teach someone with very little experience than to teach someone who thinks they already know how to dance when they really can't dance at all. They bring their bad habits onto the dance floor."

"Well, I have plenty of bad habits, Jared. Just none that occur on dance floors, at least not yet. It is Jared, right? Or would you prefer Mr. Garrison?"

Jared smiled. "It's Jared, and may I call you Christine?"

Christine smiled in affirmation.

"Perhaps, after the fundraiser, your husband will join us for dance lessons as a couple. We have very nice packages that provide couples a wonderful opportunity to dance together. We have several specials going on right now in fact."

Christine hesitated briefly. "That won't be in my future, I'm afraid."

Jared tilted his head slightly once again, held both her hands gently in front of them, and focused again on her eyes. She indeed had beautiful eyes. "Well, Christine, we have many ladies come and enjoy dancing without a partner. You may find you'll enjoy dancing with me, or any of the other certified instructors. Hollie is a fine instructor and Kyle, our general manager, teaches as well. Kyle's in the back room. I'll introduce you. I'm certain you'll love it here and the studio can meet your every need. Don't be too quick to rule out making dance part of your life."

Christine's hair floated about her face as she shook her head and laughed. The suggestion didn't seem all that funny to Jared, who provided her a brief tour of the dance studio and introduced her to the staff on site. Following these niceties, Jared took her by the arm and escorted her onto the dance floor.

She flopped her oversized cloth purse onto a bench against the mirrored wall.

"Never want that bag to be out of my sight. I feel naked without it."

Jared rightly refrained from saying what came to his mind and merely smiled. It was time to put her through her paces, like a horse new to the race track. As this was a fundraiser, however, only one style of dance, and one routine of the selected style had to be mastered. Under these circumstances, it was even more important to discover how a student's body naturally moved and what limits there were to her abilities. Jared introduced various dance styles and demonstrated each to Christine through a few steps of his own before gathering her to join him.

Jared was pleasantly surprised that Christine had natural grace. She flowed across the floor and seemed very attentive to his elementary instructions. Although Jared could easily have selected waltz, foxtrot, or the quickstep, he knew that the Latin dances drew audience favor in competitions. And Christine certainly had an aptitude for Latin movement. Her hips rolled on every step and she seemed comfortable with the sensuous rhythm. Jared had no trouble seeing Christine O'Garra as she was at thirty, a very beautiful woman with a natural magnetic attraction. She had likely dated plenty of men in her day, and made the one she had now a very happy man.

Tuesday, August 11
Tracy: New Job, Familiar Face

Tracy took a few days to adjust to living in her Indianapolis apartment before starting work at the Bookworm Bookstore, and she had made good use of the time. Her current dope manager and delivery boys weren't allowed to use; Tracy never did—not ever. Her boys, however, hadn't followed this strict policy so she had to crack a few heads. She had sent one home with enough pure cocaine that he'd certainly O.D. and disappear.

The rest of the time had been spent securing exclusive rights to sell near the strip mall and surrounding lots. She had been warned that the territory closer to the high-end franchise mall was off limits, but Tracy resolved to change that policy. This area of Indy was new, but her weed was Chicago Kush strong and she had just hired a "blaster" to distill marijuana into eighty percent pure THC wax. Her cocaine was so pure it made your fingers numb. With Tracy's high-quality products and consistent reliability, her wealthy long-time customers would seek her out. Word would spread, sales would increase, and in time, the old dealers could be paid off for the rights to sell on their territory. But she'd build slow, keep it manageable. First, she had to focus on securing and transforming the bookstore—create a private place for discreet transactions.

Only two weeks at the bookstore and Tracy had already endeared herself to her aunt by opening on time every morning, working through lunch, and sticking around to lock up. She cleaned, sorted, and catalogued the inventory, and improved the store's layout by moving shelving for better visibility and customer flow.

This morning, Nora let it slip that Amber, the brat, had already moved back home to Vincennes. Something about how "it was real nice that her sister would be there to look after her mom." Tracy smothered silently. Amber was only a half-sister, not "her sister." And now the frightened rabbit was back in their childhood home, all snuggled up in Mama's burrow with her snot-nosed kids—probably demanding free babysitting, cooking, and laundry service from the HQ.

The day Tracy last spoke to her half-sister, well over ten years ago, was at Amber's backyard high school graduation "party." The memory was still fresh and amusing. A rickety card table bravely held the burden of a grocery store cake slathered with heavy garish frosting, as well as a punch bowl brimming with green lime Kool-Aid, complete with a floating ring of slimy frozen sherbet. The table was surrounded by reptilian relatives in folding chairs balancing flimsy paper plates on their bony knees. Some party.

Tracy had provided the only spark of fun when she had offered the ever-trembling Uncle Teddy the rickety aluminum lawn chair with the worn-out webbing. Uncle Teddy had Parkinson's disease, or multiple sclerosis, or something. His hands trembled, and his head bobbled like one of those fun novelty dolls you get at ball games. Amber had been the focus of everyone's attention until old Teddy took a tumble. His chair crumpled, and his skeletal remains flew backwards onto the cement patio. The ugly exchange that followed Teddy's exhilarating crash had been Amber's attempt to regain everyone's focus. Amber fired off a stormy accusation that Tracy had orchestrated the fall "on purpose." That made Tracy giggle inside. On purpose? Why would anyone ever do something without purpose?

Tracy remained silent. Even at age fifteen she had enough sense and control to remain silent. She knew that causing a fall was against the unspoken, unwritten rules of social interaction. She mustn't bite, kick, hit, pull hair, pinch, etc., etc. But all rules have exceptions, if she planned ahead. And, she discovered, her victims nearly always tried to hide the wounds she inflicted, so she learned to help them by only bruising them under their clothing. They were easy to control once she had created secret shame and fear, lots of fear.

So Tracy had remained calm and controlled as Amber's mouth gushed like an unplugged sewer line. The things she accused Tracy of doing in their past were so lewd, so despicable, so creative, that no one, not even their relatives, could possibly believe much of it. Amber was making a fool of herself, and Tracy wasn't about to interrupt. HQ finally steered the wailing high school graduate into the house and away from the wide-eyed guests who were still patting at Uncle Teddy with concern, clucking out the possibility of a concussion. Concussion? How would anyone ever know the difference? Tracy fondly recalled that, even then, she was very good at appearing "normal." She had joined the party guests in their gestures of worry, had grabbed up the offensive crumpled lawn chair and ceremoniously marched it to the curb for trash pickup.

The only unfortunate thing about Amber moving out the day after the party was that Tracy was suddenly very bored. That was the one thing Tracy feared—being bored. Fortunately, that concern wasn't currently looming in Tracy's future—she was on to bigger things than dull, dumpy Vincennes, Indiana.

She needed a cigarette—a good excuse to stroll through the back lot of the strip mall to study the parked cars, gather information, and look for opportunities. A short, thick-chested, black man was smoking alone behind the dance studio. He wore a crisp white shirt that strained slightly at his broad chest and shoulders, sleeves rolled. Black dress slacks. Blue tie. He stood with his feet planted slightly apart, a confident manly stance. He looked familiar, very familiar. He had been studying his phone when Tracy started in his direction and as she got near, he looked up at her and smiled. Then she knew. She knew the face and she certainly knew that smile. He, however, did not greet her with any sign of recognition, so Tracy held back her knowledge. Knowledge is power and Tracy didn't give power away, ever, so she stopped in front of him and waited.

"Nasty habit. I'd really like to stop," he said as he studied the cigarette in his hand. "Can I help you? The doors are in the front."

"Oh, I know. I work at the bookstore next door. Actually, I'm trying to decide if I want to buy the place. It will be a lot of work though; it needs a total overhaul," Tracy said.

"Well, welcome to the back lot. I'm Jared. Jared Garrison. I work here at the dance studio." He stuck his cigarette in his firm full mouth and extended his hand. He gathered hers into his in a friendly handshake.

"I'm Tracy Martin," she said, and shook his hand before releasing it with a light downward jerk.

He hadn't reacted to her face and now he hadn't reacted to her name. He didn't remember her. Why would he? It had been years since she'd seen Jaden Gregory, and she had changed a lot in those years—sprouted up several inches, and exploded into full curves men now turned to appreciate. She didn't look anything like the mousey Tracy Martin he might remember from Lincoln High School. But why was Jaden calling himself "Jared Garrison?"

Tracy had been a quiet pimple-faced freshman when Jaden was a senior—he, the most popular football jock in high school—a short, leg-churning running back. One of only three black guys in the senior class, he had been the secret heartthrob of nearly every girl in Vincennes, especially for Amber. As the photographer for the high school newspaper, Tracy had captured wonderful shots of the ever photogenic Jaden Gregory in various stages of dress inside the boy's locker room. Amber had paid her handsomely for those photos in a variety of ways. Their mother would have had a conniption if she knew Amber had the hots for a black guy.

Tracy studied the man in front of her and did a quick think back. Yes, the last time she had seen Jaden he was waiting tables at a greasy hometown restaurant in Vincennes. What, seven, eight years ago? Big shot, Jaden Gregory, waiting tables and now here he was teaching ballroom dance in Indianapolis. Tracy was fascinated by this older, less athletic, still extremely handsome Jaden Gregory—a man now calling himself "Jared Garrison." Unraveling her new friend "Jared" would prove to be an amusing pastime—perhaps one she could enjoy with Amber. She tapped out a cigarette. Using a sleek silver lighter, Jaden quickly lit it for her. She pulled the air sharply into her lungs and gently, slowly, blew a soft stream of smoke toward Jaden, encircling him in a haze. Tracy vaguely recalled that he had married just out of high school, to a black girl, one of only a handful in his class—except he wasn't wearing a wedding ring.

"I've noticed a lot of overdressed ladies in the bookstore, probably your students. They're a bit older than you though." She stopped to smile down at him sweetly. Fortunately she had carefully applied her makeup this morning and was wearing a low-cut sweater that seductively hugged at her. She brushed light ash from her cashmere breast and said, "I guess in a way we're in the same line of work, making the old and tired look attractive again. Isn't that it? You dance with ladies who love to dance. I bet you're very good."

She had learned to pause after saying something complimentary. People needed time to process and appreciate the fact their qualities were recognized. Evidently, this made them feel all warm and special. She thought to add a small detail, "This is the third store I've acquired for a makeover, so I'm pretty good at that line of work too."

He looked at her strangely. He stared at her as if he were waiting for her to come clean. She had seen people look at her that way many times. Perhaps there had been an uncomfortable amount of time between her responses. She quickly added, "So, I guess we'll be smoking buddies. How long have you been teaching dance?"

"Six years." He turned on his heel toward the door, glanced at it briefly, then turned back to her. "I love it. Don't know what I'd do if I couldn't teach dance." He snuffed out his half-finished cigarette in a tiny silver box he held in his palm and added, "Well, Tracy, I've got to get back to work." His partially smoked cigarette was carefully deposited into a waste receptacle.

He turned to a black Nissan parked beside them, unlocked the door with his remote and zipped the cigarettes, lighter, and silver ashtray into a small leather toiletry bag. He turned and removed a tin of mints from his jacket, then looked up at her with his head to one side. He suddenly took her hand and smiled at her, "I'll look forward to lighting you up anytime, Tracy."

"I'd enjoy that." They both smiled before he disappeared through the dance studio's back door.

"Yes, I plan to enjoy that a great deal, Jaden," she said

softly to her glowing cigarette.

She made a quick check to be certain there was no surveillance equipment. No cameras. Although Jaden had locked his car, Tracy was able to see a notebook through the window. "One third behind me—lucky if 55 left. What next?" was written at the top of the exposed sheet—bold and black. Many people would have been mystified by the words, but not Tracy. Tracy had studied how people think. It helped that she knew Jaden's age—same as Amber's. They had graduated in the same class three years ahead of Tracy. This note was obviously his age and a frank self-question about his life's direction. Tracy had recently explored this question herself, so it was easy to decipher.

So, Jaden (no she must call him Jared), was feeling a bit unsteady being thirty years old. She recalled Jaden—Jared—as fun-loving and full of himself. But he had done fairly well, considering the direction his life had been heading when he was a high school senior. He was well-known for partying, tomcatting. And now he was a ballroom dance instructor in glorious Indianapolis, Indiana.

Tracy flicked her cigarette and reflected on the conversation. Six years in one spot meant that he was loyal and devoted to his work. The type of person Tracy could teach; teach, then control. It would be a pleasant diversion to reverse their roles—put Jaden in his rightful place. She would teach him to love her, as she had done to other men. She would become his everything—his thoughts, his actions, his words, his world. Yes, Jared would serve as a pleasant diversion from her carefully laid plans at the bookstore.

Tracy put the final glow of the cigarette out against the hood of Jaden's car. Timing smoke breaks to coincide with his wouldn't be difficult and it wouldn't be long before they'd be more than just friends. She smiled, imagining Amber's surprise at receiving photos and videos of this new Jaden Gregory. Jaden dancing with Tracy, laughing with Tracy, kissing Tracy, Jaden in bed doing all the things Tracy loved best. No, stop with the "Jaden Gregory." It's Jared Garrison. Jared Garrison. Jared Garrison. Tracy wouldn't think of him as anything except Jared Garrison again. But she planned to think of Jared Garrison a great deal. Tracy would research him online and join him—here in the back for a friendly smoke and a private chat. Indianapolis was certainly proving to be an interesting place.

Friday, August 14
Jared: How Firm a Foundation

"Love does not brag and is not arrogant. It does
not act unbecomingly: it does not seek its own..."

I Corinthians 13:4-5

Jared parked on the scruffy front yard, well out of the way of the rental truck that filled the crumbling driveway. He sat for a moment and studied the tiny house—it had aged over the years. Crisp white curls of paint clung desperately to dry weathered boards. A rusted gutter sagged above the large grimy window that stared out at him. He wanted to wash the tear-stained window till it shone as it had in June. But there wasn't time, or reason, to fight against what the years had done—it was moving day for Gran Gregory.

Eugene's tall frame was backing out the front door, and the handcart he was fighting bumped anxiously down two cement steps and onto the sidewalk. The flimsy aluminum screen door slapped shut with a tinny snap. Its torn screen waved in the slight hot breeze.

"'Bout time you show up," his brother offered as greeting.

"Good to see you too. How's Gran doing?" Jared asked.

"She's wonderin' around just looking. Fingering stuff instead of packing. You were supposed to be here on Tuesday night to get all her stuff boxed. What happened to that, huh?" Eugene scowled as he heaved a box onto the back of the empty truck.

"She told me not to come. Said she wasn't ready."

"Jaden, she's never gonna be ready to leave this place." Eugene wheeled the now empty cart aside and steadied it upright. He held his hand toward it as a command not to fall. "Lots of memories here, I know, but she can't stay here alone. We all know that."

"She said she'd move to the apartment you and Claire picked out. She's ready. She just needs time to take it in is all. Today's gonna be hard on her." Jared waited for a hint of tender consensus from his older brother, but Eugene was intent on kicking crumbles of asphalt away from the wheels of the cart.

"I'll go talk with her a bit then get her packing up," Jared said.

"Well, it's got to get done today. We're both off work and only rented the truck for twenty-four hours."

"But I gotta work tonight. Friday night's dance party

night. Missing work all day, so can't miss tonight's party."

Eugene jerked at a packing strap that dangled from the truck. "God no, you can't miss the party, Jaden. You never miss a party."

Jared found his grandmother sitting on her bed looking at a photo album. She struggled to stand when her eye caught him coming down the long hallway. Jared picked up his pace and took her by both arms to help her. Then the hug. Gran's hug.

Her body was soft and yielding, so her hug was like being engulfed by a warm foam pillow. She'd hold you, and then wait till you released, then she'd pull you back in and hold you for one more moment. And in that moment, she'd hold all of you. Your worries, your tension, your falseness would melt away for just that moment. It was deep and forgiving. Gran's hugs always made Jared want to cry, but he didn't know why.

He kissed her soft cheek and tasted the soapy lotion there. "Hey, girl. I hear you're just looking at stuff, not packing up. Whatcha got there?"

Jared helped ease her back onto the bed and settled himself near enough to feel her softness, to hear her rustle, to smell the jumble of cooking and bleach and mint. "Photos. Yes?"

"Your impy little face in some of 'em, you and that brother of yours." She took up the album and poked a gnarled finger at a photo of two skinny little boys sitting at a table: the very table waiting in the next room to be hauled off to an apartment in Lebanon. The boys had huge round eyes and they were looking at a man grinning over a platter of food. The table overflowed with bowls and dishes filled with a colorful feast.

"Probably only a couple days after you came," Gran said softly. "Look at your big otter eyes. Up to somethin' for sure."

Jared wasn't looking at his own image, he was studying the mark on Eugene's skinny arm, dark purplish black, and another on his face. Gran's finger pulled slowly across the image of his grandfather.

Although a strange mixture of memories, the mental snapshots of love and laughter outweighed the hurt. He remembered his grandfather's attention to Gran, especially at mealtime. Supper was a nightly affair that commanded everyone's full devotion to ritual. Granddad would stand at the kitchen doorway watching Gran put the finishing touches on the meal she had labored over. She would hand him a bowl, and he would reach beyond it and softly pull his hand down her wrist and over the back of her hand before taking whatever she held. Over and over, he would safely deliver the food, one bowl or platter at a time, to the dining room. He would round up Eugene and Jared and get them settled as Gran fussed with a few last details in the kitchen. During one of these waits at the table, Granddad had shown Jared how to be certain he had something securely in his hand before taking it from a lady. Jared recalled practicing sliding his hand down Granddad's over and over. "That only works on the ladies, though," he had told Jared with a hardy laugh.

Gran would finally emerge from the kitchen and remove the cover of the butter dish. It was her sign that the meal was ready. Granddad would stand up at the clinking of the butter cover and pull out Gran's chair. He would take up her left hand and tap at her wedding ring, then kiss that ring softly as she finally settled at the table with them. She would giggle like a schoolgirl and swat her hand playfully in Granddad's direction. They could finally say grace and eat.

What Jared remembered most was the way his grandparents looked at one another. They had laughing eyes. Eyes full of special secrets. Back then, Jared wondered what those deep secrets could be, and he was a bit hurt when they wouldn't share more than smiles when he asked. He still wondered.

"You miss him, Gran?" Jared finally asked, as the light and dark shadows of memories drifted about them.

"Never stop missin' people you love. 'Cept I look at that face and think about the boys he raised up—you and Eugene. No regrets there." She looked up and smiled at him, patted his leg.

Jared provided her a false, but loving, smile. They both knew that there were regrets. He had created them himself and fortunately, Granddad hadn't lived long enough to see the poor choices he had made. The photo album didn't display the mug shots taken after his arrests. One here in Vincennes, another, unknown to Gran, in Indianapolis after his last, and final, DUI. Cocaine, a kicked habit that still pulled at him, especially at night.

"Could use some help here, Jaden." Eugene's distant voice held its normal amount of annoyance. He could hear his brother stomping about the house, grumbling loudly. Jared watched his grandmother's hand turn another page. Tanisha's unmoving face stared back at his. He hadn't expected to see her photo, and his heart stopped for a moment before it pounded forward again. There were several photos of Tanisha surrounded by colorful gifts tied in shiny bows.

"When were these photos taken, Gran? Where? Don't remember ever seeing them."

"Took 'em at Tanisha's mama's. Had a baby shower for her. You not remembering 'cause menfolk not invited."

Gran's hand lifted the page to turn, but Jared held his hand at the photo and looked at his ex-wife for a long time. Unlike all the women who surrounded her, Tanisha wasn't smiling. The photo had to have been taken just after their wedding during the first pregnancy. The baby they lost would have been ten, no eleven, years old now. If it hadn't been for the miscarriage, he'd be tearing around the house, getting in the way, asking everyone silly questions right now. Maybe the baby would have been a girl, a giggly little girl with a cinnamon button nose. Jared found himself wishing Claire had come today with his nephews and niece, except they would have only slowed the work. And besides, Claire had soured since he had messed up with that last DUI. Jared still felt her crisp coldness whenever he was near her, or the kids. He remained unforgiven. Forever branded.

"No sense sitting here looking at old pictures," Gran said as she gently pulled the photo album away from him. "You best be gettin' a box and helping me get all this stuff ready to go." Jared continued to stare at the closed album. Gran shook her head.

"You just ain't found the right girl yet. She's out there. You just keep being good to the ladies. You be polite to 'em and do what they ask. You'll know her when she come, just ain't come yet is all." She rubbed his head above his ear then struggled to stand. He helped her to her feet and she sway-tottered down the hallway. The photos and the house were pulling memories he tried not to visit. He found an empty box, started wrapping newspaper around Gran's trinkets, then allowed himself the one memory of Tanisha he did visit. The day of their one, and only, wedding anniversary. He visited that memory often.

It was late at night, after Jared had finally gotten home from his second job waiting tables. Tanisha hadn't bothered to make a meal or even get takeout, so he ate ramen noodles, yet again. Things brightened for just a moment, one sparkling moment when Tanisha told him that she was expecting again. A second pregnancy. He had been hoping and praying for this. Only moments later, she told him the baby wasn't his and that she was leaving to live with the baby's father. He hadn't believed her, and he told her so. She spat at him, screamed profanities, as if it was he who had been unfaithful. He was shocked by the ugly woman who stood over him, mocking him. Even so, he pleaded with her to stay—told her he would work to be whatever she needed him to be. It didn't matter that the baby wasn't his—he would love the baby as his own, and love her through the years ahead. His wife, suddenly a stranger, had laughed at him. Their marriage was beyond repair.

Tanisha remained in the apartment. Jared moved back in with Gran Gregory. The divorce finalized. Seven months later Tanisha gave birth to a baby boy she named Tyrone. She soon remarried and the happy family settled into a new house on the outskirts of town.

Jared had set eyes on the baby only once. He was grocery shopping with Gran and had seen Tanisha before she saw him. Tyrone was sleeping in a car seat in the cart. Gran boldly approached Tanisha, said hello, and then patted the baby politely with a warm smile, wakening him. Tanisha barely glanced at Jared. Gran started in on her chatting and began her typical information extraction.

"So, Tanisha, your mama tells me you're married and

doin' good." Gran backed away from the cart slightly and continued, "Hear you and him moving to Chicago, that right?"

The distraction had provided Jared an opportunity to examine the baby who smiled up at him. As Jared stared at that little face, Gran's purse hit the floor. Stuff bounced and rolled in all directions and Tanisha bent to help her. Jared fought off his instinct to help too, instead he slipped out his phone, flipped it open, and took a photo. Tyrone had Jared's light chocolate skin and dark caramel eyes. It was as if he were staring at his own baby photo. This was his child. He could see it, smell it, feel it. He was as certain of it as his next breath.

The tiny miracle started gumming at a blue rubbery ring clenched in his fat little fist. The baby held it out, all wet and slippery, toward his father. Still gazing at the baby, Jared took the slobbery gift, stood entranced. When Tanisha saw the phone in his hand, she threw a blanket over the baby's face, hissed at Jared, and jerked the cart off in a rush down the cereal aisle.

That was the last, and only, time Jared had seen his son. Even now, Jared would dream about Tyrone, enslaved by two plump fists that reached out to him, and the enormous eyes that stared up at him from the grocery cart like two drops of dark warm honey. Jared thought of those eyes many, many times in the room he was standing in now—the small bedroom he had called his after he moved back in with Gran. The room had served him for three sad years before he moved to Indy to live with Eugene and Claire.

His fingers traced the small indent in the wall where his angry fist had landed late one drunken night. A rare outburst. He turned his attention to the chair near the window. He could still see Gran sitting there as she had done so many times. She would stay up till Jared got home from work to talk with him in the dark. He would start drinking after she went to bed. Not a lot, just enough to relax, and push the pain aside. Enough to sleep. Time slipped by. Work and talk and drink and sleep and work and talk and drink and sleep...for days, weeks, years. He lifted the twin-sized mattress slightly and pulled his arm across the threadbare box spring to be certain there were no bottles still lurking.

Jared tugged the top drawer of his old dresser open, it squeaked out a protest. The box was still there. He cradled it in his hands, lifted off the lid, and backed over to sit in the lonely wooden chair. A pile of letters, twenty of them, all addressed to Tanisha, all returned unopened. His thoughts, feelings, and hopes for a new start unread and unwanted. He sat there studying his own handwriting. It hadn't changed—small printed letters, slanting dangerously across the envelope. He sat very still and listened for Eugene. He could hear him talking with Gran in the kitchen about pots and pans. Jared quickly stuffed the box in his shirt and hurried outside to toss it in his car. He'd throw the letters away later, privately.

Jared made his way back to the small bedroom, picked up the small wooden chair and looked at it thoughtfully. A comrade, a witness to this past life.

"You know if you put things in the truck instead of standing around holding them, we'd get this done a lot faster," Eugene's voice boomed past him and down the hallway, rudely invading Jared's sad reminiscing. But he was right. Eugene was always right. So he, and the precious chair, took a slow walk to the truck.

Gran had insisted on making lunch, and stood over the

sloppy joe meat, stirring and tasting. She was leaning heavily onto the counter and rocked back and forth as she reached for more chopped onion from her cutting board.

"You need me to check those feet of yours? Looks like they're givin' you trouble," Jared said. She turned, shook her head.

"Jadie, you see that Granddad's urn is packed up proper in that there box on the table." She thrust the end of her wooden spoon at a solid-looking box stuffed with bubble wrap. She said it with her "no nonsense from you" voice.

"Yes, ma'am." He took up the box, but barely glanced at the container that held the ashes of his grandfather as he hurried through the living room. Human remains were way beyond his comfort zone.

"Gran says to use this to pack Granddad's urn." He handed his brother the box. "Here, let me take that," Jared said as he quickly pulled at the ironing board his brother held.

Eugene laughed. It was never a secret with him that Jared was squeamish around that dusty urn. Jared would keep at least three feet away from it. Sometimes he would forget, and be studying a framed photo on the mantel, or toying with a nearby trinket. He would quickly pull back when he realized how close he was to those creepy ashes.

"'Fraid he's going to jump out at you for all the hurt you've caused Gran?" Eugene's words hit Jared harder than they would have most days. Today they stung. Jared turned away with the stiff ironing board knocking at his shins and carried it to the truck.

He had spent too much of his life causing hurt. He'd provided plenty of childlike trouble for Granddad years ago. He had failed to satisfy his young wife, hadn't met her needs. Hurt Gran. Disappointed his brother and sister-in-law. A lot of time wasted and too little time left to live. *Then you die, Jaden,* he thought, but he didn't want to think about getting older, let alone dying. Having his powdered body sifted into a jar—no longer able to hear or smell or see or taste the world. No longer able to feel anything. Jared pushed these thoughts out of the truck and studied the blue flowered ironing board still in his hands. He imagined the board as a beautiful woman, someone as beautiful as Christine O'Garra. It startled him that his new student came quickly to mind, but there she was, smiling at him. He smiled back. The ironing board waltzed beautifully for a moment, through one turn, then another.

"Jaden, what the hell are you doing bouncing around in the truck? You got a herd of buffalo in there? Gran says it's time to eat." Eugene provided Jared adequate motivation to assist his partner to the recesses of the truck. He bowed to Christine and she shyly smiled back before he hopped out and headed to the house. His brother rolled his eyes as he walked through the door toward the savory aromas coming from the kitchen.

"Could get this all done today. If we stay at it," Eugene said as he glared at Jared over a fork of coleslaw. Eugene's face glistened in the hot little kitchen as he pulled the belly of his shirt up to wipe the beads of moisture off his forehead.

"Just need to get the furniture in now," Jared said.

"The furniture for the apartment. But all these appliances need to be taken outta here too, you know. Gotta get everything that Gran doesn't need delivered to the thrift store. Then get all the things she needs to her apartment and get her settled in. And the truck needs to get back. On time." Eugene wolfed down the last bit of his sandwich, grabbed an empty box from the floor and headed for the linen closet in the hallway.

Eugene was right of course. There was still a lot of work to be done, but he needed a little dessert, a grease cutter, Gran called it. Jam and crackers would have to do. Jared studied his grandmother as she poked about in the refrigerator—a faithful appliance that would soon be only a shell, stripped empty, then discarded. And yet there was Gran, still at home, causally looking for jam. Surely, she'd miss living here—the garden and her birds and the squirrel she called Howard. Eugene was right again, though. Gran's health was failing, and she needed to live where he and Eugene could check on her. Howard would have to fend for himself.

The apartment Eugene had chosen was in the same county where he served as a sheriff's deputy. Although the area was located off a major interstate, it had the same hometown feel as Vincennes. The county had the elderly services Gran needed, and could provide the assisted living housing she was likely to need in the near future. Her new apartment would be a short twenty minute drive from Jared's. The brothers had agreed to split half the cost of the apartment and allow Gran to pay the other half.

Jared now had his grandmother written into his weekly schedule. Thursdays were going to be "supper with Gran night" for everyone. She had insisted on that. Jared would shop with her on Sundays, and sit with her in the afternoon. He would drive her to doctor appointments during the week whenever possible. Mornings would be best.

By midafternoon, the truck was packed and it was time to leave the little house that held so many memories, both good and bad. Jared helped lower Gran into the front seat of his car.

"Get me that box you packed up for me. Gotta hold Grand-dad here on my lap." Gran smiled up at him from the bottom of the seat.

Jared hesitated. "Euggie's driving you, Gran. I'm driving the truck. That okay?"

Gran looked past him at the small empty house. "Don't care, just need to git." Her eyes welled up and she started crying. Jared quickly offered his handkerchief.

"You turned out real fine, Jadie, real fine." She sniffed softly. "Now, tell that brother of yours to hurry along."

Eugene retrieved the very special box from the seat of the truck and smiled as he handed the truck keys to Jared.

"You're such an idiot, Jaden, you beat everything." He lifted the box above his kid brother's head and shook it playfully. Jared cringed as he fled to the safety of the rental truck.

Thursday, August 20
Christine: Calculating Time

Seth and his parents left behind a legacy that allowed Christine to effortlessly settle into the heart of Boone County's foundational families. The O'Garra name was recognized, respected, and most importantly, associated with wealth, so community leaders eagerly welcomed her into their elite circles of influence. But, unlike Christine, their community stopped at lines on a map—bound within the county. To Christine, community was no longer a physical place—it was the self-made fabric of her relationships, each person an essential thread as they wove their way in and out of her life. She would care for all of them, and it didn't matter if they cared for her. In fact, to Christine's way of thinking, it would be much better if they didn't care for her at all. It would hurt less when they left. Even so, she resolved that all of her money (of which there was plenty) and her time (of which there was far too little), would now be invested in people.

Lessons the past two Tuesdays, another last Thursday and now again today. She began calculating her investment for the charity gala as she drove. Fifteen forty-five minute lessons would be a total of eleven and a quarter hours. Time spent chatting before and after the lesson: ten minutes each lesson. Traveling: sixty minutes per lesson. All total, nearly forty hours would be invested before displaying her used-once dance skills at the gala. And she hadn't yet counted the time she would spend shopping for a dress and necessary heeled shoes, getting her hair done and all the travel for those tasks. Then attending the gala itself. Yes, the November fundraiser was a substantial investment, hopefully one that would pay off well. At least she now knew better than to waste time changing clothes after work for lessons.

Jared had told her to shop for a bright red dress. *Had he really mentioned red? Bright red? What was wrong with muted blue or dark green?* She had already looked through Lebanon's thrift store to find a suitable dress of any color without success. She was now seriously considering purchasing a new dress for the occasion. Perhaps one that wasn't even on a clearance rack.

Christine smiled at the outrageous thought of buying a dress at full price. Seth would have been proud of her. April would have laughed out loud, maybe.

At the moment, however, Christine was stuck in traffic. She forced herself not to add the wasted minutes to her time budget total. Instead, she moved her thoughts to Jared. Jared, this mix of unborn baby and Jesse. Two sons swirled together at the start of every lesson. Jared lavished her with cheerful touches the way Jesse had years ago—an affectionate little boy with a quick smile and his head in the clouds. With Jared, Christine allowed her mind to see young Jesse reaching for her hand, bringing her a hug, delivering a kiss. A child, who needed to be touched, needed to be physically against her before settling comfortably into conversations. Jared's friendly mannerisms numbed the pain of not being with her sons—especially the living one, long-delayed in returning to her.

Twenty hours alone with Jared would be plenty of time to get to know him and share with him whatever he needed from her life experiences. If she could help him find his way, find his happiness, get comfortable with his purpose, she would have fulfilled her true mission here.

She prepared questions for Jared, ones she wished she had offered Jesse when she'd had the chance—meaningful questions that could start real conversations. She asked Kyle, the general manager, her Tuesday question and he freely shared about his struggle with a back injury severe enough to end his dream of dancing on Broadway. Unfortunately, Jared resolutely withheld any personal information from her. Apparently, life was a dance party to Jared Garrison.

Christine entered the studio, changed into her tired low-heeled dress shoes. Jared was running a bit late, so she decided it would be more efficient to hold onto her bag of street shoes and her purse during the greeting hug. Jared was strutting her way. The bags bumped about, crinkled awkwardly around him during their greeting. She decided the lumpy hug may not have been a good idea. Next time she would drop her things, hug Jared properly and gather everything up again. Her bags prevented Jared from his customary after-the-hug handholding too. She was sorry she had messed with his routine to experiment with efficiency. Time was ticking, so she took Jared's extended arm for the usual escort.

"Do you remember being born, Jared? I'm just wondering if anyone remembers being born because someone I knew was dying of cancer and he told me he was scared to die. He and I decided that dying was probably like being born. We don't remember being born and we probably won't remember dying after we've done it." Christine allowed time for that to register. "What do you think?"

Jared marched her in quick step across the gleaming hardwood. "We talked about your need for a dress, yes? Bright red is the best color for a salsa. Knee-length or shorter and it would be best if the hem is asymmetrical. And what about your shoes?"

He pulled to a stop, dropped her arm and provided her shoes a look of disdain. "You should wear higher heels than those. We have catalogs here at the studio from which you can order a proper pair of dance shoes." He watched as she settled the bags onto a nearby bench. "You should purchase shoes soon and wear them to the rest of your lessons so you'll feel comfortable in them. And I love the slacks you always wear, but you should wear a dress to lessons from now on so you feel the flow and float of a skirt." He leaned over and picked a small bit of white lint from her sleeve.

Comfortable in heels? Seriously? Feel the flow of a skirt? I just asked you if you remember being born. "I've been looking for shoes, but the ones I've seen women wearing here at the studio certainly don't appear to be made for comfort. Have you ever danced in high-heeled shoes?" She noticed that the mirrored wall made it appear that she had brought four large frumpy bags instead of just two.

Christine listened as the ever-polished Jared explained that properly heeled shoes with suede soles were a necessary part of the uniform of a serious female dancer. It was somewhat patronizing, as he had explained this before. Perhaps his shoe description was drawn out because he hadn't taken the time and effort to properly shorten his message. Or perhaps all this nattering about shoes was a convenient diversion—a way to avoid answering her questions. Christine sighed. Perhaps ballroom dancing was his purpose in life. She should share his enthusiasm for the tools of his trade and buy new shoes.

It's not just the shoes, it's the dress. He insists I buy a bright red dress. Red was one color Christine avoided wearing. There was still enough Mennonite DNA in her that made wearing eye-catching colors somewhat prideful, even offensive—an illogical remnant of early constructs. Red also sat unforgiving against her pale, nearly blue, skin. She sighed again and reluctantly resolved that she would proudly wear a little red dress in November. A dress that would be donated to a thrift shop before Thanksgiving.

"And, Christine, about the jewelry. The outfit will not be

complete without lots of jewelry, dangling bracelets, a heavy pendant necklace, and hoop earrings—those are a must. You have hoop earrings, yes?"

Christine hesitated, "I think so." She gently rubbed the top of her diamond rings across her lips. "I could wear my daughter's hoop earrings. They're small gold hoops with inset diamonds. Tiny diamonds." She lowered her hand, turned and sighed again—the sound of heartache. Jared mustn't hear it, mustn't see it in her face. She was there to dance. She turned quickly back to him and replied, "I have bracelets and I'll look around for a necklace. I'll be all gussied up, don't you worry. I've got earrings so I'm making progress."

"Good. I've missed you, Christine. What have you been doing since Tuesday?"

The list of things she had accomplished would likely overwhelm her young dance instructor. She had successfully launched a newly-published curriculum on transferring estates within farm families. It was a multi-year project she had finished after moving. Somehow, however, it didn't seem Jared's standard question was searching for that type of answer.

"Not much. I did paint the upstairs bathroom last night, though."

"I hope that husband of yours helped you." He peered at her carefully. "I see you chose pale green. There's paint in your hair." He reached up and pulled his fingers down a few strands of her hair, tugging out the paint. "That's better, yes?"

"Well, yes. I suppose a woman shouldn't walk around with paint in her hair. Can't understand why I didn't notice it earlier today." And yet again she thought better of telling him there was no husband.

Jared tilted his head assessing her hair for a moment then abruptly turned and marched to the corner of the room. He toyed with the music till he found a suitable song, turned the volume up a notch, and then spoke loudly against the pounding vibrations.

"Let's get started. We've settled on the salsa, and that requires movement of the hips and a smooth looseness of the shoulders. All that without a lot of movement in the upper body."

He had her stand beside him at the mirror and showed her the rolling movement of his hips as he swayed his arms in front of his body. She mimicked him the best she could and he grinned at her reflection. "Yes, you have the movement of the hips. We need to see those arms moving and keep your hands a bit lower." Jared observed her reflection for a time, then he took her into his arms in a standard frame, but immediately dropped his hands to his sides and took a quick step back.

"I've held a lot of women in my arms and I know what they wear under their clothing, so what is that?" He poked a finger toward her left side. Christine cringed. She normally carried her gun in her purse.

"Sorry—forgot I was holstering today. Would you excuse me a moment, please?" She turned, yanked her purse from the bench and headed for the bathroom where she stowed the gun properly into her purse. The body holster was stuffed in as well. What must he think of her? Well, at least she had gotten him to react transparently to something. Not something she said, but to something. She returned to the dance floor to find Jared pacing. He stopped abruptly and stood with fists on his hips, that handsome head of his at full tilt.

"Well, at least you now know why I never want to have that bag out of my sight." Christine settled her purse onto a nearby bench then added, "The studio doesn't have a policy against concealed carry do they? I have my license and have gotten very used to having my gun with me at all times."

His big eyes looked at her for a moment then he replied, "I don't know of any policy against it, so if you're more comfortable having a gun, feel free. It just surprised me is all. None of my other students have had reason to ask."

"Perhaps your other students are simply more careful with their firearms." Christine was enjoying his obvious unsteadiness. "It's perfectly legal and acceptable for me to carry a gun. You needn't look so surprised."

He stood silently studying her. Even though he didn't seem upset, he wasn't pleased either. "Does it bother you that I carry a gun?" she asked.

He narrowed his eyes—fighting with the possibility of engaging in conversation. He suddenly turned on his heel and restarted the music.

"Okay, let's work on the first few steps of what will become your routine. We've settled on the salsa, yes?" He popped yet another Altoid and returned to her.

"You feel like yourself again." He smiled that smile of his and Christine saw Jesse's face, but it was Jared's right hand that gently pulled at her back, and his left that pushed her hand. She moved to his lead the best she could. They worked together steadily through the lesson as teacher and student.

There were other dancers on the floor: an elderly couple with Hollie and an older woman dancing with Kyle. The woman looked to be in her seventies and was obviously having the time of her life. Christine enjoyed watching her. She was having fun. Christine fought not to envy this woman who was simply having fun.

The lesson was over, and Jared escorted her to the receptionist's computer. Wedging the remaining eleven lessons into their calendars was a bit tricky. A couple weeks had no lessons, several others were assigned two. Jared provided her a CD of music so she could practice at home. She imagined herself dancing the salsa in her living room, her kitchen, maybe even her bedroom. The very thought of such silliness made her smile. Jared tilted his head at her with a puzzled look, but she left him with only a light laugh.

Monday, August 24
Tracy: Bookstore Break-In

Tracy made a few more mouse clicks and shook her head at the glowing monitor. She had been looking for a challenge, but Nora's sloppy accounting made using the bookstore as a front so easy it was somewhat deflating. She pushed herself from the computer and wandered out into the store.

"Aunt Nora, I've applied for a new business credit card. The interest rate you're paying now is way too high. Besides, the cash back bonus points with the new card can be applied to our payments."

"Oh, Tracy, I've been meaning to look into a new card

for months and months. Just never got around to it." Nora was in front of the counter, surrounded by several large cardboard boxes on the floor. She leaned over one and sliced open the packing tape with a flourish, her bony butt hoisted to greet the rare customer who might wander in. "My arthritis is acting up terrible today. Today, of all days," she lamented.

Tracy pulled and twisted her dark long hair and started again, "We can hang onto the old credit card too if you'd like. I don't know as much about running a business as you, and maybe there's a reason not to change over to the new one too quickly." She stopped to study her aunt who was folded over at the waist with her face planted in a box of paperbacks.

"Oh, Tracy, look at this one! It's the next in that series in the Irish fishing village. I must read this next." Nora grabbed up a copy and positioned it carefully on top of her hidden "must reads" under the counter. The stack of books leaned precariously. She returned quickly to her treasure hunt.

"The insurance man will be here this afternoon to complete the paperwork," Tracy shared nonchalantly. "I'm pretty sure I have everything he'll need. The police report, a list of things stolen, damage done, and the repair estimates." Tracy stepped around the boxes, and studied the screws that held the plywood in place at the front door.

Nora had a troubled look. "It's just so hard to get good help these days. I wish my brother-in-law was still alive. He would have been here to replace that door glass before the police left. It's just a shame." She shook her head as she studied the plywood at Tracy's red-tipped fingers. "Oh, but Tracy. You've handled this whole thing so well. I've never been broken into, and here only a month after you arrive and this happens."

"Well, at least I got a new computer yesterday, and I had backed up all of your records so I was able to reload the customer database and the accounting information."

"I just couldn't believe that, really. What made you decide to backup the computer as soon as you got here? I know I'm supposed to have been doing that...that backup thing. Just never did. You young people know so much about computers and what to do."

Tracy stopped and studied the woman with interest. Was she really such a simpleton? The woman was nearly as boring as the HQ. Tracy forced herself to maintain the polite exterior she needed to herd her aunt, sheep-like, into the next decision.

"Just so you know, Aunt Nora, the police suggested that we purchase a security camera for both the front and back entrances, and when I asked the insurance guy, he highly recommended it, too. It will be costly, but having cameras installed will lower our premiums. I found a vendor and plan to purchase what we need today, if that's okay."

"What?" Nora was now thumbing through a hardback on traveling Europe by train. She set the heavy book aside and began rubbing the back of her hand gingerly.

"I need to make several security equipment purchases. Hopefully the things we need won't be too expensive."

"Oh, yes. Yes, whatever you feel is best," Nora replied. The colorful beads on the lanyard of her reading glasses jiggled cheerfully as she raised her head to acknowledge that Tracy knew best. It was exactly what Tracy hoped to hear. Tracy had, in fact, already made her purchases—security cameras, a professional voice recording system, a miniature purse camera, and a GPS tracking system. Cost was no consideration—the bookstore credit line was paying for it all.

The woman's never-ending mouth was saying, "Oh, Tracy, you've made it possible for me to just enjoy the store again. I must say, everything has worked out splendidly having you here."

"I couldn't agree more, Auntie. I really couldn't agree more." Tracy smiled sweetly and gave Nora a warm little pat before returning to the office to download the manuals of her new purchases as well as research the features of the 2011 Nissan Altima.

Tracy was soon checking public records in Vincennes, Indiana for Jaden Gregory. A DUI, one marijuana possession charge…

"Whatever is the matter with that cat?" Her aunt's fretful voice called out, interrupting a productive thread of online research.

Tracy glanced up. *The cat, always the damn cat.*

"Why? Is it sick?" Tracy called back.

"The poor thing is cowering under the gardening section again." Nora's distressed voice had wandered to the back of the store.

"Maybe the delivery man scared it when he brought in that book order," Tracy suggested. She made a mental note to stop terrorizing the cat—at least not quite so much.

Tuesday, September 22
Christine: Playing His Games

"A person starts to live when he can live
outside himself."

— Albert Einstein

Christine cringed at the sound of Jared's ricocheting footsteps. She purposefully scowled with focused attention at her cell phone and mindlessly fingered the raised dotted scar above her collarbone. Just once she wished he'd sneak up on her. The lobby of the dance studio flooded with sunlight and the polished wood floor glistened in front of her as the staccato footsteps rapped closer. It would be impossible not to notice someone approaching, so she hoped she appeared oblivious to anyone or anything around her. It wasn't until he greeted her that she looked up at him with what she hoped would appear to be surprise. There was, of course, nothing even remotely interesting on her phone.

He hadn't opened up to her in any genuine way, so she had resorted to his type of nonsense. He would gush; she would pretend not to hear. He would hug and she would yank herself away with a quick sisterly smile. It didn't help that she was in a rare bad mood and had a lot to get done at home.

Here it comes—the greeting. The hug. The hand holding. The same question.

"So, Christine, how was your week? What did you do?" His head tilted and his beautiful smile was delivered with a flash. Right on cue.

Christine tilted her head the opposite direction and smiled

at him. "The sump pump failed and the basement is wet." His frozen smile continued. "And I spilled coffee on the seat of my friend's car," she added, wondering if her eyes were twinkling like his.

How far would these superficial conversations go before he would finally reach a breaking point? Last week she told him the cat brought her a dead mouse and that she canned twenty pints of ketchup. That was true, but occasionally, she lied about her activities—slipped in something from her journal, the one in which she had recorded her childhood activities and the lives of her parents. She felt her childhood as she read about their practical skills and close-to-the-earth adventures, such as planting potatoes and mixing molasses into livestock feed. If she shared something self-deprecating, Jared would be quick to assure her that he, for one, simply could not picture her in the situation she described. Like today.

"You are one of the most graceful students I've ever taught, so I find it very difficult to believe you spilled your coffee."

Seriously, Jared?

He didn't seem much like Jesse any more. His touch felt rehearsed, the same at every lesson. He now reminded her more of her niece who performed on stage in Cincinnati. She and Jared were both very convincing actors, except Jared's theatrics were now grating on Christine. He was a smooth-surfaced fake—a very sweet, lovable fake.

As Jared re-rolled his left sleeve to mid-arm, Christine dug in her bag and quietly laid a tiny pack of hard to find Sen-Sen on the table beside his mint tin. Jared tried to mask the fact that he was a smoker by popping Altoid mints before and throughout every lesson. He never offered her a mint, so today she had brought her own candy, a strong salty licorice.

"What's this?" He examined the tiny foil packet.

"My favorite candy, but unfortunately, they're no longer made. Most people find them nasty. Would you like to try it?" She shook a couple of the tiny black bits onto her palm and tossed them seamlessly into her mouth.

He eyed her briefly then did the same. The black bits came spitting out as quickly as they had gone in with no regard for decorum, like a small child. Fortunately, Christine had a clean tissue handy to receive them from his mouth. That was the typical reaction to salt licorice from these sheltered naïve young people.

"You know, Jared, I want to thank you again for the time you're spending toward the support of this charity event. The organization provided my mother-in-law wonderful elderly housing and services." *Perhaps the event will get him talking about his own family*, she thought.

"Mavis, the owner, always selects organizations that provide great services. Hopefully my grandmother will be able to get into one of those elderly housing facilities soon."

"Oh, you have a grandmother living in Lebanon?"

He hesitated. "We need to get started, Christine," he said turning from her.

"I hope we can get enough people to shell out a hundred dollars per head to attend," Christine said, as she watched Jared plant his feet and shuffle through possible song selections.

"Well, let's give them their money's worth, yes?" He turned up the music and escorted her to the mirror where she tried her best to mimic his movements. He in turn studied her reflection carefully with his tenacious smile. She began to wonder if he was addicted to the never-ending drug of sound and movement, and it was becoming difficult to maintain enthusiasm. Still, Christine had made a promise, a commitment. So she would learn this saucy little salsa routine to wow the crowd.

Fortunately, it was good exercise and she was developing strong friendships with the receptionist, Donna, and the studio manager, Kyle, and with some of the other county "celebrities" who she had previously known only by name or title. She would pass a county commissioner coming, or a well-heeled business owner going, and they would spar with one another in friendly competitive banter.

Good company, and the dancing itself was actually quite fun and Jared was a fairly good instructor. Having served as an educator for many years, she could relate to Jared's difficult task of teaching. He was young too, probably not yet thirty. She wondered what she would have named her first son.

"Jared. Jared. Now tell me, what is the meaning of your name?" Christine slipped in as Jared headed to his Altoids.

"I really don't know. I've never thought about it."

"I will research it for you. Everyone should know the meaning of their name. A name captures a person's character. Your very essence is reflected in your name."

Jared eyed her suspiciously and headed to the Altoids yet again. The first one could barely be wet.

"God used His name, I Am, when speaking to Moses. It proclaimed His sovereignty, His power, His love. 'I Am' is a reflection of God's overpowering shield of sacrifice."

"That's nice, Christine. Real nice. Today, we need to work on those left, right slides."

"Let's try that without the music so I can hear your suggestions for improvement. My hearing isn't what it used to be." Christine's insides tightened at the lie. Her hearing was perfectly fine, better than most.

Jared hesitated for only a moment before he headed to the noise machine and returned with the requested silence behind him. Christine preferred the music of thought and conversation. But try as she might, she wasn't able to get Jared to discuss himself, his family, or his dreams for his future.

Wednesday, September 23
Tracy: Collecting Jared

Tracy was again pleased she was female. Being a woman meant she had power over straight men, men like Jared. She had enjoyed the power of her sexuality since she was twelve, and found it amusing that men believed they were the supreme gender. Yes, men controlled business, science and politics, and most believed their dominance still included women. Tracy, however, didn't put stock in anyone's opinion but her own, and she knew that a savvy woman could play both ends of any relationship—be powerful or vulnerable, knowledgeable or naïve. Tracy got whatever she wanted from men by being whatever they wanted her to be, then twisting and leveraging information. Controlling men was simple: probe their deepest fears then make all those fears come true. Every man she ever selected to be hers was eventually submissive—they were all hers, hers to cast aside in her own time. All she needed was their trust, personal information, and tangible evidence of secret things they'd done. Naughty boys all.

Not being married, her current specimen had fewer secrets and was therefore a rare challenge. She got Jared to linger long and chatty over their smoky back lot conversations. But, of course, he couldn't talk openly with his students and apparently he didn't have any trustworthy friends. It wasn't likely many people would be patient enough to listen to Jared's trickling minutiae anyway. But Tracy was. She feasted on his words, carefully catalogued details of his private life in her mind.

She would pick up right where they left off, simply ask leading questions to get him started up again. Like a little gas engine, chugging out noisy personal delights. "I trust you, I trust you," the little Jared engine puffed out. He trusted her. Tracy allowed the thick richness of this fact to drip down the layers of her plans for him. He was perfect.

She knew that the person closest to Jared's heart was his grandmother who lived in a town nearby, "Gran" he called her. He talked about Gran and about a broken marriage, about his drinking, past drug use and arrests. He confessed to being an "idiot" for wasting so much time being stupid enough to use cocaine, marijuana even. Geez, what a cute little dumbass. As tempting as it was, Tracy never laughed at his emotional ruminations. She had trained herself to watch people for signs they were feeling certain emotions. It didn't come naturally, but if she studied Jared carefully, she could hear the hurt in his voice and see it in his dark golden eyes. If he believed that she struggled similarly, he would become even more gullible, more trusting. So, she told him she was also divorced, that her evil husband had repeatedly raped her, even forced her to have an abortion. She must have been convincing; there were actual tears in his eyes when he hugged her.

Of course, she didn't ask him to talk about his childhood. That might prompt a true memory, one where he would suddenly realize that it was fourteen-year-old Tracy outside the high school locker room behind that camera snapping photos for the school newspaper. He might even remember the thoroughly forgettable Amber. That wouldn't do. Tracy wouldn't allow it. She wasn't going to risk losing Jared to their past. So, on the rare occasion when Jared mentioned his childhood or Vincennes, Indiana, Tracy would skillfully steer the conversation elsewhere, to things like life purpose and deep desires. Jared liked to talk about those things.

Her hard work had paid off. Tracy now knew what Jared wanted most in life. She wasn't certain Jared knew, but she did. It was something he would do almost anything to have—a family—a sweet little wife who would melt all over him and eagerly pop out lots of little brats. And a house—probably wanted a white picket fence too, except Tracy wouldn't dare ask. Asking something like that would be making fun of his dreams, right? Can't make fun of Jared. Not yet.

Poor, sweet Jared. All the women in his life were mewing kittens. The aged students chattered at him, pawed him, and toyed with him. And the few girlfriends he'd mentioned were no better—flighty and immature. He didn't take any of them seriously. What he really wanted was a strong woman, a listening woman, a marriage-ready woman. Tracy would be those things for him, for a time. Once hooked, Jared would experience a woman he couldn't seduce, couldn't predict, certainly couldn't control. A woman would take the lead during this little dance with Jared.

Monday, October 5
Jared: Looking this Good

"Recollect that the desire of imparting pleasure, especially to the ladies, is one of the essential qualifications of a gentleman. The truly polite man is always mindful of the comfort of those around him."

— Prof. D. L. Carpenter, Philadelphia, 1854

Any man, who knows he excels at work he enjoys, will carry himself with irresistible self-assuredness. Although this trait alone would have been enough to turn a woman's head, Jared was also very careful of his grooming and appearance. He wasn't as lean and muscular as he had been ten years earlier—his once solid body had settled with age. Although fit, there was now a bit of roundness pushing at his dress shirt just above his belt. Even so, Jared was cool and comfortable on a woman's eyes. And he knew it.

He loved clothing and had no trouble justifying the money spent on silk-lined vested suits, soft-crisp dress shirts, and top-quality leather shoes. His work required him to wear these wonderful things. Dance shoes were special ordered and could cost hundreds of dollars.

Jared entered his closet every morning like a man seeking out treasure. He would allow each piece of clothing to compete for the privilege of being worn, and would carefully select several outfits that spoke to him. Each article of clothing would be examined closely for any sign of wear. He would feel them and smell them, and then study how various pieces looked together. A suit and shirt would finally emerge as first victors.

Socks? Socks were easy. It was the one thing that wasn't supposed to matter. The wilder the patterned colors and more ridiculously mismatched to the rest of the outfit, the better. A flash of wild sock was a ballroom dancer's idiocy. Sometimes Jared would simply reach in and grab a pair of socks, thinking he'd wear whatever pair took hold of his fingers. Truth be told, Jared would often tilt his head and explain to the socks why he was trading them in for a different pair. A pair just as wild and bold, but a pair that complemented the suit and shirt already selected for the day's festivities.

And then there were the bright magnificent ties. Hung by predominate color on display racks lining the wall in his master bathroom, any number of beauties would argue for their right to be drawn around his neck. The steam from his shower gently erased any wrinkles as they hung, waiting patiently for his attention. They were difficult. The little restrictive splendors were all too striking to be excluded without careful consideration, so he would think about them as he showered, narrow down his choices to two. Maybe three.

Despite all this, it wasn't uncommon for him to change his mind—about the entire outfit. He would then carefully return each piece to its place, the tie to its rack, the suit to its curved wooden hanger, and start the entire process over. Finally, he would dress. His ex-wife, Tanisha, would often complain that it took him far longer to get ready than it did her. In Jared's opinion, it showed.

As to be expected, the top drawer of his dresser contained white cotton handkerchiefs. Folded, crisp, and clean. The final step to the morning dressing ritual was to carefully place one clean fresh handkerchief inside the breast pocket of his suit coat. A gentleman is always prepared to offer his handkerchief to a maiden in distress. Occasionally it made its way out for Jared's use, but not often.

His last act before leaving his apartment was to tidy up, carefully, as to avoid mussing his clothing: turn off the kitchen vent after it had sucked away his cigarette smoke, straighten the magazines, and put the toilet seat down. He never knew when he might bring home a guest, and women appreciated and noticed these things. He would study himself carefully and preen once more before leaving.

His appearance was, however, only part of the product he sold. He was also chivalrous and normally very considerate—to women at least. He would pull out their chairs, open doors, and stand whenever they entered a room. He would offer his arm and walk on the street side when escorting a woman down a sidewalk. Although these habits endeared him to his students, Jared would have done these things anyway because Gran Gregory had insisted that he, and his brother, Eugene, be gentlemen and treat women with proper respect. Gran insisted that they anticipate and provide for the needs of women and accommodate them without question or hesitation, so being old-school polite to women came naturally to Jared.

Ultimately, Jared's job was selling dance lessons, and a good salesman equips himself with information. This, however, was something Jared had to work at; he couldn't keep information in that handsome head of his. To compensate, he would hurry to the instructors' lounge after a lesson, open his three-ring binder, grab his favorite heavy black pen and quickly jot down all scraps from the brief conversations between dance steps. He had to do this quickly because the information shared was trivial, justifiably forgettable, and he usually listened with little effort. Gran Gregory called it lazy listening and she would have reprimanded him for his poor manners of only appearing to be engaged. It was an old habit, one he had tried to correct since his failed marriage. Unsuccessfully.

This being Monday, Jared checked the instructors' work calendar posted on the wall in the lounge, and then carefully recorded his weeks' worth of students into his three-ring binder. His plan was the same for each of them—ask his standard question and appear genuinely interested in their answers. If they shared any personal problems and concerns, he would carefully avoid offering possible solutions. Women didn't want answers—they wanted a listening ear, someone who cared. He left the task of providing answers to their husbands or friends. Jared studied his list of Monday students, all long-time regulars. He considered what repeat concerns they'd likely share with him, and rehearsed under his breath, "How awkward that must have been for you, Mrs. Clements," "Well, Madelyn, I can certainly understand why you were upset." Jared understood very well what to say, and what to avoid saying.

Today, his first student was Mrs. Nolan. Jared flipped to

the "N" tab and re-discovered that widowed Mrs. Carla Nolan had three cats: Tabby, Bailey, and Mark. It never failed to
impress her that he remembered each cat's name, their latest
illness, their favorite toys. "How are the kittens?" he planned
to say. "Has Mark gotten a new catnip mouse from you yet?
No? But, Miss Carla, you told me that the way he holds a new
mouse firmly in his paws and rolls about the room reminds you
of us dancing. How long will you deprive him of that pleasure?" Yes, that would do nicely.

He had flipped to the "O" page during his development of
the "Mark the cat message," and once again studied the stark
page of Christine O'Garra. She was married, yes, apparently
to a man named Peter Zachman. So Christine was using her
maiden name—somewhat uncommon. She had a daughter living close enough to borrow earrings from, but Christine had
shared nothing more about this daughter—not even her name.
Family was always shared in elaborate detail, except Christine
never spoke of her husband, her children or grandchildren—
precious topics to his other students. Jared picked up his heavy
black pen and tapped at the page. The only information recorded from their four lessons was a list of strange answers to his
standard question and equally strange questions she had asked
him:

"Do you think people enjoy sex just for the moment, like
animals, or is it sacred—something that binds us to another
person?"

"I just received a postcard from a friend visiting Paris.
Did you know that people killed during the French Revolution
are buried under the streets there? Do you think the happy tourists walking those streets right now would be as carefree if they

knew they were walking over dead bodies?"

"Are you proud of what your life legacy will be as a ballroom dance instructor?"

"The Amish are in the minority by choice. Would you have chosen to be black if you'd had a choice?"

"Do you remember being born?"

She had slipped two questions in during her last lesson, one at the beginning and another at the end. There didn't seem to be any topic she wouldn't be willing to discuss. And although he never answered her questions, he did think about them, would turn to her notebook page and ponder the written questions between students.

Instead of giving her an answer, he would ask, "And what did you do since our last lesson?" as he did all his students. Christine, however, never failed to provide strange answers:

"I helped my neighbor chainsaw down a dead tree."

"I mended three pairs of socks. You know, a light bulb comes in very handy for that."

"I researched dust. Did you know that eighty percent of what we see floating in an indoor sunbeam is made up of tiny flakes of dead skin, and that ten percent of the weight of a two-year-old feather pillow is made up of dust mites that eat that skin? And their droppings, of course."

"I painted the bathroom."

Yes, Christine was quirky, charmingly so. She carried a loaded gun, yet she had this innocence about her—a happy, content gentleness. And she never reacted to any of the occasional comments he made that were borderline inappropriate. He wondered how far he could go before she reacted as his other students: a "disapproving" look followed by a wink, a raised eyebrow accompanied by a chuckle, a playful hand smack in his direction. Nothing pulled those reactions from Mrs. Christine O'Garra. It was as if she were a child who didn't have enough knowledge to understand sexual innuendos.

After several lessons (How many? Jared couldn't remember), there were lots of blank lines on her page. The internet might be of help, so he took hold of his computer mouse, typed in her name: "Christine O'Garra." Several listings popped on the screen referring to a woman at Purdue University—a professor, or something. That woman had published articles titled "An Analysis of Farmers' Use of Online Financial Management Tools" and "The Unintended Economic Impact of Community Gardens." It wasn't his Christine O'Garra. Before he could scroll down, his search was abruptly interrupted.

"Jared?" Mavis snapped out. Her sudden presence in the lounge was unsettling; he hadn't heard her come in. Jared quickly stood.

"Oh, sit down. Where's your appreciation note for the August charity event with Miss Lynne? You were to get your draft to me no later than yesterday," she stabbed the words at him as he slowly sat.

"I gave it to you," Jared said. "I think."

"No, you did not, and all thank-yous were to be mailed no later than the end of September. Everyone else has theirs finished." She remained solidly planted in front of his desk, her accusing eyes narrowed.

Jared remembered writing the note—remembered struggling over the words. He opened his side drawer, sifted through a few things and there it was, laughing up at him. He lifted the rumpled page from the drawer and shivered it up toward her folded arms. She snatched the page from him with a crackle and began reading.

"I'm sorry, Mavis, it looks like I must have brought it in, just forgot to give it to you. I'll write it on a card before I leave today." Jared tapped firmly at the dark hollow mouth of his pen. It was sharp, but not sharp enough.

"I'll say you will." Mavis plopped down onto Hollie's chair and churned her skinny legs to roll herself over to the corner of his desk. She grabbed the pen from his hand and scratched at his work.

"Oh, Jared, really. How many times must I tell you it's 'I', not 'me'? You and I were a great team. And high isn't spelled like the greeting, it's H, I, G, H. Score is spelled with a 'c' not a 'k'."

The pen scratched furiously across the page as Mavis mumbled out her irritations. She finally thrust the badly stained paper back to him with a blank notecard and envelope.

"Here. You sit right here and write this out very neatly. Don't you dare seal that envelope till I check it again. Here's Miss Lynne's address. And for goodness' sake, don't address the envelope upside down this time." She rose, rolled the chair back to Hollie's desk, turned and glared down at him. She waited until Jared began his rewrite before spinning on her heel and marching from the room.

"Yes, ma'am," Jared sighed out toward the empty space that had been Mavis a moment before. He slid his notebook over the card to keep the lines straight and began to write, working carefully and methodically across the notecard, one slow word at a time.

Tuesday, October 13
Christine: Getting What You Pay For

"If you are not taking care of your customer, your
competitor will."

— Bob Hooey

Only five lessons after this, she thought with mixed feelings. Conflicts between Jared's dance competition and her
work made delays necessary. A familiar woman approached as
Christine got out of her car in front of the studio.

"Christine? It is Christine, isn't it?"

Christine adjusted her heavy purse on her shoulder. "Yes.
Yes, I'm Christine. It's good to meet you." Christine extended her hand. It was ignored. "I think you and I have the same
dance instructor—Jared."

The woman failed to introduce herself and launched into a
rambling dispatch, "Oh, Sweetie, you really need to know that
he has fallen hard for you. I've watched the way he dances with
you. The girls and I have been placing bets on when he'll finally invite you to stay overnight at his apartment. Has he asked
you yet?" She thrust her face sideways with her chin down and
looked at Christine through the corner of her eye with a tight
smile.

Christine jerked back slightly, swallowed down her surprise, "Ah, no…I…I have no plans to ever see Jared as anything except my dance instructor. What would make you ask
me such a thing?" Christine could feel the redness rising on
her neck.

The woman stared suspiciously at Christine. "Seriously?

It's as plain as the nose on your face. You're both nuts about each other. It's like he's making love to you right through your clothes. Jeannie still thinks he's gay, but the rest of us know better. He's all man. He's all man and yet he's never reacted to a student the way he's reacting to you." The unnamed woman tossed her head, "You've thrown him off his guard. Even with Jared's dark skin, I had no trouble seeing the way you made him blush a few weeks ago after the hug. I just can't figure what it is you could possibly have said to get a reaction like that out of him. He never blushes at any of the outrageous things I say."

Try as she might, Christine couldn't bite off the hard edges of her words. "Look, this conversation is beyond ridiculous. I am taking ballroom dance lessons for one reason and one reason only, to learn a dance for a fundraising event next month. At this point, however, I can't help but wonder just what it is you and 'the girls' are doing here week after week. Is jumping in and out of bed with instructors common practice?"

"There's no need to get high and mighty with me, missy. And no, we don't. In fact, I don't know of anyone who's even been asked. Anne Matthews claims he took her out for drinks after a late lesson. We call her 'Crazy Annie.' Said he went to her house and got everything that goes with it too. Nobody believes her. But there's always a possibility. None of us have given up hope."

Christine had to tell herself to close her gaping mouth. "Okay…I've only just now met you, actually, I've never met you and I'm fairly new here, but I must tell you that this is offensive and, frankly, a bit pathetic. No, really, it's…it's…really pathetic."

The woman studied the front of the studio for a moment as if reflecting on a distant memory before turning back to Christine.

"No. No, you know what's pathetic, Miss Prim and Proper? I'll tell you…being sixty-six years old, lonely, and bored to tears night after night." She planted her feet on the dark asphalt and continued to stare at the glistening glass front of the dance studio. "Until I came here, my only companions were tight-lipped church ladies who pruned up back in their forties. I felt like they were sitting in judgment of every word I said." The pace of her words had slowed and she sighed loudly before continuing, "When I came for my first dance lesson years ago I thought I'd meet some interesting people, maybe drop a few pounds by getting off the couch. And you know what? I got what I paid for and a whole lot more."

The woman rocked back and forth gently as she stared at her own reflected image on the glass panels. "I can pretend to be someone special for a little while, just a little while. It's an outrageous place, a zany place. Vanity is celebrated, gossip flows, people are manipulated, and deception is just part of the fun. It's a game we all play, you see?"

The woman dug into her coat pocket and extracted a limp tissue to wipe her nose. She continued with a faraway look, "On any Friday night, I can slather glistening lotion all over my body, stick feathers in my hair, and arrive here in a shimmering sequin gown. And when I walk through that door I am welcomed with happy music and hugs. Then I can sail my rear end around in circles and flash my puckered cleavage across the dance floor in the arms of any one of several handsome young men. Nobody here thinks it's the least bit unsuitable.

They encourage it."

She suddenly turned to Christine with a defiant look. "Thankfully, there are none of your rules about what's appropriate and what isn't. It's incredibly liberating. I know what I'm buying, missy, and I certainly get what I pay for. All the girls do. The funny thing is, we just don't want the instructors to know we know." The woman shoved the tissue back in her pocket and peered at Christine. "You understand that?" She paused again then added, "No, you don't. I can see it on your shocked face. All pinked up."

She took a long hostile look at Christine before dispatching a final declaration, "You may not be at a place where you can understand, at least not yet, but you will someday, my pretty."

And with that, she turned and sashayed away, leaving Christine gawking at the exaggerated swaying of an ample backside. Christine wondered weakly if Toto had made it out alive.

A few minutes later, Christine was sitting on the edge of the delicate lobby sofa, struggling with the changing of her shoes and her thoughts, when she heard his approach—the sound of his signature clip-snap steps, Jared's fanfare. *Just once, walk to me quietly, Jared. Just once.* Ignoring the sounds of his grand entrance, Christine continued her frustrated tussle with her left shoe. Her typical cheery greeting seemed impossible, even inappropriate. She didn't know how to avoid a very awkward dance lesson.

Christine glared down at the shiny black point of Jared's right shoe that was now positioned beside her bare foot. He suddenly knelt in front of her, took her shoe from her hand, and smiled up at her. He took both her hands firmly and laid them gently in her lap, lifted her foot and cradled it in his hands as if it were fragile. After studying her foot with interest, he reached inside her pant leg and gently pulled his hands down both sides of her calf, then continued pulling smoothly past her ankle and down both sides of her foot. He was smiling up at her through those long thick eyelashes of his. He gently twisted her foot from side to side as he tilted his head to look at it closely.

Unbelievable, he's considering kissing my foot, thought Christine. It appeared he would. In fact, it looked as if he wanted to start sucking her toes. Was he really such an innocent that he didn't realize how suggestive his actions were and how very inappropriate those suggestions? No, his actions were calculated. The woman in the parking lot was right; Jared was obviously a very experienced man who was selling little bonbon moments to hungry women in need of attention. He knew exactly what he was doing. It suddenly angered her that he was purposely disrespecting her space, her body. Except it was only her leg, her foot. Hadn't women in her mother's generation, and those for many generations before, tried on shoes with the help of a salesman? This emotional reaction made little sense. Nevertheless, she felt mildly violated. Until now, no one had ever helped her put shoes on her feet. Not even Seth. Not ever.

That vile woman in the parking lot might be able to notice a slight blush on Jared's face, but he wasn't the one blushing now. The red blotches she knew were radiating from her fair cheeks and down her neck were certain to betray her completely. She knew the rush of heat she felt would be misread as a blush of sexual desire and this angered her all the more. *Oh for heaven's sake, I'm nuts. No, he's nuts.*

Jared never said a word. Instead he lifted her foot, and tilted his face from side to side as he turned the foot once more. He looked at the bottom of it for a moment before working the shoe into position and onto her foot.

What have I gotten myself into?

"There now," he said, as he rose smoothly and leaned over her. Christine had little choice other than to accept his politely extended hand. He lifted her to her feet, kissed her hand tenderly, and pulled her into his arms to embrace her. She didn't have the emotional strength to pull away. Donna smiled sweetly at them as they passed the receptionist counter and he escorted her to the back room reserved for private lessons. "I've missed you, Christine. I really have." And yes, he delivered his standard question, "So what interesting things did you do during our extended time apart?"

After the events of the past ten minutes, her social filter had suffered a jagged rip, leaving a hole where words could slip out. He probably wouldn't give a cup of hog's snot to know what she had done during the past three weeks. She had to force herself not to spit out something she'd regret. They weren't building a long-term relationship. Still, she refused to be rude. Except, he never shared anything about his personal life. He never answered any of her questions. She had used this to justify lying to him simply for her own amusement. And now, she was feeling a bit guilty. *Oh, for Pete's sake, why am I the one feeling guilty? He's probably never listened to any of my answers to this canned question.*

"Jared, I have a confession to make. Sometimes I've answered that question with silly little lies."

"Really? At our last lesson, you told me you butchered a

deer. Do you really think I believed that?" He flashed his perfect grin.

My, what nice teeth you have, thought Christine. It wouldn't do much good to tell him that she really had traveled to Elkhart County and helped her nephew, and his new bride, butcher a fat doe. They had pressure-canned several quarts, and got the rest into the freezer. As was custom, they offered her one of the back-straps for her trouble. Christine loved venison.

"I'll tell you what, Jared, let's have some fun. From now on, whenever you ask me, 'What interesting things have you done since our last time together?', I'll provide you three answers. Two will be true and one will be a lie, but I won't tell you which is which. Sound like fun?"

"As you wish. So. Tell me about your fascinating and very busy three weeks." He held both of her hands at arm's length and looked up at her through those thick lashes—an interesting habit of his.

"I tied the cat inside an old pillowcase to give him a flea bath, I signed a contract to speak at a women's conference in January, and I burnt down my neighbor's outhouse. So what did you do with your time since our last lesson?" Jared, of course, never answered the question himself.

He tilted his face and squinted. His dark golden eyes settled on her for a moment.

"Hmm, okay, I think you would be capable of doing that to a cat. And for the remaining, you made it pretty easy for me. I read about the outhouse burning in the newspaper. Your hometown made the news here in the big city yet again." Jared smiled that smile of his.

Oh, so at least he has a sense of humor. Her left thumb

stroked at the back of her rings.

"Look, Jared. Would it be okay if we have a more serious talk?"

Jared studied her briefly, turned abruptly and inserted their music into the CD player. "We're already off to a late start and I couldn't help notice you were chatting with Mrs. Lechman in the parking lot. Just so you know, you mustn't believe what that woman likely told you. She is prone to exaggerations and fantasies." He flashed a dark-eyed glance at her as he fussed with the machine. "She's fairly harmless. Even so, everyone here knows she's a little mixed up about the...about the extent of our services." Jared popped a mint from his tin and snapped the lid closed. He turned to her and delivered one of his quick head tilts.

"Last year, we had to assign Mrs. Lechman to an outside instructor just to give all of the men here a bit of a...give us a bit of breathing room." Jared made a final adjustment to the buttons and increased the volume of the music.

He had to raise his voice to be heard. "I don't mean to speak poorly of Mrs. Lechman, but I know her well enough to guess what concerns you want to share. Concerns without merit, so if you don't mind, I think we should get started."

He quickly took up her hand and led her through the pulsating music to the glaring mirror where his reflection chuckled at her as he began dancing smoothly.

"Your Cuban motion could use polishing. Let's begin by practicing rolling those hips of yours, yes?"

Polishing!? I swear if he gets anywhere near my Cuban motion, I'll smack him silly. Christine forced a smile at the reflection. Here had been an opportunity to talk honestly about his work. A time to seriously examine his purpose here and he had brushed her away, yet again.

Christine shoved aside her thoughts about Jared the person, and focused on their work together. She had trouble keeping her arms in motion and remembering the next steps. Jared guided her skillfully, however, and by the end of their abbreviated lesson, Christine felt fairly confident that she wouldn't make a complete fool of herself on the dance floor in front of hundreds of people the first Saturday in November.

Jared escorted her across the main dance floor, provided her his farewell hug and yet another kiss to her hand. His mouth moistened her rings. Harmless spit. It would dry unseen and yet it occurred to her that he was kissing her dead loved ones the same way she did, lovingly, tenderly. She wondered briefly if she should tell him the diamonds were made from the ashes of April and Seth—man-made diamonds, one pink, the other crystal clear. No, best not.

"Can we confirm my scheduled lessons before I leave? I come this Thursday, after that I only have Tuesdays till the first week in November, right?"

"I'll check." He headed behind the counter to stand over Donna's shoulder, who fumbled about with her mouse and keyboard in search of the scheduling spreadsheet.

Christine turned her attention to a young woman waiting in the lobby. A baby in a car seat beside her thrashed at the air with his fat little hands, jiggling the seat as he kicked.

"You have a beautiful baby," Christine said as she leaned down to capture the baby's attention.

"Thank you. I think I'll keep him." The young woman smiled up at Christine.

"Are you here for lessons?" Christine asked.

"No, just waiting for my mom to get off work."

"And who's the lucky grandmother?" Christine allowed the baby to grab at her finger.

"Donna, the receptionist."

"Donna?" Christine called over to the counter, "You have a beautiful grandson." Christine looked again at the mother and asked, "May I hold him? I don't get to hold babies much anymore."

The young mother glanced over to Donna, who had become completely absorbed in watching her family instead of her research at the computer. Donna nodded her approval toward her daughter as Jared continued to study the flashing monitor.

"Sure," the young mother consented. "He's getting kind of fussy though."

As Christine lifted the baby, she was surprised by how heavy he was, and how wiggly. Donna's daughter patted her son's back then wandered over to the counter to be with her mother. The baby stared intently at Christine's face for a moment then reached for the brooch on her sweater, tugging it toward his slobbery mouth. The baby looked over her shoulder and suddenly lurched sideways, throwing his weight toward a certain fall. Although she hadn't heard Jared approach, he caught the squirming baby then gently pulled the rest of the cherub from Christine's uncertain arms with a confident tug. He held the baby and stared at its cheeky pink face.

"I'm glad his mother didn't see that," Christine whispered as she leaned over to Jared. "I nearly dropped him." Christine instinctively reached out to take back the child, then stopped and took a slight step back. Jared was looking intently at the baby as if he hadn't heard a word she said. She watched with some interest now to see how Jared handled babies instead of women. The baby's fat dimpled hand explored Jared's face with uncontrolled slaps then settled on Jared's fuzzy chin. The baby chuckled in toothless glee. The pink hand patted at Jared who smiled and held the baby close.

"It tickles, huh?" Jared said softly. "Feels pretty funny." Both Jared, and the child, looked completely relaxed in one another's arms. The baby's exploratory fingers probed at Jared's lips. Two tiny fingers dug their way into his mouth, hooked into his lower lip and pulled. Jared's soft smile nibbled at the chubby fingers and the baby squealed in delight. Jared's eyes twinkled as the baby's drool slid from his mouth and dripped onto Jared's chest, narrowly missing his silk tie. The wetness created a navy stain on the crisp blue shirt. Jared's eyes looked like deep pools of molasses as he drank in the baby. These two boys were completely lost in this moment of sweet joyful innocence. Christine stood, mesmerized.

Without warning, Donna's daughter abruptly yanked the baby away and frowned uneasily at Jared's startled reaction. She openly glared at Christine who winced. She had given this woman's baby over to a stranger—a social norm broken, damaged trust between women. Christine wondered how much it mattered that Jared was male, that Jared was black.

"You have a precious gift," Jared said, his arms still slightly extended toward the child who was quickly plopped back into the car seat by his coldly quiet mother.

"I'm Jared. I work here with your mom as an instructor." Jared extended his hand, ignored by the woman.

"I'll wait for you in the car, Mom," she said loudly as she hurriedly gathered her things. The baby started fussing, then crying. Jared rushed to open the door for mother and child as they exited. He then stood inside beside Christine, watching as the woman strapped the car seat in with a jerking motion. The woman yanked a wet wipe from a pouch and wiped at her audibly upset child. It had never bothered Christine to have Jesse or April's fingers in someone's mouth. She couldn't remember ever being upset by slobber or the giggles of her babies as their tiny fingers were playfully nibbled. Hadn't Christ used spit to heal a blind man? She turned to talk to Jared about her thoughts, but he was no longer beside her. She turned and watched as he slowly, quietly, walked back across the glistening empty dance floor alone.

Thursday, October 15
Jared: First Lesson

Christine was finally wearing properly heeled shoes, and she had on a dress, a very conservative, age-appropriate dress. But, it was a dress, not those dress slacks she always wore. And she had legs. This first glimpse of her legs made him smile at the memory of a conversation they had about a month earlier.

Christine had never made it a secret that she believed there was a God. She wasn't overbearing about it, she simply assumed everyone knew there was a God. He bit at her conversation one day and challenged her belief that God existed. "Christine, I've never seen God. Why would I believe in something I can't see, or hear, or feel?"

In response, she had asked him if he had ever seen, heard, smelled, tasted, or felt her legs. He had laughed at her ridiculous question.

"Then how do you know I have legs?" she had asked.

Well, he saw her legs today.

Although Christine wasn't as cheery as usual, she still asked one of her questions: "How do you know when someone's 'faking' it?"

As usual, no time for talk so he quickly hauled the clutter of her words aside and focused on dance—the music, her movement. She certainly could roll those hips, except she needed to relax, to experience the sensuousness of the music and move fluidly through the motions. She was, as always, too exacting. There was visible tension in her shoulders and she had a tendency to lift her back and hold her posture erect, as if she were being pulled to the ceiling by an invisible string.

Even so, she was doing surprisingly well. He was suddenly acutely aware of how little he cared if she could dance or not. He had missed her when they weren't together for three weeks in September and early October, and told her so on Tuesday when they finally danced again. Except, he told all his students he missed them—at every lesson. It was strange to say it and actually mean the words that simply dropped from his mouth. He realized, in fact, that he had thought of her a great deal over their weeks apart.

Christine seemed distant. Once they started the lesson, she simply focused on practicing the dance steps. She hadn't started their time with two truths and a lie, and she only asked that one question about being "fake."

They were dancing and he was thinking. *Look at my smile, Christine. Look at my smile.* But she didn't. She was concentrating on her feet. He stopped mid-dance and searched for her. He tilted his head and focused on her eyes. She was there, in a detached way. She had changed since his refusal to talk with her about Mrs. Lechman's conversation in the parking lot on Tuesday. He wanted to start that conversation over. Better yet, to go back to that first lesson in August, and start completely over. She had hugged him that summer day like she cared. Like she loved him. How could she? No one can love someone they don't know. And she didn't know him now.

He fought off the urge to stop practice altogether and just talk with her. He longed to discuss her questions. Why God would put Himself into an infant's body, and whether people truly have choices, and what she had meant when she said earth's life time is like a little dot. He wanted to talk. But, he couldn't. He was her instructor and it was his job to teach her to dance, not to collapse into her like a confused child.

He had to admit, he was fascinated by her, attracted to her questions. Or was it her? Attracted to her? As a man is to a woman? The possibility startled him, scared him. Date a woman who was in her late forties? Maybe even early fifties? He still didn't know her age. He could imagine the awkward looks, the ribbing from co-workers, ridicule from Eugene and Claire, maybe even from Gran. And yet, did any of that matter, really? What was he thinking? He wasn't interested in her that way. Couldn't be. The darting thoughts were making him sloppy.

He quickly turned from her and adjusted the music to

avoid those eyes. The buttons and knobs on the sound machine swam in front of him. He reached for a mint and stole a wipe to his face. Fortunately, he was able to see in the mirror that Christine was practicing her slides—to the right, to the left, to the right again. He needed to dance with her; he was a professional instructor, and perfecting her dance was his product. A product he was to deliver in less than a month to a room full of wealthy people—people who had strong potential of becoming paying customers. He turned back to her with fresh resolve and smiled. He was her instructor, nothing more. There she went again, pulling her shoulders up toward her cute ears. He gently pushed down on the sides of her neck.

"Let your shoulders relax. Let your body flow with the music, smooth and rhythmic. Stop looking at your feet. And let me lead."

Christine's detached smile quickly faded. "You've told me that over and over. Could we go through those fast swivels again too, please?"

Jared searched for her hand with his. She took it, then suddenly steadied herself firmed against his outstretched grasp. Leaning heavily onto his arm, she thrust her leg backward with a quick bend to her knee and examined the bottom of her shoe.

"I cut pieces of suede and glued them onto the bottoms of my soles. Do you think these will work?" She plunged her left foot back to the floor and quickly bent her right knee behind her back to show him the bottom of her shoe. She picked a bit of white fuzz from the suede there. "I really didn't want to spend the money to buy dance shoes and I had a piece of suede leather at home. I'll never wear dance shoes again after the gala."

Jared examined her shoe with a certain amount of admiration. Christine was certainly resourceful, and the suede was every bit as soft and smooth as what was on the bottom of professional dance shoes. He was, however, a bit dismayed that these strappy black shoes were her final choice. They were sturdy, practical shoes—matronly. He decided not to mention his disappointment with her style choice.

"Those will do nicely. You certainly have an eye for the practical. But that's good, that's good. My granddad always told me not to let someone else do something that I could do for myself." Jared had finally coaxed a genuine smile from her. Her eyes lit up and he could see that she was about to ask, yes, a question. About his grandfather no doubt. He was dead. Jared didn't want to think about death. Certainly didn't want to talk about it.

"We can go over the swivels, and anything else you'd like, as often as you need to. I am here to teach you to dance," Jared said it as an affirmation to himself as well as to his student. "You're doing very well, actually, considering our long break between lessons. You've been practicing, yes?"

"Actually, I have. In fact, I'm getting up twenty minutes early every morning, just to get in a few steps before my day starts. The routine takes two and a half minutes, so I can dance the entire thing seven times every morning, allowing for starting and stopping."

"You kill me. You and time. Do you ever just live? Not worry about seconds and minutes passing?"

Christine paused, seemed to consider the question carefully. "Earth is the only place where time exists. I value and respect it more than any other resource I have stewardship over."

As strange as that response was, Christine suddenly didn't

seem so odd in that moment. In comfortable silence, they danced the remainder of their time together, allowing the music and the movement to talk for them. Christine had to tell him that their forty-five minute session was over.

He hugged her and kissed her left hand. Her rings felt cold on his lips. He suddenly realized how extraordinary this was. He rarely kissed a woman's hand, and when he did, he reached for their right hand. It was only natural. He mused about the fact that he always kissed her left hand, her rings, the funny little bump on her finger. The tip of her ring finger, bent like Gran's gnarled arthritic hands. He wanted her to notice, to want him to kiss her. The thought made him flinch as he tapped at his notebook. He couldn't be in love with Christine O'Garra. She was old. Too old for him, at least. And yet, he couldn't stop thinking about her and how much he wanted to be with her, to talk to her. *Is that what love is? This overwhelming desire to be with someone? To talk with them?*

His pondering was interrupted when he noticed on the camera monitor that Mrs. Pierce was in the lobby waiting none too patiently, pacing. No matter, she would have to wait a few more minutes while he prepared. He turned to "Pierce" in his binder to study this long-time student. He would begin her lesson as he did for all his students—reviewing the past lesson's movements. Jared liked it best when his students struggled to deliver the steps correctly. It meant additional lessons could be more easily sold. It also allowed him to let his mind wander during the long forty-five minute session as he repeated the same moves over and over and over. He could then dance and think at the same time—enjoy thoughts of Gran and Christine. But mostly of Christine. Jared quickly snap-stepped his way to the lobby to deliver the expected greeting, the hug, and the arm-in-arm escort to the somewhat annoyed Mrs. Pierce. Soon, however, he had her tittering in demure little smiles.

He tried to create timeless youthful eyes out of the small watery ones that stared back at him, except he was already thinking about Christine. He was failing at his attempts to blur the wrinkles of Mrs. Pierce's crinkled parchment face. Her swollen bulb of a nose simply wouldn't conform to any standard of beauty today. Finally, he just started dancing with the puzzled Mrs. Pierce.

He wondered what Christine would do if he kissed her hand while they danced. He allowed himself the wicked pleasure of imagining doing just that. He was kissing Christine's left hand, gently kissing her rings and her funny little broken finger that held those rings. He envisioned himself dancing with her and pulling her hand to his face and sliding her palm down the side of his cheek until her fingers met his lips. He gently took them into his mouth between his teeth and softly nibbled at them like he had the baby's fingers on Tuesday. That would certainly get a reaction from the playful, but ever proper, Christine.

Mrs. Pierce suddenly stopped mid-step. Her slivered lips parted. "If you giggle once more without letting me in on the joke, I'll have to sit this one out. Are you laughing because you're pleased with how I'm dancing or because I look ridiculous?" Mrs. Pierce delivered a wounded look before digging under her blouse to adjust her bra straps one at a time.

"I apologize, Mrs. Pierce. I'm somewhat distracted today. You are doing marvelously as you always do. If we could start from the beginning, I'll teach you a new foxtrot step. I've wanted to show this to you for some time and I think you're ready to learn it. Are you up for that?" Jared turned before Mrs. Pierce could answer, dialed up a foxtrot and set it to high volume. Jared sighed. It was like dancing with a large bag of oranges, bumping and rolling. Keep focused. Mrs. Pierce could never remember where she parked her car. If he could just concentrate on the rest of this lesson, she would quickly forget he had been drifting during her paid time. She had paid for him, he would deliver.

Jared held Mrs. Pierce in frame briefly to adjust to the physical and mental work before him. As he studied her face, he noticed a bit of fuzz near her eye and he leaned toward her. No, it was merely an irregularity in her skin tone. He peered intently at her cheek for a moment then brushed his face across her stiffly sprayed hair. He smiled at her sweetly then sailed her off across the floor. Mrs. Pierce's pale face reddened slightly and her eyes twinkled happily. The rest of the lesson went smoothly. Jared didn't giggle, and Mrs. Pierce didn't know he was far away.

Even though Jared's binder required a fresh page for a new student, he had already filled in a great deal of personal information about his final student of the day—Tracy Martin. Surprisingly, she had pre-paid for an expensive package of lessons. It would be strange to have Tracy as a student—treat her as he would any other: hug her, escort her across the dance floor. And she wasn't softly padded and bouncy like his older students. No, Tracy was a powerful tower of curves. She'd be an armful of solid movement, firm and unyielding. It made him uncomfortable and he hadn't even started dancing with her yet.

However commanding Tracy's appearance, she was most

certainly attractive and Jared looked forward to their conversations in the back lot. In fact, he had given serious thought to asking her out. Except, she was now his student. Jared glanced up at the monitor and saw Anne Matthews and Mrs. Pierce were in the lobby studying Tracy with obvious interest. He smiled at their narrowed eyes and pursed lips, then made his way to the lobby where he hugged Tracy under the watchful eyes of his two veteran students.

"I knew you'd be surprised to see me here for lessons. I hope it's okay. I can't think of anything I'd rather do with my free time than be with you." Tracy leaned against him as she talked, her sharp dark eyebrows arched up. Mrs. Matthew and Mrs. Pierce both leaned forward and their eyebrows arched up too.

"Well, I am surprised, but it's great to have you here as a student." He hoped he sounded more convincing than he felt. First lessons always included an introduction to the types of ballroom dances, and the rhythm and basic steps of each. Jared did most of the dancing while Tracy stood watching, smiling.

"That's it for today. We'll get you dancing in no time. You've purchased a lesson package, yes?"

"Absolutely. I'm really looking forward to learning all those dances," she said sweetly. "You know, I used to manage staff on a cruise ship out of Miami." Tracy squared her shoulders and continued, "It was always so much fun to watch the dancing. I've always wanted to learn."

Jared could never keep up with all the jobs Tracy had held in her short working career. She was certainly a very industrious young woman.

"I wonder if you could do me a favor," she said. "Could I

borrow the studio's vacuum cleaner till tomorrow? The bookstore could really use a touchup and Aunt Nora keeps forgetting to buy one."

"Of course, it's in the front closet." Tracy followed him to the lobby where there was now a small gathering of women. Several approached Jared like matronly penguins, twittering brightly, arms flapping.

"Well, Mrs. Pierce, I didn't expect to see you still here. Anne, I already gave you a hug earlier. And Mrs. Clements, you don't have a lesson this afternoon, do you?" Jared delivered yet more expected hugs.

"Oh no, Jared. We're just using the studio to gather the girls till Madelyn gets here. We're all going to the quilt show." Just then, Mrs. Nolan tumbled in the door and received a hug as well.

"My goodness, Jared, you're wasting away to nothing. We need to put some meat back on those bones of yours during the holidays," Mrs. Nolan said. The women nestled together as they cooed at one another's purses, outfits, hair styles. Tracy placed her hand on her hip and rolled her eyes. Jared was finally able to make his way past the happy throng and into the closet to wrestle out the seldom-used vacuum.

Once back in the lobby, he paused to enjoy his students. They were sweet and special. Madelyn's van finally pulled up and they all announced at once that it was time to go. A few got in a third hug as he held the door open. They tumbled out onto the sidewalk as if he had turned over a box of happy puppies. He assisted each one into the open door of the van and their wild toad ride to the quilt show was off.

He returned smiling. Tracy sneered, "Geez. How can you

stand being around those old cows?"

These were his long-time students. People he had grown to know and understand. Jared eyed Tracy with disapproval. She failed to notice. Jared thought silently, *Actually, I love them. Every one of them is special. I favor some over others, but they're all brave, beautiful women I enjoy and admire.*

"They're so…so ridiculous. Dancing around at their age," Tracy said, as she burst out the front door. Jared followed without comment, the obstinate vacuum bumping at his shins. He hurried ahead to hold the bookstore door open as soon as she unlocked it. She locked the door behind him as soon as he set the vacuum down.

"Thanks, you're so sweet. And since you're here, would you be a lamb and help me move a cabinet in my office?" He dutifully followed her into a side room behind the counter.

Tracy didn't really want a cabinet moved. Once in the office, she closed the door. She pulled him toward an old yellow couch, then nestled down on it with a teasing giggle. She reached up and pulled gently on his tie until he leaned over her. She dragged her fingertip over his lips, and smiled. She released him and pulled off her sweater, shook out her long dark hair.

"Come here," she said simply, smiling up at him. She pulled gently on his tie again and tapped at his mouth. She lifted her skirt. There was no confusion about what she expected from him; she wasn't even wearing panties. He silently knelt at the edge of the couch and slowly reached behind her to remove her bra and began delivery of the request. He worked with her until she panted out soft moans, arched her back, and let loose a lusty breath-filled cry. Jared did not allow women to lie to him, so he kissed the hard pink pearls at the tips of her breasts and made certain there were rhythmic contractions against the finger he held within her wet velvety chamber. He looked up at her flushed face through his eyelashes, searching for a signal, for further instructions. Finding none, he slowly stood and gazed down at her nakedness. A sigh crackled from her panting lips as she draped one hand over the arm of the couch and fondled her breast with the other. He had to look away, gain control over his body.

"Come on, Jared, it's all good. Go ahead," Tracy said between little panting sighs. Simple as that. She reached up, pulled him into a lean and waited until he opened his pants. Quick, dispassionate, without feeling or thought. Awkward. When finished, he made the necessary corrections to his clothing, adjusted his twisted tie.

"That was very sweet," Tracy purred up to him from the couch. Jared remained silent. Tracy looked sleepy; her heavy dark eyebrows seemed to blanket her eyes. He wondered if her words had slept around with a lot of guys, too.

Jared returned to the dance studio barely twenty minutes after he had left with the vacuum. He could hear Mavis noisily burrowing about in the adjoining front office beside Donna's reception area. He couldn't see his boss, but she was raising a racket.

"Donna, I'm certain I gave you that list of email addresses," Mavis shouted. "But there's no time to look for them now, I'm late. You need to find that list and get those addresses entered first thing in the morning."

Jared moved to the counter where he could see Mavis digging in her purse for the front door keys to lock up for the day.

Mavis and keys clattered past him and out the door without acknowledgement. She locked the front door in a flash then disappeared into her car.

"Hey, Jared," Donna said quietly. Her eyes twinkled over her reading glasses at him. "Did Tracy get all her vacuuming done?" She pressed her smiling lips together firmly and then covered her mouth with a fluttering hand.

"I'm sure she will. She's gonna bring the vacuum back tomorrow." Jared straightened his perfectly straight tie, smoothed it down his chest. "I helped her move some things around."

"I'm quite certain you did. Yes indeed, I'm certain you were a big help." A small laugh escaped as Donna stood to retrieve the sweater from the back of her chair. She glanced up at the wall near the corner of the ceiling tile behind her desk and turned toward him with another smile. Jared jolted at the realization that the yellow couch was sitting just on the other side of that wall. She must have heard the unmistakable sounds coming from Tracy only minutes before. He felt his face warm as he helped Donna slip the sweater onto her arms. He knew he had turned the color of fine cordovan leather. Donna smiled her way across the dance floor toward the employee parking lot with her hand on Jared's arm. They stopped at the back door.

"Have a good evening, Donna. I guess I'll see you tomorrow." Jared opened the door for her and stepped aside to give her plenty of room. Donna patted his arm and laughed again before stepping out.

Jared saw Tracy's car was still in the lot. He locked the door then quickly made his way to the bathroom to wash his hands, his face. Back in the instructors' lounge, he sunk heavily into his office chair and dug out his favorite pen. The binder slowly opened to "M." He tapped at the page, couldn't find words to write down regarding his newest dance student. "Wears no underpants to her first lesson," was scribbled through till it was illegible. He could think of nothing appropriate to record. Instead of words, Jared drew a picture of Tracy's tattoo with his black ink pen. In his mind, however, he saw the fiery tattoo of three red and orange flames that sat just above her dark hairline. He drew the three flames on the blank line under the long list of jobs and experiences Tracy claimed her past held: "owns and runs several businesses," "teller at bank," "tattoo artist in Philly," "divorced from a violent man," "buying and updating her Aunt's bookstore (third store she's renovated)," then he added, "managed staff on a cruise ship."

He suddenly realized he had just done something he had never done before; he had had sex with a student. Jared stared at the three flames. Tracy had been a friend, now she was a student. He had spent hours with her when she hadn't been a paying client. He had openly shared personal things with her. Jared never did that with students, much less have sex with them. Except his other students had never asked. This one certainly had—boldly, directly.

Until now, he had hoped there was something special between them, perhaps something lasting. He had spent a lot of time thinking about how he was going to ask Tracy out. He hadn't wanted to move too quickly, afraid that it would look like all he was after was a roll in bed. He laughed. *Afraid of moving too quickly?* He smiled sadly. *Unbelievable.* All his plans faded. No sense dating a woman who wasn't wife material. Besides, Tracy was now a student, not a friend, and certainly not a potential spouse. Jared tapped at the binder once more, put his pen away, and gathered his things.

He loosened and removed his tie as he crossed the parking lot. Tracy was sitting in her car, looking down at something. No sense worrying about her following him. He wasn't going home, and she had gotten everything she wanted from him in the bookstore office. He carefully hung up his suit coat, then folded the tie and laid it on the back seat. He was somewhat cheered by what lay ahead for the evening. Gran Gregory was preparing the Thursday night meal. He wanted to get there well ahead of Eugene. Once that mob arrived, there was little of Gran's attention left for him. He loved the time with his nephews and niece, however, and delighted in the silly things they'd do and say.

He rapped on Gran's apartment door and waited patiently. When she finally opened to him, he said, "Hey. Something sure smells good." He pretended to head past her to the kitchen.

"Oh, no you don't. You gonna be hugged proper." And she hugged him the way only she could. When she finally released him, he felt like a warm wet noodle—a happy content noodle. He watched his grandmother turn and hobble toward the kitchen in obvious pain.

"Hey, lady. Let me take a look at those feet of yours, okay?"

"Not now, you do that on Sunday and it's not Sunday yet. Got the taters to mash up. Gotta get this meal on the table before Eugene's gang of rompsters busts in here."

"We can mash them together in a bit. Now get yourself over here and sit down." He took her by the hand and pulled at her gently. She finally relented, put weight on his arm, and slowly maneuvered around the hall corner to sink down on the sagging couch. Jared carefully removed her shoes and rolled off the tight suppression stockings. He lifted her right foot—the one that gave her the most trouble.

"You taking care of this one? This one here's my favorite." He stroked the top of her cold swollen foot as if it was a puppy. He kept his head bent over his work removing the bandages. He soon smiled up at her to get a glimpse of her reaction.

"That one wasn't your favorite last Sunday," Gran said with a twinkle and a light slap to the top of his head.

Jared paused and gently twisted the foot from side to side. He cradled it in both of his hands and held it as if it were fragile. And in fact, it was fragile, very fragile. He lifted her foot to his tilted face so he could study the sides, then he looked at the bottom of it for a long time. Even though the sores were noticeable, they didn't appear to be any larger. Not infected.

"Well, they're no better are they? But they don't look any worse either. Are they feeling worse?"

"Well today them feet are a barkin'. Just standing around more I 'spose. Glad you could take a peek at 'em, had me worryin' some."

"I'll get more bandages. Do you have clean stockings? These need washed." Jared headed to the hamper and soon returned with fresh stockings and her foot cream. "We might need to pick up another pair of these at the drugstore Sunday, Gran. Mrs. Milligan coming over every morning to help you with those feet, yes? Coming over before bedtime too?"

"Yes, Jadie. Every mawnin' and night like you would if you could. She's a right fine woman. Got so many people helping me, can't seem to remember how to do nothin' for myself."

He smiled and knelt in front of her. He applied lotion to

his hands then softly pulled his hands firmly down both sides of the calf of her leg. He continued pulling smoothly past her ankle and down both sides of her foot, then repeated the process on the other leg and foot.

"That's enough now," Gran said. "Got to get to mashin' those taters. And the butter's not outta its wrapper coat yet."

"The potatoes will wait. The butter will wait. I, however, will not. You just sit now. Just sit and be still."

Jared took her left hand and kissed it. Her wedding rings felt cool on his lips. Gran's eyes laughed at him and she swatted at him playfully. But she sat still. He massaged her swollen legs and feet for a long time and she rubbed at the top of his head and sang church songs to him. It wasn't till Eugene's family burst through the door that he helped Gran get her bandages and stockings on and worked her shoes back into position. She rubbed Jared's soft head playfully one more time before he stood and pulled her up out of the couch's depth and into his arms.

Thursday, October 15
Tracy: New Strategy

As soon as Jared left the bookstore, Tracy gathered herself from her treasured childhood couch and dressed. She held her glowing cigarette to the arm of the upholstery. The scorch marks were beginning to take the shape of the third lick of flames to match her tattoo. Her father's original mark was centered at the bottom, the heart of the fire. Tracy made Jared's mark especially deep and noticeable then sniffed the heavy burnt air with satisfaction. She turned off the tiny camera that strategically sat on her desk. She couldn't watch the video—not yet.

Tracy hurried to her car to wait for Jared. He came, he always came. He never looked around to notice that she was there, in her car waiting. His routine was like clockwork: he'd remove and hang up his suit, take off his tie, fold it and place it neatly on the back seat of his car, then jump in. He'd sit there for a few minutes writing in his stupid notebook, put on his seatbelt, and finally, finally, he would speed off like a wild man. Tonight, he seemed in a bigger rush than usual to get somewhere.

She waited until he was out of sight. The light would stop him. It always did. He was probably heading to the mall again anyway. She pulled out of the lot and saw that he was only two cars ahead of her, except he was in the left-hand turn lane. He wasn't going to the mall. She forced the gas pedal down to keep up with him, but had to slam on her brakes as an old pickup truck veered without warning, or reason, blocking her. She nearly smacked into its rusty bumper. The truck slowed to a crawl. Nearly stopped.

The vinyl on Tracy's car seats peeled back in sheets from exposure to the choice words she lashed out at the old man driving the rusty heap. The rickety truck swung a tad to the left in preparation for a wide right turn, then violently bumped its rear tire over the curb and shambled unhurriedly into the lot of a rundown convenience store.

Jared's car was out of sight, and the car in front of Tracy slowed at the yellow light and ground to a halt. By the time she was able to finally speed around all the offensive cars, Jared was long gone. Tracy tore forward and wove in and out of traffic for several blocks before conceding defeat. She may be a sociopath, but she wasn't stupid. Fuming and cursing, she turned back.

The old truck was still parked at the side of the crusty cement block store. Tracy jerked into the lot, grabbed up two glass beer bottles from the floor of her car, and wedged them under the truck's bald tires. She was doing everyone a favor by keeping him off the road.

This ridiculous rushing after Jared had to stop. She had what she needed—the GPS tracker had been sitting in a locked cabinet for weeks. Unfortunately, Jared always locked his car, and he always carried his keys with him, sometimes even in the dance studio. She'd never have the opportunity to attach it to the underside of his car, and besides, it wouldn't last long out in the weather. Best to plan, and wait. Not knowing where Jared was ate at her. Where did he go? Why? Who was he with? He might leave her just like her father.

She drove slowly back to the bookstore and flopped onto her yellow couch. She was still there long after darkness settled over Indianapolis, laying in night-wrapped silence. Splintering light from passing cars hit the storefront glass and flashed through the open door of her shadowy office. She lay there, smoking, thinking.

Complacent, sweet little Jared. The August Jared had been like a new cell phone. Fresh and fun. She had enjoyed learning his features, pushing his buttons, studying his applications. She especially loved the way he did whatever she asked without question. "Pick up that cigarette I dropped," "Get your sunglasses so I can wear them while we smoke," "Bring the vacuum to the bookstore," "Please me, Jared,"... anything...anything she asked, he did. No questions, no delays.

Even so, her long-term plan wasn't going well. He wasn't responding to her "I'm the perfect wife and future mother of your children" strategy. She had told him how much she looked forward to having babies of her own to love and care for. Even so, he hadn't even asked her out on a date. He hadn't said a word throughout the entire vacuum-borrowing event. Not a word before, during, not a word after. He simply zipped up and fled.

Maybe Jared sensed her oddity and was uncomfortable around her. Damn that HQ, and damn that psychologist, tagging her with "reactive attachment disorder"—a teen hurrying toward becoming a sociopath, maybe even a psychopath. She could see herself even now, sitting, listening, raging in red silence as the HQ and the doctor talked. In her mind, the doctor's juicy eyes had bulged just before his head popped off in her hands. Tracy had long ago decided that if she were to be labeled as "ill," she'd simply redefine the label to suit herself. To her way of thinking, a sociopath was a gifted person who was more intelligent, more focused, and more likely to get what they wanted. Everyone put themselves first. They'd be fools not to. Perhaps other people simply weren't very good sociopaths. Damn, why should she care? She would never lower her personal standards, never adopt a subpar lifestyle to make other people comfortable. The label had been useful though—she had carefully researched "sociopath" to better avoid being identified as one. She was different, special really, and rare. She just needed to perfect the appearance of "normal" so she could streamline her plans for people. People like Jared. Except, something had gone wrong.

Tracy unlocked a cabinet and pulled out several bags of marijuana. She flipped on her desk lamp, took out a pack of papers, and started rolling tight joints. She lit another cigarette and slowly pulled the smoke in deep and full.

Originally, this focus on Jared had been about getting back at Amber. Thoughts of her sister, Amber, buzzed around her mind like a troublesome gnat, in her eyes, on her lips, up her nose. The humming thoughts of Amber blurred into Jared. They turned over and over in Tracy's mind. Jared was making her life miserable. He needed her. He just didn't know it and convincing him was getting tiresome.

Perhaps a change in motivation, find his underbelly, a weakness. Maybe it was money. Tracy put the tidy bag of rolled joints into the cabinet and drew out several stacks of money, mostly twenties, some fifties, a few hundreds. She stacked them until the tower tumbled onto her letter-less keyboard with a clatter. Jared wanted a wife and family, yet he had not responded to her offers to fulfill those dreams. Perhaps he'd respond to money, knowing he needed it for his future family.

Weed? Cocaine? Something else? Maybe. Once a user, always a user. Trouble was, he hadn't indicated an interest, and she wasn't about to put herself in a position of weakness by telling him she could provide him drugs. Once he started using, she'd have him, except that wouldn't be fun. Addicts were easy, predictable, and incredibly boring. One thing was certain, she would have him. Sweet Jaden Gregory would be hers. Although it was getting tiresome, she would give him one more chance to "fall in love." Perhaps offer him more couch time. He was quite skilled.

He was skilled at dancing, too. She had wandered over to the studio several times over the past several weeks—simply sat and watched the comings and goings of the students, the way the instructors sold their product, the way the business moved and flowed. It hadn't taken her long to see how they had "extended" their product—selling women a feeling, perhaps even more off the dance floor. Who would know? One thing was for certain, little Jared was a favorite toy. The way the old biddies coyly nuzzled into him at every opportunity was quite flirtatious. Nauseating, but flirtatious. Tracy settled herself on her couch, let dangling ashes fall to the floor before she brought the cigarette back to her mouth.

Poor Jared—constantly surrounded by weak, pleasure-seeking old women. Wealthy, pleasure-seeking women. Tracy reached over her head to finger Jared's scorch mark as she lay in her dark burgundy thoughts. A very small, interesting idea sparked, one that would be challenging and profitable. Very profitable. She rolled this new idea up out of the deep and through her mind. She would take time to explore it, develop it, and then she'd give him one more chance. Only one, before she'd think more about this new plan for sweet Jared.

Tuesday, October 27
Christine: Invest in the Future

Christine had rarely seen, let alone talked to, the studio owner, Ms. Mavis Deporre, but luck was with her immediately after her afternoon lesson. Mavis was behind the counter with Donna.

"I said twice on Tuesday, and once on Thursday. Tuesday at ten o'clock in the morning, and the afternoon slot's the same, one o'clock. It's not difficult." Mavis handed a pen back to Donna with a flourished wave of her hand. Donna smiled weakly at Christine as Mavis turned with a spin and moved with speedy determination toward the front office. Christine moved quickly to head her off.

"Ms. Deporre? Excuse me, Mavis?" Christine's voice apparently opened a small crack in her cloak of invisibility as Mavis stopped abruptly, turned and delivered Christine a perturbed look.

"I'm glad to have caught you, Mavis, and I know you're very busy. I just want to let you know how much I've appreciated your studio donating time to the Community Services organization. And I've really enjoyed learning how to dance. Jared is an excellent teacher."

"Well, he should be, shouldn't he? And I hope your little event is a big success. I won't be there of course. Kyle will be," Mavis rippled out.

"I wonder what the policy is on tipping, or providing Jared a gift of some sort, especially as I am not a paying client."

Mavis violently shook her head. "No, absolutely not. A tip is not necessary. I pay him for his time with you." Quick birdlike movements accentuated her resolute message as she turned away.

"But I need to show Jared my appreciation. I don't feel comfortable not providing a gift," Christine said to the back of Mavis's bobbing head as it rushed toward the doorway of the front office. Mavis's sudden turn and Christine's persistence collided in an awkward bump. Mavis stepped back and looked at Christine as if she was encountering the most ignorant person imaginable.

"Well, get him a pair of socks."

"Socks? Why would I get Jared socks?"

"Men who dance wear crazy socks under their trousers. They all do," Mavis said. She suddenly swept past Christine and onto the dance floor where Hollie was teaching Mr. and Mrs. Hull a new waltz move. Without warning, Mavis grabbed Mr. Hull's pant leg and jerked it up. "See? All male dancers wear crazy socks."

"So I see," said Christine, who had barely arrived in time to get a glimpse of both Mr. Hull's bright scarlet sock and his spindly white leg. Mrs. Hull giggled at her husband's startled reaction to being publicly accosted.

Jared had returned from a back room and was characteristically clip-strutting toward them. "Jared! Show us your socks," Mavis's demand barked across the floor. Without a moment's hesitation, Jared stopped and dutifully raised his pant leg to provide everyone a good look at his flamboyant green and gold striped sock. Although he looked rather puzzled, he never said a word. He just stood there with trouser leg raised, waiting for further instruction.

"See? Even Jared wears crazy socks."

"Yes, so I see. Again," Christine replied, certain her face had noticeably reddened.

Jared smiled at Christine before flashing his second sock at her. He looked uncharacteristically childlike, as if he were wading in a puddle. Obviously enjoying his audience, and still holding his pant legs high, Jared turned and waddled back to the lounge. He was acting abnormally silly, but still charming, of course.

"And I'll show you another," Mavis cut through her words and sailed back to her front office where she showed Christine yet one more pair of socks, beyond garish, adorning her desk with their bright pink and blue florescent dots. *Wouldn't it have been more appropriate to show me this pair first?*

"I plan to give these to Kyle. A tie would be suitable also—a tie or a pair of socks. But no tip," Mavis decreed. She spun like a top on the heel of her stylish dance shoe and left Christine standing alone with the highly offensive socks. *Lucky Kyle.*

Christine had planned to stop at the mall before heading home anyway, determined to use this opportunity to shop—invest in her future. Her mission was to break through her own self-limiting attitude, disrupt her tightwad approach to consumerism. To do so, she had decided to spend an outrageous amount of money on high-quality cosmetics. She was nearly out of foundation—purchased over two years ago by April at a drug store. Inevitably, the products Christine had bought since were disappointing—too dark, too bright, too orange. At fourteen dollars per fluid ounce, the little bottles of foundation were a financial investment, not an inexpensive use-once-and-trash consumable. Except, she needed help, hence the department store. Their products could be tested before purchase, returned if she wasn't satisfied. Christine convinced herself that she'd save money in the long run.

Christine never felt like she fit into society, and when shopping, those feelings of awkwardness were nearly overwhelming. The mall and its products mystified her. *Why do people spend these outrageous amounts of money for clothing?* She realized that she was different than most of the people who lived in this particular area of the world at this particular time in history. She was the odd one, she was strange and foreign. She could relate to what alien beings might feel when visiting Earth.

Her mission was twofold. First, she would purchase cosmetics with the help of an expert, and then find a gift of appreciation for Jared—socks, perhaps, but no tie. She had seen him in a different tie at every one of her lessons. He didn't need another tie.

The glistening glass and sparkling mirrors in the cosmetic department battled for attention, leaving Christine a bit lost, dazed. She slowly circled each counter, avoided touching anything for fear that by doing so she would be signaling the closest beauty consultant to rush to her aid. Christine was trying to find the oldest, most experienced saleswoman available.

As she turned the corner of yet another sparkling display, she saw a beautiful young saleswoman and in that instant, Christine saw April, alive and healthy. A scant moment later, she crashed back to reality. Similar experiences were common. She'd be going about her day and hear a voice that was Jesse's. Or she'd smell blueberry muffins and immediately be in her kitchen, baking for Seth. This moment of recall was so unexpected, however, and so powerful, Christine's knees buckled, she stepped backward and sunk onto a nearby stool.

She struggled to maintain control, but refused to look away. This girl looked so much like her daughter that Christine wanted very much to go over and give her a motherly hug. A second later, she felt an overwhelming need to gather herself and run from the store. The young woman's long flowing hair cascaded down her back, like April's—the reddish color, the cut, and way it drifted as she moved. The girl turned and reached up for a small container on top of the divider and her hair fell away from her face long enough for Christine to see her earrings. They were identical to the little gold and diamond hoop earrings April had been wearing the day she died.

Christine's eyes welled up, she stood unsteadily. She had to leave, there was no choice. She reached for her purse to locate a tissue. She had not been without colorful purse tissues for over two years—another investment she had decided would be perfectly acceptable considering her circumstances. She knew she would be crying a lot, so she had resolved to look as beautiful as possible while blowing snot and crying her eyes out. Even though the cheery tissues were scratchy and stiff, they always made her feel a little better. Just a little. She glanced once more at the precious April-like girl as the tissue finished its hurried work at her face.

"May I help you?" a voice behind her asked. Christine turned. A friendly face of her own age was studying her from behind a nearby counter. The woman looked at her quietly, gently smiling. Waiting. *What kind of help is she offering,* wondered Christine as she stuffed the wet wad into her purse. *A hug would be appreciated.*

Instead of asking for the much-needed hug, Christine replied, "Yes, thank you. I'm...I'm here to do something I've never done." It seemed a silly, childish thing to say. Christine hoped her red eyes and nose weren't too noticeable. "I'm here to select a line of makeup. I've got an aging face, but it's the only one I've got, and I rather like it and thought it time to take better care of it." Christine looked at the woman who was still smiling patiently. "I was hoping to find a person with a lot of experience to help me. Have you worked with cosmetics for a long time?" Christine's nervous ramble finally slowed to an uncomfortable end.

The woman nodded. "You've come to the right place. My name is Mary, and I have helped hundreds of women select personal products for their skin and faces for over twenty years. I would be happy to help you find exactly what you need." The woman's pleasant look and friendly patience provided Christine the validation needed.

"Thank you so much," Christine said clearly and out loud, but Christine wasn't thanking Mary, at least not directly. It was a prayer of gratitude. She accepted the chair, carefully positioning it so she would be facing away from the April look-alike during her experience in indulgent consumerism.

Mary asked a lot of questions before collecting various products from display cases and placing the line-up on the counter. Christine actually enjoyed having them applied with such skill and pampering. "You are a gifted artist," she commented as she looked at herself in the mirror. Mary's smile seemed genuine. Christine had never spent $500 for appearance's sake in her entire life. This day, however, she purchased nearly every product suggested.

As Mary bagged the purchases, she said, "You have beautiful rings, Christine. I don't think I've ever seen anything like that pink stone. What kind of gem is that?"

"It's a pink diamond. These diamonds are both very special." Christine did what she always did when people asked about her rings—kissed them twice. People looked at her strangely, but she did not explain. Christine was certain many people wouldn't understand or appreciate this tangible reminder of her lost loved ones.

Her cosmetics purchase had been easier than she thought it would be. Like the rings, the cosmetics were another rare investment in freedom of choice. She refused to feel guilty for investing in herself, not any more. The gift for Jared, however, proved to be much more challenging. The socks were all of poor quality—the yarn twist wasn't tight enough and the fiber length was too short. The socks would all leave nasty bits of fuzz all over the floor when removed. Christine smiled at her memories of the battles she and Seth had had over his cheap socks and the mess they left behind on the bedroom carpet— worse than the feathery fuzz she imagined floated off Liberty. Christine reluctantly weaved her way back to the parking lot without socks.

The car keys jangled in protest as she yanked them from their typical hiding place. As she searched for the right key, it struck her that she already owned everything she needed to make Jared a perfect gift. She even had the right-sized drill bit.

Wednesday, October 28
Jared: Perfume Research

Kyle had taught her last week. Today, unfortunately, it was his turn to teach the statuesque Miss Tracy Martin. It was still strange to see her name there on his list. Jared sighed. His relationships never worked out. His last steady girlfriend had gotten quite serious—nearly moved in with him to make his apartment their home. Then, he had invited her to a Friday night dance party. Regrettably, the night ended badly. Very badly. She complained that he hadn't danced with her, seemed surprised by the way he held his students and the way he lightly flirted with them. He thought he had sufficiently warned her of the nature of his work and the methods he used to satisfy paying clients. Still, she had failed to understand, and took what she had witnessed as a clear sign that he wasn't a suitable partner.

Jared shook the hurtful memory aside and turned his thoughts back to Tracy. She wasn't the person he thought she was, hoped she was. The couch time had twisted their relationship, damaged it somehow. It was merely a passing pleasantry for her, one she had demanded of him. Now at smoke breaks, she'd fire out her petty demands and wait for him to deliver as if he were a well-trained pet, a dog that was expected to wait in her shadow and jump up at every command. And he did.

He wished he could go back to the "old Tracy." That Tracy cared about him, understood and accepted his work. She had listened and she remembered things, too—would bring up little details he had shared weeks earlier. Easy to talk to. Easy to trust. Now, she was shifty, wave-like. She'd subside and be calm for a time, then build up an attitude and push at him. Was she still a friend? If so, it was an uncomfortable friendship, especially now that she was a student, a student who had demanded non-student benefits on her dirty yellow couch.

Even amidst all these swirling thoughts and feelings, he provided his customary greeting, the expected hug. After all, he was a professional. Throughout the lesson, Tracy filled the space between them, claimed it. He was reminded of Gran's moving day when he tried to move the refrigerator across the kitchen floor by himself. Pushing and pulling with little to show for his effort.

Jared ended the lesson very much on time, retrieved his coat, and leaned his spent form against the doorway of the instructors' lounge. "Hey, Kyle. I just finished Tracy's lesson and we're heading out. Are you planning to be here a while?" he asked.

"Nearly finished. Booking flights to Vegas for that comp in December. I'll lock up. So, where are you taking Tracy tonight?" Kyle smiled, no, smirked. "Dining? Then home?"

"I'm escorting Tracy to her car. What she does from there is her business. She's a student, you know."

"Oh, sure. Right." Kyle's narrowed eyes peered up at Jared. "Come off it, Jared. You've been sniffin' around that long-legged pussy for months. Lots of amazing inches to explore there, Buddy. It should take you all night."

Jared wanted to smack Kyle's slimy smile clear off his face. He envisioned himself doing just that, watching it sail across the room and splat against the wall. Jared glanced at the vandalized wall for a moment, imagining Kyle's gooey lips stuck there. He turned away as he slipped on his coat.

"Look, Kyle, I don't know what I can say to convince that

dirty mind of yours that Tracy and I are not seeing one another. I have no intention of dating her, or anything else. If Mavis hears that kind of talk, I'll be in trouble. So knock it off." Kyle simply smiled wider into the glare of the computer screen.

Jared's newest dance shoes had been delivered that morning housed in a hard plastic shoe box that sat solidly on the desk between them. Jared lifted the box and tested its weight. It was rigid and sturdy. The shoes had certainly cost enough to live in a well-designed durable box. He toyed with the idea of dropping the corner of it on Kyle's mouse-driven hand. Instead, he gently set it down and tapped purposefully at it with his fingertip, pleading with the sharp corner to help calm his intense irritation.

"Why aren't you using the computer in the front office?" Jared asked. That got Kyle's attention. They both knew why. Kyle liked to visit websites that weren't appropriate for work, and Kyle shared the front office computer with Mavis. The pesky thing was set to record all visited websites. Jared smiled at Kyle, who pushed the shoe box across the desk toward Jared to provide himself more space for his evening's entertainment.

"Just stop about Tracy, okay?" Jared said.

"Rumor has it that you've already gotten more than friendly with her," Kyle said calmly, maintaining his steady fascination with the computer. "She's obviously into you, Jared. If you'd like to expand your time with her off the floor, your secret's safe with me." This time Kyle looked up at his co-worker thoughtfully. "Really, you need a girl and Tracy's really into you. She told me so herself."

"I'm not interested. She's not my type," Jared said firmly as he gathered his belongings. He left with a shake of his head and rejoined Tracy near the back door, then dutifully set his things down to help her with the coat she was still holding. She leaned against him as she slowly slid into the sleeves. He couldn't help but notice how beautiful her dark hair looked against the bright pink fabric of her coat. She held onto his arm for a moment before turning to him.

"I was unsteady on the dance floor today. I can't seem to get the hang of being sensitive to your lead."

"You did fine, really you did. It's only your third lesson."

"I hear there's a Halloween dance party this Friday," Tracy said. "I'm working late tomorrow to finish up the monthly inventory so I can come."

Oh great, now she's coming to Friday night dance parties, Jared thought, as he smiled at her. "That would be great, Tracy. Just great."

He grabbed her elbow and started to open the door. Sheets of rain pelted the cars; water rushed across the lot and gargled through drain grates with bubbling force.

"Oh crap, look at this. Wait here, I'll get the umbrella." Jared headed back to the lounge.

"What did you forget this time?" Kyle didn't bother to look up from the glaring monitor.

"It's raining like crazy and I didn't want Tracy to get wet." He circled the desk looking for the seldom-used umbrella.

Kyle turned from the screen. "Perhaps you ought to get Tracy wet. I bet you'd find her quite enjoyable. Or should I say, find her even more enjoyable the second time?"

"For real? Just stop, already," Jared said with force. There was a time when Kyle's sexual references would have been hilarious. Jared wondered when crass had stopped being funny as he made his way back to Tracy. Even though the rain had slowed to a steady pace, they both unlocked their cars from inside the building with their remotes. Jared finally delivered a nearly dry Tracy to her car.

But before he closed her door she exclaimed, "Oh how stupid. I forgot my shoes inside. Not sure where." She looked so distraught it was only right to offer to retrieve them for her.

"Oh, would you? That would be great. I need them tonight." Jared knew exactly where the shoes were, he had watched in the monitor as she stuffed the bag under the lobby sofa before her lesson. He wrestled the umbrella back inside the heavy glass door, ran quietly across the dance floor, retrieved the shoes, and ran back again to avoid any more exposure to Kyle's vulgarities.

When Jared paused at the door to fight with the umbrella, a flash of pink outside caught his eye. Tracy. She was no longer in her car—no, she was getting out of his car. Jared watched as she shut his passenger door and quickly jumped back into her own vehicle. She had set him up to get something from his car. This wasn't the first time a woman had taken some personal item of his as a keepsake. Jared recalled a past student who regularly wandered into the instructors' lounge and stole things from his desk. Kyle was right—Tracy had a crush on him. It made things awkward, but it was understandable. He'd let it go. Whatever she just took had to be small, insignificant. He shoved at the glass door, opened the umbrella, and made his way out to her through the slowing rain. He held her bag up into the umbrella so it wouldn't get wet.

Tracy's car window lowered and she said, "Thanks. It's very sweet of you, really. I can't believe I forgot my shoes."

The outer strands of Tracy's long dark hair were hanging damp and limp about her face.

"I can't believe it myself," Jared replied, smiling down at her. "Hey, I'll probably see you tomorrow. Have a good night." He tapped on the hood of her car and lowered the umbrella.

Jared left the back parking lot before Tracy, who waved at him through her rain-stained window. He wasn't worried about her following; he was headed to the mall to do some research. He realized he had forgotten his clothes on the bench in the studio when he helped Tracy with her coat. Mavis would admonish him for his forgetfulness in the morning.

Once parked, he sought for something missing. He really didn't keep much in his car. His pens and notebook were right where he had left them. His extra tin of Altoids. A couple spare ties were folded neatly on the back seat undisturbed. He checked for his new gloves in the compartment between the front seats. He located only one. No sense looking further, Tracy had taken the other. The gloves had been a birthday gift from Gran. Jared sighed, then winced. Gran would wonder why he never wore them come winter.

He turned his attention to his mission by checking his notebook for the names and personal details of the saleswomen he would likely encounter. He checked his face and hair in the visor mirror. Fortunately, the rain was now only a misty drizzle. The walk through the lot was time well spent as he visualized the saleswomen's faces, practiced their names out loud, and considered which of their personal details he would call to mind during conversation.

He paused at the store entrance and flipped the lone glove in the trash. No sense keeping it—a painful reminder of his loss. He hurried to open the door for a woman pushing a stroller, and to get a glimpse of the baby, then he finally entered one of the few places he always felt comfortable and appreciated—the mall.

Today, he had a "shopping list" and would probably spend a good hour at the cosmetic counter. Even so, it was unlikely he'd make a purchase. He rarely did. He realized a long time ago that his presence added to the look and feel store managers wanted their buying customers to experience. A savvy young man dressed in an expensive suit just might increase sales. He didn't have to buy a thing to help them make money.

He hoped the little strawberry blonde would be working, and smiled as he recalled how much she reminded him of a walking Barbie doll. She couldn't hide that outrageously built body under that smock. He hadn't recorded her name, and would need to start all over with flirtatious small talk, but her help could actually be quite valuable to his research. He needed to find the perfumes used by two students, one being Christine. Christine had a clean scent, like winter air, like fresh icy lemon water. Jared regularly updated his knowledge on the latest products from the perfumer houses and was considering which artist had created Christine's scent.

He wove his way through the clothing racks and walk-danced around mannequins toward the front of the store. Yes, the Barbie doll was at the counter and she was not helping a customer, not yet. Seeing her now, it surprised him how much she reminded him of Christine. He hung back to give himself a few moments to study her. Yes, her pale coloring and her dark blue eyes were very much like Christine's. Jared approached the counter and selected a Chanel perfume from the row of offerings. He merely held it near his face—spraying would pollute the air and the opportunity to experience other perfumes as the artist intended. It was a familiar scent and several students came to mind as he inhaled.

A second bottle was lifted, one with the shape of a full-bodied woman. He slowly pulled his finger down the side of the voluptuous bottle as he drew a deep breath through his nose. Yes, another student came to mind. He had purposely positioned himself out of sight of a familiar saleswoman. He wasn't shopping, merely hooking the blonde and he smiled shyly when she approached.

"May I help you?"

He continued to hold his head down as he looked up at her—studying her Christine-blue eyes. "Yeah, um…I'm not very good at these things. I want to find a perfume for my… aunt."

He tilted his head and studied her face. This girl didn't merely resemble Christine—she could easily pass for a young Christine. This would prove to be an enjoyable hour, imagining this young woman as Christine at a younger, innocent age. Christine still seemed to be genuinely naïve and inexperienced in many ways; it wouldn't take much effort to transform this salesgirl into Christine for a few pleasant minutes.

"Do you know if your aunt already uses a favorite perfume?"

"I don't think so. She doesn't think she needs nice things. But I wanna find something that will make her feel special. She's my favorite aunt."

"She's very fortunate." The little doll's soft pink mouth smiled.

"I think she'd like a perfume with a citrus undertone," Jared said.

"A citrus undertone? Apparently you know a little something about perfume," the salesgirl said with a soft laugh. She set her elbows on the glass countertop and leaned forward, revealing just a hint of rounded cleavage. She blushed, quickly pushed her weight back to her feet and stood upright.

"It's just an expression I heard. I…I hope you don't mind me saying this, but I couldn't help noticing just now that you smell wonderful. What are you wearing?"

"I'd love to share it with you, but this store doesn't carry my perfume. It's called Almond Delight." She lowered herself back to the counter toward him.

"Perhaps you could share it with me later," Jared said while wondering what deep discount drug store sold such an overtly sweet stench. He glanced up at her quickly and noticed that she was still blushing slightly. "But right now, I'd like to check out some of your bestsellers."

Jared did indeed enjoy his research that afternoon. He sampled fifteen perfumes and successfully identified one as Mrs. Clement's—a heavy peony base lightened with poivre. Unfortunately, there is a limit to what olfactory glands can handle, even Jared's. So, regrettably, he was unable to experience every perfume in the store. Fortunately, however, he did fully experience the all too familiar sparkle of a woman flirting.

So, although he was disappointed that he had not found the scent of Christine, he was pleased that the Barbie doll and he were on very friendly terms. He asked for sample scent cards of two of the perfumes he "liked the best." One was Mrs. Clement's perfume. He had collected nearly every student's perfume and stored these sensory records along with their written re-cords in his ever growing three-ring binder. When the Barbie doll turned to spray the perfumes onto stiff cards, Jared quickly slipped a nearly full bottle of Chanel in his side pocket. Old habit. The fragrant sample cards were handed to him, accepted with a smile for his new young admirer.

"Guess I'll have to come back when I've made up my mind. Do you have a business card?"

The doll smiled back. "Of course," she said.

She turned and fingered out a white and pink business card. She then reached under the counter and brought up a cloth quilted purse, dug inside, removed a small bottle then sprayed its contents on the card. Jared guessed this would be Almond Delight. She scribbled something on the back before extending it toward Jared, who reached well beyond her fingertips and slowly slid his palm across the back and side of her hand before releasing the card from her.

"Thank you," he said, concentrating on her blue eyes. Even her blush was Christine-like. He glanced at the front of the card and captured her name before turning it over to read the flowery sloped invitation, "Call me sometime," followed by her phone number. He kept his head bent and looked up at her through his lashes.

"I'd really rather not have to wait to call you. What time do you get off work?"

Wednesday, October 28
Tracy: Fun at the Local Mall

"The human heart is the most deceitful of all
things, and desperately wicked. Who really
knows how bad it is?"

Jeremiah 17:9 (New Living Translation)

It had gone exactly as planned. Her sweet Jared had helped her by being so damn polite, retrieving her shoes just as she knew he would. He never suggested that she come to the studio the next day, never offered to bring the shoes over to the bookstore later. He heard her request, knew he could satisfy her need, and simply said, "Okay. I'll get them for you." All she had to do was jump into his unlocked car, shove the GPS device into the deep dark recess of his glove compartment, and get back into her car.

Tracy didn't trust the device, so she had waited until he left, then returned to the bookstore and fired up her computer. She watched with interest as Jared's car pinged out its location every five minutes. Ping—the back lot. Ping—an intersection. Ping—the mall. Again, the damn mall. What could the little man possibly be doing at the mall yet again? Tracy clicked away from the GPS tracking surveillance site to record several transactions from her drug trade, then clicked back to the tracking site again—still at the mall. Even though Tracy had managed to successfully follow Jared to the mall several times, it would be good to do more on-site research.

She trolled the lot and soon found his car near an anchor store. He was at the perfume counter openly flirting with a little blonde number. It wasn't difficult to blend into the racks of clothing among the hustling movement of shoppers. Tracy observed Jared unnoticed.

Tracy was not only watching him, she was using her phone to video his every move. She seethed silently as he expertly hit on the pouty pink mall slut. As she watched Jared on the small screen in her hand, however, she was delighted to see him palm pocket a bottle of perfume. *Well, well. Jared shoplifts.* Yet another juicy tidbit to add to her collection, captured nicely on video. The cloth flower attached to the dress Tracy was holding received a brutal crush and a smile before she turned off the phone camera and moved to the next dress.

She wondered if her little lump of brown sugar had been spotted for the theft as she slipped behind a protective wall of coats. Security wouldn't nab him until he left the store. This could get very interesting. After an eternity of flirting, the blonde provided him perfume sample cards and a business card. Jared left without making a purchase. He strutted out into the mall and Tracy waited, hopeful. Nope. Security was not providing him an escort back into the store. He had gotten away with his petty theft. No fun of that sort, so now it was time for some fun of her own making.

The coats had provided an effective bunker for making a plan, one that would keep this little blonde bitch from becoming a nuisance. Tracy leisurely wandered toward the perfume counter where the girl stood staring out toward the open mouth of the store, fluffing at her fuzzy mane—probably looking for Jared's distinctive saunter far down the mall by now.

"Excuse me," Tracy said. The girl didn't turn, barely nodded. "I noticed you helping a very handsome black man just now." That got the girl's attention. Tracy picked up one of the perfumes and sprayed it liberally onto her neck. "That one's a bit flowery for me," Tracy said with an exaggerated wave. Her long red fingernails flashed through the pungent air.

"Looked like the two of you were thoroughly enjoying your conversation." The girl's back stiffened a little, but her look confirmed the need to put the plan into action, so Tracy added, "I actually saw him earlier today. He's a patient at the clinic where I work. I just started there a few months ago, but a co-worker told me all about him. Jared? Jaden? Josh? Why can't I think of his name?"

"It's Jaden. Jaden Gregory," shared the little blonde with a knowing nod. Tracy fought to control her surprise. *He's using his real name with this little bitch?*

Tracy said, "That's right, Jaden. Jaden Gregory. And did you know that he's the son of one of America's top twenty wealthiest African American men?" The blonde looked surprised. Tracy continued, "Yeah, he's only in Indianapolis for an appointment at the clinic and to go to his box seat at the pro-football game on Sunday. Has a fully-furnished apartment here in Indy, a car parked at the private airport ready and waiting. He just flies into town from L.A. for a few days now and then."

"Really? I mean…he's really wealthy? He seemed pretty normal to me," the little blonde said with a flutter. Her huge blue eyes sucked at Tracy for more information.

"Normal?" Tracy let loose a light laugh. "I guess that depends how well you get to know him and how you define 'normal.' My friend at the clinic dated him briefly, but she lost him. That's how I know about the apartment and all. He'd make some girl a great catch. But she wasn't the girl for Jaden Gregory."

The blonde stared at Tracy, leaned across the counter and whispered, "I've got a date with him tonight." She smiled, sweet little cheeks all pinked up. Tracy held the perfume bottle tightly to keep from slapping those Kyle-like cheeks.

"You do?" Tracy puffed out a little sound of surprise. "Oh, I envy you. That's great. I…I hope you don't mind me asking if you made plans."

"No. We didn't make plans, only that he's going to pick me up right after work."

Tracy leaned onto the counter and said softly, "It's not really my place to say, but do you want some advice? I mean, what my friend shared with me might be helpful."

"Oh, sure! That would be great." The little blonde's head thrust forward and her pouty rose mouth opened slightly. Tracy wanted to reach up and snag that pretty mouth with her fingernail.

"Well, you'll have dinner of course, maybe a few drinks, and then you'll end the evening at his apartment." Tracy held the girl's eye and was very direct about this vital fact before continuing. "I mean, you know that, right? That's what he expects, what he needs."

The little blonde took a slight step back and stared at Tracy. "Yeah, I know. That's my plan too, of course." The blonde forced a quick smile as her little red face turned toward the perfumes and her fingers quickly arranged the bottles in a tight row across the glass countertop between them. Her neck had reddened too, and it was quite clear that the girl had no such plan until that moment.

"I'm sorry, maybe I'm sharing too much," Tracy said.

"No, no really, I want to hear what your friend said about Jaden."

Tracy looked at the girl steadily as if she were considering her words carefully. "Well, she said that she regretted not being more open to some pretty kinky stuff. He likes women a bit pushy and a little freaky in bed." Tracy noticed a slight raise to both eyebrows that sat above the blue eyes. The cheeks flamed brightly.

"I'm not saying he's dangerous or anything. She just said she wouldn't hesitate to be more open if she had the chance to do it over." Tracy took one of the bottles from the carefully placed row and sprayed it on her wrist. "You'll have fun. I'm certain of that. But…" Tracy took a long whiff at her wrist and looked steadily across the counter at the girl.

"But, but what?" the anxious words bounced out.

"Well, just be careful. Be careful if he gets slow and quiet. That's when he's fighting back an urge to hurt someone. My friend didn't catch on the first few times. Not serious hurt. Just a bit rough. Some guys are like that. You know that, right?"

Tracy could see that the little blonde did not know. She didn't know anything about people who would purposely hurt other people—Tracy's favorite type of people.

Tracy hurried on to reassure the sweet little thing. "But just so you know, my friend wishes she had him back. The rest of what she said sounded like he's a really nice guy. Just let him do whatever he wants." Tracy stifled a giggle as she watched the girl struggle.

"He might make up some weird stuff about what he does and where he lives and all just till he gets to know you better.

He told my friend he was a dance instructor when they first met. Funny, huh?" Tracy twisted at the top of one of the bottles and the cap popped off and clattered across the smooth glass. "Those really wealthy people probably have to do that—make up stories about who they are so people won't just use them for their money. I can't imagine that kind of life. It would be living the dream." Tracy completed the conversation with a playful wink before heading home.

Thursday, October 29
Jared: In Morning Light

"Searching too hard for happiness will make you
absolutely miserable."

— Unknown

He had already dressed for work and now he sat waiting, watching. The leather chair squeaked ever so softly as he adjusted his legs to more comfortably admonish himself. A long list of stupid choices rolled through his mind, the first, and most obvious, inviting this girl to his apartment for the night. She was still in his bed at 9:30 a.m., sleeping soundly the way twenty-year-olds do. A string of slobber flowed from her parted pink mouth creating a dark puddle on his pillowcase. There was a purity about her that certainly wasn't apparent the night before. He resisted the urge to touch her hair, afraid it would waken her.

He had told himself he wouldn't do this anymore—have sex with a girl he didn't even know. He had had plenty of time to think between making the date with this girl and picking her up. He could have bailed, but he didn't. No, he pulled in beside her car early, paced outside the mall door and then, suddenly, he had this girl, Christine-beautiful, glowing at his arm. Even though he knew he was about to make another mistake, he had strutted her to his car like he was caught in a tide, an irreversible wake.

When she had asked his name, he shocked himself when he blurted it out—his real name, Jaden Gregory, and she had called him Jaden all night. It was nice. Throughout their meal he had hoped she would settle, just be calm, and slow down. But, she seemed to quickly push their evening toward what they both knew would be part of their shared experience. Jared had been fairly certain they'd land in bed too, but he found himself wanting to delay the process, to just talk and laugh, and talk some more. When he asked her a couple Christine-like questions, she just looked at him strangely, probably the way he himself looked at Christine. She chatted about her television shows, fashion, and spent time texting invisible people who regularly intruded into his time with her.

Now she was in his bed, sleeping. He couldn't remember her name and it was awkward to wake her without it. He suspended his irritation long enough to appreciate the color of her skin and the way her soft hair floated around her face, and then he revisited their night together. Once in the apartment, he had questioned whether he even wanted to have sex with this girl. She asked for a drink, and he obliged. But he hadn't given her what he knew she needed as she sat with him. No music—none of the usual rhythmic vibrations stroking her ears. He hadn't carelessly rested his hand on her leg as they talked, or tenderly caressed her arm. He hadn't drifted his hand across her soft breast or casually brushed hair from her face, hadn't hesitatingly kissed her neck, her mouth. He had simply sat with her on the couch and held her in the stillness, wanted to just hold her and be. Just be. He wanted to ask her questions—real questions about things that mattered, but he didn't know how.

Typically, he initiated the gradual build-up toward the inevitable nuzzling walk to the bedroom. This time, however, it was the girl, slightly drunk, giggly, who finally pulled him from the quiet couch. He didn't want to hurt her feelings, didn't want to embarrass her by suggesting they wait and just talk, just be. He couldn't explain it, so he didn't try. He didn't even want to undress her, except she guided his reluctant hands to start the process. He silently consented and undressed her slowly, leaving her bra and panties. He tenderly pushed her hands aside when she attempted to remove these herself, shook his head at her and kissed her fingertips.

Then every part of her was all over him to get him undressed. He had to stop her frantic tugging by taking her hands gently into his yet again. She wasn't ready. He kissed the palms of her hands tenderly, placed his finger on her lips and whispered softly to her to calm her. She seemed uncertain what to do; her huge blue eyes stared at him. Jared could feel her body tighten and shift away. She seemed almost frightened and he started to question if she had any experience at all, wondered if she really wanted to be in his bedroom, except, she had pulled him there.

She watched, wide-eyed, as he removed his belt and dress shirt, his shoes, his socks. He pulled back the bedspread and laid her against the crisp white sheets then rested his face against her shoulder, ran his hand against the tiny soft hairs on her arm and watched each one spring back up as his hand moved over them. He stroked the girl's neck where the scar would be if she were Christine and kissed her there tenderly, allowing his tongue to imagine it felt the scar's little raised bumps. After his fingertips softly caressed the exposed mounds of her breasts, he removed her bra and panties, then slowly stroked her every curve, every crevice. He traced a long path the length of her body with his fingertips, kissed that path gently to its end. She shuddered and he worked with her until he was certain she was satisfied. He would have been almost content to stop when she finally lay slack in his arms. Although his body pleaded differently, his heart was comfortable with the thought of just being with this beautiful Christine-like creature. But that moment didn't last.

He finished undressing himself, she watched, strangely quiet. He rolled her over and leisurely dragged his hands down the length of her back. Her skin, silky soft, warm and submissive. He caressed the cute dimples at the base of her back, explored the crease where her sweet little ass mysteriously became a leg, and slowly pulled his fingers across her inner thigh. She reacted again to his touch and kisses, and felt her yielding, rising, falling into the intensity. His body, and the girl, assured that the rest of their time together progressed as predicted, as she had wanted. He pleased her, and she him, and afterward he was able to do what he had really wanted to do all along, simply hold her. He experienced her long after she had fallen asleep. The base notes of her perfume had mellowed, leaving a mildly spicy smell. Her taste, like soft pink pepper. The way her stomach gurgled and her chest rose and fell. Silent pain seeped through him, a stinging pain he had been holding, tightly shoving down. The light from the bathroom reflected on the soft feathery hair that floated, halo-like, above her head, and he allowed the golden wisps to dance on his open palm as she slept. This girl didn't even know him. He was totally and completely alone.

Later in the darkness he had wakened her with kisses, tender and slow. Even though her eyes opened wide and alert, she hadn't stopped him. Not since the quick ugly time with Tracy had he had that experience, unsheathed, risky, satisfying. Totally dishonorable. He had focused solely on his own needs, one physical, one emotional—a pleasurable, guilt-filled decision, using this girl to fade the ugly experience with Tracy. When the golden girl lay still again, sleeplike, he held her as his reproachful heart crackled silently inside him.

Fortunately, the feelings were slowing now that it was morning. The morning always fought off the confusion that grew only at night. Jared sat in his bedroom watching the early sunlight flow over the beautiful girl as she slept. Her hair, like fine-spun gold, danced across her white shoulder. She looked so much like Christine. He leaned back in the chair, crossed his legs, tilted his head comfortably, and gazed at her. He relived his favorite moment from the night before: a rare simple, lingering, kiss when he had her soft and sleepy in his arms. They had simply relaxed into each other, lying mouth to mouth, breathing together, simply being together as one. Being one. After he had watched her drift off, he fantasized that she was Christine, his young wife, asleep in their home, completely relaxed, content, and secure. But even then, the emptiness haunted him in the hollow darkness.

The morning Jared now sat perfectly still, dreamily watching her sleep. One of her hoop earrings had come unclasped, and was lying on her cheek. He'd help her close it when she awoke so she wouldn't lose it. She was very young. It was much more difficult to determine the age of a young woman. Jared reflected on her face and bare shoulder and decided she was likely twenty or twenty-one. Maybe only nineteen. *Stores in the mall don't hire teenaged girls, do they?* Jared tried to push down the sudden distress of the possibility that she was only a teenager. He stood up and took her business card from the dresser. It had only her name: "Rachel Sensen," the store's contact information, and of course, her phone number scrawled on the back. Rachel Sensen, a funny, strangely familiar, name. This wasn't helping. He had to know for certain she was of age.

He left quickly, and quietly, to find her purse in the living room. It was made from quilted cloth with green, blue and black flowers, a much smaller version of the one Christine carried, except Christine's had paisleys. He had two paisley ties, one yellow, black and red and the other two-tone blue. Jared chastised himself for getting distracted by paisley, unzipped the purse, and dug about for a wallet. A

nearly empty bottle of "Almond Delight," tampons, a porta-
ble razor, a wad of mangled jewelry. He paused long enough
to sniff at a package of Zig Zag papers. There was just a hint
of marijuana and, damn, it smelled good. Jared sucked in a
deep breath and let it out with a soft whistle. He shook his
head and shoved the package to the bottom of the purse.

The realization that there were typical things missing
briefly slowed his frantic search. No condoms, no birth control, no plan B pills, and he thought wistfully, foolishly, that
"maybe, just maybe." Jared smiled a "just maybe I got her
pregnant" smile and deeply inhaled the mingled scent of the
purse's treasures.

A swollen wallet was finally pried away from the rest of
the contents. It bulged and strained against the abuse of Rachel's squirreling. He freed the snap and the wallet popped
open in relief. She had three credit cards, crushed receipts,
clothing hang tags, and a little metal buckle, all stuffed in the
snapped side.

The driver's license was in the zippered side, wedged
between a gift card and a coupon for hair conditioner. He focused his full attention on finding her birthdate, captured the
numbers in his head and slid the license back into its sleeve.
He did the math as he quickly worked to zip the wallet shut,
and no, thank God, no, she was not a teen. She was twenty-two years old. He relaxed.

He struggled to recall what side of the purse the wallet
had been in when he had started. *Idiot, just choose a side and
get away from the purse.* He finally got it zipped and settled
back on the couch before releasing a breath he hadn't known
he had been holding. Rachel hadn't walked in on him, and

she was well out of her teens. There was still no sound from the bedroom and he enjoyed a slow release of tension. Relief was sweet. He looked forward to returning to his chair—building on the fantasy of having young Christine as his life partner.

First, however, he made his way to the kitchen, poured another cup of coffee and lit a cigarette. He pulled on the swatches of his daydream and decided to muse again over what house shopping with Christine would be like. She'd want a garden. In his mind she stood, child-like, with her nose buried in a flower. The cigarette was snuffed and he returned softly to the bedroom for his time alone to observe a woman sleeping. The leather squeaked slightly as he settled. He watched as her eyes twitched. Her lips trembled ever so slightly. Her breathing was mesmerizing, the in, the out, the in again.

She was still naked under those sheets, and he had all morning to be with this lovely adult woman. Not enough time to repeat the evening before, but he could enjoy her once again. He loosened his tie, paused before unbuttoning his shirt. She really did look very young, and she really did look very, very much like Christine. Even though her hair was redder than Christine's, it was still blonde, and it floated about in wisps the same as Christine's. He tilted his head and blurred his vision. She could be Christine, or at least her daughter. A daughter of Christine's would be this lovely. She could indeed be Christine's daughter.

Jared sat bolt upright and tightly gripped the chair's padded arms. This could be Christine's daughter. The thought hit him so hard he nearly cried out. She had a daughter, yes? Yes. Christine mentioned plans to borrow earrings from her daughter to wear to the gala. Jared stared at Rachel's earrings. They were exactly as Christine described, gold hoops with channeled diamonds. He pulled in a deep breath trying to push down the new, more powerful anxiety. He needed to think, so he forced himself to look away. He stared up at the light-filled drapes and brought his fists to his mouth, tapped his mouth with the back of his curled thumbs.

Rachel was the right age to be Christine's daughter. She lived and worked in the area. He stole a glance at her. How could anyone look so much like Christine and not be related? If this is Christine's daughter, her last name would be O'Garra and that was decisively Irish. People with red hair were always Irish, yes? That reddish-blonde hair of hers may not be her natural color, except there was no way for him to know for certain: the rest of her body was silky smooth and completely without hair. Jared took just a moment to reflect on how women could do this to themselves, shaving and waxing for their partner. No time for that thinking, not now.

Her name was Sensen. Sensen? Not O'Garra, and not her father's name of Zachman. Jared knew that name, Sensen. It was connected to Christine somehow. Suddenly, it came to him; Sensen—the vile "candy" Christine enjoyed. Nasty little black squares that tasted like salty sweet tar. Who has the last name Sensen? He'd never heard of anyone with that name. He hadn't taken time to look at the name on the driver's license. Was it Rachel Sensen? He simply couldn't be certain, he hadn't looked. He had only focused on discovering her age. For all he knew the name on the license could easily have been O'Garra or Zachman. He used a false name at work, why couldn't this girl? He certainly understood why this gorgeous young woman would want to conceal her true name from customers as well as from men she enjoyed as one-night-stands.

And the purse, it was the same as Christine's, only smaller. The purse, the name of the candy, the earrings, Rachel's age, and definitely her looks. Jared pulled all the pieces together and the only possible conclusion put him near panic. This girl was Christine's daughter. How could he have been so stupid? What if Rachel wanted to date? He had unprotected sex with her. For God's sake, what if she were pregnant? Before this moment, that thought was delightful. Now the possibility was abhorrent.

Even though she had initiated getting together, and was far from an innocent virgin, he had slept with Christine's daughter. How could he look Christine in the face after this? He envisioned himself saying, "Hey, Christine, I'd like to roll around in bed with your hot little daughter again tonight, if you don't mind." Stupid idiot. Perhaps Christine would never know. Never know? Idiot, of course she'd know. Rachel, and her dad, would attend the fundraiser gala to watch Christine dance. How much time did he have to straighten things out? When was that damn fundraiser? This weekend? In a couple weeks? Why could he never keep dates in his head?

Surprisingly, his fear revealed something he had known, but had never fully and conscientiously acknowledged. He didn't want to hurt or embarrass Christine O'Garra. He loved Christine O'Garra. He loved Christine O'Garra in a way he had never loved any woman, not even his wife. He wanted to spend his life with her, enjoying the silly things she said and did. He wanted to explore answers to her weighty, slightly crazy, questions. He wanted to have deeply meaningful conversations with her late into the night, every night. He wanted to be with Christine. Gran would say "get old and ugly" with her. That would suit him fine. In fact, it was the only thing he had ever been completely certain of in his life. Except Christine O'Garra was married. She was taken. She was married to a man she never talked about named Peter Zachman. He forced his thoughts to return to the awkwardness of his immediate situation.

Rachel had been part of this—the vixen had toyed with his natural desires. He hadn't even wanted to go to bed with her. Rachel didn't even know him, and yet she agreed to come here and spend the night. The risk she had taken made him sick to his stomach—he could be a sick pervert for all she knew. How could she behave like a whore when she had Christine as a mother? She had sold herself to him for a meal and a few drinks. Jared could only imagine the pain this child had brought to Christine over the years. He suddenly wanted to grab Rachel by that pretty golden hair, yank her out of that bed, and shake her. He left the room, nearly ran to get away from her.

As he paced in the small kitchen, he was shocked to see the oven clock blaring a bright red 10:45. Couldn't be. His phone, however, confirmed the time. Unbelievable, he had sat there starry-eyed for well over an hour just watching Rachel sleep, fantasizing that she was Christine. But she wasn't Christine, she was Christine's daughter, and he had had sex with her, twice.

He had to get her out of here before he did something he'd regret. He was glad she had followed him in her car to his apartment. At least he wouldn't have to drive her back to the mall.

Water was running. She was finally up and he needed to get her out of his apartment—now—immediately. He stumbled and cursed around the coffee table as he bumped his way through the living room and back into the bedroom. Several sharp taps on the bathroom door were needed to get her attention above the rushing water.

"Hey, Rachel?" Tap, tap, tap, tap. "Hey, girl, I know you probably want to take a quick shower and all, but I need you to leave so I can get to work. Okay, baby?"

"What?" an answer was shouted out. The shower continued. "I'll make it quick."

He forced himself to remain calm, and on the outside of the door. A steady firm approach was needed. He worked up resolve.

"No…Rachel, stop the shower. I need you to leave now. Right now. This minute," he said firmly, but calmly.

The shower ran for a few more seconds then abruptly stopped. The door opened just a crack and one of Rachel's blue eyes peered at him through the small sliver. Funny, now she was modest?

"Really, babe, I need you to get dressed and head out before I leave, and I need to leave right now. Not in a few minutes. Now." This time his voice had more force and he leveled a steely look at the big blue eye.

"Are you serious? You can't wait just a couple minutes?"

Jared turned and quickly scooped her clothing from his dresser, shoved the door open and pushed the crumpled mess at her. When she failed to take the pile, the clothing plopped onto the tiled floor in front of the very naked Rachel. Jared steadied his eyes on hers and with a firm, steady voice made it very clear that he was indeed very serious.

"Just get dressed and go. It was a mistake to have you here

at all and you need to leave right now. Now, get dressed and get…out." Jared turned and as he marched across the bedroom, he yanked his tie back into place, pulling it a bit tighter than necessary. A nail file from his dresser drawer nervously poked at his thumb, trying to help him steady the emotions through every slow second Rachel remained unseen, unheard. The words he had snapped at her now seemed too harsh.

Moments later, the bathroom door flew open and Rachel steamed past and around the corner. She located her shoes under the coffee table and wedged them roughly onto her bare feet, stuffed her socks into her pants pocket.

"You're a piece of work, all sweet and sugary last night, and this morning you're a freakin' bastard. If you needed me outta here so fast, why didn't you wake me up, huh?"

"Rachel, you should know better than to go to a stranger's apartment. You don't even know me. Let me help you with your coat," Jared said, almost tenderly now. She glared fiercely at him.

"What? Are you my mother? My dad? You know what? I don't care if you're the richest man on earth, you're weird, and you can just forget ever calling me again. Where's my phone number? Hand it over." Jared headed back to the bedroom, wondering what Rachel's strange "richest man on earth" comment was all about.

When he returned, Rachel was roughly shoving her arm through a sleeve of her coat. She shrugged off Jared's attempt to help her with the other, snatched the business card from his hand then tossed her purse, Christine-like, onto her shoulder. She stomped to the door, still yanking on the second protesting coat sleeve.

"Look, Rachel. I'm sorry if I came on a bit strong, but…"
He received a blistering glare. The slammed door reverberated
as Jared began paying the price for what had been, until the last
few minutes, a very enjoyable evening…and morning.

Friday, October 30
Tracy: Every Five Minutes

Tracy watched Nora struggle to understand the account
statements and smiled at the aged furrowed brow, the senseless flipping of pages. "Aunt Nora, it's okay, really. I know it's
confusing for someone who's not good with numbers. I studied accounting in school and I understand why you had trouble
keeping the financials straight."

"Oh, Tracy, you've been an angel, really." Nora finally
set the stack of papers down and glanced about the room. "I
just can't believe how well everything is working out. I'd been
thinking about selling for a long time, but never told your mom.
You coming here is the only reason I decided to keep the store
open at all."

"I guess it was just supposed to happen. You sell the store
to me, so you can enjoy your retirement years. We just need to
settle on a fair price, one I can afford, over time of course."

"Oh, Tracy, absolutely. You finish the inventory, and get
a second estimate from someone, then we'll settle the matter.
This store will be yours by the start of the new year." Her wa-

tery eyes blinked. "It's just that I've put my heart and soul into this place. Tough to let it go."

Tracy would miss her aunt; she had been helpful. Cleaning, talking endlessly to the batty people who wandered in—helping provide the overall appearance of a legitimate store. Yes, Tracy would miss her. Miss her like having a dependable car repossessed. Tracy sighed. Sacrifices had to be made.

"Aunt Nora, I'm counting on you to fill in for me and spend time here chatting with people about books and authors. I know you like doing that and I'll still need help until I find a dependable employee."

Her aunt smiled weakly. "Oh, Tracy, that would be wonderful. I'd love to come in from time to time." She patted at Tracy's arm then padded off to the front counter to get lost in her newest "favorite of all time" book.

Tracy turned her attention to more pressing matters. She had installed the voice recorder in the ceiling between the back of the bookstore and the dance instructors' lounge and was dying to know if it worked. She plugged her headphones into the speaker and listened intently to a captured conversation between Kyle and Hollie regarding which of the six "original" dance routines Hollie would teach the new wedding couple. Evidently, waltz number four was the pick because of the groom's limitations. Geez, who gave a rat's ass what dance they stumbled through, or whether they danced at all? No one would be watching. All the wedding guests would be lined up at the free bar getting an early start—a typical friends and family drunk fest.

Tracy was, however, very pleased with the quality of sound. The recorder had picked up every foot shuffle, every chair squeak, as well as the slippery slobbering of Hollie and Kyle making out after their tough decision about which dance routine to teach the betrothed.

Enough fun—on to real business. She typed in her special account password and entered several recent drug sales. Cash flow was easy, but her boys were causing trouble. She was certain one of her runners was skimming cocaine—cutting her high-quality goods with Levamisole. He was stealing profit and damaging her reputation, so she had spent much of last night schooling him up at his hole of an apartment. Tracy pulled at her fingers as she thought about her time with the manager. It wasn't likely he'd make those choices again. But there were other challenges—like Boyle, who was accusing her of running on "his" mall turf again. And marijuana wouldn't be profitable for much longer; no matter how sweet her quality, future legalization would hit her sales hard. Dealing was certainly interfering with other, more enjoyable activities, like Jared.

She reflected on the time spent watching him at the mall, replayed her talk with the little blonde and bubbled at the possibilities. Jared would pay a high price for his night of fun. Later this week, she would return to the perfume counter and let the blonde know the terrible news about Jared. No, no, it was Jaden for the little blonde—his blood results tested positive for HIV. Of course, it was Tracy's duty as a health care professional to track down possible victims; it was only right to tell the girl personally. That would put an end to that. She hoped he liked the blonde, a lot. Perhaps, he'd try to contact her over and over, be confused every time he got her voicemail. Maybe he would visit the perfume counter and there would be an ugly scene. The blonde might get fired. Tracy smiled at the possibilities. Yes, it was time Jared learned not to toy with little mall sluts. Any woman, other than Tracy, was now off his menu. She would teach him, he would learn. One way or another, he would learn.

The GPS tracking software was installed on the bookstore computer and she had not revisited it since installing the device, so she settled in for a look. Fortunately, the location system had captured the fact that Jared had been at the mall the entire time Tracy knew he had been there. He left soon after the mall closed, stayed in the area, then was back to the mall at 10:15 p.m. Afterward, the car traveled to what she assumed was his apartment because it had sat in one spot until yesterday morning when the system showed his car was on the move at 11:10 a.m., arrived at the dance studio, then sat all afternoon. The steady beeping indicated that his car was now only a few feet from where she sat. Today was Friday and Jared was at work. Good system. Good boy.

Unfortunately, there was no way to know if Jared had dropped the little bitch off at the mall Wednesday night and if she went home alone from there, or if she had followed him to his apartment in her own car. Maybe Jared hadn't spent the night with the little minx. A weakness in the system. The blonde's face would reveal the truth soon enough.

Nora had left an hour ago, and Tracy decided to close the store early to pick up her costume for the Halloween dance party. She had a special gift to give to Jared tonight—a standing "open-door" invitation. She checked to be certain the newly-made key worked smoothly in the bookstore's back door, then placed it in the outside pocket of her glossy black purse. She could easily find it there, when the time was right. Maybe she could get it onto his key ring unnoticed; that would be a fun twist. She had written a lovely invitation to explain the key, one she was certain Jared wouldn't be able to resist.

Friday, October 30
Jared: Halloween After Dance

Dressed as a nurse in a plunging neckline and stiletto heels, Tracy arrived in time for the very last dance of the night. At least she had sense enough to remove the ridiculous shoes. Even in bare feet, she towered over all the party-goers. By midnight nearly everyone had left. Nearly. Tracy was lingering, loitering. Jared finally gathered the needed courage to set things straight.

"Hey, Tracy," Kyle said loudly as he slid up to her, openly staring at her ample chest. "I hear you let people do late night shopping at the bookstore. You up for some fun later?" Jared was a bit surprised that Kyle was so open with his suggestion, except he was grinning at Jared, not Tracy.

"Oh, I've made some plans, Kyle, only not with you," Tracy said with a chuckle. She too was looking at Jared. Everyone was acting strangely this evening.

"Tracy, can I talk with you a minute?" Jared asked.

"Certainly." Tracy winked at Kyle as Jared pulled her toward some privacy.

"Look, I know you'd like to get together with me—your little theft on Wednesday, you coming on to me, the time in your office. And I'm flattered, really." Even though Tracy's smile pulled at him, he knew he had to continue. Set things straight between them, make things clear and final.

"But, I'm not into you that way. You see? I'm not interested in dating you or anything else." Jared hoped she didn't start crying like the student who had fallen hard for him a year ago. Tracy lowered her chin and gave him only a blank cold stare, so he continued, "I don't mind that you want something of mine. But why did you take a glove outta my car? I really liked those gloves and they were a gift from Gran."

Tracy's eyes narrowed. Her dark red lips pursed tightly as she frowned sourly at him. "What are you talking about? I didn't take your gloves."

"No, you took a glove. One glove. From my car on Wednesday after your lesson." Jared's accusation was direct and unwavering. The number of lies from her were adding up, some of them fairly outrageous, so it was no surprise that she was lying now. Just this morning, Kyle had shown him Tracy's social media page. Although the photos she had posted of him dancing with her were fine, the bold comments there were totally out of line. Strangely, Kyle had found Tracy's audacious claims of successful conquest amusing.

Tracy stood glaring down at him. He couldn't fight that look. "Forget the glove. I don't want it back. But you gotta take those lies off your Facebook page. Instructors aren't allowed to date students, and I could get in a lot of trouble if Mavis saw the comments you posted." Although it was difficult, Jared looked directly back at those icy eyes until he saw a slight softening.

"Oh, Jared, Kyle told me he liked them, thought it was funny." Tracy brought her hand to her face before extending it toward him. "If you're serious, I'll take all the photos down. I promise. I just wanted to impress my friends—make them all jealous. You understand."

"I dance with lots of women. I'm not romantically involved with any of them. And I'm not romantically involved with you."

Tracy's face was flush and her eyes flashed at him. She was irritated, no, she was angry. It radiated from her, pulsed out at him. Perhaps he should apologize.

"Really?" She pressed her fingernail to her mouth briefly. "Well, lucky you 'cause tonight you get a chance to change that. I delivered a personal invitation for you to join me for some fun later. It doesn't seem like you've got much going for yourself." Tracy snapped away from him. Jared watched her jerk her bright pink coat on with Kyle's help and then head for the back door. Kyle glared at Jared before he turned and marched to the lounge. Apparently, Kyle had been playing cupid. Incredible.

Jared sighed and headed to the lone coat on the rack. He patted at something in his pocket, couldn't remember what he had left there. A second one of his drawings? Tracy's distinct musky perfume wafted from the emerging envelope emblazoned with his name in thick bold lettering. So this was her "invitation for fun." He quickly checked the rest of his pockets to be certain he still had his cell phone and key lanyard. His handkerchief was there and the carefully folded paper he had placed in his breast pocket was still there, too.

The unopened envelope and its contents were torn to pieces in the bathroom. The flush swirled the floating bits before they were sucked down with a gulping gurgle. All, save one.

One floated back at him and lay helpless just under the surface of the water where the ink bled pinkish grey.

Darkness fought against the buzzing glare of the pole lights as he crossed the parking lot. Tracy was watching him from her well-lit car—just sitting there. She waved gaily at him, childlike, as he jumped in his car and locked the doors. She wasn't going to follow him home. He wouldn't allow it. He scribbled in his notebook, fiddled with his phone, watched leaves being ripped from a tree and flung past her car by the harsh wind. She didn't budge. Jared briefly considered confronting her. About what? Sitting in her car? He finally went back inside, quickly locking the studio door behind him.

He could hear muffled Kyle and Hollie noises coming from the lounge. Awkward. Jared coughed loudly, and purposefully created even more racket than normal as he walked across the dance floor. A desk lamp blinked on in the lounge followed by low voices and soft giggles. Jared, in turn, flipped on the overhead studio lights and looked at his place of work. An empty room. How many hours had he spent dancing here? How many women had been in his arms on this floor, and what did he have to show for it? A little money. A little fun. A lot of nothing.

He had given Hollie and Kyle sufficient time, so he wandered nonchalantly into the lounge. These two birds. On again. Off again. Merely comforting one another in an attempt to cloud their own loneliness. He understood.

"Hey, you two," Jared said in their direction. Their silly attempt to appear to be working on a routine at Hollie's computer was comical. Jared wasn't laughing. Several drawers of his desk were opened and closed again quickly. He wasn't looking for anything—just needed to waste some time, hoping Tracy would give up and drive away. He opened a drawer. Rummaged about. Closed it. Opened another. And there it was—the last thing he expected to find. His glove. He had just accused Tracy of stealing what he was holding in his hand. He hadn't asked her, he had told her that he knew she was a thief. Jared sat and sighed deeply at the limp glove. The soft leather was buttery and smelled woodsy, like prestige and freedom. But it was very alone—no partner, no future purpose. He slowly put the glove on and watched his fingers bend closed. They opened and closed again into a fist. Hollie and Kyle sat looking at him through the corners of their eyes, likely wishing he'd just go away.

"Any big plans tonight, Jared?" Hollie asked.

Jared studied his glove lovingly, thinking of the day he had unwrapped his birthday gift—this glove and the one now in the trash somewhere at the mall. He sighed heavily again as he guided the soft glove across his cheek.

"Oh, I don't know, Hollie. It's nearly one o'clock in the fricken morning. I'm sure I'll find something to do before bedtime." He glared at them both as he tugged off the glove, stood and tossed it into the trash.

He could hear their stifled laughter behind him as he turned off the studio lights. He should go out and apologize to Tracy about the glove. He paused at the back door to gather his words before stepping into the night. Tracy's car was there, but there was no sign of the vindicated thief whose invitation had been flushed, unopened, unread. He hurried to his car. An apology could be offered, later, another day.

Thursday, November 5
Jared: Last Lesson

Christine's final lesson. This woman was intelligent, playful, sensitive and centered. She lived what she believed. How could he not love her?

He was timing his breathing as they danced, synchronizing it so that he pulled her spent breath in, and he returned his out to her. He pulled in the peace, and energy he tasted in her breath. He wanted a part of her, any small piece, and he wanted to become part of her in return. They'd danced together for three months and she didn't know him. He hadn't told her anything meaningful about himself. But why would he? He never let any of his students know the real him. None of them even knew his real name. Christine didn't know his name. The realization stabbed at him as he held her.

"You need to allow me to push and pull you on a pivot through the eight swivels, Christine. They need to be very quick."

The nearby chairs tempted him, begging him to pull her to them and finally talk—honestly talk. He needed her to hear him, to understand. He desperately wanted her to listen to him, trust him, affirm him. He needed one of Gran's hugs, but there would be no supper with her tonight, a church group had taken priority. Sunday was far too far away. Far too far.

"Let's start at the beginning one more time. The routine needs to flow without hesitation from start to finish. And smile, Christine. Show the audience you enjoy dancing."

He moved toward the machine and Christine stepped toward her nasty little licorice candies. He was all too certain of its name, Sensen. Rachel's name. He briefly considered talking openly about his time with Rachel, come clean and take Christine's justifiable heat right now, not wait until Saturday in front of a crowd. That would be smart, that would be brave. He waited silently. Her left thumb stroked the back of her rings as she shook a few black bits of Sen-Sen into her open palm. She popped them into her mouth and turned back to him. She stroked her rings until he took up that nervous left hand and kissed it gently, tasted the diamonds. She eyed him wearily.

"Allow me to come to you after you make that turn. Let's start again in frame at that spot."

Even though her breath now smelled of salt and licorice, he held her and inhaled her still. His time with her was limited, and the strange smell of her candy mixed with her perfume, like a lemon winter, was unique and pleasant. She smelled like laughter and peace. He would never experience forty-five minutes alone with her ever again.

"Nice job. You practiced that arm extension, yes?" He pulled her toward him. As rehearsed, she slipped under his arm and turned.

He didn't try to make her look any younger today. A younger Christine would be Rachel. In the unlikely event that Rachel had talked to her mother about her date with a black man, she'd certainly refer to him as Jaden, so at least there was a delay in the inevitable conflict, at least until Saturday night. The fact that he even lied about his name would make it all the more awkward, painful, laughable. The humiliating conversation would likely occur in front of all of his coworkers and in the presence of Rachel's dad, a lucky man who had married and had a child with Christine O'Garra.

"Christine, I honestly believe you will take first prize on Saturday."

His habit popped a mint, then Jared inhaled deeply and tried to smile at her like it was August again.

Saturday, November 7
Christine's Gala

Christine sat staring in the mirror at the mass of curls perched on the top of her head. The stylist continued to poke at them, insisting the molded extravagance would stay put well into the evening. Never having had her hair fussed over to this extent, she hadn't allowed enough time for the appointment. Nothing could be done about it now. She couldn't take a deep breath with all the hairspray in the air. She tried to relax, just enjoy this strange experience. She would apologize to Jared, to everyone, if she were late.

Christine, however, arrived at the banquet hall for the 3:00 p.m. dress rehearsal promptly at 2:45 p.m., just as Jared had instructed. Jared was not there. No instructors or fellow students were. Alone, she felt as if she were trespassing into the sophisticated elegance. Crisp white cloths draped the large round tables and the back of each cloth-covered chair was adorned with a dense white bow. Snowy tapered candles stood waiting at the center of expertly arranged mounds of rose centerpieces. Christine caught her breath at the sight of the roses—white roses. Even now, she could see Seth laying white roses on their daughter as she slept. He would sit by her bedside to wait. And wait. When April finally stirred, her thin blue fingers would tremble around a rose blossom, weakly pull at the soft white petals. Seth would sometimes sit and talk softly to April for an hour, or more, stroking her face with roses until he would see that rare precious smile. The memory moved Christine to reach out and finger the petals as April had done. Before the tears could come, she softly kissed away the thoughts and studied the rest of the room.

The white monochromatic table settings were striking against the rich red carpet and the heavy drapes that hung opulently from floor to ceiling at the windows. Although the room was empty, she could hear staff in the back rooms loudly discussing preparations for the evening through metallic clattering of pots and pans. She walked across the temporary dance floor, pulled out a chair at the clearly labeled "Table 6" and offered it to her angel.

"This is where I'll look for you this evening, Liberty," she thought aloud. She claimed the next chair, dropped her cloth purse to the floor where it sat limp and shabby among the opulence. The well-loved purse would get the night off, traded out for the dressy one waiting on the kitchen table.

Christine dug her dance shoes out from a reused plastic shopping bag, put them on, and then sat delaying. Funny, she had no trouble wearing a ring made of April's ashes, but this... this was different. She sat and looked at the crumpled bag at her feet for a while longer before leaning over and pulling out a small jewelry box. The overhead lights caught every facet of the tiny diamonds. It had been nearly two years since April had worn these earrings. Tenderly, she unsnapped the latch of one and slowly pushed the stem into her right earlobe. The slightly curved stem poked a gentle pain much less significant than the pain her heart was experiencing. After the second found its place in her left ear, she tilted her head from side to side. They felt strangely foreign tickling against her neck just at the bottom of her earlobes.

It was now 3:00 p.m. and the other dance couples had arrived. Still no Jared. Had she taught him nothing? Not even the importance of time? Boredom and agitation finally motivated her to once again examine the hem she had sewn in the full-priced red dress. Although it wasn't as good as the manufacturer's hem, it was barely visible and she knew she was being overly critical of her work. She always was. She dropped the hem and smoothed her dress before looking up to see Jared grinning at her. *Finally.* What was the sense in asking her to be early if he was going to arrive late? She offered him the customary hug.

He walked around her with his head at that familiar angle. "Christine, you are gorgeous. The dress fits perfectly and the short length is good. An asymmetrical hem would have been better, though." He stepped back to examine her closely.

Christine felt the inspection went on silently a little too long so she said, "So, you approve of the dress, but how did I do with my makeup?"

"You look ravishing, Christine."

"I haven't put any makeup on yet. I had to skip that to get here on time."

Christine found Jared's reaction to this fact delightful. He stopped, stepped closer and said, "Well, you are ravishing all the same."

He never stops. What a schmoozer. Okay, once this evening is over, I'll be rid of this crazy world of gushing compliments and lavish lying.

Suddenly, Jared took hold of her arm and pulled her toward him. He brought his face very near and for a moment it seemed he would kiss her. Instead he reached out and pulled gently on an earring. She felt his hot breath exhale on her cheek as he studied it with a slight scowl.

"I like the earrings. These are your daughter's, yes?" His expression didn't fit his comment. But he said he liked them. Christine chose her words carefully. This night was reserved for fun. *Do something physical.* She flicked both earrings at him with the back of her index fingers. The simple act enabled her to control her emotions and keep her voice steady and strong.

"I'm glad you approve. And yes, the last person who wore these dangly trinkets was my daughter. What do you think about the rest of this jewelry? Did I put on enough sparkle to suit you?"

She had adorned herself with every piece of gold jewelry she owned, including two small necklaces she had never worn. Many women would have felt comfortable and quite normal wearing several bracelets on each arm, rings on both hands, and of course, necklaces. To Christine, the jewelry clattered about in protest.

"Well, the bracelets are good, but I had suggested a pendant. Those little things are nice, but they're just chains. A bold pendant would have made a bigger statement."

She was relieved he hadn't touched the delicate necklaces at her imperfect neck, but annoyed that he remembered his suggestion to wear a noticeable pendant. The only pendant she had ever owned had been hammered flat on a cutting board. It now rested in peace at the bottom of a landfill somewhere.

"I'm fairly certain I don't want to hear anything a bold pendant necklace would want to state anyway, Jared."

After a quick run-through of the dance routine, Christine and Jared selected chairs at Table 12 and set their place cards to indicate the seats there were reserved.

"Hey partner, I hate to dance and run but I really have to get home and finish getting ready. And I have to get a second coat of varnish on my table, too," Christine said.

"Where's the other one?" Jared asked smiling warmly.

"The other one what?"

"That's obviously one truth and one lie. I want another truth from you."

She smacked his arm, he laughed. Easy for him. Refinished furniture was a lot of work. Fortunately, she could take off these horrid shoes and slip her coveralls over the dress to do the job. She had gotten a first coat on the tabletop yesterday, but today had been eaten up by the hair appointment and waiting on Jared.

Christine reentered the building at 5:55 p.m., complete with makeup and, except for her firearm, fully dressed. The snazzy purse was too small, her dress too tight. The adjoining rooms were filling quickly, and the low rumble was occasionally spiked with loud distinctive greetings and laughter. She moved among the happy crowd, greeting people and thanking each one for attending. Near Table 9, she spotted a familiar face—Donavin Bayer. So, he was finally back in town.

Donavin was actively engaged in conversation with a

woman as Christine approached him from the back. The woman stared up at her over his shoulder with slight annoyance.

"Donavin, you old Scotty dog. I didn't expect to see you here." Christine nudged his shoulder playfully.

Donavin turned, and after a moment of startled unawareness, he jumped from his seat to greet her. "Christy." Donavin snatched her up in a quick embrace and held her back for inspection. "Christine O'Garra, I didn't recognize you. I don't think I've ever seen you in anything but slacks." Christine caught the twinkle in his eyes—eyes that took a quick glance at her left hand. Donavin took up her hand and lifted it to his face. His hand was warm—calming somehow.

"I see you're wearing the rings. They're beautiful."

"I absolutely love them, Donavin. It's a little strange though, and I don't tell people what they really are." Christine could feel his eyes studying her.

"You clean up real nice. But what have you done with your hair? That is your hair isn't it? Can I touch it?" Christine turned her curls toward him so he could get an impish poke at the unnatural mound of stiffness adorning her head. Donavin patted them playfully.

"And look at you." Christine brushed at a bit of white fuzz on his lapel. "I can't honestly say you clean up as well as most men. I recognize this tired old suit from events at Purdue years ago."

"Only you would know. I've been hoping we'd get together, but I just got back Thursday. Did you get the postcard I sent you from Paris?" Before she could answer, Donavin leaned into her. "I had to change my cell phone number. I hope you haven't been trying to call me."

"When did you change your number?"

"Back in June, I think." He grinned at her. He knew full well she hadn't tried to call him. But he hadn't called her either. The dog received a playful nudge to the chest.

Grabbing her purse, she quickly extracted a pen and her small notebook. She recorded her office's direct number and her email address, tore the page from the book, and handed it and the notebook to Donavin. He recorded his phone numbers at the top of the page complete with a little message.

"That Europe project has eaten me alive for months, but it's finally winding down. I plan to start spending more time for myself, doing things I enjoy with people I want to be with. You're at the top of my list, Christy, so I'll call you soon," he said with a smile.

"I'd like that," she replied, as the Director of the Community Services Agency cleared his throat at the podium, shuffled his notes. Christine provided a quick hug to Donavin and continued, "Maybe we could meet at the shooting range. I'm a better shot now so you don't need to worry as much as you used to when I'm holding a gun." A short hug sealed their agreement to be in touch.

Christine provided a few more hurried greetings as she made her way to Table 12. Jared had graciously positioned both of their chairs to face the podium. A thoughtful gesture. She had seen Jared at their table when she arrived, but he wasn't there now. She stood over the table and smiled down at Kyle briefly before taking her seat.

Her feet already hurt. She'd have to endure the torture of the shoes for hours. She once again extracted the notebook and pen then laid the purse on the linen covered table behind her. A moment later, the Community Services Director finally woke up the microphone. As the crowd slowly quieted into listening mode, Jared appeared and quietly slipped into his seat. Christine delivered some eyebrow his direction as a mother would a naughty child. She then smiled to reassure him, patted his leg. What could he possibly have been doing to be late this time? Her nose decided smoking.

Her pen was poised to capture information, and to help her actively listen. The speech entailed the many services of the valued non-profit. As Christine dutifully recorded the elderly housing information, Jared grabbed her notebook and jotted silliness in the margin.

She made quick eye contact with Donavin and gave her short dress a gentle tug. Donavin snickered into his napkin before turning away to take a sip of water. Finally, the closing was delivered, followed by polite applause and the horrid little Master of Ceremonies took his place at the podium again. The man's jokes were tasteless. Crude.

When she glanced over at Liberty's chair, she was shocked to see that her angel, though not summoned, was there in full view. A woman was sitting in the same chair, her likeness a hologram within Liberty. The poor woman squirmed and adjusted her green scarf before brushing restlessly at her lap.

Liberty was glaring at a woman sitting in the chair Christine had used to change into her shoes a few hours earlier. The tall young woman looked familiar. It was the salesgirl from the bookstore beside the dance studio. Christine had visited the store once after a lesson and had seen her in the dance studio as well. Christine watched as the stately beauty stood and navigated her way toward the lobby.

Liberty then rose slowly, majestically, watching the beautiful salesgirl walk away. He leaned over the table with his usual fluid elegance, and unhurriedly spit into her water glass. Christine sat stunned. She had never envisioned Liberty doing something immature, wrong. She certainly never expected to see him behaving like an ill-disciplined teen. April had done the same thing to Jesse once, and Christine remembered being more disappointed that her action lacked originality than in the fact that April had spit in someone's glass. Liberty never looked in Christine's direction—he merely looked pleased and leisurely faded away. His feathers disappeared long after his body paled to nothing. The scarfed woman squirmed in her chair and blinked about the room.

"Are you okay? Can I get you something stronger than that lemon water?" Jared asked.

Christine's surprise must have been obvious, and Jared was perceptive enough to notice. It was kind of him to pay attention to her, considering the room contained several attractive young women at their finest. Women like that tall salesgirl.

"Thank you, no. No, I just now noticed something I'd never known about someone and I'm just surprised and a little disappointed, I guess." Christine turned to Jared and patted his hand with reassurance.

"Did you notice the tall young woman who works at the bookstore beside the studio is here?" she asked.

Jared jerked his head out toward the crowd. "No, is she?"

"Do you know her?"

"I don't really know her. I smoke with her sometimes is all." Jared's eyes continued darting about the room.

"Oh, so you're a smoker, Jared?"

"Well," he stammered out, "not any more. I quit."

Christine pursed her lips and lowered her chin sideways at him. "Jared, you can't hide the fact that you smoke with breath mints." Jared gave her an apologetic look, and then reached for his wine glass. Christine felt compelled to speak with the woman in the green scarf. She might know Tracy and reveal something that would help explain why Liberty would do something this strange to a bookstore clerk.

"Excuse me for a moment. I need to ask a quick question across the room. If the waiter comes by, please let him know I ordered the steak." Jared looked distressed.

"I'll be right back," she assured, then made her way across the room for introductions and a sociable chat. The nervous woman in the green scarf was friendly enough until Christine asked about Tracy. At that, she crisply claimed that she knew nothing whatsoever about the bookstore clerk. Christine thanked her, stood, and leaned over the table slightly, and yes, there was a bit of white fuzz floating in the water. Christine recognized it immediately as Liberty's feather fuzz, those downy bits of linty softness that clung to chairs and the carpet. The vacuum cleaner even had a tough time pulling them up. Sometimes, she had to bend over and pick them up a bit at a time. Christine turned and smiled at the thought.

Jared was staring at her from across the dance floor, his head tilted, tapping the back of his naked wrist in the universal symbol for "hurry up." *Right, Jared, you're telling me to hurry?* Christine smiled all the more as she moseyed over to Table 5 to chat with the Regional Planning Commissioner, who was being served his meal, and only then did she make her way back to the obviously impatient Jared. Thankfully, the rest of the table had only just been served so she hadn't kept anyone waiting. That would be rude.

She and Kyle picked up their conversation on the pros and cons of socialism, where they had left off after her last dance session. He was an interesting young man. Jared, however, was another matter. Interesting? Yes. A conversationalist? No. The gift she had made for him was tucked in her tiny purse, waiting for the right moment to present itself. It wouldn't be proper to give him a gift with other instructors watching and listening.

The young waiter removed her plate from the right and she quietly motioned to him to lean down to her. "You are doing a fantastic job. You're even serving and removing correctly," she whispered softly in his ear. The young waiter was a bit pink when he turned toward her, and she couldn't resist touching his cheek. Jared looked at her oddly.

Both Kyle and the other instructor left the table as the dessert of mint chocolate mousse was served, and Christine saw her chance. In her attempt to quickly locate her gift for Jared she discovered a white rose had found a home in her purse. Although the rose was a sweet gesture, Jared had created a noticeable hole in the once lovely mound of roses.

"Just a little something to help you remember tonight. Do you like it?" Jared asked.

"You really shouldn't be tearing apart the flower arrangements. The evening isn't even half over, and these could be taken home and enjoyed for at least a week." She smiled after the mild rebuke and set the rose aside.

"Jared, give me your car keys."

As predicted, he did not hesitate, nor did he question her. He simply reached into his suit coat and removed a lanyard of keys, handed them to Christine with only a slightly puzzled look. Once again, Christine marveled at his trusting nature, humbly doing as instructed, no matter how absurd the request. She pried open the key ring and slipped the small silver loop onto it quickly. She was pleased with the result as the Winged Liberty dime joined the keys with a soft musical tinkle. The candle flickered as she studied the effect with pleasure. She rubbed the dime softly between her fingers before handing the lanyard back to Jared.

"That is known as a Mercury dime, but it's really a Winged Liberty dime. The artist intended it to represent Lady Liberty wearing a cap with wings. Those wings represent freedom. Freedom of thought. Freedom to pursue your passion, your hopes and dreams."

"It's beautiful, thank you."

"I wanted to give you something that would remind you to live every day completely, with purpose. Life's too short not to." Christine's hand rested at the mark on her neck before she played with the foreign necklace nearby.

Jared held the dime by its edges and simply stared silently at it, turning it back and forth between his thumb and forefinger.

"You taught me to dance," Christine said, and paused to study this young man who knew so little. "You still don't understand how much I needed to learn. I needed to learn how to buy myself things, how to wear my hair in curls in a short red dress. I needed to learn how to enjoy myself. That it's okay to spend time and money on myself." Christine realized that she finally believed the things she was saying and had to press back tears. Jared looked at her strangely as he fingered a key on his lanyard.

Christine continued, "I plan to show the video they're making of us dancing to my family, who will be more than a little surprised, I assure you. Many will be happy for me, some will not. I've learned that your work brings people joy. It brought me joy, and I want to thank you for that. People fail to tell one another how much they appreciate the work of others, and I didn't want to do that to you. You are very special to me."

Jared took her by the hand and kissed it. "Thank you. That means a lot to me, especially coming from you." He was still holding one of his keys, and although he looked at her expectantly, there wasn't more to say. Christine hoped the dime wasn't too big or heavy. Men don't like bulky key chains. He put the lanyard back in his pocket slowly and leaned over his empty dessert cup.

"Christine, I thought your family would be here tonight. Your husband? You mentioned a daughter." He looked about the room as if expecting someone to suddenly materialize.

It surprised her that he didn't know she was a widow. Had she never told him? No, she had mentioned it casually to Donna, maybe to Kyle, but not to Jared. No, she had never forced herself to tell him, not after all the "your husband" references he had made during lessons. She was certain her lost children had not been discussed with any of them. What could it hurt now? She wouldn't be seeing him again. Even so, she didn't want to see the typical look of pity, especially not from Jared. This wasn't a night for sadness. He had asked, though, and he deserved an honest answer. Perhaps a reminder that people die would help Jared live more fully. She would tell him about Seth. And about April.

"I'm not married," she said.

Christine caught a twinkle in his eyes as he leaned out from the table to allow the young waiter to clear his place. He smiled broadly at her. "Well, marriage doesn't always work out. I'm divorced as well."

Christine was surprised. She had never heard him share anything personal.

"Everybody knows Christine's a widow," Kyle said.

So much for holding back information, thought Christine.

Jared flashed a glance at Kyle, who never looked up from his dessert.

"But you have a daughter. Those are her earrings. Why isn't she here tonight?" Jared asked. "I was looking forward to meeting her."

"My daughter is in another place, a place of higher priority. So, no, there's no family here tonight. It's just you and me dancing."

"But what could be more important than watching her mother dance?" Jared asked.

Had she not just told him that April was dead? She hadn't told him that bluntly, but apparently she needed to. Everyone lives forever, so although April was clearly still her daughter, answering this question continued to be difficult. But, no more games with Jared.

"Jared, I had a daughter, but she died nearly two years ago. She was wearing these earrings when her life ended, and this is the first time I've had the courage to wear them. But I forced myself to so I could create new memories about them, enjoyable memories." Christine smiled at him through her tear-filled eyes. She refused to cry.

Jared sat very still. He didn't look at her for some time—

just stared at the white roses, tapping at the sharp point on a wayward salad fork. Christine regretted telling him. She had told herself she wouldn't share these details of her past life with people. They were going to dance in just a few minutes and she had dumped this news on him. It was a mistake. Jared turned to her, smiling? No, he wasn't smiling, not in the moment that followed. Perhaps it was a grimace. She felt suddenly uncomfortable and stood to leave. Jared rose and provided her a hug. He wasn't smiling any more.

"I'm very sorry. I didn't know. I wish you had told me earlier," Jared said.

"I'm glad I didn't. I'm a little sorry I shared all this with you now, in fact. It's not a good place or time to discuss loss." She glanced around, hoping for somewhere else to be needed. "Excuse me, Jared, I need to remind the State Representative how important he is to our organization." She turned away quickly, then back to add, "Come find me when we need to line up for the dance."

At Table 10, she extended her hand to the state legislator for a second time in less than an hour to express appreciation for his attendance. He likely thought she was extremely forgetful.

Saturday, November 7
The Gala as Heard
and Experienced by Jared

Finally, the day of the gala, and of course, two neckties were fighting. Both satisfactory, neither perfect. Jared finally pulled his favorite black vest from the closet and started the debate again. The plain red tie won out. The red and black remained in his hand. He laid the vest and both ties out on the bed and headed for the kitchen. He needed to smoke, come back to the battlefield later.

It was after noon already and he couldn't afford to be late. The gala was at a golf club somewhere in Boone County. He dug about at the kitchen table trying to find the address. Christine would be there early. He had told her he wanted to be the first couple to rehearse, hoping they could just sit around and talk until guests arrived. He needed to tell her about Rachel in private, but what to say exactly? "Oh, by the way, I had unprotected sex with your daughter a few days ago, but it's you I really care about," just didn't seem to be a good lead-in for a meaningful discussion. Other words, poor possibilities, stumbled in and out of his head.

He hadn't mentioned the gala to Gran, and was glad he hadn't. Although the event was in Lebanon and couldn't be more convenient for her, she didn't have a hundred dollars for a ticket and she wouldn't have allowed him to pay her way. Eugene had heard about the event, but had to work. Just as well. Jared didn't want the distraction of having family at a dance contest, especially with O'Garra/Zachman family in the mix. Jared's stomach seized in protest as he envisioned Christine and family glaring at him over their elegant meals.

What did it matter? None of it made sense anyway. Christine was married. Even if she weren't, they were too different to be a couple. They were, in fact, about as different as two people could be. They were opposites in social standing, race, income and education levels. She was old enough to be his mother, literally. None of that mattered; he couldn't imagine being without her. But that, unfortunately, was his future reality. Jared grimaced and studied the smoke from his cigarette, a rare second one, maybe it was a third. He busied himself with his final choices for the evening. The battle of the socks raged even longer than the one between the ties.

He eventually found the right building and headed toward the noisy laughter and buzzing talk coming from beyond the lobby. To Jared, Christine was the only person in the room. She was holding up the bottom of her dress, studying it carefully, obviously unaware how much thigh she was revealing. Even though a sight such as this would not normally spark a memory of something transparently pure, it did for Jared.

The memory was of a children's event at Eugene's church last Easter—one of little boys jamming their fists into their pants pockets, tugging at their neckties, and of little girls in frilly dresses that twirled even when standing still, dresses that begged to be lifted and examined. The resulting full front "panty parade" filled the pews with muffled snickers and squirming mothers. Finally, the Sunday school teacher gently patted the unruly dresses down with a whisper and a smile. Sweetness and purity—qualities he needed a reminder of now and then. Christine seemed to embody such innocence.

He would miss her. But he couldn't think of a way to

continue a relationship, especially after the awkward unfolding of his encounter with Rachel. Painful silence or a heated exchange, either way, it was sure to be a memorable and very painful evening. He pushed the dreaded premonition aside and walked toward Christine with a smile, determined to at least enjoy this moment.

He said what years of practice prompted him to say without heart, hesitation, or thought. After the words dropped from his mouth, he wished he could take them back and offer her different ones, words he had not already used hundreds of times with other women. At least this time he believed them.

"You look gorgeous."

He hugged her, inhaled her, and experienced that familiar citrus winter freshness. He took more than his normal moments to hold her, mere seconds, but more, before he released her for a final time. *Get a grip, idiot. This is a married woman with a twenty-two-year-old daughter.* He stood staring at her, wishing he could escort her to his car and just drive away, somewhere, anywhere. He pulled himself back, kissed her hand, felt her rings briefly on his mouth. He held her by both hands and tenderly caressed the little Gran-like bend on her ring finger. The Christine who stood facing Jared was a very beautiful woman. *Idiot. I'm a child to her. She's too old to be beautiful. Focus on her faults, her imperfections.* And thus he forced himself into expected character.

"Nice dress. Latin dance costumes reveal more cleavage, of course, but for you, yes, it suits you. It's the right color, too. So much better than that blue number you brought to the studio to show me." He walked around her to complete a full inspection. "An asymmetrical hem would have been better, but the length is perfect. You were afraid it would be too short. It's just right to show off those thighs of yours during the swivels in our routine."

"You have never seen my thighs so you wouldn't know if they're worthy of being shown off." Christine narrowed her eyes at him. "You've gushed all over this little dress. How did I do with my makeup?"

He laughed at her. "You look ravishing."

"I'm not wearing any makeup."

At first he didn't believe her. She had to be wearing makeup. He always noticed these things. When he focused on her, however, he saw a chin covered with pink splotches, poorly defined eyebrows, and small eyes framed by dark circles and thin blonde lashes. She indeed had nothing on her face: no foundation, no concealer, no mascara, no blush, no lipstick. She was completely naked from the neck up. What kind of woman walks into a room dressed in a fancy little red dress, hair stiffened into extravagant curls, gold jewelry dangling, and not wearing makeup? It didn't matter, she was beautiful. No matter what part Jared examined, this woman was beautiful. Face, dress, curls, jewelry. Her earrings. He grabbed her arm as she walked past and pulled her close. Rachel's earrings. He kept his face near her ear for a moment to get a good look, just to be certain. No amount of eye blurring could change the fact that these were Rachel's earrings. He stood back and held her hands in his, this time to steady himself.

"I like the earrings. These are your daughter's, yes?"

She paused, and reached her hands to the earrings, tugged them gently. Her fingers flicked them at him, making the tiny diamonds sparkle gaily. He heard Rachel's laughter through those happy little hoops.

"I'm glad you approve. And yes, these are my daughter's. I was glad she let me borrow them," he heard her say.

"I'm quite certain they look better on you than they do on your daughter," Jared murmured.

Christine had fortunately secured permission for them to be the first couple to rehearse. Jared was quite pleased with how well Christine moved through the steps and motions. She had indeed been an excellent student. He wished they could dance it again one more time so he could relax and concentrate on Christine instead of the dance moves. As soon as they were done, however, Christine announced that she had to run home and finish getting ready—and something about varnish. She snatched up that big cloth purse of hers, fluttered her fingers at him, and made for the door. Jared felt cheated. So much for spending some down-time with her. Time to talk—to confess and hopefully clear the air before her family arrived.

Jared relocated their assigned table, and considered again whether they had selected the best chairs. He had mentioned to Kyle that Christine's family would probably attend, so it would be best to leave two chairs to her right available. Kyle had only laughed, called him an idiot, and plopped his suit coat onto the chair seat beside hers. Jared wished he could just move Kyle to another chair, ideally to a different table. He was likely to say something suggestive, offensive. Regrettably, his coworker wasn't going to be his biggest challenge. Christine's husband and daughter held that honor.

While the other couples practiced, he sat and envisioned himself and Christine on the dance floor. The minutes on his phone blinked slowly forward toward 6:00 p.m. He wandered to the downstairs dressing room and changed into the outfit he had brought for the event: crisp black suit and vest, white dress shirt, shimmering red tie. He considered what he should transfer into his pockets, decided he would take only his lanyard of keys and a folded piece of artwork he had created, for luck. The rest would stay tucked away in a toiletry bag under his carefully hung day suit.

Back at Table 12, Jared carefully hung his suit coat on the back of his chair, waited, and watched happy people enter the building and find their tables. He plucked one of the white roses from the centerpiece to present to Christine when she arrived. He cradled it in the palm of his hand so she wouldn't notice it until he could give it to her. Growing ever more nervous, he gently tested the skin on his thumb against a thorn near the bud.

It had to be 6:00 p.m. by now and Christine was never late. Then finally, finally, she was at the doorway admiring the trophies to be awarded. Although he searched for her husband, and for Rachel, Christine appeared to be alone as she fluttered about talking to nearly everyone between the door and where he stood waiting.

Each lucky person received only a brief moment of her attention until Table 9. Her presence there incited an excited reaction from a man about Christine's age. The dignified thin man greeted her with the exuberance of someone who had just stumbled across a long lost treasure. They did more than chat, they hugged, and laughed, and hugged again. The man actually raised her left hand to his face and kissed her, studied her rings. Christine pulled a small notepad from her purse, quickly extracted her ever-ready pen. They exchanged papers, no doubt phone numbers. Jared stroked at his chin as he watched the man tuck the paper inside his suit pocket with a soft pat to his chest. The man's hand found hers again quickly. The man stared at Christine as if he wanted to eat her. Jared knew that look. Still holding her hand, the man moved past her, pulling her toward the door as if he would flee from the event and make off with her. Christine laughed, pulled him back, and shook the notepad in his direction before he finally released her.

The ever smiling Christine moved on to the next table, but Jared studied the thin man for some time before turning his thoughts back to more immediate concerns. Concerns like the impending arrival of Rachel Sensen and Peter Zachman. He should have been preparing for his work by going through dance steps in his head. Jared's mind, however, jumped from Rachel back to the man at Table 9—a very responsive man who was far too familiar to Christine and far too obvious regarding his intentions. It didn't matter, did it, really? She was a married woman—a married woman who was openly flirting with every man in the room. All her talk about God and life. Her husband was so late he was likely to miss the meal. Maybe he was out of town. Her hot, fast daughter was late too.

Jared cursed softly as he dug into his suit coat for the cigarettes he had left in the dressing room. Although the podium stood poised for action, it didn't appear anyone intended to start talking soon. He quickly made his way through the crowd, and out into the lobby, where he scurried down the steps to retrieve his cigarettes and lighter. Once back upstairs, he maneuvered through the dwindling crowd at the front door and made his way far down the sidewalk where he hoped he wouldn't be seen, or at least not recognized. A quick smoke, just to settle.

He had carelessly brought the rose, so he fished out a cigarette and slid the rose stem into the cigarette pack. The glow of his lit cigarette calmed him as much as the smoke that filled his lungs. Fortunately, it was unseasonably warm and no jacket was needed. He scanned the parking lot for any sign of Rachel's car or Rachel herself. No Rachel. Happy, well-dressed people hurried past him arm in arm, people who had someone. As he nervously scanned the lot again, a familiar voice approached from behind.

"Don't you look marvelous, Jared." It wasn't the expected Rachel-sounding voice, one that would have called him Jaden. Turning, he was surprised to see Tracy. It was disorienting.

"Tracy? Why are you here?" He reached to his chest to touch the folded picture he had drawn and hidden in his breast pocket of himself and Christine, except he wasn't wearing his suit coat. His lost fingers tapped at his black satin vest.

"I so love these types of events, and thought this was the perfect opportunity for me to come watch you and that beautiful partner of yours. What's her name again?" She bent over and yanked at the bottom of her tight dress before reaching toward him. "I could use a smoke myself."

"Christine. Her name's Christine O'Garra." Jared dutifully dug out another cigarette and handed it, and his lighter, to Tracy. Her steady gaze was unsettling.

Tracy shivered her shoulders. "It's a bit nippy out tonight. Winter's coming." The top of her dress overflowed as she needlessly hugged herself.

Why was Tracy here? Her words were now fuzzy and unheard. *She works in a small struggling bookstore and she lives in Indy. Maybe she's searching for investors for the store.*

He stopped his thoughts, realized he no longer cared to

understand her, to know her. She wasn't a friend. She was simply a student, an impulsive, slutty, short-tempered student. Even so, she was talking, he ought to listen.

"...you don't seem too surprised. Perhaps we'll get together sometime, away from work," he heard her say. She smiled down at him before she tossed the remains of her cigarette into the landscaping.

He couldn't believe she continued to suggest they get together. He wasn't interested in her. *Why couldn't she get that?*

"Hey, I better head inside. Gotta get back to work," Jared said before taking her by the arm and heading toward the door. He paused at the waste can to deposit his cold cigarette, and then escorted her into the lively building. He excused himself in the lobby, headed downstairs to return the cigarettes and lighter, and to escape Tracy.

Back upstairs, the speaker began just as Jared slipped onto his chair beside Christine. During the details regarding dollars and services, Jared watched her scribble furiously at the little notepad. If she turned the page he'd lose the opportunity to see what the thin man had written, probably his phone number, maybe a message. Jared couldn't quite see the top of the paper so he teasingly snatched the notebook from her lap. He raised his finger at Christine to keep her from taking it back. He reached over and gently drew his hand over the back of hers and down her fingertips to take the pen from her then jotted: "This guy is a bit stuffy. He needs to dance." As he wrote, he was able to read the thin man's note: "Our future will brighten by being together. So looking forward to it, Christy. With long-held affection, Donavin." Jared tried unsuccessfully to memorize the ten-digit phone number before handing the notepad back to Christine with a grin. She smacked him playfully. *Donavin. The man's name is Donavin. He wouldn't forget that name.* Mr. Donavin was being quite forward with a married woman. A woman whose husband hadn't bothered to come watch his beautiful wife dance.

They sat quietly. Jared watched Christine as she listened. Occasionally, she looked about at people at nearby tables. Jared brushed at a few fuzzy little bits of white fluff from his black vest. He finally had to pick them off with his fingers. They'd likely float back onto him if he just let them go, so he looked about for a moist place to anchor them. The only obvious option was the roses, so he carefully placed the fuzz onto a petal and rubbed it gently to assure the fuzz was attached.

He couldn't remember what he had done with the rose he had plucked for her, so he reached for another and pulled it gently from the arrangement, and then slowly slid it across the table and into Christine's slightly open purse that lay behind her. He rested his arm on the table behind her chair, snuggled it closer. He wanted to hold her, but he wanted to smell her purse even more. The smell of an open purse—a perfume he couldn't find at the mall, an erotic mixture of mint, fig-scented lipstick, silky face powder, ink. An aphrodisiac. He eyed the purse longingly. Jared glanced around and noticed Kyle's eyes smiling knowingly at him from behind Christine's back. Kyle delivered a barely perceptible shake of the head to Jared. Jared pulled his arm away and ordered it to stay in his lap, away from Christine's purse. Kyle snickered.

Christine continued to be a delightful distraction. A few closing remarks were delivered and the podium was finally surrendered to the MC. Jared twisted to locate his drink, and when he returned to his observation post, Christine was staring intently across the room. She looked upset, somewhat shaken.

"Are you okay? Can I get you something to drink?" he asked. She sat, eyes narrow and unwavering.

He looked in the direction of her intense scrutiny. He could only see people, regular, everyday people. She wasn't looking at the man named Donavin, no; Christine was looking in the direction of Table 6. Tracy was striding from that table, probably heading to the cash bar. Christine, however, stayed focused on a seated woman in an ugly green scarf—a very ordinary, very fidgety, woman.

Christine's gaze finally returned to him. "Did you notice that girl from the bookstore is here?" she asked.

"Who?"

"That beautiful, very tall girl who works at the bookstore beside the dance studio."

"I don't know her," Jared replied. He squirmed in his seat as he looked toward the lobby.

Christine was looking at him strangely. "If the waiter comes, please have him serve my meal. I ordered the steak."

She rose so suddenly that Jared had a difficult time properly standing. She walked directly to the woman in the scarf. He watched for the short time Christine talked with the unknown woman, thankful that she left the table smiling and that Tracy had not returned. He motioned for her to join him, but in her Christine-like fashion, she stopped to chat with some fortunate elderly man.

As he waited, he put on his suit coat to prepare to eat. Scanning the room once again for Rachel, he noticed that Tracy was now standing over the nervous scarfed woman. The look on Tracy's face seized his full attention, a steely, threatening look. Tracy glared down at the woman and spoke a few words. Tracy suddenly jerked her attention to a man nearby then turned and steamed out of the room. Jared wondered what it was about this green-scarfed woman that made other women so upset.

The annoying waiter, whose entire evening was focused on refilling Christine's water glass, began serving meals. Jared stood as Christine returned, helped her into her chair. He took a moment to search the room once again before taking his seat and placing his napkin on his knee. *Where the hell was Rachel? And where was Christine's sorry excuse for a husband?* Jared attacked the chicken on his plate as if it had personally offended him. There was something satisfying in having control over something, even if it was only the simple act of eating.

Kyle gulped his food down, wiped at his pink face, and left to settle the music lineup. Jared had been waiting for a moment like this to ask Christine about her very absent family members. But when he turned to her, she lifted her finger at him and reached for her purse. Jared watched her hand hesitate, and he knew her fingertips were exploring the unexpected rose. She extracted it slowly and gave Jared that look of hers. He was suddenly ten years old, watching his grandmother's stern disapproval as he squirmed in the pew during a long hot sermon. Evidently he had been wayward.

"I thought you'd like a memento of the event. Do you like it?"

Christine studied the flower arrangement. "You really shouldn't be tearing apart the decorations, Jared. The evening isn't even half over, and these should be taken home and enjoyed for at least a week."

"Well, I hope you enjoy that flower for at least a week, and that you'll remember me for at least that long. Do I have your permission to dance into your dreams now and then?"

"Dreams are where I work out problems, so I have no doubt you'll show up there now and then. But thank you for the rose. It's very sweet of you." She patted his hand as if it were a remorseful puppy.

"I have something for you, too." She reached back into the purse. Jared hoped it wasn't a very, very small, fully-loaded handgun.

"Give me your car keys," she said.

A strange request—he hadn't had that much to drink. Quickly, silently, he reached into his jacket pocket, removed the lanyard, and handed her the keys. She huddled over them for a few moments, working at something, then looked at him with smug satisfaction before handing them back. There was a small round dime attached to the ring, glimmering against his keys.

"That is known as a Mercury dime," she said, as he held it in his hand against the table to steady it. "The artist intended it to represent Lady Liberty wearing a cap with wings. Those wings represent freedom of thought."

"It's very nice, Christine, thank you," Jared replied quietly. Although the dime sparkled at him from between his thumb and finger, it was no longer the focus of his attention. There was a fifth key. He only had four keys. *Four, right?* Even though Christine was talking to him about the dime, his ears were waiting for an explanation about the key. *Why did she give me this key? What is it to?*

"Thank you for teaching me to dance. You are very special to me," he heard her say.

Jared took her hand and kissed it. "Thank you. That means a lot to me, especially coming from you." He studied the key, attentively waiting. Kyle returned, breaking into their secluded moment. She stopped talking, now delivering only a soft smile. Evidently, an explanation of the key required privacy, so he slipped the lanyard back into his pocket, patted at it, and winked at Christine. She would tell him later. Even though Kyle was eating his dessert, he was watching them, listening. Although not ideal, Jared decided it was time to ask about her family. Obviously, Peter and Rachel were not coming.

"I thought your family would be here tonight. Your daughter? Your husband?"

Christine held her spoon in mid-air briefly.

"I'm not married," she said quietly.

The pesky waiter was reaching for his empty dessert cup. "Well, marriage doesn't always work out. I'm divorced as well," he replied, not yet settled into the full significance of her words.

"Everybody knows Christine's a widow, dumbass," Kyle said tersely. He swore out loud in front of her—spit foul words over her chocolate mousse.

But Christine wasn't married. Once it sunk in, it took a lot for him to keep from jumping up and doing a "happy dance." Instead, he took up her hand, considered pressing it to his lips, kissing her funny bent finger, her rings. He had a hard time shaking these thoughts as he stared down at her hand.

"I'm sorry, I didn't know." He looked up at her thoughtfully. "Your daughter's earrings look lovely on you, Christine. I had hoped to meet her tonight. I imagine she is nearly as lovely as you. What's your daughter doing tonight? Does she live in the area?"

Christine slowly scraped at soft swirls of chocolate mousse with her spoon. She set it aside and looked at him.

"My daughter died two years ago. It's something I choose to tell very few people, so I guess that makes you very special. She had these earrings on when she died, and this is the first time I've ever worn them," Jared heard her say.

Rachel was not Christine's daughter. Rachel was not Christine's daughter. That's all he needed to hear. He understood that perfectly. Relief flowed through him. Christine abruptly stood and Jared jumped up and hugged her. She seemed put-off by his spontaneous reaction.

"I'm sorry. Sorry to hear about your daughter."

Christine looked at him through the corner of her eyes, her face turned toward the exit. She looked confused. She finally said, "Look, I need to go over and speak to the State Representative for a moment. It's my job to do a little hob-knobbing here tonight."

Jared's hand fell from her arm and she drifted away. The red dress flowed lightly across the floor, stopped at Table 10, where Christine extended her precious hand to a well-suited man and to the mousey little woman by his side. She then made her way quickly to another table and yet a third to graciously talk with the Master of Ceremonies. She radiated a friendliness that made people smile and laugh as they spoke with her. And although he enjoyed watching people respond to her, they were near her, and he was not. The buzzing crowd finally enveloped her completely. The rest of the gala, dance competition and all, swirled past far too quickly.

On his drive home, his mind traveled through his upside down day. Everything had hit him unexpectedly, except winning the contest with Christine. But he didn't care about winning at dance. He had lost the love of his life to a thin man. Yes, he had weaseled out of an embarrassing confrontation with her family, one he had stressed over for days, but the daughter and husband didn't even exist. And to top it off, his cell phone had been stolen. Kyle, and two instructors from the other studio, had lost their phones, too. And how had he missed seeing lipstick and snagged threads on the lapel of his suit during his inspection this morning? He reached up and brushed the lapel, pulled at a limp thread.

A crazy mix of ups and downs. The biggest up was that the unmarried Christine had put a key on his lanyard—an unexplained invitation. Yet, why would she consider spending any more of her valuable time with a lowly dance instructor? She wouldn't. Then why had she given him a key and a dime that symbolized freedom of thought. *That was it, right? Freedom of thought.* Just what kind of thoughts did Christine have in mind? A spark of hope.

Although it had been a long, emotional night and Jared was tired, he was forced off the interstate. He pulled up to the gas station on fumes, running on empty again. *Thank God, I can sleep in tomorrow,* he thought as he paid for ten dollars in gas and a couple packs of cigarettes. He examined all his keys carefully as he walked back to the pump: his car key, his apartment, Gran's apartment, the studio, and a fifth key. It would fit a door lock. To her house?

As the tank filled, Jared studied Christine's other gift. Winged Liberty's face twinkled from the dime proudly. It would gleam at him like this twice a day, no three or four times, every day. It would be a constant reminder.

The pump thumped to a stop and he tightened the gas cap with a turn of several clicks. He sat in his car and rubbed gently at the dime. He had seen how that man, Donavin, looked at her, trailed her with his eyes throughout the evening. Jared reluctantly admitted that they seemed right together, and it angered him. He had to call it what it was: jealousy. Regret, too.

For months, Christine had nearly begged him to talk, to share his beliefs and feelings by answering her crazy questions. But he had refused, afraid his answers would be childish, stupid. Now she was gone. The dime would remind him of Christine and his loss, yet he treasured the connection it symbolized. He would carry this glistening hurt, but not with his keys. He removed the dime from the lanyard. He'd leave the key—keep it with him ready to use, in case. He removed his small silver pocketknife, pried open the ring hanging from the knife and slid the dime's loop onto it carefully. Somehow, they seemed to belong together, the knife and Christine's symbol of freedom. He didn't have the energy to think why.

Instead, he chose to relive his gala dance with Christine. Over and over they danced, then he imagined she was beside him in the car—they were heading home. She smiled shyly and picked softly at her dress. He reached up and loosened his tie, the real one that still bound him at the neck. He always undressed himself, always, so now he imagined it was Christine's hands that slowly undressed him. They were no longer in a speeding car as she removed his tie and freed him of his workday restrictions. She slowly unbuttoned his stiff shirt, released the shirt tail from his pants. She removed his cufflinks and unbound his hands. His arms felt the soft fabric as the shirt dropped to the floor. She lifted off his white undershirt, and pressed her palms against him. "So I see you really do have a chest," she said.

They both smiled, and the heart that beat there replied, "Lay me down, Christine, lay me down and love me."

Fortunately, there wasn't much traffic on the highway as his distracted mind drove back to his empty apartment in Indianapolis.

Saturday, November 7
The Underground Gala

Tracy arrived fashionably late to the fancy little event in the northern suburbs, the home of wealth. Nora had been easily convinced that having the Bookworm Bookstore listed in the program as a donor would be a savvy business decision.

She sped through the parking lot, cursing loudly. All the choice spots had been taken by insolent Mercedes, Lexus, and BMWs. Fortunately, there was an open spot at the door where she shoved the car into park and secured a handicap hang tag to the mirror. Her skin-tight dress was harshly tugged and a black sequin purse snatched from the seat before she began her processional march up the curved walk toward the glowing building of light and music. She slowed. A man, a solidly built short man, was smoking on the sidewalk. Always time to bum a cigarette. She knew full well that the average man could see better than they could think, so as she walked, the dress was slithered a bit higher from the bottom and pulled a bit lower from the top. He had been looking at the building, but turned as she approached. It was Jared. As always, Tracy's stars were aligned. She firmly applied her best display smile for her Sweet Coffee Bean.

"Don't you look marvelous, Jared?!"

Jared jerked toward her and fought to steady his focus. His surprised look was delightful. He seemed puzzled, annoyed. *Well, good.*

"Tracy…what a surprise," was stammered out before he suddenly reached up and tapped his fingers on his chest.

Hmmm…a sign of intimacy. Tracy moved just a tiny bit closer, easing into his space until he took a small step back.

"Thought I'd come watch you do some real work. Dancing with that older blonde woman, right?"

He sputtered out the name of his student and handed over his smokes. He shook his foot to settle his pant leg in place.

"Haven't seen as much of you as I'd like to, Jared. Surprised you haven't come over to watch *me* do some real work by now. You know I'm there late nights, and the back door's always open for you. But you know that. Maybe we can have more fun away from work—go somewhere else." Tracy waited, only Jared wasn't biting. Not even a nibble. She had already given him an engraved invitation and a key to the bookstore at Halloween, dammit. *Ignored the key. Ignoring her face-to-face invitation.*

Puffing rapidly, his eyes played over the parking lot. He barely glanced at her. She set her jaw, tense and tight. No one ignores Tracy Martin. She forced a smile on her continuing challenge, except, quite suddenly, Jared was tiresome. He was, in fact, a pain in the ass. Certainly no longer fun.

Here on this sidewalk, Jared had blown his last chance to warm up and her plans for him abruptly shifted, then settled firmly in her mind. She would keep playing the friendship game, outwardly. He would still be hers—in a different way than originally planned, but hers all the same. He'd be more fun in the new plan and she was looking forward to schooling him up, but she'd need to research and prepare, contact the right people first.

Jared made some pathetic excuse for hurrying inside and grabbed at her arm. Once inside, she watched him flee down a set of stairs. The program listed Jared and his partner, Christine O'Garra, along with five other "celebrity" competitors. Christine's photo was of a ghastly pale woman, smiling brightly.

Tracy pulled in a deep breath through her dark red smile. She felt completely at home surrounded by these sparkling wealthy people. She smiled at them in confident acknowledgment that she was one of them, of their type and influence. Her natural charisma would eventually generate her well-deserved fortune. It would take time, strategic planning, and a lot of hard work, but in the end she would be wealthier, and far more powerful, than any of these haughty bastards.

During her procession through the festive crowd of narcissists, she noticed Jared's student, Christine, seated across the room. The empty chair beside the pasty white woman would certainly be occupied by Jared soon. Fortunately, Table 6 was in direct line of sight of the precious couple, yet Tracy could easily blend into the crowd to watch. She staked claim to a chair and sat on it with authority. She immediately felt uncomfortable—a strange restlessness. The insipid woman next to her, who nervously jerked like the bookstore cat, had snatched a better choice of seats. Fortunately, Catwoman had to pee—she even said so before she left to visit the litter box. Tracy chuckled silently as she watched the tailless fanny wiggle away.

The olive green scarf Catwoman had left on her chair begged to be moved, so Tracy rose quickly to oblige. Tracy tossed the scarf onto the seat of the rejected, offensive chair. The man across the table watched her wordlessly over the top of his eyeglasses. Tracy smiled sweetly at him as she moved her purse from chair number one to the much more comfortable chair number two. The man continued his steady observation, looking mildly uncomfortable.

Oh, thought Tracy, *switching chairs must be yet another breach of social protocol. Who knew? Who cares?*

By the time Catwoman returned, Tracy had established her rightful place at the table and was sipping her fluted glass of lemon water. The woman flashed Tracy an irritated look, likely wanting to hiss. Tracy could always count on the protective silence of social etiquette in these situations. Just in case, though, she delivered Catwoman a direct, defiant stare. Tracy could see the thoughts behind those cat-like eyes—*say something, or silently let the matter go.* The cost of confrontation always outweighed making a fuss about little things that ill-mannered people did, impolite people, like Tracy. The hideous scarf was lifted and stroked repeatedly before Catwoman finally settled quietly into her assigned seat. *Got your fur up, but you're a polite old pussy.*

The evening was off to a good start. Now, all she needed

was a drink. "Be an angel and hold my seat," she loudly demanded to the man beside her as she quickly stood and leaned slightly to reveal her cleavage to him. Her tablemates suddenly silenced themselves to cast their judging eyes on her. "Thanks ever so much," she loudly countered before making her way through the crowded room toward the cash bar in the lobby. She glanced back to see them shifting in their chairs, nearly laying on top of one another to talk about her.

She selected a slicked-backed geezer at the bar, sauntered over and rubbed against him as she unsnapped her sparkling purse. "Oh dear. I always forget my wallet when I change purses." Tracy sighed loudly.

"Well, allow me," boomed out her selected dope. After a leering look, he extracted a smooth leather fold-over from the breast pocket of his glossy suit coat. He fingered out a crisp twenty. "This ought to get you whatever you need. Give this pretty gal the change, Bruce."

"Very kind of you. Thank you so much." Tracy rewarded him with a slight brush to her bosom as he turned to leave. She accepted the wine and abundant change from Bruce, who winked at her before she turned away. Tracy, smiling back, refrained from sharing her thoughts and headed back into the noisy room. Her tablemates were obviously enjoying themselves, chattering like monkeys. The sudden silence as Tracy approached was striking. Catwoman picked at the fringe of her ugly scarf with intense interest.

"Meow," whispered Tracy over the top of her wine glass. She pulled her chair far from the table, turned it around to face the podium, then made herself very comfortable by extending her long shapely legs straight out, crossing them at the ankles.

Catwoman noticeably bristled at yet another social violation and Tracy congratulated herself on her excellent timing as the man at the podium cleared his throat into the microphone.

She painfully endured a drawn-out lecture on the importance of the event's featured group—a bunch of Boone County bleeding hearts. Apparently, the organization managed an annual budget of over seven million dollars. That perked Tracy up considerably, and she studied the non-profit staff table, weighing various possibilities. She caught herself in the act of planning how to get hired into their financial department, and had to force herself to concentrate on her purpose for being there: to watch Jared. Gather information. Maybe now look for future clients for her expanding business.

She looked past the podium across the dance floor at him. As far as she could see, neither he, nor the ever pale Christine, had brought a guest. Unbelievably, Christine was listening, even taking notes as the lecture droned along. Jared, however, was watching Christine watch the speaker. He would smile intermittently at his dance partner, glance at her notes now and then. Once, he even took her notepad and added his own message, apparently an inappropriate one from the way Christine smacked his knee with the notepad upon its return. Tracy snorted into her nearly empty wine glass and coughed as she watched his sneaky arm slide across the table behind her.

The podium windbag studied his notes again before launching into some drivel about little kids. Tracy could remember several events during her "formative years" and had no intention of listening to silly shit about the importance of "early connections with caring adults." She abruptly flopped her purse onto the table, stood, and made her way back to the bar. There was sure to be a man on a white horse somewhere in the lobby. There was, in fact, a group of men who had escaped the pleading torture from the podium. She decided to stay awhile, get to know some normal people.

Tracy was collecting information from a wealth-dripping widow when polite applause rose then slowed, signaling that it was finally safe to head back to the table and eat. She slithered herself past her new drinking buddies with an expensive wine in hand and surveyed the room briefly. Although she never allowed herself to lose control, the alcohol buzzed up the fortitude to start the painful process of mealtime conversation. Tracy looked across the room and was surprised to see Christine's butt parked in her conquest chair—sitting beside Catwoman, comfortable and chatty. After a moment, Christine stood, pushed the chair into place, leaned over the table briefly, turned and smiled. Then Christine found Jared with her eyes, delivered one of her sugary sweet smiles across the room to him before she clucked over to a nearby table. *Damn, that woman smiled all the time, talked endlessly.*

Tracy leisurely weaved through the swarm of snobs—all too uppity to speak to her. The evening yawned before her. What a crock. Why should she force herself to endure the snotty conversation, gag down the fussy meal, the dancing? Good God, the ludicrous dancing. Why should she sit and watch tottering old bags bounce about in the arms of their ever-delighted instructors? She should be with her crew. Most of her sales were made on Saturdays and she should be out there confirming her rightful place, making sure they secured payment, keep them from pinching out cocaine or weed for themselves. She had run into a long-time cocaine customer in the lobby, though.

Maybe new clients could be secured here, but it was too public, too many unknowns. At least the Master of Ceremonies was entertaining.

Tracy set her wine down and stood behind her chair. She reached for her water glass and lifted it to her lips as she considered whether or not to leave. It seemed strange that Catwoman was smiling up at her. Tracy stopped suddenly. There was foreign whiteness floating on the top of her water, clinging to a slice of lemon. Spit. That bitch, Christine, had spit in her glass. Christine had spit in her glass and her co-conspirator, the Catwoman, was knowingly smiling. Instantly, rage consumed Tracy, flowing out red pounding in her head. She felt her teeth grind and a twitch pop from her left eye. Even so, Tracy refused to give Catwoman the satisfaction of a reaction of any sort. She merely set the glass down unhurriedly, gently, and smiled back. She pictured herself grabbing the dripping scarf and wrapping it around and around Catwoman's throat. She saw herself pulling firmly on the olive-fringed ends until both the life of the woman and Tracy's rage floated up and out of the room together. Although Tracy had a lot of experience controlling rage, Christine's premeditated assault and this vile woman's obvious reaction of smug delight was more than Tracy could manage in a room full of snooty elites. The insipid woman was still smiling. Tracy breathed deeply in and out. She unclenched her fists then gathered her purse with a slow, controlled movement. Her neck was pulsating, her jaw ached. She turned to leave.

"They're serving the meal. I'd be happy to speak to the waiter on your behalf. Did you order the beef or the chicken?" asked the swirling man to Tracy's left.

He dared to ask her about beef or chicken? The words

"Go to h— " flew from her throat and out her mouth before she could choke them back, the words stabbed out crisp and harsh. Fortunately, she snapped her mouth closed before all of "hell" sprung out. Tracy inhaled deeply, exhaled slowly, fought to find and deliver the expected reply. She forced a smile toward the startled asshole and said, "I believe I ordered beef, thank you. I'll be right back."

Once the words were out, the fury of emotions quickly recoiled and she watched herself move through the lobby and out the front door. She'd smoke and calm herself. She would take needed time to think and plan. This level of excitement would result in many hours of planning. It would be fun, really, to make plans for Christine. Tracy looked down at her trembling hand; it was holding a lit cigarette. She had made it outside and into the safe darkness. She envisioned the flashing glow of the cigarette pressed against Christine's pink cheek. She played the scene over and over in her mind before actually touching the amber to her own wrist briefly, softly, steadily. Tracy silently studied the dark smoldering circle before lifting it to her face. She deeply inhaled the coppery metallic odor of burnt flesh. That sweet, familiar musky smell. The pounding slowed a bit, the frenzy fell to just manageable.

Oh yes, now she would enjoy the evening. Even though she would continue to watch Jared, this Christine woman had her attention now. Christine and Jared seemed to truly enjoy one another and they'd probably continue to spend time together after tonight. If Christine cared about Jared, he would be very useful. She needed more information. Tracy nearly finished her second cigarette before tossing it into nearby bushes. She twisted her alligator stiletto purposefully onto a rose lying on the sidewalk. Its softness yielded a submissive pop, like a soft pleading sob. She pulled in a deep breath near her copper-scented wrist once more before returning to the enjoyment of the evening ahead.

The real excitement was probably downstairs; Jared had gone there earlier. Fortunately, the meals were being served as she descended the steps. She could explore unnoticed. All the lockers in the women's dressing room were locked. Christine's things were probably behind one of those sheltered doors. She might lose Jared because of this damn dangerous woman, this old cougar, the properly pale Christine O'Garra.

Tracy stood very still, listened to be certain she was alone, and then made her way to the men's locker room. A stimulating mixture of men's cologne and stale sweat hung in the air. She paused to enjoy the feeling of a place used only by men— surrounded by their clothing, leather bags, their pervasive virile scent. It would be a waste of time to rummage through the many abandoned items tossed on benches. Instead, she looked for a tidy collection, quickly found Jared's quality leather grip sheltered under a carefully hung suit. She searched the pockets of the coat. No keys. Blast, he nearly always took his damn keys, didn't at Halloween, but nearly always. She was, however, able to procure a notebook and phone from his bag, then quietly made her way back to the women's locker room to settle into a bathroom stall. The little fool had no security code on his phone. What was he thinking? Anybody could steal a phone. As expected, Tracy found an extraordinary amount of information about Jared's contacts on his phone. She slipped it into her purse.

She couldn't take the notebook, too obvious. She carefully studied each page and learned a great deal. Jared was sick. He was gaga in love with that aging bitch, Christine, the spitter. She tore a blank page from the back of the notebook and scribbled down several helpful details. His booze store and what he bought, Granny's church and neighbor lady, names and phone numbers of several women, somebody named Euggie. She stuffed the page into the bottom of her purse where it wouldn't be able to tattle on her by working itself back to the top. She carefully reapplied her lipstick with ardent self-appreciation for her full lips. She kissed the mirror, leaving an inflamed stain on her cold reflection. After a final admiring glance, she returned to the men's locker room and placed the notebook back into Jared's sturdy bag and zipped it shut.

The carefully hung suit coat requested her attention. She pictured Jared dangling on the hanger inside the suit, hanging there before her, at her mercy. She thrust her face deep into the opening of the suit coat and rubbed her cheek into the rich sheen of the lining. Tracy inhaled. Tobacco and mint. Gingery cologne, sweat, musky manliness. The same smells as she had enjoyed on her couch with him. She stood back and studied Jared's clothing, wondering how it dared to be so sensuously intimate with her. The lapel begged to be touched and she provided herself a risky moment to rub it—her long flaming nails clicked in delight. She pulled the lapel to her mouth. It scratched at her tongue and lips. She bit down.

Biting—that old atrocity of toddlerhood that so often shamed her mother. Tracy held the lapel in her angry red mouth and clamped her jaw against the dry cloth until it yielded to her. She growled through the fabric, grabbed at the suit and found herself quite stimulated by the smell and feel of Jared's clothing against the tension of her mouth. By the time she released the moist battered lapel, she was tempted to go back to the women's room and finish pleasuring herself. Instead, she dug through a few more bags and jackets, freed three more cell phones and wedged them into her purse. Best not to make Jared the only target. She picked fuzz from her teeth with her precise nails and swallowed the bits with a certain amount of satisfaction. No—pleasure.

She was missing the party upstairs. No worries, the life of the party would soon arrive to the delight of the precious guests, just as soon as she deposited these phones under the seat of her car. She'd leave immediately after Jared and Christine's dance, then find a quiet place to search through Jared's phone, take careful notes then trash the phones. Wipe them clean and toss them in a deep grassy ditch.

Sunday, November 8
Christine's Morning After

Christine drug herself through the shower late Sunday morning. It was extremely rare for her to miss church and she was wondering how best to use her guilt-ridden time. The house needed to be cleaned. There were purses to finish sewing for Christmas gifts. There was fifty pounds of rice waiting in the kitchen to be oven-canned and added to her emergency food provisions. Pondering over her work list, she flinched when the phone rang. It was the crisp light tune reserved for general incoming calls. It wasn't family; they'd be at church, and besides, she had assigned them all different ring tones. Someone she didn't know was calling on a Sunday morning. She debated answering as the phone jingled out several seconds of readily available temptation right there beside her coffee cup. Dare she hope it was Jesse? She snatched up the phone.

"Hello?" Christine moved her coffee aside and instinctively reached for the notepad and pen that always waited to serve her at the kitchen table.

"Good morning, Cinderella."

"Donavin?" It took a second to register the voice. "Well, this is a surprise. I didn't expect you to call me, at least not quite so soon."

"You sound disappointed. I can hang up and call you later. Say, in ten minutes?"

"Silly. I'm not disappointed. Just surprised is all."

"I couldn't wait to tell you again how marvelous you were last night. Apparently you're very good at keeping secrets, Christy. I would never have guessed you could salsa with such…conviction."

"Well, I only let the real me out once a year and you were never around to see it until last night."

"I kinda like the real you. I like the other you too, of course. In fact I've always liked you." His voice had a slight endearing stammer. Christine stifled a giggle.

"Well, anyway, we didn't get a chance to catch up last night. I was hoping you might like to get together sometime."

"I'd like that." She paused, uncertain what else to say. "Would you like to come over for dinner?" Christine could barely believe she had said those words. She wished she could draw the offer back into her mouth and slow herself down, but it was too late. He had already accepted and would arrive at 5:00 p.m. with a bottle of wine, no less. She didn't have the heart to remind him that she didn't drink.

She spent the rest of the morning cleaning the house and planning the evening meal. She very rarely shopped on Sundays. Today, however, she had no choice, her cupboards were bare. Bare by Christine's standards.

Even though her grocery cart had a ripped bit of white plastic bag wrapped around the right rear wheel, the cart moved without protest. The torn bag slapped out a scratchy tap against the floor in time with the music. It playfully swiped at her feet when she swung the cart to make a right turn into an aisle. Then she saw him.

Although he was dressed in jeans and a sweatshirt, she knew it was Jared's back—his stocky solid build, the way he placed his feet apart and planted himself into the floor. He was talking to the deli clerk as he received a wrapped package. An elderly woman, who was leaning heavily onto her shopping cart, took the package from him with an unsteady hand. Christine didn't want Jared to notice her. She was nearly finished shopping, and needed to get home. But she wanted to watch this real-life Jared, so she pulled her cart backward, slowly. The wheel unwound the bag onto the floor as she retreated quietly into the soup aisle.

This was very likely his grandmother, the one who lived here in Lebanon. Jared placed another paper-wrapped item in the cart and consulted the list in his hand before showing it to the elderly woman. He nodded at her and pointed toward the east side of the store. Christine smiled as he lovingly patted the woman's arm, then helped turn the cart. The old woman glanced back at Christine and smiled before she hobbled away, rocking side to side with the trusted support of the cart. Jared's back was to Christine as he bent and swiftly picked up the scrap of bag Christine's cart had littered and threw it away in a near-by trashcan. It was a smooth fluid motion Christine had seen from him many times.

Jared and his elderly partner made painfully slow progress toward the dairy department. Christine was happily touched by what she observed; she had been right about him. Although he was an accomplished actor at work, here was the real Jared. Patient and caring toward his elderly grandmother. A young man who picked up other people's trash. She was pleased to have witnessed him as a real, genuine person. He was even wearing real clothes. She successfully snuck through the checkout without another Jared sighting and headed home.

It had been a long time since she had made a meal for a guest, and she found she enjoyed fussing over the details. The preparation was finished and the meal was in a "holding pattern." She heard a gentle rapping. Donavin must have discovered the doorbell didn't work. He was peering in at her through the glass as she approached the front door.

"Glad to see that you lock your door," Donavin said, as he removed his coat and tossed it causally across a nearby chair. "Something certainly smells good. Reminds me of a chicken dish I had once with curry and apples." Donavin grinned. They both knew he had raved about her chicken curry with apples in her dining room years before, a lifetime ago.

Christine simply smiled. "We'll have to eat in the kitchen

like family. I'm refurnishing an old table for the dining room but I just got the second coat of varnish on it yesterday."

"Nothing would suit me better," he said as they made their way to the back of the house. They reminisced over the meal—relived their experiences with Seth. At one point, Christine reached past the tissue box and handed Donavin the nearly empty bottle of April's perfume. Even though using it to keep her daughter tangible was a very personal quirk, she shared it with Donavin. Christine enjoyed his insights on how the five senses, especially smell, can generate memories. Shortly after they had cleared the table and washed the dishes, the conversation took an unexpected turn.

"I'll miss dancing. I really will," Christine said. "Not only was it fun, it was good exercise. I won't miss some of the silliness that went on between the people there. Even so, I'll miss the dancing."

"Funny you should say that. I don't know if you know it, but I took dance lessons as a kid and didn't stop until I was in my late teens. I was quite good, even competed for a short time. As I watched you dance last night, I kept thinking about how much I miss dancing. I would love to find a regular partner so I could start up again." He looked at her expectantly for a moment before adding, "What do you say, Christy? I'm a bit rusty, but I'd love it if you would take lessons with me."

"I don't know. I'd love to spend time with you, of course, but…" She sat and looked at him.

"I'm not asking you out on a date. Quite frankly, I'm not ready for that either. Let's both agree that we'll spend time together as friends, just friends, nothing more. No flowers, no possessive jealous rants, and no sex, I'm sorry to say." He smiled at her and Christine knew she was blushing, again. She sat quietly, considering the opportunity.

"Let's just dance together, Christy. Everyone needs to spend time having fun with a friend," he said. He had a point.

"But, I really don't know how to dance. I simply memorized the moves to one little salsa routine, that's all."

"Well then, it sounds like you need lessons, too," Donavin said. He had another point.

Christine decided not to walk on this one. "Agreed," she said. "Just as friends. Dancing friends." She took him by the hand and it didn't take him long to move skillfully through several of her salsa moves, except it felt very different with Donavin, and it didn't feel like "just friends."

"I know the dance studio provides lessons for couples in the late afternoons. What week day would work best for you?" Christine asked.

"Thursdays are best, then Tuesdays." Donavin flopped himself onto Seth's big ugly couch and settled in comfortably.

And so it happened that the day after the gala, the day she knew she'd be free of the absurdities of the dance studio, she and Donavin agreed to become dance partners.

The next day, Christine called and successfully scheduled weekly lessons on Thursdays. Mavis seemed very excited, and eagerly reminded her of the benefits of dance. She informed Christine that unlike her lessons for preparation for the gala, she and Donavin would be assigned to various instructors. Even though Jared may be one of their instructors, she should not expect him to be their only teacher. Christine assured Mavis that other instructors would be perfectly acceptable.

"Oh, and Christine, please wear proper shoes and attire.

No sneakers or flat shoes. And you look marvelous in dresses. I'm certain your partner would agree."

"I'll try to remember to wear a dress to work on Thursdays, Mavis. Thanks for the tip."

Thursday, November 12
Jared: New Students

"The single biggest problem in communication is
the illusion that it has taken place."

— George Bernard Shaw

Jared drummed his pen on his desk. All morning, his desire to avoid Tracy had been more powerful than his need for a cigarette.

"We could insert a cross body lead before the arm check, then follow it with a double arm turn. Would that be better?" Hollie asked. Her eyes squinted as she nudged at his elbow. "This TV promo is important and you're not even listening, are you, Jared?"

"I'm listening. I'm listening." He had heard that last part at least. "It all sounds good to me," Jared said as he set his pen down and quickly read through her suggested choreography. He pushed himself away from the desk.

"Sorry. Need a quick smoke."

"Really? There for a while, I thought maybe you quit,"

Hollie said.

"Good idea, but not today."

He passed Diane with a smile as he headed out the front door. He'd take a leisurely walk and smoke instead of risk a conversation with Tracy, except he didn't want any students to see him smoking, so he rounded the corner toward the back door anyway. He had been waiting the days away and not even Tracy could dampen his spirits—not today. He glanced up and saw her pacing, looked annoyed when she saw him, as if she had expected him earlier.

"Hey, Tracy." Jared tapped out a cigarette and lit it for her as always. Her cheeks caved in with the effort of pulling heavily on the cigarette, amplifying her cheekbones. Red fingernails clacked out sharp snapping sounds as she twisted the cigarette quickly back and forth. She sought out a bit of tobacco from her tongue with those long, long nails—tweezed the speck from her cracked yellow tongue and smiled sweetly.

"Where have you been hiding all morning, Jared?" She stared at him, blew smoke his direction. "You seem a little jumpy. What gives?"

Jared flicked his lighter on and off a couple times before lighting his own cigarette. Finally he drew a deep breath and let out, "Just working. But, you know…I'm still finding it strange to have you as a student. I mean, we're not supposed to spend time off the dance floor with students. I guess us smoking together could even be a problem. Technically, I mean."

Tracy continued tapping her cigarette long after the ash had fallen. "I was a student when you came over to my office—spent time on my couch."

He watched her mouth tighten around the cigarette. There

was a sharp glare at the corner of her eyes. Her smoke-filled breath streamed out, "If it makes you that uncomfortable, I'll stop taking lessons. I'd still have to pay for them, though, right?"

Jared studied a small crack in the sidewalk intently. It was shaped like a jagged fork, like a three-flamed tattoo.

"Look, I think it's best if we just smoke together when it happens to happen, and if you want to learn to dance, then I'll teach you. But that's it. I've already told you this." He dug into his pocket, popped a mint and waited. She said nothing.

"I just want you to know it's strange for me, you know?" Jared said. He sought for a hint of understanding, a smile, a nod at least.

Tracy's tight lips pulled on the cigarette and a tight stream of white smoke slashed between them.

She finally said, "I'll try to keep from being too friendly to you in the studio so no one will know how it is between us." Suddenly, she leaned over and kissed his cheek.

He glanced up at her smile then stood staring at his mint tin, rubbing the lid with his thumb. He watched as she walked off, then he went back to wait some more.

Time plodded along painfully, slowly peeling itself out of his way. Lunch was a hurried affair as if rushing would make late afternoon arrive sooner. Jared tapped his pen on his notebook page at O'Garra. He had filled in as much information as he could from the gala. No husband, no children, well-respected in the community, seems to know everyone in Boone County. Jared had come to a decision. One he had never made before. He was going to break studio policy and ask Christine out for dinner. He still couldn't believe she was coming. Mavis had casually mentioned that Christine had called on Monday to schedule regular weekly lessons for Thursday afternoons. He had been flying high all week waiting for this day, for this afternoon. Christine had repeatedly suggested that she wouldn't use the dance skills or her shoes once the gala was over, except she had signed up for a full series of lessons. It was surely a sign, a sign that she wanted to be with him. Yes? Obviously, Christine O'Garra enjoyed being with him and wanted to keep dancing. And she would finally be able to tell him about the key she had put on his lanyard.

Jared glanced at the lobby camera monitor for the thousandth time and jolted at the sight of Christine. Of course she was five minutes early. Christine O'Garra was always on time. He quickly made his way out of the lounge to greet her properly, take in the hug he thought he'd never get again. He kissed her gnarled finger and her rings. He held her at arm's length and soaked her up. She was back in slacks and the hair had fallen to its natural position. She was strikingly lovely. He double-checked, and yes, she was wearing makeup and it was perfectly applied to enhance her eyes. Those beautiful blue-grey eyes. Surprisingly, she was wearing the same little hoop earrings. The earrings momentarily unsettled him till he reminded himself that there was no Rachel. Worrying about Rachel was a habit he would gladly break.

"So, just when I thought I was rid of you, back you come for regular weekly lessons. You just couldn't get enough of me, huh?"

She rolled her eyes at him. "I actually had to be talked into it."

The door suddenly flung open and in came the thin man—

the Christine-kisser from the gala moved quickly to Christine and hugged her warmly, saying, "Always running ahead of me. Hey, I brought you a little something." The man extended a small, very feminine white and pink bag to Christine. "I noticed you were nearly out, so I picked this up for you."

The two of them intimately worried over the ribbon that tied the bag as if they were enjoying a private celebration. Christine smiled shyly and carefully, slowly, opened the small bag and removed a bottle of L'Eau d'Issey. A Japanese perfume. Jared should have spent more time searching outside the mall. She expressed her obvious delight, far too openly for Jared's liking. He had stopped thinking about this man since Mavis told him of Christine's return. This man named...Donavin, here at the dance studio. What was he doing here?

The laughing Christine placed her hand on Donavin's arm and said, "Oh excuse me. Jared, this is Donavin Bayer. Donavin, this is Jared Garrison. Jared prepared me for the dance competition, so you can understand why he still looks a bit weary. I'm certain he's somewhat distressed to see me here again. I was a rather stubborn student at times."

Donavin extended his hand, "Glad to meet you, Jared." Donavin's grip was as powerful as his voice. Both had a dominance that demanded full attention. Jared found himself quickly developing a bristling dislike for this man.

The thin, detested Donavin boomed out, "Yes, yes indeed. I greatly admired your work on Saturday. You and Christine did a great job. Very impressive. I can't wait to get started."

Can't wait to get started? Get started at what, Doughboy? Jared thought, but managed a nod then said, "Will you two excuse me for just a moment? I'll be right back."

As he turned on his heel and started his quick retreat, he heard Christine say, "He probably forgot his Altoids, again. Would you help me with my shoes, Donavin?"

Jared felt his jaw tighten as he rounded the corner into the safety of the empty lounge. He stood reluctantly at the whiteboard schedule. The students, and their times, were clearly listed for the week. Jared always transferred the list into his notebook, never bothered to look at it again. He now read the list carefully and completely, and under Christine's name was clearly written "& guest." That meant a couple's lesson. Mavis had told him he'd see Christine's name on his schedule, and that's all he had bothered to read, "Christine O'Garra." *Fool. Stupid, idiotic, romantic fool.* Jared stabbed at "& guest," smeared it, not caring that black dust clung to his finger.

Christine, and this Donavin Bayer, would be at the studio every Thursday for lessons. Jared felt bile bite at his throat before swallowing hard. Perhaps they were just friends. Yes, just friends. They had been delighted to see one another at the gala, so they had to have known one another before Saturday. Except they had exchanged phone numbers. That didn't make sense. So they weren't close.

Maybe not, but Donavin had bought her perfume and he had noticed what kind she was "nearly out of." Jared knew where women kept their perfume, in their bedrooms. Mr. Bayer worked fast. In less than a week, he had accomplished what Jared failed to achieve in three months. And now he was forced to teach this unpleasant man how to dance with Christine. He slowly retrieved his tin of mints and made a sluggish return to the lobby. He wouldn't be breaking any studio policies today.

Surprisingly, Jared learned more about Christine in the

forty minutes that followed than he had in all the hours he had spent with her alone. He discovered she had left a job at Purdue University to move to Lebanon, that she had a son named Jesse, and that her husband's name had been Seth. Evidently Seth and Donavin had been college roommates, great pals, and great admirers of Christine. Well, why not. Jared could understand that at least.

He felt for Christine when he heard that Seth had died less than two years ago and that their only daughter, April, died only months before Seth. It wasn't she who shared all these details of the very private life of Christine O'Garra—it was Donavin. Christine finally had to shush him with a pat and a small smile.

Jared realized he could learn a great deal about Christine by spending time with Donavin. Unfortunately, time at the dance studio was filled with prying eyes and ears, and their time with Jared would, and should, be spent learning to dance. It was also very likely the couple would be regularly assigned to Hollie, and sometimes Kyle.

"So, I understand the two of you will be back in a week, yes? Well, I'm delighted. You know, the studio also provides Friday night dance parties as part of your student package. I hope to see you at tomorrow's party."

"Oh I don't think so. I've got to work fairly late tomorrow and Donavin and I will be up at the crack of dawn on Saturday. We have a lane reserved at the shooting range."

"Oh, Christy, we should try to get to the dance parties. I need to try out these new moves or I'll lose everything this boy here has taught us," Donavin's voice echoed across the floor.

Jared's focus, however, was entirely on Christine when he said, "I must confess I have developed a keen interest in shooting sports and the safe use of guns because of you. I'd love to learn how to shoot someday." Jared smiled in fond remembrance of his close encounter with her firearm during a lesson. He now looked from one to the other waiting for a response.

Donavin offered the invitation hoped for. "Well, why not join us Saturday morning? The lane's reserved from eight till nine. I have several guns and can show you how to fire. What do you say, Christine? Should we show this young man that your many skills extend beyond the dance floor?"

Christine delivered Donavin a wilted smile then steadied her gaze at Jared. "Are you serious? Do you really want to learn about guns and how to use them?"

"Absolutely! Or don't you think I should?" Jared, who was enjoying her somewhat puzzled blue eyes, added quietly, "Perhaps you want to enjoy your date alone?"

Christine quickly said, "No, no, it's perfectly fine for you to join us. I'm just surprised you want to. You never expressed any interest to me and, as I recall, I gave you a perfect opportunity here at the studio to discuss guns."

Jared simply grinned at her, looked at them both as if he were making up his mind before saying, "Yes, I think I will come. That's early for me, of course, especially with Friday's party going on till midnight, but I'm very interested and I doubt I'll get another chance." Apparently he was going to break the studio policy against spending time with clients off the dance floor after all. Although not the way he had planned, broken all the same.

Christine scribbled the address of the shooting range down in that notepad of hers and tore out the page. It seemed she flinched slightly as Jared carefully extracted it from her hand. Christine's pleasant voice was muffled by Donavin, who opened the door for her and walked her to her car. Jared watched from the lobby as the pompous man leaned over her at the open car door, as if he had corralled her. This man had something Jared wanted. Something Jared needed. He had Christine, maybe. Jared watched Donavin pat the top of her car, shut the car door, and walk briskly to a sporty silver Lexus— slick and bold, like its owner.

"They seem like a very nice couple," Donna said from her receptionist nest.

Jared started at her voice. She had obviously been studying him. He managed a half-hearted smile and wondered if she had overheard Donavin's invitation for Saturday. With Donavin's booming voice? Of course she had. Donna simply smiled. Jared smiled back, then quickly escaped to the lounge. He checked his schedule, the one on the wall this time, and cringed slightly to see that Tracy would be here any minute for her lesson. Fortunately, she was Kyle's student today.

Saturday, November 14
Tracy: Expanding Business

Perched on the counter stool just outside the office door, Nora called out to Tracy occasionally with tidbits from the bulk order discount catalog. Tracy scowled at her monitor. She'd have to finish her drug sales accounting and do Jared research through her aunt's uncontrolled chirping. Maddening.

The GPS continued to blip out steady updates of Jared's location from the bookstore computer. If it weren't for an oddity early this morning, Tracy would have termed Jared chronically predictable and boring to stiffness. His car had been out in the middle of nowhere about ten miles west of Lebanon, far from Granny, far from his precious Christine. Tracy studied the location of the car and noticed it had been parked in one place for nearly an hour. She pulled up a satellite map of the area. He had been at a shooting range. This was troubling. Very troubling. But much more fun.

The system provided a detailed history of everywhere Jared drove, so she knew that he often went up to Lebanon—too often to merely be visiting Granny. He had his little black butt parked on North Meridian Street on Sunday late afternoon, Monday night, Wednesday night, and again on Thursday until 11:30 p.m.—late nights for the hardworking Jared. It hadn't taken long on the county auditor's website to find the names of people who owned houses on Meridian Street. Of course, there it was, O'Garra. Christine owned, and probably lived in the house that Jared visited so often. He was in love. How sweet. How nauseating.

Tracy took time to visit the lovely little town of Lebanon late Thursday night just to see what her boy was doing so often and so long at Christine's house. She parked at the armory and walked two blocks. Fortunately, she had seen him before he saw her. Instead of being inside with the fair Christine, he was out on the street, just sitting in his car like a dope. Tracy physically gagged at the sight of the lovesick puppy staring up at Christine's house. Such a pathetic romantic. Like they were back in high school.

Tracy had done research on Christine, too. She easily found the obituaries of both her husband, Seth, and her daughter, April. April O'Garra, age twenty-two. Perfect. In less than five minutes, Tracy had April's Social Security number. She applied for several credit cards in April's name using the O'Garra address in Lebanon. It was something to even things up with Christine, but not enough. Not nearly enough.

On Thursday, Tracy saw a man who looked a great deal like the one who hugged on Christine at the gala. He was just leaving the lot, so she immediately wandered into the dance studio and asked Donna about the man in the sporty silver Lexus. Donna merely eyed her suspiciously, smiled, then told her that she had "nice hair." *Damn that Donna. Only a matter of time.*

Although Tracy hadn't spoken with Jared on Thursday afternoon, she knew he was there, hiding in the instructors' lounge, pushing down an urge to smoke. She had seen him run out the back door after Kyle had her dancing in his arms. Tracy had actually been glad she had been assigned to Kyle. She needed his help, again. It was obvious at the gala that Christine cared for Jared. This made it easy. Hurt one, hurt the other. It would be easier to hurt Jared than Christine, and she was making plans to do so—hurt Jared, and help herself at the same time.

As always, Tracy had paid attention to small details in order to make her plans. She studied the women who pranced into the bookstore before and after their dance lessons. These were wealthy women. Foolish, hungry women. Foolish, hungry, lonely, and wealthy: a perfect combination. Tracy wanted some of the guaranteed profit from that combination, and today she would start her focused preparations. If it was possible for a plan to be perfect, this was it. Perfect. Tracy turned off her computer, leaned on the doorframe of her office, and waited.

Five minutes before the Bookworm Bookstore would close for the day, the bell at the door jingled and a man entered. He had a sturdy build and stood tall. Nora peered out over her reading glasses at him as he sauntered past the front counter, but didn't provide her customary greeting. His cowboy boots thrust forward down one aisle of shelved books then turned abruptly in the opposite direction. The dark eyes above his pockmarked cheeks darted about the store before he headed toward the back and finally settled at the small gardening section.

The urban cowboy lifted a hefty hardback from the top shelf and thumbed through a garden of bonsai trees. He stood studying two miniature trees encircling one another on a dog-eared page. Tracy made her way leisurely toward the bookstore customer as he removed a photo from the fold of the book. "I can offer you a twenty percent discount on that." Tracy spoke loudly enough for Nora to hear. "You can walk out of here with that beautiful book under your arm today. Can't do that shopping online."

"No indeed. Still lots of things people can't do online," the man said as he rubbed the photo of a well-dressed black man between his fingers. He glanced up at her briefly then continued his study of the man in the photo. Tracy needed no further introduction to know that this was Lonnie Deel—the man she had invited to join her today after hours.

"Well, take all the time you need. Let me know if I can help you find anything in particular. We have books of every sort." She made her way back to her aunt who had draped her coat over her arm.

"Oh, Tracy, this always seems to happen. No customers all day then right at closing someone comes in to browse." She gave Tracy a distressed look then fretted with her purse.

"It's okay, you go on ahead. I'll stay and lock up. I don't mind. Really I don't."

"Oh, Tracy, and it's a Saturday too. I so much appreciate you being here on Saturdays now with the holidays coming."

"I don't mind working weekends, Aunt Nora. Really. We both have Mondays off, and it's Friday nights that I need for myself, and of course during the week for dance lessons, cleaning my apartment, and such. Looks like this carpet could use a vacuuming. I'll do it once this gentleman leaves."

"I really don't know how I've managed without you. Oh, Tracy, you've been a godsend." Nora clucked out a quick meaningless apology once again and finally left. Tracy was certain she'd strangle that woman if she said "Oh, Tracy" one more time, swore she'd etch it onto her grave marker. Tracy waved sweetly at Nora through the front door as her car pulled out of the lot, immediately locked the door, put up the closed sign, and returned to her lone customer.

"Tracy, right?" the man asked.

"Yeah. Glad you could come in. I guess you're at least a little interested."

"Worth a talk anyhow. Got me curious. I checked around and some of the boys have heard of you. Said you had it together dealing dope, but some are saying you're muscling off your field. Not too smart, that." Lonnie's crooked smile pulled at one eye and his bent nose hooked to the left. "Boyle talked ugly 'bout you. Tagged you up with plenty of names. Nasty ones," Lonnie said.

"I can get ugly when necessary, too," Tracy responded. "But my preference is to work with people who are smart enough to see the advantages of being partners rather than enemies." She invited Lonnie into the privacy of her office, offered him a seat and a cup of coffee.

Once settled, she set him straight. "Boyle's not serving his customers. Someone like me has to step in just to keep people happy. He moved into heroin a while back thinking the money was easy, but I don't wanna get caught up in the crossfire dealing that shit. I only sell the sweetest cocaine and wicked fine weed. My clients can pay the price for high-quality and they don't have to run the dark mean streets to buy. Boyle's got his place and I'm not trying to muscle in." Tracy knew Lonnie got his girls heroin from Boyle, and she didn't want to cause trouble between the two.

"Boyle's just mad 'cause he has to manage his couriers is all," she said. "They're stealing him blind, and he'd better step up and line 'em up or he'll be bowing to them. He's been around a long, long time and now he's just scared 'cause he knows that the oldest dog has to fight twice as hard."

Lonnie's eyes revealed a fresh appreciation for her. "Pretty free with your facts there, girl."

"I just tell it like it is." Tracy stood and lifted a file folder from the top of a cabinet behind her. She sat back down, opened it, and jotted a note. After studying it for a moment she added, "And I am nobody's 'girl.'"

She finally looked up from the folder and peered at him. She made another quick note on the paper in front of her, closed the folder and pushed it far out of his reach. Lonnie set his cold coffee down on the corner of the desk and studied the folder. He squirmed in his chair and looked about the room.

Tracy continued, "I didn't ask you here to talk about dealing drugs, or Boyle. Thought you and I could talk some about my own idea. Something fresh. It's more in line with your type of work. I've been doing some research about how you operate your business, and I hope we can work out an understanding before I get started."

Lonnie leaned forward in his chair and took the pen from her desk. He unscrewed it slowly and let the spring pop the stem back and forth against his thumb.

"I saw your boy out back like you said. Pretty," Lonnie said as he studied the movement of the spring. "Still not seeing how you plan to manage that piece, though. He work both ways?"

He's not working for me at all, yet. And no, he'll be strictly a ladies' man."

"No shit?" Lonnie Deel looked up from the disassembled pen and made little humming sounds as he shook his head. "Won't work. Never been money from women much. Not enough willing to pay for service. Too shy, too cheap, not enough blow off in 'em to make 'em wanna spend the money or take the chance."

"Well, you're the expert, but that could be changing. I've

got a different product here. I'm not trying to take business from you, or anybody else, and you'll have no trouble from my boy. And someday, I'll have several to choose from. They won't be on the streets or online either, only getting new business by word of mouth. I'm just marketing to the rare wealthy lady who needs to feel special now and then. A lady who can easily pay for an exceptional experience, something she can't get anywhere else."

Tracy pulled at a large desk drawer, removed a second folder, and handed it to Lonnie. The photos of Jared dancing with bedazzled older women brought a small tight-lipped smile to Lonnie's face.

"These nice old ladies wouldn't blow a stop sign. Not seein' 'em paying for a roll with your boy. Look like they're having enough fun with him legal-like," Lonnie said through another tight smile.

"Those women won't be clients—just need them as part of the front. Paying customers will come from outside, and they won't be buying by the hour like your tricks. My product will take all night. Lady might just need a companion, but she'll probably want, and need, a lot more by the end of her evening."

Lonnie laughed. "For sure not gonna make money now. Gotsta turn a lot more than one a night." He shook his head and looked at her as if she were a child, tossed the closed folder of photos on her desk.

God, this man was stupid. Stay sweet, stay calm.

"I see your concern, but let me tell you how I see it a little differently," Tracy said.

She unlocked the side drawer and offered him a joint. He accepted. Tracy carefully chose a joint for herself that she knew contained only tobacco. She chatted with him about the storefront and her accounting system as they smoked.

Lonnie inhaled deeply and steadied a rare direct look at Tracy. "See lots of cover. Good cover. Still don't see money in one trick a night. No way."

"Yeah, in your world. But, I'll get ten times what any of your johns pay for the best of your girls. My customers are wealthy women. Very wealthy, bored, lonely women."

"What's your price?" Lonnie seemed genuinely interested.

"First time's only a small fee, say a thousand dollars. After that it's thirty-five hundred for four hours, plus she's gotta buy five hundred dollars' worth of books to help keep my front looking legitimate. She makes a referral that pays, she gets a night free. One free for every paying sister she sends my way."

Lonnie snorted and laughed. "You're crazy. No broad gonna pay at all, let alone those prices."

"You don't know my customers. I do. I've studied them." Tracy pushed herself from the desk and stood. She walked over to the coffee maker and poured herself another cup then returned to her chair, settled in. She tucked the back of her hand under her chin and leaned toward Lonnie with her elbow on her desk.

"Here's the thing, Lonnie, you and I could both profit if my idea works. I've got the books set up, got the front, got the boy, even lined up my first client. And I'm willing to cut you in on five percent of the profit for the first six months so you know I'm paying my dues. Show you my books and everything. You're the manager everybody knows around here. I know that." Although Tracy's wandering nails clicked at her keyboard softly, she never took her eyes from Lonnie's face.

"Yeah. I see you done your homework. That's for sure. You've got a great setup here. Everything a growing business needs. Can't say you're not creative." Lonnie dragged out the final morsel of mellowness from the joint and quickly rubbed the remains between his hands over the nearby trashcan.

"But still not seeing a lady, not even you, managing a man, not a real man. Men think different, ya know. Need to be in charge, wanting ladies to give it to them. Ladies want to please 'em. That's what ladies do, they please men. Not seeing it the other way 'round enough to make it work."

"This boy will let me lead, Lonnie. He's already used to pleasing women—doing whatever they say, whatever they want. He's sold himself to them for years. Tuned up a few of 'em in bed, too, I'd bet." Tracy examined the back of her wrist carefully and rubbed on a faded red mark gently. "In fact, I know he has, and you're right, he is fine. Had a nice long piece of him myself and I'd pay for more." Tracy giggled. Lonnie looked away.

Tracy allowed a final puff of smoke to sail up where the recording wire entered the ceiling. "See that wire up the wall and into the ceiling there? I've been recording what goes on in the instructors' lounge where my boy works now. The things that go on in there would make you blush, Lonnie." Tracy smiled at her guest and future partner.

"I've done my research. He'll be ready. Promised my first customer I'd deliver by Christmas," Tracy said. Lonnie looked like he actually believed her. He should, it was the truth.

"Look, Lonnie, I just want to be certain you understand what I'm doing here before I get started. Don't want any misunderstandings. Getting in each other's way might get us both on the hook. I'll send your customers your way, and you send my customers to me. I only want clean though, no diseased low-class women messing with my merchandise."

Lonnie took one more look around the office. He scratched at his chin as he studied Tracy's yellow couch and finally said, "Yeah, girl." He caught himself. "Yeah, Miss Tracy. I'm good with that." His chipped front tooth made a special appearance in a full grin.

Tracy handed Lonnie a stack of bookstore business cards and a dozen rolled joints. "Tell any wealthy, healthy, horny ladies to call and ask for me by name. Tell them to ask for a book on bonsai gardening. I'll have to interview them before they become customers." Tracy stood to clearly signal that their business was finished. "Only high-class mind you. I have very high standards."

Sunday, November 15
Jared: Gran's Gift

As Jared pulled into the church lot, he saw Gran making her way down the front steps, clinging to the rail, rocking and pausing at each step. He felt a twinge of guilt. Normally he was on time to slip inside during the closing hymn. He stopped the car at the foot of the steps and popped out.

"Hey. You should have waited for me inside."

"Not gonna find my groceries hiding under the pews." She smacked his arm playfully, and then took hold of him for the final step toward the car. She soon sat beside him, chattering miles away, as Jared's full attention mulled at the events of the previous morning—yet again.

Today, as always, Gran insisted on approving every item before it went in the cart. And as usual, Jared was beside her through each slow movement she made, but today he had to fight to stay focused on meeting her needs. He hoped he was acting normal, but knew his torturous thoughts were likely betraying him.

"You can put that bread in the cart now," Gran said. "You been holdin' it like a baby up and back two aisles. Nearly got it squished back to dough." She narrowed her eyes at him then gazed back at the deli display. In the next aisle, the price labels of the cleaning products blurred as he told himself not to think about Donavin, the theft and the phone call that still hadn't come. Swirling thoughts. The frozen fish told him to call Donavin and Christine as soon as he got home and explain, make it right.

"Maybe tomorrow," said the magazine at checkout. "Today, you are helping Gran and should be with her fully, not thinking about how stupid you were yesterday." The magazine made a good point.

Only thirty minutes on her feet, and Gran sat exhausted in his car, so he was surprised to hear her say, "Gotta go to the five and dime now."

"The drugstore? Didn't Claire already pick up your prescriptions?"

"Yep, Claire finally got that right, but I gotta get something else."

This meant she wanted to purchase a gift for someone, nothing expensive, only personal. She had a knack for knowing what people liked. It wasn't until he was checking out that he saw the box of crayons. The little sneak had gotten them into the hand basket without him seeing. He shook his head and grinned at her. She had not failed to buy him a new box of crayons every six months since he was a kid.

"Gran, you're amazing. You never forget."

"No, and I won't neither. Those crayons are your time traveler. I've seen how you dig them out of the bag and sniff at them, and I know where they take you, too, right back to Vincennes. Sure would like to see the place again myself."

She, of course, was right. Crayons took Jared back to the kitchen table in Gran's small house where he had spent many happy hours creating colorful worlds on paper. He drew places he planned to travel someday: mountains, jungles, oceans, carefree destinations to explore and enjoy. Gran still had several of his paper worlds stored safely in her dresser drawer. He had enjoyed looking at them on her moving day in August.

Gran was the only person who knew that he still enjoyed drawing with crayons. His creations were no longer wonderful places, only tinted movements, wild blurts of color. A few months ago, the drawings had morphed into crude portraits of a beautiful blonde woman and a handsome dark man. Last Sunday, he had purchased heavy-weight paper in this same store to support the heavy crayon strokes he passionately lavished at his kitchen table. Last night, his well-worn crayons could only manage heavy strokes of light orange with a brown swirl of color twisting around and around the orange. He was carrying one of these with him, carefully folded and tucked away in his inner coat pocket. He reached to feel for it, and allowed the sharp corner to press against his fingertip. The small pain dulled his sadness, but not the anxiety that had started Saturday morning—had grown since. *Idiot, don't think about that now.*

He felt Gran tapping his shoulder. Startled, he couldn't remember checking out from the store, or how they had both gotten into the car. He hadn't stolen the things in the lumpy bag he held on his lap, had he? He opened the bag to be certain it contained the much needed crayons. Gran looked at him strangely for a time then reached over and pulled her purse from the floor. She extracted a few dollars from her wallet, grabbed his hand, and stuffed them into his palm.

"Here, you're not gonna be buyin' me my things and the crayons aren't a gift if you go buyin' 'em with your own money."

Jared knew then that he must have mindlessly swiped his credit card at the cash register. Gran wouldn't have argued there in front of the cashier, but it had long been understood that she would pay for her own things. He and Eugene had given up trying to argue with her on this, or anything else for that matter. He sheepishly grinned, then slipped the limp wrinkled bills into his pocket where they were supported by his folded crayon masterpiece. He tapped the sharp corner of the stiff paper once again to experience a slight stabbing before removing his hand and starting the car.

"Sorry, Gran. Just thought I could slip that one by you somehow. But you know I make good money teaching dance. And it's really no problem for me to buy you things now and then. Don't have anyone else to buy things for."

"Son, I'm worried up with what's on your heart, not carin' at all 'bout what's in your bank account. I want to know what's going on with you lately. You're one drifty character. Always been bad, but not this bad. You just staring off like everything disappeared. Love's only reason for that. So, who's this girl that got you all dreamy stupid, Jaden? And don't mess with me, it's got to be a girl. She somebody I know?"

The idea that it could be someone Gran knew was comical. The only women he and Gran both knew were relatives, doctor's office receptionists, and store clerks. Even so, she was right. Yet again. He was in love, he thought, and he knew he had been overindulging in daydreaming. He just couldn't seem to control his thoughts from drifting toward Christine. And now the events of yesterday added to the swirling. But he wouldn't think of that now.

"No, Gran, you don't know this girl," he replied.

"So, I'm right, though. You've been mooning over a girl day after day. And every night, too, I suppose. You visit her regular, or you just moping around alone—all sulky and sad?"

As much as he wanted to, he couldn't find the right words and any stammering would only expose him to Gran's curiously probing questions. He hadn't sorted out his feelings well enough to confide in her and he wasn't certain how she would react to Christine: her race, her age, her family history. He must have sat there driving silently for a long time to elicit the rare stinging reaction that came next.

"You keep your pants zipped least till you make her a proper wife and know her family and such. Don't want to share babies with no strangers." She had his full attention now.

"I haven't had sex with her. Doubt I'll ever get the chance."

"You still livin' reckless. Yes? You too pretty not to have 'em if you want 'em. Shouldn't be havin' 'em without the ring, and all. But you're sure enough sugar with feet to look at just like your granddad."

Her slight smile was likely due to a distant memory. She suddenly turned and fixed a sharp look on Jared. "You pinin' away over somebody else's woman? She married then?" When Jared didn't respond, she moved on quickly. "That's got hurt all over it. Can't say it doesn't happen though. Happened to me once. Couldn't get that man outta my head, but your granddad never knew. He's too busy pokin' every young thing that would have him."

Fortunately, the defensive driver coming toward Jared in the opposite lane was able to swerve out of the way. The blaring horn faded away behind them as he steadied the car. *What? What was she saying?* Jared stole a quick glance at his grandmother before returning his eyes to the road in front of them. This was news. He assumed the relationship between his grandparents had always been the way he remembered it: loving, caring, affectionate, certainly not adulterous. Even though Granddad had died a few short years after he and Eugene moved to Vincennes, he could still remember how he'd hold Gran's hand as they walked. How he'd opened the car door for her. Bring her flowers from the empty lot. Sing silly songs to make her laugh. He did anything she asked, when asked. Never a question. Never a complaint. Jared couldn't recall a time when his grandparents had even raised their voices toward one another. He was suddenly very curious about this cavity in his family history.

"Are you sayin' that you and Granddad cheated on one

another?"

"Not certain you're old enough to know," Gran smacked as if that settled the matter. She reached into the store bag and drew out the chalky pink candies, the wintergreen mints that reminded Jared of Pepto-Bismol. She struggled to open the troublesome cellophane bag. An upcoming gas station provided the perfect place to pull over to help her. He slid into a parking space and gently took the bag from her hand.

"I'm thirty years old, Gran," he said softly as he reached inside his coat pocket for his pocketknife. The dime there glimmered and he rubbed Liberty's face softly before opening the knife.

Gran was studying him thoughtfully. "Yep, you're thirty years old and still stupid as a stump. Hope you wake up smart enough to keep yourself zipped up till the right girl come along. She show up and you still rootin' around other girls—why'd she stick around waitin' for you? 'Cause you pretty?" Gran eyed him as if he might actually reply. "Ha! Best wise up, son. Wise up real fast, too."

Jared closed his knife and handed her the open bag that crinkled happily. "So, Gran, you're saying what exactly? That if I stop having sex, the right girl will just fall into my lap or something?"

"Lord, I raised a stupid boy. No…you gotta go get her. If you're just sittin' back waitin' for her to see you? Well, that's dumb." Her gnarled fingers reached into the bag and pulled out a mint. She shook it at him.

"So here's what you need to know. You need to know that smart people get happy by gettin' wiser and doing stuff, not just gettin' older. People miss it—miss it all the time, and stay stupid thinking that if they just live long enough there'll be happiness. It'll just come. If'n they that stupid? Then they get mean and mad at everything and everybody when they get old."

Gran smacked at the mint and crumpled the bag closed as she continued, "And old creeps up on 'em. All of a sudden they're old, and lonely, and then they die. Bitter and mad at ever'body, even God Himself. You'd best be getting smart and find yourself a good girl to get old and ugly with. Somebody to take care of you and not just in bed making babies. But that's important too, mind you—just that bed stuff is easy—too easy and soft. Them long hard hours outta the bed, there's where the love grows…or dies." Gran paused and looked at him for a moment, shook her head. "I don't want to die seeing you like this, all sad and alone. Nobody to love."

"I do have somebody to love, Gran. I've got you and Eugene and everybody."

Gran scowled sourly at him. "You know full 'nuff that's not it. You been sulking around like a sad camel and it's 'cause you don't have your girl. You need to go talk to her. Ain't no love without words. Words and things you do between the words. You gotta go get her."

He hadn't heard Gran raise her voice like this for years, not since his arrest in Vincennes, the last one she knew about. She was angry then because he had been stupid, and she was angry now. He was being stupid. He returned his attention to the dime and rubbed it gently. He let the silver face tilt back and forth before finally returning the knife to his pocket.

"You're right, Gran. I've got some wisin' up to do." He watched her fold the top of her mint bag down again as if she were really done. He straightened himself, got the car turned around, and pulled out of the lot.

"Hey, I've got one more stop to make. Would that be okay? You getting tired out?"

Gran studied him carefully. "Don't you mind me none, I'll nap while you shop. Where we goin' now?"

"I've got to buy a very special lady some flowers."

"Well, glory hallelujah for that." Gran opened the bag, fished out another mint, offered one to Jared. She knew he never ate those things. Gran chuckled at him. He was struck again by the many similarities between his grandmother and Christine.

Jared turned the car onto Meridian Street and slowed to a crawl in front of the familiar house. Christine's black and white cat was sitting on the front porch struggling to lick at his white chest. Although there were lights on downstairs, the curtains were drawn. The curtains were always drawn. He noticed Gran's ever watchful eye prodding at him as they sped off toward the one florist open on Sundays.

"I won't be but a minute, Gran. It's kinda cold so I'll leave the car running. I'll put your groceries in the trunk where they'll stay cold. Okay? You keep that door locked now, you hear?"

"Jaden, I told you I'd be nappin', so you just take all the time you need in there. Don't you mind me none."

"You've got your cell phone, right? You just call me if you need anything or if you just want to get home." Jared was still getting used to his new cell phone. He tapped at the display to assure it worked properly, and that he had remembered to charge the battery.

"Mercy, such fuss. You'd think I was a little bitty child. Go get your posies."

Jared grinned at her. He came back out with not one, but two, flower arrangements. The rest of the afternoon was spent settling Gran and her acquisitions into her apartment. She nudged around at her cheery flower arrangement as he brushed out her hair the way she liked. He allowed himself to fully sink into her goodbye hug. It fortified him for what he was about to do.

The sweet mound of white roses trembled on the car seat beside him. He pulled past the house slowly then slipped around the corner onto the side street. As he pulled behind the house, Jared's heart crumpled at the sight of Donavin's silver car. The realization was clear and painful; Christine would never be his. And now he was helping Donavin get closer to Christine through dance. He circled the block to consider his options before slowing to a stop in front of the place she slept, she ate, she lived. He saw no sign of life from the massive brick house. The roses were cool and soft at his fingers. He lifted them to his face. He held them carefully as he approached the dark steps, stood staring up at the house. *Knock on the door. Talk to them. Tell them.* Crisp air bit at his face and at the hands that held the gift—his heart. He should throw the roses back in the car, pound on the door and talk to them about yesterday. The glowing white roses shuddered in his hands at the thought and his final decision hit him fully—he wasn't ready to see the look on Christine's face following his confession. He quickly scrambled up the steps and placed the precious roses on the porch just outside her front door. They were left there unannounced, alone in the cold. He was fairly certain he made it back to his car unseen, unheard. An unnoticed coward. A fool.

Sunday, November 15
Christine: Unexpected Roses

The anniversary of April's death would always be hard, worse if the day fell on the weekend. And today, of all days, Christine made a rare mistake—she sat in a pew behind a young family with a little blonde-headed girl. The next hour was a series of cringes and mental readjustments as the little head bobbed, hair floating only a few painful inches away. Two blue eyes turned and gazed at Christine through the reading of scripture of an unexpected baby who would become John the Baptist. The words sat stoically in the Bible on her lap. She pressed her right thumbnail into the tip of each finger, counted one, two, three, four, and started again, over and over. As soon as the echo of the closing hymn faded, she made her way through the bustling crowd and across the parking lot with a steady determined stride. Her trembling hand slammed the car door. And, at last, she lost control. Through tears, she texted her niece that her supper offer was appreciated but declined, and headed home to be alone. And so she was alone—the rest of the morning and into the afternoon. She applied April's perfume liberally to the backs of her hands and sat on the big ugly couch with her hands to her face. She almost never watched television, but there she sat as the day drug by slowly, painfully.

Around three in the afternoon, she had a fight with God—wailed at Him like a child.

"I've lost my only daughter."

I lost my only Son.

"You gave your Son, you took my daughter."

April's work was complete. She is here so you can com-

plete your work.

"I just want to stop. I am jealous of them both."

Your work's not done. Everyone gets exactly the right amount of earth time.

"It's too painful. The earth can go on without me."

Earth is the only place where time exists. You need to use it to serve, to teach, to love. I won't change what is best for you. No loving parent would.

"I want to come home."

I know.

Christine decided to bake something, anything. She banged out loaf pans and mixing bowls, started rounding up ingredients, angry at herself when she found cinnamon had been shelved after nutmeg instead of beside curry where it belonged. Finally, she stopped, leaned on the window of the back door, and sighed out at the leafless trees. She imagined Liberty on the stoop trying to catch a season-hardy moth with the tips of his wings. Playing with moths, when he should be inside acting sad and serious like a proper angel. Liberty was male again and Christine smoldered silently. The mixing bowls and pans sat abandoned.

She nearly visited the little suitcase in the closet to review the tangible justification for her bitterness. She spoke to the living King of the universe daily, and yet she refused to give up her wounded emotions. *Why should she?* She tried so hard, yet lived in non-confident assurance that she would live a joyful eternity. She poked at her unworthiness, her ineffectiveness, angry that she wasn't experiencing peace. *I didn't even make a difference in Jared's life. He never opened up to talk with me. I care so much for hurting people, but nothing good ever happens. And yet I remain faithful. Who deserves peace more?*

By 5:00 p.m. she realized her desperate need to be with a caring human being and called Donavin. He immediately offered to come over. It would have been inappropriate to ask him to stop and buy white roses. On this date last year, she had bought a dozen white roses, and had enjoyed them all week thinking about April's smile. When the flowers finally wilted, Christine ripped off the petals and spread them on the sidewalk in front of her house. The tiny dry petal bits hugged to blades of grass at the sidewalk's edge for a week before they drifted off. She had planned to make white roses an annual tradition, but today she hadn't found the energy to keep this promise. *Having roses is not important,* she thought. *It was only a promise to yourself.*

Donavin pulled his car into her backyard drive, opened the kitchen door and hugged her. No knock, no words—just hugged her till her body relaxed then held her as she cried. Finally, they sat at the table. She wanted to tell him about the roses, but forced the piercing regret from her mind. Tissues and pats and a couple more hugs and they set to work in the kitchen. His company quieted her heart, lifted her spirits.

"Can't believe that's all there is to making pumpkin bread," Donavin said as he wrapped the last loaf, fumbling with a ribbon she had cut for a bow. They were gifts for the office.

Christine laughed at him. He took her by the hand and pulled her onto the couch where they sat and watched a movie. Christine allowed her head to settle heavily onto his shoulder, nearly closing her eyes.

"I should be getting home. It's late," Donavin announced. She jerked her sleepy head from him, shook it, and laughed.

They both knew he'd be up for hours yet. She was certain she looked as tired as she felt when Donavin reached to take her hand.

"Do you want me to stay here overnight, Christine? Flop on your couch again?" Donavin seemed sincere.

Christine nearly said yes, instead said, "No, that'd be great and all, but you'd just keep me up to all hours wanting to walk downtown for late night Chinese and watching movies like we did Friday night. I have to work tomorrow, Buster."

"I don't." Donavin grinned at her.

"Donavin Bayer, I get very little sleep with you around." Christine poked him playfully. "But thanks for coming. I needed you here, especially today."

He provided her a reassuring hug before slipping on his coat. The white moth was still bouncing around the lightbulb at the back steps, and Donavin paused briefly to swat at it. Quite the moth, neither an angel nor a full grown man could stop its frantic dance. She watched till Donavin was out of sight then made her way upstairs.

Although she got into her pajamas, she didn't go to bed. Nearly every evening at 11:00 p.m., Christine would check on her neighbor. Mr. Zachman's upstairs light would always flicker on between 11:00 p.m. and 11:05 p.m., signaling that her elderly neighbor's routine was intact. But she could only see this from her front porch. She donned her slippers, went downstairs, and pulled the old green coat from its sturdy hook by the front door. Even though the coat was long, it didn't cover her pajamas. No matter. She snuggled her head deep into the hood then opened the heavy oak door with a struggle. Just outside, she stumbled over something. Her front porch light was out and she chastised herself once again for forgetting to replace the bulb.

She assumed that she had fallen victim to a wayward pile of bagged doorknob advertisements. "Legal litter" she called them, or perhaps, Lord forbid, a new phone book.

She knelt in the darkness groping for the offensive bags of trash and found her fingers nestled instead among soft, cool suppleness. Clammy and cold, like the face of a dead person. She drew her hand back quickly just as Mr. Zachman's upstairs light came on. There was now just enough light to see what it was she had tripped over. White roses. She was bending over a mound of beautiful white roses. She sat down hard on the rough cold cement and stared at the roses for as long as Mr. Zachman's light glowed. Then, in the dark, she groped for them and cradled them on her lap. Christine buried her face in their shivering softness and cried.

Christine had no doubt that the roses were a gift from God. He knew the grief of losing a child, and He knew how much she needed white roses today. Even so, a person had delivered these precious flowers to her front porch—not God, not Liberty. The list of possible people who would give her white roses was very short. Donavin was at the top of the list, except he obviously hadn't brought them. Family may have had flowers delivered. Her brothers and sisters, nieces and nephews knew the significance of this date and had been thinking of her. Several had texted a quick note. But, there was no card. Her family would have sent a card. No, only one person could have brought her white roses arranged in a little, gala-like, mound. Jared. Jared had dropped off roses and left without speaking with her. *The little stinker.* He had probably found April's obituary online and knew this would be a difficult day. She resolved to contact him and thank him, although she could never be able to help him fully understand how special his gift had been.

Monday, November 16
Jared: Reflections of a Full Weekend

Jared squinted up at the lobby camera monitor to be certain it was indeed his long-time student. Yes, Mrs. Anne Matthews was tapping at the locked front door, nearly fifteen minutes early for her regular Monday lesson. Older white women, Jared observed, were never late; in fact they seemed to show up far too early. Nothing else to do, nothing else to live for. Let her wait. She knew the studio opened at noon on Mondays. He watched as she cupped her hands over the glass to peer into the dark studio before finally disappearing from the camera's view. *Probably went to the bookstore*, thought Jared. Let Tracy deal with Mrs. M. for a few minutes. Nope, there she was again, back at the front door. Yes, this was Monday. The bookstore was closed on Mondays. His fingers took turns drumming at a sharp corner of the plastic shoe box on his desk. He finally snapped it open, stroked one of the glistening shoes with his thumb, then closed the box with a crackle.

Kyle had on headphones, listening to potential songs for his next competition. He seemed to spend more and more of his time in the lounge rather than in his front office. Jared was struggling with whether or not to apologize for several short-tempered comments he had made earlier. Was it any wonder he was being ignored by his co-worker?

Jared answered the phone and tried to listen to Donna's excuse for not coming to work. The tapping at the front door was a bit more persistent now. Jared clattered the phone back to its cradle and sat shoving his thoughts around—guilt, anger, confusion, all because of Saturday morning, and of course, his pitiful flower delivery. He had had a rough weekend.

He sighed heavily and opened his notebook to the "M" tab. Matthews, Anne. Age sixty-eight, (no she had a birthday a couple weeks ago, so she was sixty-nine now). Widow, two children: Amy and Justin, seven grandchildren: Bryan, Joanna…Jared didn't care for Mrs. Matthews; she perspired after the first few dance steps, and wore heavy perfume in a futile attempt to mask the fact. Her syrupy stench would hang on him all day, and he had forgotten to bring a change of clothes. Perhaps being outdoors for a few more minutes would help Mrs. Matthews "blow the stink off." Christine had said this once during a lesson. Christine was such a strange woman. She picked the most unpredictable moments to say very honest, but strange, things.

"Hey, dope. Isn't that your student freezing her ass off at the front door?" Kyle asked suddenly.

"She can wait until the studio opens," Jared sharply replied.

"Geez, Jared. It's ten after. Where's Donna, anyhow?"

Jared quickly pushed himself out of his chair to rescue the excessively fragrant, and likely frigid, Mrs. Matthews who stood at the glass door hopping from one foot to the other.

"Oh my goodness, Mrs. M., I hope you haven't been out here long. Donna is normally here by now. Let's get you in and warmed up." He rubbed at her shoulders as he pulled her into the studio lobby, then gave her a rare wink and his customary sparkling grin. This, of course, was followed by a hug, a disgustingly smelly hug. It wasn't long before he had Mrs. M. working through the steps of her foxtrot, a routine Jared had used so many times over the years he could do it in his sleep. This was just where he wanted her, a place where he could allow his mind to drift to more pleasant thoughts, like that day in August when he first met Christine. As much as he wanted to float to Christine, however, he found the events of the past two days crowded out any drifty enjoyable thoughts.

He had stolen Donavin's handgun on Saturday morning. There it was, the staggering reality of what he had done required him to say it over and over in his head so he would believe it, even now, two days later. *I stole Donavin's gun, I stole Donavin's gun...* Petty theft was a remaining stubborn vice of Jared's youthful past, but this was serious. It wasn't lifting a little inventory from a store; this was real theft, and it was personal. Even on Saturday, it had seemed as if he was watching someone else steal the gun, instead of actually committing the crime himself. Thinking back, he couldn't recall any willful intent. Anger combined with opportunity. It just happened. *Tell that to the judge, certainly he'll understand. Idiot.* Jared's knee buckled slightly. He steadied himself with a soft apology to Mrs. Matthews who smiled at him with her normal moist enthusiasm. They danced on as Jared reflected on the gun that now lurked in his bedroom dresser drawer.

Donavin had made the theft all too convenient, as well

as justifiable. He had been an ass the entire morning by strapping himself to Christine in an obsessive fashion. He didn't only stand against her back to show her how to hold and fire, he mounted her. Jared played the scene from Saturday morning out in his mind as he danced. He had stood helplessly by, watching the two of them court one another, playfully poking and preparing for their next target shooting contest. Infuriating.

Mrs. Matthews suddenly stopped. Jared noticed the wince. "Jared, you've never held my hand quite so tightly. Are you afraid I might run off?" She rubbed her fingers gently.

"I'm sorry, Anne. I just want to be certain I give you the proper leads to follow." Jared took her offended right hand and kissed it. The pacified Mrs. Matthews readily returned to proper dance frame and they began again. And so, of course, did Jared.

He had been a fool to think he would be able to gather information from Donavin while shooting guns. They all wore heavy earmuffs the entire time. No one could hear a thing, so no one bothered talking. After the first half hour, Jared was ready to ignore all the rules of gun safety and stage a slight "accident" just to scare the shit out of Donavin. Maybe whizz a bullet through the flimsy tin roof. It would have been believed. Jared had no experience with guns, and accidents do happen.

After forty agonizing minutes, Donavin had snapped his handguns into separate cases and asked Jared to transport them all to his car. No, it was a directive, not a request. Donavin threw his keys in Jared's general direction, hadn't bothered to go with him to the parking lot. Clearly, a jabbing, silent slur: "Here, Little Black Sambo. Lug my prized possessions to my fancy car. I'll toss you a quarter later." Although Donavin hadn't said the words, Jared felt the intended message and burned with anger.

Once Jared had the trunk open, it wasn't difficult to un-snap one of the cases, slip the pistol out and re-snap the case. He slid the gun into his coat pocket, returned the keys to Donavin, thanked them both, shook Donavin's hand and kissed Christine's. Simple as that. He was halfway home before he started thinking clearly. No rational person steals a gun from someone who will miss it the same day and will know without a doubt who stole it. *What was the plan, Jared? Stupid idiot.*

Except Donavin hadn't called. And funny thing, Jared was getting comfortable with the gun. Last night, he had played with it—dry fired it at people on TV. He'd give it back to Donavin at their next lesson. No, better to call him and ask for forgiveness first. Except, Donavin would certainly ask him for it back soon, best to wait and apologize then.

Jared bumped Mrs. Matthew's generous backside into the small table that stood against the mirrored wall. His Altoids slid and the table sputtered. Jared ignored his obvious indiscretion and the look Mrs. Matthews delivered. He turned his smile on her.

"You are doing splendidly, Mrs. M. Have you been practicing with one of your grandchildren this week?"

She looked like an overstuffed mummy, so he quickly turned away. Her thick perfume mixed with perspiration, her clammy hand in his, it all made Jared's stomach a bit queasy. He forced himself to think of something more pleasant than stealing guns or dancing with Anne Matthews.

Jared's thoughts danced well past the forty-five minute lesson, but Mrs. Matthews didn't seem to mind his careless-ness. Jared had never seen her quite this damp; there were dark stains on her dress and her face was red and glistening. Just like his heart—a sweaty limp mess. He offered her his handkerchief, a gift from Gran initialed "JG." Jared allowed Mrs. Matthews to wipe abundant moisture from her face, and it didn't surprise him when she stuffed the handkerchief into her purse with a sly smile. Only a petty theft. He smiled back, held his breath, and bravely provided her a parting hug.

Thursday, November 26
Jared's Thanksgiving

Thanksgiving, as Christine would say, had a name and its name said it all. Jared realized he was thankful, thankful for Gran Gregory and thankful that this morning he did not have to dress in suit and tie. The soft T-shirt, the tossed-about sweatshirt, and velvety worn jeans felt great. On Sunday, Gran had insisted that he just sleep in on Thanksgiving morning— get to the family feast whenever he got there. He had laughed and kissed her cheek. It was a game they played every year. He played as well as she, and had told her he would do just as she wished. It was now six in the morning, and he was heading to Lebanon to help her prepare the meal and set the table as he always did on Thanksgiving morning.

Today "family" would include Gran's neighbor, Mrs. Milligan, and a few elderly friends from Gran's church. He was looking forward to meeting them and listening to their choice tales of youth. Old people said the most outrageous things, things that were in complete conflict with their feeble demeanor. Eugene's family would be there too, of course.

The morning and the meal that followed had gone according to plan, and Claire and Eugene were clearing the table and washing up after the meal. Normally Uncle Jared was the target of much romping and rolling about on the floor of Gran's small living room. But today, subdued in the presence of strangers, they had to be coaxed onto the full-sized couch by a stack of books. Having met Mrs. Milligan several times, they felt comfortable cuddling under the sharp corners of her arms. The bribe of dessert later, if they sat still, helped, too. Jared and Gran nestled together on the smaller couch at the far side of the room and simply watched. Jared sucked up the sweetness of home. There's no home without family, and Gran had family and friends, and the warmth of the moment melted into him.

"Those children sprout up a mile between visits," Gran said.

"Sure do." Jared tilted his head and studied the precious contents of the room.

"You speak to that girl yet, Jaden? You tell her your feelings?" Gran pulled at a thread from a nearby pillow.

"Well, that girl's not gonna work out. She's got another guy. Someone who will be good for her."

Gran lowered her face and peered at him from over the top of her eyeglasses. He could see those eyes studying him through her lashes. "Not as good as you'd be though, huh?"

"Certainly not as good as I'd be to her." Jared smiled then turned away. His fingers found a ceramic flower blooming under a lamp. A petal was chipped and he tapped on the sharpness gently. He pulled in a deep breath and turned back to her. "It was a great meal, Gran. I have a lot to be thankful for, and you're at the top of my list." Jared reached over and patted at a wayward puff of her hair, softly smoothed it into place.

"You know something, Jadie? You turned out fine. Wasn't too sure couple years back." She hiked her dress up just above a rough dry knee and pointed at its dusky fullness. "See that there?"

Jared looked at her, puzzled. "You got sores there now too?" He sat up and leaned over her lap, his eyes poking at her dark ashen knee.

"Nearly wore these knees out praying over you. Was your granddad that got 'em roughed up first. Got me some camel knees praying 'bout that man. He got 'em all toughened up for you, so you'd better thank him, too, while you is sayin' your thank-yous." Gran's giggle hid behind her hand.

"Well, keep praying. Can't say it doesn't help, but can't say it's helping any either."

"Helped your granddad. Took time, but he come around." She pulled her skirt back toward the room with a soft huff. "You a lot like your granddad. Look like him, act like him. When you talk, I swear I'm hearin' his voice. Told him when you was just little that we'd have trouble with you 'cause you so much like he was. He just smile and say you'd be one to take the scenic route. Build yourself a powerful testimony to share when you get round to growin' up, straightening out."

Jared winced at the "straightening out" part, serving to further strengthen his resolve to call Donavin, apologize and return the damn gun. He forced his focus back to the love beside him.

"Was Granddad happy?" he asked. It was a Christine-flavored question. He waited.

"Was he happy?" Gran repeated. She sat a moment. "Can't say for sure. Not something you can say 'bout somebody else. Too easy to hide hurt. Lots of people push it down hard for a long time. He had me, so he couldn't be too much in misery." Gran winked at him and grinned.

"Yeah, you're a pretty special lady."

"Not gonna argue with you on that. You need to get over this gal that got away and find somebody else. But good girls aren't out dancin' all spangled up, you know, and you best be puttin' clothes on 'em. You wanna find a girl worth havin', you best come take me to church." Gran lowered her voice and patted his leg. Her hooked finger leveled a bony poke across the room. "Miss Hawkins over there's got a young friend at church who comes and sits with her every Sunday. Cute as a button. Prettiest thing you ever saw is Miss Sharon. Goin' to nursing school." Gran paused to peer at him through her lashes. "Might be too skinny for you, though. You like 'em all round and fleshy."

"Oh, Gran, I do not. I just want a girl to love is all." He tapped harder at the sharp ceramic flower and his leg started jiggling uncontrollably. Gran was certainly in rare form today.

"Well, there it is. You can still blush." She grinned at him. "You'll find that gal, Jadie. You just need to settle a bit. Just now figured out what's important—this here." They both listened to the little engine struggling out, "I think I can, I think I can," up the mountain for a few moments. "But you ain't gonna find an angel dancing among your Jezebels."

He stared in his lap as she quickly added, "I know you

doin' good in that dancing of yours, makin' a living at it. Be more happy knowin' you're living as the man God made you to be." She paused and studied him. "I'm proud of you. You know that? You just forgot where you left your dream, is all." She patted his jumping leg until it slowed to a halt.

"Best I get to the kitchen before that Claire sticks my things in all the wrong places. Couldn't find my ladle for weeks after she took over to clean up the last time."

Jared stood quickly and pulled her up with both arms. He steadied her until she could make progress toward the loud clattering from the kitchen. Mrs. Milligan was now halfway through *The Very Hungry Caterpillar*. Her hands munched playfully at his nephew's belly and they all giggled.

Going to church with Gran and Eugene. He remembered going to church all through his childhood, except he couldn't see Granddad in the pew with them—only him and Eugene in dress slacks, shirts, complete with clip-on bowties. The endless squirming, Gran's scolding pinch at his shoulder, the pastor's final Amen and the release of his captives. He and Eugene would tear around the outside of the building. There'd be hell to pay if they were caught playing under the pews or running in the sanctuary. He attended church with Gran until he was in his early teens, then no amount of cajoling could get him out of bed on Sunday morning. He wished he could go back and change that. He wished he could change a lot of things.

Thursday, November 26
Christine: Burnt Peanut Popcorn

Thanksgiving wouldn't be complete without popcorn from a saucepan with melted butter and slightly burnt peanuts, at least not to Christine. She had spent the day at her brother's farmhouse, her childhood home, surrounded by a hoard of nephews and nieces, their babies and blessings. Although the joyful company was welcomed, it was exhausting to Christine who, by now, was used to the steady sound of silence in her own house. She had asked Donavin to stop by at 7:00 p.m., so they could both unwind from their respective family affairs. When she told him about the popcorn, he laughingly agreed to bring Vernors soda pop.

He arrived on time as promised, visibly troubled. She pushed aside the urge to ask for the reason until they could sit quietly together. The pantry yielded the cooking oil and the two-quart Mason jar that held black jewel popcorn. The heavy saucepan clanked to the range, and the butter and peanuts stood ready on the counter. A large empty bowl waited on the kitchen table to receive the fluffy white offering. The first pop signaled the need for steady shaking and periodic release of steam from the lid. Donavin watched with child-like fascination. A frantic kernel escaped from the elevated lid and shot across the room with a loud ping.

"Hey now!" Donavin laughed. "This is more dangerous than being at the shooting range with you."

The popped corn rose quickly in the hot pan and pushed at the lid. Christine was quicker than the mushrooming mass, and she dumped half the popcorn into the waiting bowl, then returned to the range until the popping slowed and stopped. The empty saucepan melted the butter and burnt the peanuts ever so slightly, the way Grandpa Steiner had done when she was a girl. A sprinkle of silvery popcorn salt, and her traditional masterpiece was ready.

"I haven't had your burnt peanut popcorn for years. Seth always shoved muffins at me during those weighty Monopoly competitions of ours, but I always loved your popcorn the best." He crunched greedily at his mound of white puffs.

"You know, Christy, the neighbors are probably starting to talk about the fact my car was in your driveway overnight Friday." Donavin had made her blush; she could feel it. "I'm just teasing. What I really wanted to say is how much I've enjoyed spending time with you, and sacking out on the couch again." Donavin brushed a piece of popcorn from his chest.

"Actually, the neighbors are more likely talking about you wearing women's clothing in public. Why did you grab my mother's old coat when you walked downtown for your late night Chinese?"

Donavin laughingly replied, "It was handy and comfortable, and you put the front door key in the pocket. You don't mind me wearing it do you?"

"Not in the least. It's practical. That's why I hang it there by the front door, like Mother always did." She paused briefly before finally raising the obvious and overdue question, "I noticed when you arrived that something's troubling you."

Donavin allowed a few pieces of popcorn to drop from his fingers back into the bowl. "I finally got around to cleaning my guns after our time at the shooting range, and when I opened one of the revolver cases, it was empty," he said, then glanced up at her. "You know that stubby twenty-two caliber revolver you like? The black one? It's missing."

"I cleaned both of my guns the day after. It's not with me."

"I know you don't have it, Christy. You would have told me if you had it. I figured you wouldn't be the type to put off cleaning the way I do. And, of course, I'm right about that." He stole an attractively scorched peanut from her bowl.

"So, you lost your gun. When did you use it last?"

"I just told you, at the shooting range on the fourteenth—the Saturday we were with Jared." His implication was clear.

"You think Jared stole your gun?" She must have misunderstood. Donavin couldn't mean to accuse Jared of stealing. Stealing a gun?

"There isn't any other explanation. All the other guns are there. If a thief got into my house, he would have stolen all of my guns, not just one."

"Jared wouldn't take your gun. That's ridiculous."

"Really?" Donavin fished a peanut up from the bottom of his bowl then studied her carefully. "What do you really know about the ever smooth and smiling Jared?"

"I know he puts other people's comfort ahead of his own. I know he's kind and thoughtful and…and polite," she said.

"Polite? He's polite so that means he wouldn't steal from someone?" Donavin set his popcorn aside and rubbed his hands together. He reached across the table for her hand and toyed with her rings.

"Look, Christine, you're one of my favorite people in the whole world. In fact, I've always been a little soft on you even when Seth was here." He looked away and studied the cooking oil on the counter. He turned back to her and added, "But you are not a good judge of character. You believe everybody's honest and will be kind and thoughtful the way you are. You never think about people as evil. But they are. People are nasty. I don't think you want to believe that, but it's true."

Even though Christine was listening, her thoughts were watching Jared holding a happy baby whose little fingers probed at his mouth, Jared's sparkling eyes, his soft whispering laughter. She was watching Jared patiently help an elderly woman do her shopping—smiling at her wizened face and lovingly patting her arm. Christine could still feel the roses he had left on her front porch the anniversary of April's death. There was genuine caring there. She knew Jared.

"Christy, sometimes I can't believe you're really so naïve. You work for a public university, you've helped thousands of people improve their lives through education, and yet you know so little." Donavin was studying her face. She felt like interrupting, but held back and waited for more. She was certain there was more.

"You limit yourself to eight favorite cable television channels, all very conservative. Eight, Christy." He paused.

"I don't have time to watch a lot of television," Christine replied.

"So I've noticed. There's a lot of things you've never found the time to do, isn't there? You've never been to a comedy club, have you? Or to a bar? You've never even tasted liquor, have you? You've never gotten drunk."

Christine narrowed her eyes at him slightly, but Donavin was carefully brushing salt across the table with his fingers.

"Have you ever smoked weed? No. Of course you haven't. You probably never even tried a perfectly legal cigarette."

He waited for her to respond, and then finally looked up at her silent face.

"You've never stolen anything in your life. Not even a pack of gum. Have you? Really, you don't get it at all because you don't understand how normal people think and act. You're like a child."

Christine, of course, blushed, red with anger, not embarrassment. *Who did he think he was berating her for not engaging in worldly activities such as these?* She pushed her chair from the table and stood over the sink. She used her fingers to strain the little bit of Vernors left from her glass, washed her ice, and strained out the water. She put the glass of clean ice in the freezer to use later. She still had her back to Donavin when he continued.

"Did you know that I was never in your kitchen in West Lafayette? I never got to go into your kitchen, Christy. I was always fascinated by your house and all your projects. Herbs growing on every window sill, morel mushrooms strung by string to dry, rounds of cheese aging in the breezeway. Seth never let me near you. Did you know that? He'd steer me away from you like you were insignificant—like I'd be bored by you. He always did that. Even in college. Then I thought maybe he didn't trust me or something." She turned to face him, turned and said nothing.

"You know what? It wasn't about me. It was about you," Donavin said firmly.

"What are you talking about? What about me?"

"He always protected you. You guys married when we were still in college, then he sheltered you. He kept you away from everyone and everything, like a modern-day Rapunzel.

Untainted for his own enjoyment and use."

His words bit at her. She turned away and gently pushed the electric yogurt incubator farther away from the sink and checked the time. It had been ready for over an hour. The proteins would certainly be firmly bound.

"My yogurt's done. I need to get it in the refrigerator," she said.

Christine could feel itchy redness on her neck as she snapped the white lids onto her yogurt containers and set them into their storage pan. Donavin sat silently watching her. It was a process, yogurt-making. Putting it away had never taken her so long. He waited.

She finally returned to the counter and started wiping down the incubator.

Donavin continued. "Seth kept you isolated so he could have you all to himself, keep you doing just what he wanted all the time."

Christine wheeled around and held onto the edge of the counter with both hands at her back. "That's not true. Seth and I enjoyed our life together and I've never wanted to do any of those things on your nasty little list. Seth never kept me from doing the things I wanted to do." Her voice had a quivering controlled sharpness. She glared at him in what was as close to anger as she ever allowed others to witness.

Donavin pushed his chair from the table and turned it slightly toward her.

"Seth kept you a prisoner in your own home. I was there to see it, Christy. You did everything for him and he never let you out of the house except for work." He paused and took a deep breath.

"Finding that Monopoly board back in the summer got me thinking about you—you and Seth. It brought back some interesting memories. I remember one late night long after you had gone to bed. I left the game for a few minutes to use the bathroom, and when I got back, Seth suddenly went upstairs to check on you. Like you were an infant." Donavin picked up his bowl and studied it. "You know what? He thought I'd gone upstairs. He thought I had gone upstairs, so he had to go up there and check on you. It really bothered me, but I never talked to him about it." Donavin looked up at her and held her eye for a long time. She stared back at him, scarcely breathing. Her head hurt. She wanted to reach up and rub at her eyebrows, but she didn't move. Donavin set his bowl back on the table and looked at her again.

"I remember once when Seth and I were working on a big project together after graduation. The entire engineering team was delayed for a whole week. Twenty people put on hold, and do you know why? Because he went with you to a conference where you were presenting a research paper. You didn't need him there, but he still went with you. He had to keep watch over you. Make sure you didn't get near the wrong type of people. That way you'd stay naïve and dependent. And you did. Seth was more like an overprotective parent than a husband to you."

Donavin's unyielding frankness pricked at the disquieting custodial relationship she experienced with Seth. One of reluctant silent acceptance she had always felt, but had never admitted existed, certainly never addressed. She reached toward the scar on her neck, a silent cry caught in her throat when her hand found the tiny raised dots. Whispers of a first baby Donavin never knew of, miscarried a month after her wedding in white. Seth would have loved that little baby as his own. He had loved her, sheltered her, yes, but loved her. Donavin had no understanding of Seth or their shared struggles, and yet there he sat, making unfair assumptions, tossing out hurtful accusations. She refused to cry.

She turned back to the sink and yanked at the faucet handle. She forced water to flow through her fingers briefly, then she watched it fight its way into the saucepan. She suddenly dumped it out just as the water heated. The greasy pan required hot water. She added a quick squirt of soap and watched the bubbles form on the surface of the newly-arrived water. She grabbed the washcloth then quickly replaced it with a prickly scouring pad. She scrubbed at the bottom of the hot pan with penetrating focus as a tear dropped into the hot water that churned at her fingertips.

"You're angry," Donavin said. "You're very angry. So why don't you yell at me, Christy? Why don't you tell me to go to hell? I deserve it."

The pan wasn't clean enough so Christine scrubbed it harder. The scouring pad poked at her fingers. She had to say something.

"So you're saying that Seth was an ogre and I'm kinda like a child trapped in an adult body. I have a rare…social disability. I'm not…not normal," Christine spoke loudly into the bubbling water.

The brutalized sauce pan was clean. It had been clean many scrubs ago. Christine dumped the angry water into the sink and banged it through a clean stream of scalding water. She grabbed a nearby towel and rubbed the pan with intense fervor. The defenseless towel was twisted onto a nearby hook with one quick movement. She turned to see that Donavin was watching the hand holding the pan.

"No, you're not normal. Thing is, I don't want you to ever become normal as everyone else defines it. If people changed to your kind of normal, the whole world would sigh out in relief." He paused, took a deep breath, "It's just that you still don't know how weirdly wonderful you are."

Christine set the very dry pan onto the drain pan and turned to look at her friend. Donavin remained quite still as if he had broken something between them.

Donavin hazarded into that fragile moment, "I do want to know what goes on in that head of yours, though. I want you to tell me what you're thinking and feeling." A deep sigh escaped from him. "And I want you to give me the finger when I deserve it. Like right now. Give me the finger, Christy."

She stared at him then down at her hands. Her moist red fingers looked as angry as she felt. Her thumb stroked the back of her sparkling wet rings.

"It's the one in the middle."

She slowly stretched her right arm and the back of its hand in his direction, middle finger fully extended. Donavin laughed heartily.

"That's a pretty good start. Next time the finger needs to take a quick little shove toward the ceiling."

Christine laughed and drew her offensive hand back into proper position.

"Don't go using your new powers all over town, girl. I'll keep that part of you just for myself." He grinned wickedly at her. "Next week maybe we'll work on saying shit right out loud."

Christine grabbed the wet dish rag at her sink and hurled it at Donavin's grin, laughing when it found its mark with a sloppy smack.

"Whoa! There's a bit of spirit," he exclaimed, as he peeled the wet rag from his face and stood.

"Well, you keep talking like this and you might have to get used to those kinds of things."

"I'd love that," he said as he carefully positioned the cloth back at her sink. His body was a bit too close, so Christine sat back down and reached for a tissue. Simply held it.

"Christy, I guess I got us a little sidetracked. We need to finish our talk about Jared. Honestly this time." He returned to his chair and sat with her. He took her hand for a moment then released it.

Christine pulled the box of tissues closer and took a second one. She wasn't crying exactly, but her eyes watered. "I just can't believe Jared would take your gun. I know you believe that's the only explanation, but I just can't believe he'd do that."

"That's because it doesn't come naturally to you, to mistrust people. You don't think about other people's motives. What people want is usually something very selfish." He smiled gently at her, took her hand again.

"You remember that lady you told me about in the parking lot? Jared's long-time student? We laughed about what she told you. How Jared was a great salesman; he sells them a good time. He's not for real and she knows it; everybody there knows it, except you. He's a con man. He might have bedded one or more of them, from what she told you."

"She made that part up," Christine said. "To be honest,

though, I've had a few uncomfortable feelings in the direction of Jared being a con man. Kind of fake in most things he says and does. But that's just Jared; he's a silly little flirt."

"You haven't noticed the way he looks at you? The way he touches you?"

"Well, yeah, but that's just his product. It's what those other ladies are buying. He does that with everybody, not just me."

"It's different with you. I've watched him just like that woman in the parking lot watched him. And here's something else I don't like about our dance instructor. I don't like the way he looks at me, either."

"What do you mean?"

"He's in love with you, Christy. It's obvious to everyone except you. Jared doesn't look at me—his eyes shoot flames at me. He's crazy jealous of me because he wants you, and he thinks the two of us are a lot more than just friends."

"You're crazy. He's like Jesse to me. I could be his mother."

"Doesn't matter. He lights up when he sees you. He holds your hands then hugs you forever."

"Jared hugs everybody."

"He doesn't hug me," Donavin said with some peppery sass.

"I mean all the women in his life; all his ladies get hugged. Jared's a hugger, you dope."

"Yeah, but he kisses your hand for gosh sake. You don't see that as a little odd?"

"Well, yes, but I think he does that with all his students."

"No he doesn't. He kisses your left hand and holds onto it

for a lot longer than necessary. He doesn't kiss any of his other students' hands. I've watched him."

It did seem odd now. It upset her that it took Donavin to point it out.

"If he doesn't have a thing for you, why does he kiss your hand?" he asked.

"He wants something," Christine said, but stopped because she didn't know how to explain.

"I'll say he does," Donavin said.

"No, I mean he wants what that finger represents." Christine extended her left hand toward him. "And I want it too. I had it once and I'd love to have what this finger represents back again," she said.

Donavin took her hand and kissed it the way Jared always did. Then he looked at her like she was a bit nutty. "I'd like to have what it represents too, but that sounds pretty out there."

"Well, maybe. But look, even if Jared is a great salesman and is goofy over me and jealous of you, there's nothing there to suggest anything close to what you're accusing him of—stealing a gun."

Donavin cut his fingers through his hair and said, "So here we are with a missing gun, a guy who's totally obsessed with you, and then here's me, the man he hates."

"He doesn't hate you. And just how did he take your gun at the shooting range anyway?"

"I've thought about that. I actually gave him a perfect opportunity. Remember? He offered to take my guns to my car for me because he was leaving early. You needed to finish shooting so I stayed with you. Jared went to the car, returned my keys, and then left with a quick goodbye. Thinking back, I don't know why I allowed the guns to be out of my sight. Really stupid of me." Donavin sighed.

Christine returned to the counter and put away the things that cluttered her world. She spied the neglected lid to the saucepan, returned to the sink to wash it, then placed it with its mate on the drain pan.

"I've got to report my stolen gun, Christy. If it's used in a crime there'll be a knock on my door, and I'll be the one in deep trouble."

"You just now discovered it was missing. If Jared has it, he hasn't used it in a crime. He wouldn't."

"He might have and just hasn't gotten caught," Donavin said.

Christine shook her head. "No. Jared isn't out there robbing banks with your gun."

Donavin placed both elbows on the table, raised his brows and stroked at them. "You're right; even I know the kid's got some sense. He's got a good job he seems to enjoy. What would be the sense in blowing it by using a gun on someone? He probably took it just to get at me. But he might have sold it by now, or he's trying to. Teaching dance can't pay well."

"Well, if he did take it, he's probably regretted it ever since. It was a childish, impulsive act," Christine said. "He had to know you'd discover the gun was missing. Can you imagine how awkward it would be to give it back to you at this point? Really, Donavin, what's he supposed to do? Come up to you before a lesson and just give a gun to you?" She finished putting away the saucepan and stood by his side.

She touched his shoulder and said, "Let's just ask him. Give him a chance to get himself out of this mess. What's the worst that could happen? He might deny taking it, and we can explain that we'll have to report it as stolen and hope he comes clean. Or he might just agree to give it back."

"Makes sense. As much sense as anything I've got to offer. He really ought to pay a stiffer price than that, though. I don't want him to lose his job or anything, but we're giving him an easy out."

"I wish we had his phone number, not just the one for the studio," Christine said. "We'll have to call him there and tell him we need to stop over and talk. What do you think? Is that the best plan?"

"Guess so. Wish I didn't have to head out of town first thing in the morning. We could have talked with him at tomorrow night's party. One thing's for certain, you are not going there to talk with him without me. At this point, we can wait till Monday."

"I won't do that. It's your gun that's missing." She paused to sigh. "You know what, though, I don't want to take any more dance lessons if that's okay with you. It was your idea to start these lessons and you signed a contract, but I don't want to take any more lessons from Jared. If what you're saying is true about his feelings, he's one mixed-up young man."

"Sure, Christy. I'll just pay off the entire contract and we'll stop going. I'll dance with you here in the kitchen whenever you want. Only when, and if, you want to."

Christine didn't feel like dancing. Not even a little bit. She did feel like praying. There was, in fact, an overwhelming feeling that she must pray.

Friday, November 27
Tracy: Friday Night Party

Finally, after three weeks of focused premeditation, the party she had planned so carefully was about to begin and the timing was perfect. Jared was unsettled around her, yet he still trusted her and wanted to please. Tracy's eyes narrowed as she again thought through every move she would make, like a well-trained athlete prior to their main event. She was indeed ready to let a little wild out on that man.

Best to put on a smile, so she delighted in the snapping sound of her new stilettoes down the narrow hallway from the dance studio's back door. The unusually thick leather straps and huge ankle buckles made them quite a find. Most women would have looked ridiculous in their heaviness, but Tracy had the height and long legs to pull off wearing them beautifully—a proper pedestal on which she confidently stood. Tracy loved her new, sharp, snappy shoes—loved them so much that she had incorporated them into her planned time with Jared. As Kyle approached, she smiled the smile she knew he liked, then provided a fleeting kiss to his fat cheek. He did the same for her, and then ogled her as if she were naked, vulnerable, and his for the taking. So much so, that Tracy wanted to punch him. He bowed slightly to her. She smiled that because-Kyle-likes-it smile again.

"Welcome to the annual turkey trot." Kyle stuck his hands in his armpits and flapped like a bird. Tracy forced herself to giggle. He expected a giggle. "Most of our students don't shop on Black Friday, so we open our doors and throw a party instead." He paused and leered at her feet. "Nice 'chews,' Tracy."

This man noticed things about a girl—things like new shoes. Fortunately, he was clueless when it came to other things, like her true plans for the evening as well as her plans for the shoes.

"You can't dance in those things. You'll break your neck," he said.

"I have no intention of dancing in them—just thought Jared would like them."

"They're fabulous, but I'm sure you'd both prefer no shoes at all." Kyle paused to appreciate himself. "We don't have a lot of people coming so you should be able to get him to yourself for a good piece of the night."

"That's the plan." She winked at him and his cheeks glowed. Poor Kyle—thinking all she wanted to do was get with love-starved Jared for a little cuddle time—a frisky desk-top quickie. A collaborator as simple-minded and trusting as Kyle was very valuable.

Kyle helped pull her coat off her shoulders and said, "He's been a royal pain-in-the-ass lately. A little fun in the teachers' lounge will do him a world of good." Kyle nodded at the small happy crowd as he hung up her coat. Their boy, Jared, was snuggling a woman's oversized purse in the faraway lobby. He opened it at his nose and the owner snatched it back with a sharp playful laugh and a slap to Jared's arm.

Kyle leaned into Tracy and quietly added, "Good thing Mavis couldn't make it tonight. I'll keep an eye on you about three songs in and send him your way when the time's right." He smiled and turned toward the lobby to head off an old duck who was balancing a covered platter and a huge fur coat in her arms.

Kyle took the coat from her and exclaimed, "Oh, Mrs. Pierce! So glad you could make it. And what's this? Cookies? Marvelous. I'll take your coat—you just head those cookies over to the refreshment table." Kyle expertly launched the cookies and Mrs. Pierce toward the merriment and returned to Tracy with an armful of fur.

"Be sure to block the door with the bench like I told you, Kyle. Don't want people wandering in while Jared and I are having our fun."

"I won't forget." Kyle smiled with admiration at Tracy before taking one more stroke at Mrs. Clement's coat. "Feels like a plump pussy." He grinned wickedly at her. "Hey, gorgeous. If Jared doesn't finally fall for you after tonight, I'd love to line up for a chance to win you over."

Tracy pursed her lips and narrowed her eyes at him as he sailed off toward the tittering collection of partiers. She carefully dug to the bottom of her purse and pulled a small pouch to the top. She hung the purse with her coat and strutted to the refreshment table. Jared remained in the front lobby laughing with some old bedazzled bird. The woman actually had a feather in her hair. Tracy stared at him until he finally looked at her, acknowledged her with a forced smile, then quickly turned back to his aged companion.

Kyle commanded the small cheerful group to attention and loudly acknowledged each instructor. Appreciative applause followed each unnecessary introduction. For the first dance, Kyle grabbed hold of a musty old gal and Jared was lapped up by the woman who owned the plump pussy coat. They began twirling through a lively foxtrot. Tracy patiently watched with complete indifference. Three dances later she was still watching, and now waiting, waiting for an opportunity to catch Kyle's eye.

Unfortunately, the Old Maid's club had worked out a fairly efficient system of "taking turns with Jared," and time off the floor to flirt with a young attractive woman wasn't on their rotation schedule. As soon as a dance was over, the wind-sucking biddy in his arms passed him off to a fresher matron standing at the mirror. Tracy could see how this worked. She grew bored and decided it was time.

She envisioned the rest of her evening, swift and precise, then found Kyle's eyes and nodded at him over the top of the woman he was dragging across the floor. He smiled knowingly and winked. Poor naïve Kyle. Helpful, though, very, very helpful.

Tracy retrieved her purse from the coat rack, and when she was certain everyone was fully focused on dancing or on conversation over cookies and punch, she slipped into the instructors' lounge and calmly, quietly, closed the door. She carefully made her way across the room in the dark and flicked on Jared's desk lamp. After removing her shoes, she re-buckled the straps, and then slid both shoes onto her left wrist. They dangled like heavy leather bracelets. Her arm trembled and the shoes danced at her wrist. The music stopped and she heard Kyle's muffled voice giving instructions to the party goers.

She jiggled the computer mouse, pushed the monitor button in firmly so it wouldn't go to sleep, and turned its throbbing light toward the side wall. She peered about and started at the sight of a plastic box. Lifting it from the desk, she was surprised by its weight. It was hard and solid and perfect. She couldn't have designed anything better suited for her purpose.

She set the box on the floor against the side wall.

Tracy lifted a sleek black pen from Jared's desk, appreciated its weight, then dug into the side drawer and pulled out his three-ring notebook. She thumbed to O'Garra, but a quick gleaning yielded nothing new. She drew a familiar graphic of three flames at the top of Christine's page, turned to her own page and grinned. There was the same mark. Jared had drawn her tattoo there. Sweet. She smiled knowing that there would come a day when Jared would wear that tattoo—properly branded as hers.

She shoved the notebook back into the drawer, removed a small pouch from her purse and set it on the desk. After carefully positioning the purse so the camera would capture the fun ahead, she finished what she had started earlier that evening—preparing and sharpening her nails. She had carefully prepared them and now only a final filing was needed. She raked the emery board back and forth and tested them against her skin until she was certain they would meet her needs. Her satisfaction was perfectly timed with Jared's entrance. He stepped into the dim room, closed the door and blinked toward her.

"Tracy? What are you doing in here?" He seemed genuinely annoyed.

"Didn't Kyle tell you, Jared?" She smiled up at him. "I was hoping to get a chance to talk to you." Tracy sighed heavily. She leaned toward him across the desk. "I haven't been completely honest with you." She noticed the soft scraping sound of Kyle pushing the bench in front of the closed door outside.

"Really, Tracy? You want to apologize about lying to my co-workers about us dating? Maybe come clean about your work history? Confess to being a slut?"

She hadn't expected him to be so forward and direct. She felt her face redden and her eyes narrow. She forced her eyes to widen into place again and smiled warmly at him.

"I guess I deserved that, Jared." She paused and looked up at him, looked him in the eye. "I'm sorry. I've done some stupid things, said stupid things. But I've been desperately hoping you'd change your mind about us. And I've been holding back—I haven't been honest. But it's never good to hold back feelings." Tracy sighed, placed her elbows on his desk and lowered her head onto the back of her hands. She peered up at him again. She could see Jared soften. His shoulders lowered and his mouth relaxed. Back on plan.

"But I can't help it, Jared. I've tried to stop these feelings I have for you, but I can't push them away any more. Can't stop thinking about being with you." She paused to deliver a soft smile. "Come here. We've gotta talk." She remained seated so he'd feel more relaxed—she knew she had to sit and passively wait. She extended her palm and kept her chin lowered to help him along.

As predicted, Jared walked over and stood beside her. He was back to his normal, polite, submissive self. Tracy turned off the desk lamp. The room dimmed to the monitor's soft bluish glow. She stood and slowly purred toward him, slid her hands up his chest and gently pushed his jacket off his shoulders, loosened his tie. Jared simply watched her face. She pulled the tie gently to one side, then unbuttoned his shirt to his waist. As expected, Jared didn't stop her. He wanted to please her. He wanted to please all women.

"You're not doing much talking, Tracy," he said. But he

didn't stop her—didn't take her hands or step away.

Tracy took his right hand and lifted it above their heads as if they were dancing. She allowed a shoe to slip past her fingers and onto his wrist. Then she leisurely pressed at him— shepherded him against the wall. Leaning over him, she took hold of the top of his ear and pulled her fingers down its curves. She gently tugged his earlobe as she kissed his mouth. A small tender kiss, one that relaxed him. Her shoes dangled danger- ously near his closed eyes. But those eyes suddenly opened and he turned slightly, then leaned a push toward her with formal intent to create space between them. *Oh, so he will push back.*

"Sorry, gorgeous, but I can't do this with you. I could lose my job," he said as he started to shrug his jacket back up. She couldn't allow that, especially not that. Tracy quickly pushed the jacket back down again and nuzzled him firmly against the wall.

"Oh, Sweetie. I just need a little attention. I won't keep you long. Just a little fun in the teachers' lounge. One of my fantasies."

His face glistened slightly. He forced another smile and shook his head in the dim throbbing light. He pulled in a quick breath—as if he were considering words. Words. No more time for talk.

When he pushed his weight from the wall again, she quickly reached behind him and grabbed the toe tip of the shoe that hung from his wrist and yanked it behind his back. With the unsettled jacket, he couldn't stretch his arms out to push her away. The moment she saw his surprise, his confusion, she flashed her thigh into his crotch, lifted his body so only the tips of his toes were touching the floor and set her bare foot on the rigid box. After strengthening her grip on the sharp stiletto shoe bound to his wrist, she shoved him harshly and felt the shoe spike twist against the wall at his back. He gasped. Even with the bunched up jacket at his back, the spike had to hurt—a lot. He was making little panting sounds. Drowning noises.

Although Jared struggled, he was suspended and pinned tight. He managed a raspy, "What the hell? Are you crazy?"

"Shut up. Do you want someone to hear us? Come in and see us here in your office?"

The chance of that was very slim as the music now boomed out its steady beat. The wall vibrated slightly through Jared's squirming.

"Let me loose," was gasped out. His useless left hand was trapped deep inside the sleeve of his jacket. It weakly swatted about—helpless, pitiful, funny-looking.

Keeping him on his toes, Tracy pressed her forearm and weight into him at his chest. She leaned over, took his lapel in her mouth, looked up into his eyes as she bit into it. He stared wide-eyed as she slowly released the tension in her mouth and brought her lips up to his face. He had a delightfully puzzled look—more shocked than confused now. It was a look Tracy had seen on other people many times and now it was Jared's turn. His soft lips pulled to one side as she dragged her cheek across them. She tasted fear as she brushed her mouth against his, playfully nibbling at his full lower lip. He was more than frightened now. His eyes betrayed him, but the firmness between his legs implied both pleasure and consent.

"Well, I see you're enjoying yourself." She laughed softly. "Glad to be of help."

"Let go of me, bitch." Jared spat at her. Literally spat.

Droplets of moisture splattered her face.

That was the wrong thing to say, and definitely the wrong thing to do, sweet Jared. She lifted the other stiletto to his stomach and slipped it off her wrist. The point sat like an icepick gently prodding at his belly button. She held the shoe tightly then crushed her body against his until she felt the shoe push into his softness, then twist between them as the pressure finally forced the point to one side. Jared made a sound like a crushed kitten.

Tracy shoved her hand up under his jaw. His head sharply bounced against the wall. She quickly slid her prepared fingertips through the opening in his shirt and raked at his undershirt, snagging the soft cotton. The ripping of his shirt was a satisfying sound.

"What the hell?" Jared's voice was now only a weak whisper.

"Shut up. Just shut up." She sucked his lower lip into her mouth and pulled the inside of his soft flesh between her teeth and bit a soft crunch from the full softness there. Jared's throat squealed, but Tracy absorbed his panicked vibrations with her mouth. The sweetness released—seeped onto her tongue. Tracy sucked at Jared's soft lip, swallowed his freakish chirps with satisfaction.

As she sucked at him, she pulled a small sampling of skin away from his chest, twisted into it with her sickle-sharp nails. A warm wetness nuzzled onto the back of her finger at his chest. She tapped her fingertip at his wet stickiness. She finally released his mouth from its snare and pulled back to study his face. Jared's wide eyes swelled into her gaze, the golden-brown dots swam in two white reflective pools. His panting gasps were overpowered by pounding happy music. She relished this moment. His frightened face beaded in sweat, but his body remained perfectly still. He was quiet now. She had seen this type of quiet many times before.

"Hush now," Tracy whispered into his parted mouth. She licked his bloody lips. Maintaining forceful pressure on him with her thigh and her forearm, she slowly pulled her hand from his shirt, and lifted the long red fingernails to his face. A smear of blood sat red on red against the sharpened nail. A bit of dark flesh and black hair protruded from the tip. Tracy stared into Jared's eyes then she slowly took the fingertip into her mouth and sucked it clean. Her tongue licked at the pointed tip.

Enjoying every moment, she gradually released Jared a tiny bit at a time—slowly easing pressure from his neck, from his chest. Her shoe clattered from his stomach to the floor as she pulled her body from his.

"Now sit," she commanded. Tracy lifted her foot from the box and let him loose. His body slid down the wall. She took hold of his tie as it passed and pulled it playfully as he sank. For a moment, he swayed from the bright silk noose. She kicked the box out from under him just before his butt hit the floor. His legs collapsed and folded him into a fetal position where he stayed quiet and unmoving. She studied him silently in the pulsating computer screen light, then dropped his tie.

Only five minutes, yet she had obviously created a lifetime of confusion. Jared's head dropped heavily and she rubbed the top of it in slow circles. His short cropped hair ripped off into her nails and she pulled at small tufts held between her fingers. She twisted her nail into his scalp and cut deep into the dark cloud of fuzz. She tapped at the small pool of crimson that sprung from the gash.

His childish mouth was blowing shiny pink bubbles. She reached down and drew her finger across his lips to capture the filmy wetness, then released its sweetness from her fingertips with the tip of her tongue.

"There now, Sugar. There now. We've had our fun and now we need to talk."

He sat on the floor like a small frightened child. Tracy paused to admire her work. She hadn't damaged her boy, not too much, physically. The wounds barely showed—he could easily hide them. And he would. He'd never mention these little wounds and they'd heal nicely, never noticed. The other wounds wouldn't heal so quickly, likely ever. Yes, he would hide all of this—give her power over him. Tracy smiled at the pathetic huddle knowing he was now hers. Finally.

"I've tried to tell you, but you haven't been very responsive. I need your full attention...Jaden." The name was hissed out in a harsh whisper through her clenched teeth. She watched for a reaction. None. He hadn't heard his name. Yet.

"From now on, you will give me your full attention. We'll get along just fine if you do what I say. Just keep me happy."

Tracy gathered her shoes and rolled the office chair close to him where he could see her. She sat. He didn't look up. Not yet. The silent Jared waited obediently. She studied him thoughtfully as she strapped on her shoes.

"Now then, we both know how you give into temptation at the mall. I have a great video of you slipping expensive perfume into your pocket." She paused. Best to let that sink in. Jared appeared to find the floor quite fascinating. Although she waited patiently, he remained silent. That was good.

Tracy reached for her small pouch on his desk, located a lipstick and pulled the waxy curve across her mouth leaving a trail of rich redness. She dragged her finger across her mouth and felt her face to assure a bit of stickiness had smeared off her lips. She slowly returned the lipstick to the dark recess of her purse and pulled a tissue to the top.

"I've been meaning to tell you how sweet your grandmother is, too. I mean, you've talked about her a lot, but I never thought you could be so attentive to a crippled-up old woman. No dancing with Gran, though. Poor Granny is all worn out, can barely walk. It must require a great deal of patience to be with her." This got a look. There was just a hint of sharpness to his eyes. She had his attention.

Tracy felt again inside the pouch and pulled out a small tube. She leaned over and sprayed a healthy dose of the pepper spray on Jared's cheek, then on his damaged lapel. She rubbed the back of her hand into the moisture there and lifted her hand to her face, inhaled deeply. Jared coughed softly, spraying flecks of pink from his pouty mouth onto his shirt. His legs splayed out onto the floor as he sputtered. She returned the spray, leaned back in the chair, placed her sharp pointed shoe under his droopy chin and lifted his face until his eyes met hers. The back of his head thumped against the wall. He was able to take her foot in his hands, but he didn't shove it away. His eyes got big again.

Tracy leaned down to his glistening face to deliver her next message in a clear sharp whisper. "But Jaden, I'm really disappointed by your unhealthy admiration for Mrs. O'Garra. Quite unnatural—a woman her age." It appeared he was looking at her, except his eyes weren't focused. They were round, filled with panic. Big, and round, and misty. That was good too. There was a brief flicker of fire in those big wet eyes. He might have heard his name this time. Maybe.

"You mustn't drive past her house any more. I don't like it. Do you hear me? I don't like it. And you can't teach her ever again. You are not to call her, or talk to her ever again. Do you understand?" His round eyes continued their blank stare and blood oozed from the top of his lower lip, nearly slipped off his chin onto her precious shoe.

Tracy thrust her words at him in a stabbing coarse whisper, "It's very simple, Jaden. If *you* get near her, *I'll* get near her." She waited patiently until she was certain he understood. She wanted to hold him like this for a while, relish him. The dim throbbing light pounded on his boy-like face, his eyes muddy and soft. She leaned back in the chair and studied him before she finally beckoned her pointed foot to release the bottom of his jaw, and the chin dropped without a sound.

"I have plans for you. Plans that require your full attention. I'll be in touch very soon to share the details with you. I have a job for you. It's a job you'll be very good at." Tracy watched the glistening crimson seep through the fuzzy black fleece at the top of his head.

"But for now, you'd better just sit here for a bit and pull yourself together. Then head straight home and get some rest. It's been a big night for you." She placed the heavy plastic box back on the desk, gathered her purse, mussed her hair and reached back to unzip her dress. She picked up the heavy black pen from the desk, reached behind her head and raked its metal sharpness across her exposed back.

"I don't need to tell you not to mention this to anyone,

Jaden." She studied him. "No, I don't have to mention it." Her eyes were watering from the pepper spray as she sauntered to the door. Perfect. After pulling the door open just a crack, she paused to be certain no one was in the hall then she opened it all the way and carefully, quickly, pushed the bench back against the wall, away from the doorway. Just before leaving, she flipped the lounge's ceiling light on. After closing the door, she backed up to the coat rack and pulled her pink coat from among the leather and fur.

She peeked around the corner of the hall just far enough to see the edge of the dance party and to catch Kyle's eye. Thankfully, he wasn't dancing. No one was dancing. The biddies were huddled around the refreshments. Kyle smiled brightly at her, opened both palms and raised his enormous eyebrows. She turned her head from him with an exaggerated shake. He maneuvered his way toward her across the floor. She quickly struggled into her coat as he approached.

"So, how'd it go in there?" Kyle quickly smirked out, "Have a good…" He stopped and watched her button her coat. "Why are you leaving? What's wrong?"

"I'd rather not talk about it, okay? Didn't go as planned, that's for sure." Tracy dropped her head and worked at another button with trembling hands. She glanced up at him with her water-filled eyes.

"Hey now," he said quietly—almost a whisper. He removed a clean handkerchief from his suit pocket and gently backed her into the privacy of the hall. He placed his hand under her chin and gently wiped the smudge of lipstick from the side of her mouth. Tracy milked a tear from her eye and let it swim down her cheek. Kyle caressed the tear off her face, then handed her the handkerchief.

She made her voice thin and quick, allowing for long pauses. "I'm sorry, Kyle. I just didn't expect…I'm not a prude or anything, but…I guess I didn't know Jared as well as I thought." She sniffed then twisted at the end of the fabric handkerchief, child-like, and turned away. She dabbed at her eyes and delivered a popped laugh. "I hope I'm not smearing my makeup. It takes a girl a lot of time to look this good." She turned back to him with a teary smile and handed him his handkerchief, which he ignored. Kyle's worried look confirmed her effectiveness. He took her arm and quickly escorted her across the room toward the privacy of the front office. As they passed the gauntlet of gossips, Tracy made certain her tear-stained face was on full display. The flock of birds circled and twittered over their plates of cookies in delight.

Kyle successfully delivered her to the office where they were out of the reach of prying ears and eyes. He closed the door, took her by both shoulders, looked into her eyes for a moment, and then lowered her carefully onto a chair. He brought his office chair around to her and sat with one of his knees between hers. Intimate yet not inappropriate. Nice, Kyle, very nice.

"Okay, what really happened in there?"

Tracy fussed with her purse. She unsnapped it and took out the tissue and handed Kyle his damp handkerchief with another smile. "Like I told you, I just wanted some fun, you know. Just a little kiss or two, but…" She made the next word catch in her throat. "But…he got rough. Kyle, it just surprised me—the way he pressed me against the wall and held me there."

She twisted at the tissue until it ripped in two. "I told him

I didn't like it," she whispered. "But he wouldn't stop. I wasn't liking what he was doing next. He was liking it, but I wasn't." Her eyes fluttered up at him then fell quickly. She sucked back a small crackled cry and softly continued. "He wouldn't stop, Kyle. He wouldn't stop and he was getting really rough, so I bit him. I bit the inside of his lip. I bit it hard enough to make it bleed. That got him really pissed and I got really scared, so I shoved him off me and left." Tracy blinked to push one of the tears from her eye onto her cheek. She let it slide down to her trembling lips before lifting her hand to wipe it from her mouth.

Kyle looked stunned. Frozen. He finally leaned back in his chair and released a loud sigh. The chair squeaked nervously when he leaned toward her again.

"Tracy, you just stay here, okay? You don't go anywhere." Kyle stood abruptly.

"Oh please don't make trouble with him. It was as much my fault as his. I mean, I started this whole thing. And I don't think he's feeling too hot right now either." She squirmed in her seat. "I kicked him too—right where it counts."

"Good for you, Tracy. I bet you can kick pretty hard." Kyle actually grinned at her.

Tracy stood, lowered her chin, and held her hand out to him. "Thank you, Kyle. You're so sweet." She let another tear dribble unrestrained down her cheek then dabbed at it as it slowed to a stop.

He took her hand and kissed it. Patted it softly.

"Kyle? Kyle, I hate to ask, but would you…" She paused and ripped at the tortured tissue and allowed bits to fall to the floor. They would be little daily reminders for Kyle until vacuumed.

"What do you need, Tracy? Anything I can do, I'll do."

She stood and slowly began unbuttoning her coat. Kyle stared silently at her, his eyes growing larger at each button's release.

"It's kinda embarrassing, but would you mind zipping up my dress?" She quickly turned and allowed her coat to drop softly onto the chair between them. Tracy could feel his eyes on her exposed back. He finally brushed around the chair. His hot fingertips prodded at the base of her spine and found the zipper tab. The zipper purred softly past her lacy panties and bra as he slowly pulled it up. His hand lingered for a long moment on her warm back where she had scraped the pen against her flesh. Tracy felt his gentle touch on the swollen mark before finishing with the zipper. Kyle rested his reassuring, firm hands on her shoulders before giving them a gentle squeeze. He opened the door, closed it softly, and left without a word.

Friday, November 27
Jared: Gotta Hide This

His sprawling legs trembled as he looked down at himself unsteadily—hoping the body belonged to someone else. His jacket sleeves were still bunched at his elbows. A limp tie lay on his shoulder, still tight at his throat. There was a quarter-sized scarlet stain on his light blue shirt. Tentatively exploring inside, he found that the undershirt was indeed ripped. He pulled the damaged T-shirt a little to one side to dab gently at his chest. His mouth filled and he forced himself to swallow, fought with his stomach to stay calm.

He panicked at the thought of being found there, cowering on the floor like a badly beaten dog—a pathetic heap. *How could he hide all this?* He could have bitten himself. People do. But there was no hiding the blood on his chest. After shrugging out of his jacket, he rolled onto his hands and knees then got his feet under him. When he sat back on his heels the pain called out a raw ache that radiated from deep in his stomach and out his back. It felt like barbed wire was being pulled through his belly and out the other side.

Even the top of his head hurt. He reached up to rub the sharp echoes of pain away, and his hand returned wet and red. The room floated and rolled. The chair he reached for strangely flowed away, left him queasy. The harsh coldness of the dirty floor fought with the painful heat in his mouth, his stomach, his back, his chest, his head. His eyes watered. Uncontrollable tears dribbled down his face. He fought to convince himself he was overreacting. *Only tiny points of pain and only little bits of blood, Jaden.* But his mind couldn't convince his body—it refused to hear the message of reassurance as he swallowed more thick blood. He slowly stood then bent, his hands gripped at his knees as he fought to control his stomach.

Kyle came in as Jared lurched for the trashcan and threw up. He lifted the can quickly and hugged it to hide his chest. Bits of Mrs. Pierce's cookies slobbered past crumpled paper and across the slick cover of a discarded catalog. At least there would be no need for a lame excuse for leaving. He wasn't well—obviously. Jared lowered himself to the floor and fell onto his rump with a thud, still cradling the can in his arms.

"What the hell went on in here?" Kyle snarled. He glared down at Jared as if he were angry.

What the hell did Kyle have to be mad about? A dirty trashcan?

"Just got sick to my stomach. See?" Jared leaned the can in Kyle's direction.

"Okay, smartass." Kyle grabbed the can and set it down with a steely clatter. "You've gone too far this time. *Way* too far." Kyle's voice pounded as Jared brought his hands quickly to his chest to hide himself. He struggled to hold his head still, trying to focus on Kyle's words. "I can't cover you on this one." Kyle's mouth moved and words fell on him like sharp sleet.

Can't cover for me? What is he saying? Jared grabbed at the dark heap that was his suit coat, struggling to his feet with his back to Kyle. He fully buttoned his suit and pulled his tie to one side to cover the scarlet on his chest. Kyle talked, but it was only babbling. Jared pressed his palms to his face, then turned to face Kyle. He hoped whatever sounds he forced from his mouth would make sense.

"Not sure what to say. Just feeling pretty sick is all." Blood glided around his tongue as it sought to nurse the pulsating wound. Metallic moisture slipped quietly down his throat. Jared forced his mouth closed so Kyle wouldn't see, lifted his hand to hide the pink oozing.

"Yeah, I'd say you're pretty sick all right. Get your black ass outta' here. I'll deal with you later. Unbelievable. What were you thinking? Are you high on something?" Kyle's harsh words rose above the happy melody vibrating around them. When the music stopped, he abruptly fell silent—gave Jared a smoldering look.

"You little shit," Kyle said quietly before turning on his heel and marching from the room. Jared could hear Mrs. Matthews and Mrs. Nolan laughing as they passed the closed door toward the bathroom. They would be talking about him. Wondering where their little Jared had gotten off to. Music began beating into the room again.

Jared wiped his mouth with the back of his hand and sat heavily onto his office chair. He took out his handkerchief and wiped frantically at his favorite pen, the sturdy shoe box, the arms of his chair, his face. He put everything in its place, even so, normal didn't return to the familiar space. He held the handkerchief to the inside of his mouth and allowed it to drink bright red blood. Bile rose in his throat and he dry heaved into the handkerchief until his stomach relaxed.

Finally, he made his way to the door and pulled it open a crack. A foxtrot rhythm flooded past him and he caught slivers of color on the dance floor at the corner of the hallway. He hurried to the coat rack, threw his coat over his arm and fled out the back door. God forbid that anyone see him.

Put the car in gear, step on the gas, stay in the right lane. He focused intently on the license plate of the car ahead of him, the yellow lines on the road, on the brightness of the red at each light. He crept up to his second floor apartment, dreading the possibility that someone would see, that someone would ask, someone would wonder what happened. Someone would know.

Saturday, November 28
Jared: Buzzards in the Bedroom

In the quiet dark of 3:00 a.m., just when Jared was drifting to sleep, Tracy's face was on his again, bouncing his head against the wall. And the entire event played in his mind, for the hundredth time. He was still trying to force it all into some sense, it was too ugly to have really happened, but it had. Even uglier than the event, though, was knowing she had choreographed their time together, had planned it well.

When she first pressed against him, he thought she was only having a little rough fun, just kicks. Women had forced themselves against him before: lifted a silky thigh between his legs, rubbed at him aggressively. Rarely, but it happened. Those women, however, had backed off when Jared didn't respond the way they hoped. It was always awkward, not being able to please them. Even so, he had always corralled his urge to comply and politely made it clear he didn't play rough. It had always ended there.

Not with Tracy. Her kiss was abrupt and acrid, like having wet ashes shoved in his mouth. She tasted cold. Then hell broke loose. So fast. His brain, stunned by her quickness, caught up well after she had total control. His anger should have taken action, but, instead he had tumbled into muddled confusion. It swallowed him and he had sluggishly watched her as though he was watching from a distant place, not hearing her at all, not wanting to care, or feel, or think about what was happening.

Even now, hours later, her smell and taste clung to him. He lay in bed, envisioned himself doing things he wished he had done, should have done: shoved her off, hit her savagely, left the room. The man he should have been had reported it to Kyle and Hollie. Only, he hadn't done any of those things; instead he had remained quiet, motionless—with the power and determination of wet bread. He did nothing.

He rolled in his bed, stopped suddenly when his stomach twisted out a pain that radiated from his bruised back to his navel and back again. He lay still, pulled at small frayed thoughts in the darkness. He had to have given Tracy a reason, something to make her think he wanted that kind of experience. He had to have. He couldn't remember saying anything. Something he did? His thoughts jumbled about and left him. Struggle as he would, he couldn't make sense of what happened.

His tongue wouldn't stop massaging the swollen raw wound inside his mouth. It was pulsating and tasted of blood. The woman was sick. He should have stopped her. But what would he have done differently? Call for help? Like that would make sense. Bring everyone running to see him dangling under her like a stick puppet?

No one would have believed him anyway. No real man lets a girl beat him up, especially not a black man. And no girl makes a guy bleed. Not ever. He'd never hear the end of it if this ever got out, especially from Kyle. He was still afraid he had been seen. Acid rose in his throat, and his mouth watered uncontrollably. He coughed the moisture into his fist and pushed the memory of throwing up away yet again. Ignoring his bruised stomach and back, he fought off the heavy blankets and sat up. Where were his pillows? They had left him. He rubbed the back of his neck with both hands, pulling at the taut cords. The tight knots found there snapped under his heavy fingers.

He mindlessly rubbed his head and confronted a spongy bump there. The soft start of a scab peeled away, releasing sticky blood yet again. He cursed himself for momentarily forgetting what it was and tapped the wet seal back in place. He shivered in the cold and dug about under the covers for the undershirt he had struggled to rid himself of an hour earlier. He had been fitful and hot then. As he jerked the shirt down to cover himself, his fingernail carelessly raked across the cut on his chest. *If there's blood on this shirt in the morning, I'll trash it too.* All of his clothes lay crumpled together in the garbage bag that lay abandoned in the hall just outside his apartment door. He flinched at the thought of losing his suit, blood-soaked dress shirt, molested tie, the glorious gold and red striped socks, and his shoes. His shoes—his new buttery-rich leather shoes. *Maybe I should go get the bag. What if someone looks inside and sees my clothes? They'll know they're mine and ask questions. God, Jaden, stop. Who would look in a tied up garbage bag?*

He pressed his fists firmly against his eyes, trying to force the sight of Tracy out of his head, but she, and her cruelty, were still there in the strobes between the blackness. Her taste clung to the wetness in his nose. Her sour breath filled the room, and his mind hit replay yet again. The vinegary kiss, her fingers pulling his ear, struggling to think, sudden swift pain, the embarrassment of an erection…

His thoughts swirled. More questions than thoughts really. Dark dots and dashes, like a thousand frightened blackbirds, a few settled long enough to make sense, only to leave him more confused. *Why didn't I just shove her off? Fight back? Just leave?* She had sucked at him, not just his body—him. She had dragged him off somewhere. This wasn't him. He was self-assured, confident, cocky even. Jaden liked and admired Jared as if he were thinking of someone he knew. He didn't want to peel back the thoughts of Jared and confront him fully.

A toilet in the apartment above flushed, and he could just hear padded footsteps overhead. The darkness was suffocating, enslaving. Maybe he had died. Maybe he was lying under the streets of Paris stacked up with other corpses, buried in the dark, just listening to happy tourists walking the sidewalks. He didn't remember dying, but he didn't remember being born. He couldn't be dead. Dead wouldn't make his entire body ache. He fumbled under the covers for the half-empty bottle of vodka that had crept into bed with him.

He'd visit Gran. Her soft healing hugs and chatter and laughter, today and again on Sunday. Yes, he'd go to Gran. She'd rub his head and sing, and…and ask him how he cut the top of it. She'd rub it and ask. She wouldn't take a reason that made no sense. She would know. She could sense trouble. Best to wait. Tell her he was too sick to visit.

He groped for the lamp and flicked brightness into the room. Hours earlier he had pummeled his pillows as he raged out his anger. They lay in a cold defeated heap on the floor, crumpled and aching like he and Eugene had been as little kids. Jared wouldn't think about that. He just wouldn't. But he could hear the dust mites sucking his skin off the feathers in the pillows. *To hell with them, the bastards, the buzzards.*

He blinked at the strange normalcy of the rest of the room, then pulled open the drawer of the nightstand. He gingerly pushed the loaded gun aside and took out the framed photo of Christine and him dancing at the gala forever ago. He pulled his finger down the length of her image and smiled at how joyful she looked. He had made her smile. Her image swam in his hands and the photo trembled back into the drawer.

He pushed the box of twenty unopened letters to Tanisha aside as his fingers prodded for the old cell phone that was kept charged and ready. He flipped the phone open and pushed the familiar buttons, frantic to find the photograph. The baby's eyes glowed up at him like warm drops of honey. He reached in the drawer again and pulled out a blue teething ring, brittle and cracked with age. He put it around his fingers and caressed the dry cracks.

Jared stared at the baby in the phone for a long time, pulled his legs up toward his chest and cradled him in his hands. A sudden sharp cry escaped. He sobbed at the little face, brought it to his cheek and held it there. The empty sheets desperately wiped at him till his heaving body slowed and stopped. The phone finally flipped shut and clattered back to the drawer followed by the teething ring. He reached in again.

He gently lifted the gun and felt its cold heaviness in his hand.

Monday, November 30
Jared: Calling in Sick

"We tell lies when we are afraid... afraid of
what we don't know, afraid of what others will
think, afraid of what will be found out about us.
But every time we tell a lie, the thing that we
fear grows stronger."

— Tad Williams

He finally took a shower, the first since Friday night when he had frantically washed himself in the hottest water he could stand. Scrubbing, lathering, scrubbing again till his dark veneer had reddened and ached. This morning, after his shower, he tried to shave, except his hand wouldn't stop trembling. The razor threatened his slack jaw. He couldn't stand to look at that face, his hollow eyes. After several failed attempts, he finally covered the top of the mirror with one of his crayon drawings from the week before—orange and brown dancing lines that whispered the past. It hid the reflection of his eyes. He forced himself into his typical morning routine: selected a suit, a shirt, socks. Normal routine. When the ties shrunk back from his extended fingertips, he grabbed a handful and tossed them in a crumpled heap on the bathroom counter. He focused on the button at his neck then knotted the first tie slowly, concentrating on the silk rather than on the unsteady fingers that guided its movement. The tie whimpered to be freed. He yanked it off and let it slip to the floor, then reached for another. Twenty minutes later, empty-handed, he ripped the paper from the mirror and confronted the man who hid there.

"Stop it, Jaden. Stop letting this get to you." He said it loudly and watched the mouth move the words into the space between himself and the man he was staring at, the man he had become. "You will get dressed, and you will go to work, and you will tell Kyle what happened." For several moments, Jared got lost in his own reflection. Finally, he forced himself to bend down and pick up a tie, any tie. His victim lay in his hand, limp and sacrificial. He put it on slowly, tightened it at his throat. He looked at himself in the mirror, then savagely tore the tie from his throat and left it lying lifeless with the others on the floor.

He'd take one more day. One more day to think things over. He'd call in sick. Just today. It was after noon so he was already late anyway. He tossed his shirt onto a heap of beaten blankets as he made his way through the bedroom and into the living room to find his phone. It was hiding among the empty bottles on the coffee table. He sank onto the couch and tried to steady the device, practiced talking aloud as his finger stuttered across its face. He poked at the icon several times before he successfully activated the phone, scrolled to the studio, jabbed at the number. Damn, the phone was ringing. He'd have to sound sick, but better than he felt.

"Hey, Donna. Yeah, it's Jared." He didn't listen to the words she said, he listened to her voice. Her voice sounded normal, like an ordinary day. Any ordinary day.

"What's that, Donna? I'm sorry. I'm not feeling well... Yeah. She is? She's there? Yeah, okay." He waited. He had heard Donna that time. He forced himself to stand, tried desperately to frame up what words to say to his employer.

"I was afraid you might do this. Calling in sick at a time when you should be here to talk. We need to talk, Jared." Mavis's sharp words stuck in his ear.

"Hey, Mavis. How's it going?" Jared said uselessly.

"Kyle called me this morning and I came in special just to talk with you both about what happened Friday night. I just can't believe this. Really I can't."

"So Kyle told you what happened on Friday?"

"Well he had to, didn't he? Kyle is the general manager of the studio, Jared. He's not your pal. He's not your buddy, is he? This is terrible. What if this girl presses charges?"

"Presses charges?" Jared heard himself ask. His knees jelled up, he fell back onto the couch and grabbed at a bed pillow that had wandered out into the living room during the night. It was clenched over and over in his fist.

"Look, Jared. This is serious. You're doing a great job here as an instructor. Students ask for you by name. You've brought a lot of business to the studio and your paycheck reflects that. It does, right? I pay you well." Mavis didn't wait for a response. "But I told you that you had one chance to show me that there'd be no more trouble from you. I didn't give you a time limit on that chance. This isn't a DUI, or drug use, but if this girl presses charges, you're no longer employed here." Mavis suddenly stopped. He heard her office chair squeak.

"No! Donna, not now. I'm on the phone with Jared. For Pete's sake, I'll be with you in a minute." Mavis's brittle voice rose above her normal irritation level.

"Okay, listen carefully to what I'm saying. Are you listening, Jared? You will get over to the bookstore and apologize to that girl today. Today, do you hear? No…No, here's a better idea. You write her an apology and walk it over to her and let's all hope to God she doesn't press charges. I don't care how sick you are, you get in here this afternoon and just do it." She hung up.

Jared wished he had the guts to call her back and quit his job loud and rude. He didn't. What would he do without his job? How could he make his rent? His car payment? Phone? His clothes? His beautiful clothes. He had thrown out his new shoes Friday night. *Idiot.* He liked his work. He was damn good at his work. His students loved him. "They love me, yes?" he said aloud, softly.

His wobbly legs knocked at the coffee table as he made his way to the bathroom to stare at himself again. He pulled his lip out and examined the swollen bite. It looked like a deep red crater with an angry yellow lava rim. He pushed some of the yellow onto a tissue. How many times had he bitten it back into bleeding since Friday? Over and over. It looked no better today than it had that night. It actually looked worse. The cut on his chest was not much better either. Like the scab on his head, he kept snagging it, ripping it open. Jared's finger gently rubbed at the new soft scab that lay under his T-shirt.

He missed Gran. He had called her yesterday morning. She thought he was calling to see if he could go to church with her to meet that girl, Sharon. He would have loved doing that. Instead, he told Gran that he was sick, and he did what he had done all day Saturday—sat on his butt and drank himself sleepy and stupid.

He had planned to do the same today, except now Mavis had delivered her orders. He was out of vodka anyway. His stomach heaved at the thought of writing an apology to Tracy. It would be helpful to know what Kyle had told Mavis about Friday. How could he write an apology without knowing? How could he look at Tracy without throwing up? Taking her by the throat?

He made his way to the kitchen, shook out a bowl of corn flakes, splashed in some milk. The milk had soured to tangy. The entire bowl was tossed into the sink. He was surprised to see the crayons and the artwork at his table; he didn't remember drawing. The papers were filled with reds and black and bright Tracy-pink. Jared grabbed up the papers and crumpled them into the trashcan. *Drunken idiot.* The lid slammed closed with a harsh clang.

He cleared a place at the kitchen table to write the damn apology. An apology. The thought turned his stomach again, this time worse than the smell that lingered in his nose and the taste loitering in his mouth from the sour milk. How was he going to find the words for an apology? Take it to the bookstore and give it to Tracy? Stand there and watch her read it? Watch her smile?

The kitchen chair screeched angrily across the floor as he reached for paper and a pen. He sat at his kitchen table and waited for words to come. The pen loomed over the clean bright paper, a dark glob of dry inky fuzz clung to the tiny ball as it threatened to smear its darkness onto the page. He brought the pen up close to his face and studied the teeny-tiny ball of the pen where his own skin flakes stuck together there with the ugly ink. The pen sunk toward the page again, but it froze just above the paper. Jared finally pulled in a deep breath, closed his eyes, and felt his breath escape across his motionless hand.

He set the pen down and reached for his crayons, found the box nearly empty. Several crayons were hiding under a greasy cold pizza box, three of these broken. Four more had slid under his stack of fresh paper and he found several more rolling about under the table. A pale green had been crushed and lay in its own bits under his chair. He gathered the scattered children up and arranged them by color back into their protective home, still five missing from the family reunion. He fingered the tops of the few that were still new, their shiny flat points glistened.

Jared sat and listened to the emptiness, remembering the harsh, raspy whispers she had thrust at him. *What had Tracy said, Jaden? Stop thinking about what happened. Think about what she said. Her words.* He laid the crayons down gently and took up the pen. He made a small dash on the fresh clean paper and wrote:

She knows about Gran, but I told her about Gran.

She knows that Gran walks slow, so she watched me and Gran.

Jared stopped and stared at the written words. He never told Tracy where Gran lived, but she had watched him with Gran. Tracy had followed him to Lebanon and watched them— probably knew where Gran lived. He felt angry that Gran had been violated by Tracy's eyes. He twisted the pen back and forth against his thumb and forefinger. Jared added to his list.

She doesn't want me to see or teach Christine. She threated Christine.

Jared stopped again and looked at the word "threated." He was certain he hadn't spelled it right. Mavis wasn't there to correct him. Mavis wasn't there to tell him to comb his hair, make him brush his teeth, or force a damn tie around his neck. He took up his pen and scratched over the misspelled word till the dark spot ripped through the paper. "Threatened," that was the word he meant, but there was now only a dark hole where the word should be. His loved ones were threatened.

He pushed himself from the table, stood and looked out the kitchen window into the parking lot. He studied his car, parked cockeyed in a spot reserved for visitors. He never parked his car there. Never. His jaw hurt. *Think about Tracy's words, Jaden.* Tracy had threatened Gran and Christine. Another memory slowly seeped through: Tracy had called him Jaden. She knew he was Jaden Gregory. Tracy knew a great deal.

Jared leaned against the counter at the sink. He closed his eyes and steadied himself with both hands as he bent at the waist. Tracy knew his real name, and she had used it as she threatened the two people he cared most about. She had said something else too, but try as he might, there was no capturing Tracy's parting words from Friday night.

He opened his eyes and was confronted with the sight of his sink. It smelled of sour milk and rancid grease. Bits of wet cereal were drying slowly to the side. The bowl and spoon sat perched on layers of cold dirty dishes, silverware, cups, glasses. Wet and slimy. The sight, the smell, and the thought of that sink, reminded him of Tracy. "Damn you," he choked out. He tore at a paper towel and attacked the speckled bits of cereal. He flushed the sink's contents with a quick burst of water. The dishes stayed put, wet and ugly.

The bookstore wasn't open on Monday. He dropped the tattered paper towel in the sink. The sudden realization embraced him like a soft hug. The bookstore wasn't open on Monday. He could call Mavis back and explain that he couldn't do what she asked, not today. Tracy wouldn't be there today. He'd call Mavis and be sweet, and tell her how sorry he was and that he would work on his apology for Tracy. He'd tell her that he'd be there tomorrow. Tomorrow afternoon and everything would be okay.

Although Mavis seemed as annoyed at his second phone call as his first, she couldn't argue with his logic to delay. Jared pushed his luck a bit by letting her know that he really was sick and he really wouldn't be able to work today. Mavis checked his schedule and saw that he only had Mrs. Jenkins late in the afternoon. She said Kyle could take that lesson, but reminded him that he had already missed his lesson with Mrs. Matthews.

"By the way, Jared. We lost a couple students today. I just got off the phone with Donavin Bayer. He canceled all scheduled lessons for him and Christine O'Garra. You remember, she's that woman you danced with at the charity gala. I told him there would be no refunds, but he didn't care. Just paid off the entire contract and canceled all future lessons."

"Did he say why?"

"Didn't explain, just said he needs to talk with you when you get back. Fortunately, I told him you had called in sick today. Probably wants to thank you for giving them quality instruction." There was a brief pause. "There's no reason to think he's upset, is there?…Is there, Jared?"

"No, Mavis. I have provided Donavin and Christine my normal high-quality instruction," Jared said as firmly as he dared.

He could hear Mavis drumming rhythmically at something. Her chair squeaked again followed by the soft rap of a door closing.

"Jared, this is just crazy. You are an excellent dance instructor. That apology better be good. Get in here tomorrow with it already written. I'll look it over and correct your mistakes. Then you will rewrite it onto a proper notecard and hand deliver it to that girl…with Kyle." There was a lengthy pause. "And Jared, I've made the decision that you are on leave without pay for two weeks. It doesn't matter if she presses charges or not, your behavior was inexcusable. Right here at the studio. Inexcusable." Another abrupt hang up left Jared staring numbly at his silent phone.

He sat quietly at the kitchen table, and then wrote the apology just as if he meant every word. It was freeing to realize that it didn't matter what words he used. Mavis would change it all anyway and he'd re-write her words carefully for Tracy to smile over. He'd play Tracy's game, or pretend to. Jared could be very good at pretending, too.

Desperate for a cigarette, he found a half-smoked stub in the kitchen. It was straightened and relit. He was out of booze. Got to get to the store. Too early. Too sick.

The drug dealer on the first floor whispered up through the floor. The craving for cocaine, the overpowering itch, had to be ignored, over and over throughout the day, and especially at night.

"It's no big deal, Jared," the itch was saying. "Pull in a few sweet lines of white confidence. Feel that lively cocky pleasure for one sweet hour," it said. "Energize," the first line said. "Just once more," echoed the line beside it.

Jared pushed the sound away. But the pothead on the third floor would be happy to share a joint. Sometimes Jared got a strong whiff of it in the stairwell and he'd pull in the drifts as he climbed the stairs. A rush of mellow desire flooded through him.

"You won't care if you get high, Jaden. Just fade away,"

it sang.

Up through the floor, down through the ceiling, the foul lullabies came. Not daring to eavesdrop longer, Jared shoved the memory from his nose, pushed it from his head. He snatched up his lanyard from the bowl in his bedroom and headed to his car.

The closest liquor supplier was just past the hospital, only a couple of miles away. Jared had stocked up there only last week. A homeless man, just inside the door, softly asked for money as Jared entered, but he slipped outside before Jared could dig in his pocket. The tattered man stood outside begging at someone else. Jared made his purchases, held back his change. It was cold, and the wind whipped at his cashmere dress coat as he shifted his package to extend his small gift. The man quickly pocketed the money then grabbed at Jared's hand, smiled, and carefully placed a small folded paper into Jared's palm saying, "Bless you and have a Merry Christmas now, ya hear?"

Jared shook the hand that held his briefly and smiled back. "You do the same," Jared said before returning to his car. "Jesus saves" was written on the little white paper. Jared tossed it into the paper bag on the seat with the bottles, smokes, chips, and Twinkies. He should get real groceries, but he had what he really needed so he navigated a fast food drive-thru then headed home. Home—an empty apartment.

Tuesday, December 1
Tracy: Apology Accepted

Nora had forgotten the Christmas decorations at her house, again, and had just left to get them when the bookstore phone rang.

"Oh, hello, Kyle." Tracy forced herself to smile so her voice would sound genuinely pleased. "Well, I guess so. I mean, there're no customers right now, so it would be okay…No, my aunt isn't here." Tracy then smiled a real smile and said, "Really, Jared wants to apologize? Well, of course it would be all right. Yes, this is a perfect time. I'll see you in a few minutes then." Tracy hung up and hugged herself. Jared had remained quiet, lied about Friday night by remaining silent about the truth. *But an apology? Seriously? Who does that?*

She allowed herself the quick pleasure of clicking on the edited sound file she had just created—a recording of the events in the lounge on Friday. The only sounds she kept were his frightened squeaks, smack-filled sucking noises, and soft coughing. Lots of soft, moist coughing. As she listened, she wondered if a ringtone could be created with the sounds—assign it as his ringtone. She reluctantly closed the file and Jared was sucked back into the hard drive. Tracy admired her keyboard as she shut down the computer—all the lettering had worn off from the scratching of her hard nails. She checked to be certain her new acrylic nails were all firmly attached and smiled. "You are one very special girl, Tracy," she said aloud as she stood to straighten her tight, short skirt and fluff her hair.

She stepped out into the store area and watched both Kyle and Jared as they walked past the exterior glass wall. Kyle opened the front door for Jared and the bell jingled merrily. Music was playing softly overhead, Bing was dreaming of a white Christmas. Jared entered the store carefully, looking at his feet as if he were stepping into a busy dog park. He looked ghastly. Red watery eyes. Unshaven. Nonetheless, he squared his shoulders and looked directly at her. Tracy was a little surprised at his ability to boldly make eye contact. Kyle was still wiping unseen dirt from his shoes onto the mat. Tracy quickly winked, then smiled at Jared who lowered his head and turned back toward Kyle.

"Well?" Kyle said harshly, as if to a disobedient child.

Jared turned back toward Tracy. "Could I talk with you for a minute?"

"Sure, of course. Come into my office, it's more private." She smiled, placed her fingernail into her mouth and caught Jared's eye as she turned. His eyes snapped away.

The moment she turned at her desk to face him, Jared thrust an envelope toward her. She leisurely sliced it open with her nail, read it slowly. Jared had brought her a sweet little written apology.

Tracy glanced up at Kyle who stood behind Jared, his slightly bowed face was flush and his eyes searched her for a reaction. Kyle had obviously been told to escort the little monkey over to her. Hold Jared on a leash to be certain the apology was sincerely delivered and that the perverted animal didn't bare his teeth at her. It was a delightful moment.

"Well, this is lovely, Jared. I didn't expect to receive an apology from you at all, so this is very nice. A nice surprise," Tracy said quietly with as much sincerity as she could manage. She looked up from the note at him, and waited. Jared remained silent until Kyle pulled at Jared's chain via a sharp poke to his back. Jared visibly winced. Kyle must have hit a tender spot bruised since Friday.

Jared dutifully responded to his prompt. "I…I don't know what came over me. I guess…I guess I lost control. Very unlike me. I'm very sorry." Jared's eyes flashed at her for a moment, then he held his head upright, stiffened his back and stared steadily at the wall behind her. Kyle's face beamed over the back of Jared's squared shoulder. His monkey was performing nicely—well trained. *Nice, Kyle. Very nice.*

"Well, I really…" Tracy's voice cracked. She looked away quickly as if struggling with tears. She was struggling not to laugh, but that would never do. Tracy kept her back to her guests, placed her hands on her cheeks and pulled them across her face and down under her jaw slowly. She stepped over to the couch and rested her hand on the back cushion before she finally got control of her emotions and turned to face the boys of dance.

"I'm ready to forgive you, Jared," she said. Keeping her voice even and steady, she stepped toward him. His feet shuffled back from her slightly. Fortunately, his trainer was close at hand. She caught the sight of Jared's firmly clenched jaw and flinching narrowed eyes as she bound him in a hug. His body was stiff and unyielding. He lifted a heavy rigid arm in a proper gesture of response and touched her back only lightly, briefly. She whispered soft and quick in his ear, "I'll be in touch. We'll get started very soon." His face was glistening when she released him. His averted eyes never left the carpet as he turned without another word and hurried out of her office. Tracy followed him out into the store area and watched him leave. The bell on the door jingled gaily as his image hurried past the glass panel wall outside. Burl Ives was having a Holly Jolly Christmas in the ceiling.

"He's really sorry, Tracy. He's embarrassed. I hope you can see that," Kyle said behind her. Tracy turned and watched Kyle search her face. She returned to her desk with Kyle trotting at her heels. He was wagging his tail and trying hard not to jump up on her or lick at her hands. *Good boy, Kyle. Good boy.*

"Oh yes. I saw the Jared I thought I knew just now, the sweet Jared." Tracy studied the notecard again. The words were locked together neatly—they marched in perfectly straight lines across the page. Every word correctly spelled. It was a nice little piece of physical evidence proving that Jared had done something wrong. She might need it later. Mavis had made him write it—a very foolish move as a business owner. But Mavis had gotten Jared to comply, and that was good. *Good girl, Mavis.*

"Kyle…do we really know Jared?" Tracy asked as she closed the card and slowly returned it to the envelope. She set it on her desk and turned to look at Kyle who was placing weight on one foot then the other in a little swaying dance of nerves.

"He's not getting off lightly. He's on leave without pay for two weeks. Don't worry, he won't be bothering you again." Kyle rubbed the back of his hand and made soft scratchy sounds. "He'll lose his job if you press charges. You have every right to…but…but just so you know."

"Seriously? I'm not that fragile. And I don't want to hurt him, certainly wouldn't want to see him lose his job over this." Tracy smiled at Kyle who let loose a deep breath, open-mouthed.

It was perfectly true. She didn't want Jared to lose his job. She wanted potential clients to come to the bookstore then go over and watch her sexy little Jared dance. Evaluate her product first-hand. They could simply walk back to the bookstore at their leisure and pay in cash. Get on the schedule. It was perfect. Kyle rudely cut short her delightful planning.

"Mavis told me to offer you a full refund and a cancellation of your dance lesson contract. If you want."

"Oh, no…no, I want to learn how to dance. It just won't be with Jared…I'll…can I schedule my lessons when he's not working?" Tracy tapped at the envelope on her desk with her fingernail. "I love my lessons with you, Kyle."

The big puppy nearly licked her face, instantaneously wide-eyed, his bright smile bridging two pink cheeks. "I can arrange that I be your instructor from now on. Come over later and we'll schedule our lessons together," Kyle panted out. She wondered if neutering would curb his energetic twitching. He stood, bouncing slightly as if he wanted to say something more, only he couldn't make that big of a decision.

"Tracy?" he finally blurted out. "Tracy…can I have a hug too?"

"Of course. I'm sorry. You've been so nice through this whole mess." She hugged him and pulled away before he did. Kyle was easy. Kyle was predictable. Kyle was boring.

Tracy wished she was as certain of Jared. Yes, there was clear progress, except he'd been so controlled—had made eye contact, held his head up and squared those handsome shoulders of his. On the up side, he had complied with his employer's ridiculous demand to write and personally deliver an apology. Although his repentant appearance was only an act, he was motivated and had done exactly as he was told. That was good. Apparently, he needed his job—perhaps he even liked teaching dance to old ladies. And now Jared knew that it was she, Tracy, who controlled whether or not he could keep that job. Jared was complacent, Jared was quiet, and Jared was scared. That meant Jared was ready. Sweet Jared Garrison. Everyone's favorite dance instructor would now be so much more. It was time to tell him the good news, explain the details of his new work responsibilities.

Thursday, December 3
Jared: Four O'Clock Meeting

Was it dark or was the bulb out? Morning? *Just stop banging.*

"Stop banging!" Jared shouted at his apartment door. "Who the hell is it?" His head swirled and protested against the effort of creating and delivering words. Stale drunkenness held him on the couch. The tormenting noise continued to worry the door. Steady soft tapping, scarcely there, growing stronger, loud and persistent then suddenly softer again. No voice behind this endless banging.

The string of his sweatpants caught in his fingers as he rolled over to sit up. His stomach growled and tattered magazines slipped about under his rump. He stood wobbly and knocked his shin into the coffee table. The offensive obstacle received a soft curse.

The tapping continued, softly now.

"Stop. Just stop," he croaked as he steadied himself. He stumbled across his living room and flung the door open to confront whoever was there. Anything to put a stop to the banging. His eyes squinted and blinked into the harshly lit hallway and his head rolled in confusion as Tracy's pink coat brushed quickly past and into his apartment.

"Get out of my home." Jared's voice was barely a whisper. "Get out." Barely a sound at all.

Tracy stepped back to him and flipped the lights on at the wall plate. She pulled his hand from the knob and closed the door quietly. Her toast-colored eyes burnt at his face as she bolted and chained the door.

"Your home, Jared? This is an apartment. You don't have a wife and kiddies." She looked at him briefly then reached for his face with her hand. He jerked to one side. She paused and smiled at him, then backed away and looked about the room.

"I like what you've done to the place." Tracy opened the door to the coat closet then walked to peer into the kitchen briefly. She closed the living room drapes with a rolling purr.

"Get the hell out," escaped from between his teeth.

She orbited his living room then flipped on the light at the bedroom door. She stood smiling at his bed for a time then turned the light off again. Her presence sucked comfort from every place she paused to study, leaving Jared paltry snatches of air as his heart pounded. His eyes followed her every move about the room.

She turned and leisurely moved toward him again. Stopping briefly at the door of the half bath, she said, "Not too fond of the smell, though. It was much better smelling the last time I was here."

"When were you ever here, Tracy? Here in my apartment? I don't always remember things, but I would have remembered that," the unsteady voice pushed out.

The tower in pink drifted toward the huddled masses that were his living room furniture. She slowly unbuttoned her coat and flung it aside. Its glow stained the back of his couch.

"Oh, you weren't here at the time." Tracy lifted a pair of knit boxer briefs from the seat of a chair. "Nice color for you, Jared. Blue is a good color. Let's remember that." The underwear was tossed on the floor as she settled into the chair. "Have a seat. We need to talk about business."

"I have no business with you." Jared hadn't moved from the front door.

"Oh, of course you do. You'll soon have two successful and very satisfying careers. You'll be working for me and for the dance studio. I told you all this. Surely you didn't forget that!" Tracy provided him an exaggerated tilt of her head as she gazed at him.

"Why the hell would I ever work for you? Your bookstore never has customers."

Tracy threw her head back and laughed at the ceiling. Her feet delivered little stomps into his carpet. She rolled her head back and forth on the back of the uneasy chair and laughed as she watched him. Her waxen eyes never stopped watching him.

"Jared, Jared, Jaden." She laughed out his names. The ugly laughter ended abruptly. "It is Jaden isn't it? Jaden Gregory." She glared at him and suddenly stood. Jared flinched and focused on her movements as she circled him. She stopped and stood between him and the bedroom, wall-like. He pulled at short, shallow breaths watching her.

"Come on. You're a good dance instructor. Your students love you. No, they love the way you make them feel, not you, really. I see that. I actually respect how you tease their money out of them, but we both know some of them want much more from you. Something *off* the dance floor, Jaden. That's one reason you use a fake name." She studied her long fingers for a moment, stretched them, then she looked up at him.

"I asked Mavis for your address—rotten bitch wouldn't give it to me. Told me you didn't want students calling you, searching for you online, following you home. Now why would they do that?" She paused and studied him for a moment. "You know why. I know why. Let's get real—you could give them what they really want if it weren't for that silly dance studio policy. You'd be happy to please them if only you could. I found our short time together *very* pleasurable."

"I don't use my real name at work 'cause I'd rather keep my past arrests private. I teach women who wouldn't understand." Jared's eyes tried to locate his mislaid phone amongst the rubble on the coffee table. "And my students come to learn how to dance. That's all. They come to dance. I've never spent time off the floor with any of them and I won't start."

"You did with me, Jaden. Yes, you certainly did." Tracy chucked and thrust her chin sideways at him. "Got our time together on video, too." She paused. "But we don't want your current dance students to join in that type of fun; they'd talk. There are plenty of other women who'd love to spend time with you—lonely women who just want an enjoyable evening with a handsome man. And they need a man's touch. A real man, not some quick-bang kid in his twenties. They need a man who can make them feel special, someone who can satisfy them." Her dark hardness held him against the door.

"You can please them, Jared, and they'll pay for what you'll give them. Well, they'll pay me, then I'll pay you. And nothing changes at the dance studio. Everybody wins. Our ladies are happy, you're happy pleasing them, you get paid for your work, and you keep dancing. And I'll be happy too. That's important. Keeping me happy is very important. It's the most important thing you'll do from now on."

"You're crazy. I'm not doing that." Jared clutched at the knob at his back, but the door was securely bolted, locked. Jared glanced at his partially closed bedroom door. How many obstacles were between him and the nightstand drawer? Too many. The biggest one was Tracy. He considered taking her by the throat and throwing her out. He stared at his hands and clenched his fingers.

"Jaden?" Tracy took a step toward him. He responded with a flinch.

"Sit," she commanded.

Jared blinked at her. Her eyes drilled into him until he finally obeyed. The newspaper on the chair cushion crunched softly under him. "No...you sit on the floor," she harshly whispered, slap-like. He sat very still, quiet prey. She came and stood looming over him until he slowly slid onto the carpet. "Good. You stay right there and listen very carefully." She tapped the top of his head before working her way back into her favorite chair, her eyes never leaving his.

"This will only be as painful as you want it to be. You do exactly what I tell you to do, when I tell you to, and I'll do some things for you." He looked up at her, briefly, waiting.

"Here's what I'll do for you, okay, Sweetie? First of all, I'll be certain you don't lose your job teaching dance. Mavis likes you, really she does, except she has standards. No drugs, no DUIs, no fondling students in the instructors' lounge like you did with me at the bookstore. It's a great video by the way." Tracy paused and quickly added, "Oh, and I've got another video of you shoplifting at the mall. Maybe Gran would like to see them sometime. Maybe Mavis, huh?"

Jared lowered his chin and studied a stain on the carpet.

"And I got some great photos of you buying cocaine outside the liquor store the other afternoon. My salesman had to wait quite a while for you to show up, but you finally came." She smiled at him. "Mavis would be especially upset to see those photos, and we don't want to upset Mavis."

"I didn't buy any cocaine. I haven't bought cocaine or used for years. Mavis makes me get drug tested whenever she wants. She says go to the clinic and I do. Sent me over there on Tuesday to pee in a cup."

Tracy laughed. "Well, Mavis has business sense. Yes, she does. I like that Mavis. Might take a clue from her and have the clinic run regular tests on you, too. Lots of nasty STDs out there and I need to make sure you stay clean and healthy for our customers." Tracy extended her hand and picked at a long red nail.

"Jared, you need to learn to listen to me. I said I had photos of you buying cocaine—I never said you actually bought any and I never accused you of using. No need to start again, is there? Waste perfectly good snow on you and put your job at risk? Besides, you can't do your best work if you're jazzed up and sloppy with our clients. Wouldn't make sense, now would it? Course, later, once you're making money to pay for it, it wouldn't hurt to let you take up a line now and then, especially when you need to work long hours."

Jared remained quiet, waiting for what he knew she would say next. She didn't fail him.

"And here's what else I'll do for you, Jaden. I'll leave your granny alone and I'll leave sweet Christine alone, too. You stay off Meridian Street and I'll let Christine play house all cozy and peacefully alone. Why is she always alone, Jared? I've seen you on her street plenty of times. I park at the armory and walk over to watch you sit in your little black car. Why don't you ever go in and visit with your sugar-mama?" Tracy smiled and waited. "You're pitiful, really you are."

Jared had been listening very intently. He envisioned his pen jotting down her every word. From where he sat, he could see the bottom of the kitchen table and knew a pen and paper sat there waiting. He stared at the table intently.

"Look, I don't want to hurt Christine, she seems so nice and all. I'll let you decide if I need to pay her a visit. I will if need be." Tracy studied a dirty coffee cup that sat on the end table. She rubbed its rim with her fingertip. "I really don't expect all that much in return." Jaden said nothing.

"Money is tight for you I bet, you being off work and all, and right before the holidays, too." She stood and retrieved her coat from the back of the couch, slipped it on, buttoned slowly. "Tell you what, sweetmeat. I'll give you your Christmas present early. Just a little employee bonus before you even get started." Tracy reached into her coat pocket and pulled out a wad of folded bills, one hundred dollar bills. She laid the money on the coffee table, held it under her finger as she studied Jared.

"Leave it right here for you," she said. "We have an agree-ment now, Jared—you and me. You come to the bookstore on Monday night. The store's closed, but I'll be there. I've got our first customer ready and waiting, so we need to work out the details. What fancy hotel to deliver you to, and such." She sauntered to the door, unchained it, flipped off the light. The darkness is thickest when the lights go off, and in that darkness the voice said, "You will do what I say. You will do exactly what I tell you to do when and where I tell you to do it." Sound-lessly, she opened the door and left.

Jared sat very still for a few moments then made his way across the dark room to the window. He slowly pulled back a handful of drapes and waited until he saw Tracy on the side-walk. She crossed the lot and got into what he knew was her car. He stared at that car as it drove down the street—stared at it until it turned the corner and was out of sight. He let loose the breath he had been holding and tugged at the fabric in his fist. Grey shadows whispered and their huddled laughter echoed in his ears. He listened to the sound of air rush through his nose. His jaw tightened and he felt hot anger flash through his stom-ach and chest. Then slowly, he relaxed his fisted grip on the hapless drapery. His breathing became steady and strong.

Enough, he thought. *Enough.*

He managed to turn on the lamp then hurried to turn on every light in the apartment. He pulled open the microwave, the oven, the refrigerator to allow the light out. He needed light to flow inside him, needed his heart to start beating again. Needed to move and sweat and pull in deep breaths of air. Feel the flow of life. He headed to the bedroom to put on his running shoes, and then suddenly stopped in disbelief at the sight of his apartment. He wandered back into the living room, maneuvered the maze back into the kitchen.

Gremlins had invaded every crevice of his home. Crispy wads of balled tissues, like colossal popcorn puffs, littered the rooms. Cigarette butts sat broken and crushed in filthy plates that teetered on the end tables. More cigarette remains were crumpled in mounds on the tile floor in the bathroom, three in the bathtub, one floated in the filthy toilet. His broken headphones dangled like a dead squid from a doorknob. There were dirty dishes in his bed and empty vodka bottles everywhere—under his desk, at the foot of his closet, even one in an open dresser drawer nestled in a dirty wad of undershirts.

Jared picked a few things up, dropped them again in a kind of stupor. Could he have made this mess himself? His anger grew, and with it came energy, and he attacked his apartment with an enthusiasm he hadn't felt for days. He lovingly collected the vintage vinyl records that littered the floor, painfully threw out those that were cracked. The loaded dishwasher hummed and he sang. Jared dragged bulging garbage bags from every room, down the steps and pitched them into the parking lot dumpster with eager relish. He vacuumed, then scrubbed at his carpet with furious intent. Energy built up and grew as he worked—the laundry and ironing of his clothes, the folding of his handkerchiefs, the sorting and careful inventory and arrangement of his ties. He jerked a pink and red tie from the rack and tore it to shreds. The ties on the bathroom floor were scooped up and trashed.

There was no food, and he was hungry. It was a real, healthy hunger and he resolved to get to the grocery—buy decent food. Fresh fruit. Carrots. He dressed in jeans and a wonderfully clean crisp shirt and grabbed his keys out of the bowl on his dresser. His pocketknife glistened and he lifted it to study the face of Liberty and the wings of freedom on the cap. He smiled at the dime and slipped the knife into his pocket.

He was disgusted by what waited for him in his car. He had driven to get vodka on Monday, yet didn't remember the car looking anything like this. Didn't recall the degrading stench. The passenger seat was smeared with stiff slime, the gear shift knob was encircled by dried blood, and the smell, even in the cold, the smell was sickening. He opened all the doors and let it air out. He finally slammed all the doors and returned to the apartment to get what he needed. Even though it was bitterly cold, he cleaned out his car.

He checked under the seats and found ticket stubs, coins, a condom. Thank God, no empty liquor bottles. The glove compartment popped open. The only thing he ever kept there was the car registration, proof of insurance, and the dog-eared car manual. Nevertheless, today, everything was checked and made clean, including the never-used glove compartment. He stopped and stared at a strange red light that blinked out at him from the dark deep recess. He reached into the yawning compartment and lifted the dark box out carefully. Although he had never seen one, he was fairly certain it was a tracking device. A little gift from Tracy. Fine. At least now he knew how she had known where he lived, where his grandmother lived, where Christine lived, where he shopped for vodka.

Although the urge to rip it from his car and toss it into the dumpster was nearly overwhelming, he forced his hand to place it back into the dark depths of the glove compartment. He'd go

to the grocery, come home and think. F
good meal. He'd sit at the kitchen tab
and draw and write down all he knew
to get all the trash out of his life. All

Jared's phone trembled in his pocket and ne ...
out. A text from an unknown number. He took a second look
before deleting it.

"Congrats J. Pregnancy test positive and could only be
yours. Take good care of me. Love T. ☺"

Thursday, December 3
Jared: Lost Babies

Jared pulled into the parking lot of Gran's apartment com-
plex far too late for supper. The loaded gun was in his glove
compartment, snuggled up next to the tracking device. Tracy
would know he was in Lebanon.

No time for the cranky elevator, he took the short flight of
stairs where Eugene answered the door and greeted him with a
snort and his usual dismissive stare. He was holding a plastic
snap lid container, likely some morsel from Gran's kitchen.

"Where the hell have you been? Gran's worried sick." Eugene's accusation wasn't well hidden in the question.

Just say it, Euggie. Tell me I'm an ass—an idiot.

"Great to see you too. Where are the kids?" He needed to
see the kids—needed their energy, and laughter, and life. But,

knew they weren't there—the apartment sat silent at the way.

"Claire took them shopping—Jeremy needed new pants for the Christmas program. Gran wants to be sure you have that date on your calendar and you don't schedule work or a party over it. It's a week from this Saturday. You think you can remember that? Need me to write it down?"

"I'll remember. Is Gran doing okay?"

"Could be better, but she's making it around. Says she can't find her potato peeler. Had to peel the potatoes with a paring knife."

"I guess if that's the worst thing happening, she's doing pretty good. I'll help her find it before I leave."

"Look, I gotta go. Not getting together for supper next week. Gran's church is wrapping Christmas presents for the homeless shelter that night." Eugene studied his brother a moment then added, "Hey, show up at the kids' program on time to pick her up, okay? That's not too much to ask, Jaden."

Eugene called out toward the living room, "Hey, Gran, I gotta go. I let Trouble in to sit with you a spell. Thanks for the cake."

"I'll make you pie at Christmas, Euggie," Gran hollered back.

Eugene delivered his kid brother a quick guy hug, paused in the hallway and turned. "Look, try not to keep her up too late tonight. She seems tired. And could you try not to cause her any more reason to worry?" With that, Eugene marched the length of the hall and disappeared down the steps.

Jared closed the door softly, feeling glad, yet a little guilty for missing supper with Gran and Eugene. The kids always provided plenty of noisy distractions to keep Eugene from beating on him about whatever improvement he felt Jared needed. Claire never hid the fact she was merely enduring a family obligation, quietly suffering through the time her children had to spend with their disreputable, and highly irresponsible, Uncle Jaden. Kids. He missed the kids. For the hundredth time today, Jared pushed away the possibility of becoming a father. *Tracy was a liar, yes? You give her power when you believe her lies.* But maybe she wasn't lying. He hoped she was pregnant. He hoped not. Hoped so. Hoped not. *Stop, Jaden, just stop.* He pushed himself away from the door and his torturous thoughts and made his way around the corner where comfort and peace sat waiting.

"Hey, Gran. Sorry I didn't make it for the meal." Jared leaned down and kissed his grandmother's soft face. "I left you a voice message about me coming late." His hand drifted gently across her crumpled paper bag cheek. The soft wrinkles disappeared under his fingers. "Eugene tells me you lost your potato peeler and that you're tired."

"Didn't lose my peeler. Claire stuck it some silly place at Thanksgiving. Just can't find it." They grinned at one another—enjoyed a little shared Claire ridicule.

"And the tired part?" Jared tilted his head and studied her. She did look tired. Tired and vulnerable. Even so, she raised her arms to him and struggled to stand just to hug him. Her hug. Jared felt himself melting into the softness of love as she held him then pulled him close the second time, and this time he did cry, just a little. Not enough that Gran would notice.

"Don't know anybody alive who's not tired now and then. No different for me," Gran replied as she sunk back onto the brave couch. Jared turned and surveyed the room to provide himself a secret wiping of his face. He quickly looked away from Granddad's ashes that now sat on a shelf at the far side of the room.

"Maybe I should make my visit short so you can get to bed," Jared said.

Gran said nothing behind him. Nothing was said by either of them for a time.

"You need me to look at your feet?" His hand secretly wiped yet another tear. He could feel her watching.

"Mrs. Milligan took good care of me this morning already and she's comin' back at bedtime too."

Jared finally turned and looked beyond Gran at the mirror above the couch. His eyes were wet and his face looked like it had been smeared with molasses. There was no hiding the hurt reflected there. He placed his hands on that face and pulled them down his nose and across his shiny cheeks.

"That's good, Gran. That's good," he said as calmly as possible—a steady convincing voice. He finally sat on the couch beside her, then reached over and tapped at the sharp chip at his favorite ceramic flower that grew under the lamp. Gran studied him, and waited. She always knew when to just sit and wait. They listened to the dishwasher splashing and knocking. The glasses clinked. And clinked. And clinked.

"Gran? Did I do right by Tanisha? I mean…not Tanisha… the baby." He paused and sought her face. "Should I have made her…" Jared pulled the ceramic flower off the table and held it in his lap. He cradled it in both hands.

"That was my baby, Gran. I know it. I knew it then. And you knew it too, right?" Jared stared at the flower and tapped at the broken petal. "We never talked about it 'cause I was out drinking, and smoking pot, and being stupid, but we both knew it back then too."

Jaden noticed her eyes water up. She was digging for the tissues she always kept in her dress pocket as he steadily tapped on the chipped flower.

"You dropped your purse for me," he said. It was something he had always wondered. Really, always knew. He hadn't meant to say it out loud, and the words seemed to echo coldly. He couldn't take them back, so he sat and studied her some more. She looked at him uncertainly before she trembled a grin at him through her tears. She pulled at the side of her nose with her tissue.

"You dropped your purse on purpose ten years ago in the grocery store with Tanisha so I'd have time to look at my son." Jared said it firmly this time as he watched her, and he could see she understood. He saw it in her dark shiny eyes.

"Lord, I didn't think you knowed that. I did. I did just that. Dropped my purse so as you could study him some in that grocery cart." Her lips quivered as she rubbed at them with her tissue. A tear slipped out and Jared reached over to wipe it from her cheek. Her skin felt like a soft worn quilt under his fingers. Like the quilt she covered him with years ago.

"I'm sorry we never talked about the baby," her voice softly rushed out. "Bout the babies, really. The babies."

Although Jared started at the word "babies," she was right. There had been two babies, two lost children.

"Two lost babies," he said softly as his finger tapped the sharp petal. He gathered the misplaced thoughts about Tanisha and the children he had lost and looped them through his mind, yet again.

Gran's voice had turned bitter. He got there in time to hear her say, "…just like that hussy not tellin' you. She didn't lose that first babe…" She caught her breath, flashed a look at him through the corners of her eyes, and hurried on, "Never seen nobody wantin' babies more than you. Me and you never talked about that first bitty baby, or your little boy baby moved up to Chicago." She let loose a deep sigh.

Jared smiled sadly at her. "No, we never talked about the babies. Tanisha plenty, but never about the babies. Lost one, and gave the other away without a fight, not even a word." He set the chipped flower back on the table and turned toward her. She was studying him through her tears.

"I didn't do anything. I just let her go and take him away. I should have made her stay." Jared's remorseful words fell onto his lap and sat heavy on his open palms.

"You couldn't make her stay, Jadie. She wasn't ever the right girl for you. Never was quite right. Never wanted what you wanted and she cheated on ya." Gran wiped at her nose. "'Sides, what'd you do different? She didn't want you near that baby. You try to drive to Chicago and see him? When? How?" Gran patted at his trembling leg and rubbed at it. "She married to a fancy rich man and you trying to see their baby? You didn't have no money for him. Wouldn't have worked. Nothin' you could have done different." She gave his leg a final pat and left her hand there.

"I could have done something. Would be better than what I've got today, huh? Nothing's what I got by doing nothing."

Gran tilted her head then shook it at him. "Doin' something better than doin' nothing. 'Cept you couldn't have done nothing different."

"I let my son go live with his mamma without me. Let him go live with some strange man who better be loving him." Jared's voice caught in his throat; he paused. His teeth gritted as he turned his head away from his grandmother. His body rocked slightly, rocked back and forth as he breathed in deeply.

"He better be hugging him, and playing ball, and fixing him food, and reading to him. And talking. Just be with him, talking." Jared rocked and his tongue forced his clenched teeth open to probe the wound in his mouth. "Damn it, he better be." He reached over and took one of her cleaner tissues for himself. "And Tanisha. What kind of mama takes a baby away from his real daddy? That was one mean bitch." Jared winced as the angry curse flew from his mouth. Gran wouldn't approve.

"Can't argue with that. No, you say it right about that woman," Gran replied.

Jared sat deep in thought for a few moments rolling their conversation through his mind. His eyebrows pulled together as he turned to his grandmother—someone he trusted.

"What did you mean just now? You said Tanisha didn't lose that first baby. Gran, what did you mean? She and her mama were just getting home from the hospital when I got home from work that day she lost the baby. Didn't even call me out of work to be with her. She cried some, then got real quiet. Couldn't get her to start talking after she lost that first baby." Jared finally slowed his rambling and waited. Gran's watery eyes never left his face.

Gran stared at her lap. Her finger started tracing a big blue flower on her dress. "She murdered that little not-born-yet babe. Murdered it at the clinic and kept it secret from you.

Didn't want a baby, so she killed it. Heard it from her Aunt Mae when word was going around that she was expectin' the second time."

Jared sat stunned. "You didn't just say that. I'm not hearing this. Right?"

Gran just sat poking at the flower on her lap, tracing it round and round, waiting. Jared finally took in the words and studied them, the meaning, the timing, and he knew. He knew it was true.

"Tanisha had an abortion without telling me. You... you never told me?" Jared knew his voice was raising, but he couldn't pull it down. "Why, Gran? Why didn't you tell me?" Jared's angry voice shuttered through the words as he tried to calm them, hold them back.

"Would only add hurt on top of hurt, wouldn't it? You losing your hussy wife to a rich man and takin' your baby with her to share with him. You didn't need to know 'bout the first baby getting murdered. Now didja?" Gran patted at his leg quickly, then slowed her pats as Jared's breathing calmed. He sat very still as quiet tears streamed down his face. They fell on his shirt, they fell on his lap, they fell silently as he, and his beloved grandmother, reflected on their shared history, struggles, and loss.

"I'll never see my babies. I'll never see the little dead one, and the one in Chicago will never even know I'm his dad, never know I even exist."

"Oh, you'll see the first one for sure. Babies go to heaven. You'll see that one when you get there."

"All babies go to heaven? You sure?" Jared blinked. He'd never thought about where babies live forever. Just never thought about it.

"Course they do. Unborn ones, tiny ones just born, little runaround babies. All of 'em go straight to heaven. God don't send nobody to hell. Only go to hell when a person's old enough to choose to go there by not takin' God's own baby to love on."

Jared considered her words carefully then said, "Better a baby live in heaven than have a bad mama, a mama like Tanisha, or worse even…have a dad who just isn't there at all. Like me."

"Now you talkin' bad 'bout yourself and it's not so. You gonna make lots of babies the best daddy in the whole world someday. Know it for certain," Gran said, but Jared didn't hear anything more from his grandmother. He was thinking of Tracy.

"She's evil. She's cruel, and selfish, and evil. Should never be a mama to anybody. Better he wasn't born if he's not loved, if he's treated mean and hateful. Some women just shouldn't be mamas," Jared said with a steady determination. There were no more tears, and his hands had stopped shaking and he held them in his lap and rubbed at them. Gran sat and watched the hands work back and forth and forth and back. They both sat and watched the rubbing hands.

Jared finally said, "Tired of doing nothing. Not gonna do nothing any more. Just sit and let hurt roll over me. Not anymore. Letting evil people bring babies into the world unloved and hurting." He stood and looked down at his somewhat startled grandmother. She was brutalizing a wet tissue, clenching and re-clenching it.

She studied him carefully. The dishwasher angrily pumped at the dirty water as they looked at one another. "Can't do nothing about neither baby. Too late, and 'sides, doing something stupid worse than doing nothin'. Can be a lot worse," she said.

Her dewy compassion and calm presence threatened to smother his resolve. Even so, he said, "Won't know till I try." Gran, now far away, went on talking. Her voice was muffled, unheard, among his thoughts, his plan. Doing nothing was no longer an option.

He left Gran's apartment and headed north to Meridian Street. Christine's cat scampered into the dark street, its white bibbed chest flashed at the car's headlights. He had to brake quickly when the animal paused to spotlight its panic before darting up the steps to Christine's porch. Jared pulled into his normal spot in front of her house, turned off the car, and hunkered down in the darkness.

Thursday, December 3
Tracy: Night Tracker

Had she not warned him? Had she not made it clear not to go near that damn woman's house? But there he was in Lebanon. Nasty little cur. Yes, he went crying to his granny's apartment for hugs and kisses, and that was okay, but now he was at Christine's. His car had been sitting on Meridian Street a long time, far too long for a quick farewell peek into the widow lady's windows. Little voyeur was sitting in his car with binoculars to her bedroom window. Maybe he had finally weaseled his way inside.

Jared was hers, he had to be. She wouldn't allow him not to be hers, hers alone. She certainly wouldn't allow this Christine O'Garra woman to interfere. Obviously, her bad boy needed more training. Tracy felt the pulsing in her jaw and shifted in her chair as she pulled at her long dark hair. Tonight had been reserved for working on a bookstore website, developing a link for women who had a special interest in bonsai. Now she would have to travel to Lebanon and work her backup plan to deal with this deliberate violation of her orders. She opened her desk drawer and dug out a pouch of tuna.

Hopefully, Jared had sense enough to follow instructions after her delivery. If not, she would follow him in person. Perhaps another lesson at his apartment was in order over the weekend. Tracy sighed. She'd have to get off work.

Friday, December 4
Jared: Early Morning Delivery

Even though the heavy thump at his apartment door was loud enough to wake the entire second floor, it didn't wake Jared. Startled him, yes. After his body jerked, Jared shivered, and felt the cold sweat of dread radiate from him. He sat and waited with energized panic on the couch while the lamps glowed out their eerie buzzing light. He barely breathed as he listened for any other sound. When only silence followed, he crept to the securely locked door and peered out the peephole into the hallway. No one. He kept his eye at the door and waited. No sound. No movement. Nothing.

He worked his way around the furniture to the window and pulled back the drapes in time to see Tracy's car pull out of the parking lot. He flicked on another lamp and padded quietly to the door. He looked out one more time before finally twisting back the bolt and unchaining. He felt slight pressure and heard a small whispering brush at the bottom of the door as he cracked it open.

A cat lay at the foot of his door. Its lifeless body fell across the doorway as the door fully opened. Jared stared down at the white, clover-shaped patch emblazoned on its little black head. And although he couldn't see it, he knew the cat's chest was white, a brilliant beautiful white.

Friday, December 4
Jared: Murder on the Mind

Jared drove past the house on Meridian and turned onto the side street. For once, he was glad to see Donavin's fancy car in the back driveway. He circled the block near the armory and parked. It was time. It was time to sit and wait. She'd come.

He sat and watched the houses. Lights flicked on. Lights flicked off. Children were being tucked into bed the final time. The soft trembling glow of television sets. A dog barking. Families living together, breathing together, sharing stories of their day, their dreams, fears, tears, and laughter. Being one together. Jared started his car to warm himself. *Gloves would be nice, damn it.*

He looked in at the tracking device lurking in the deep glove compartment; it blinked out a steady beat. She'd come. She'd been here last night killing a cat and she'd come again. *Come and get me, Tracy.*

Jared bent his chin to his chest and studied the loaded gun on the seat beside him. He'd probably get caught, might even turn himself in. He saw his grandmother's face at the trial, his brother holding her in his arms glaring out his rebuke. Then prison. Not the county jail in Vincennes or Indy this time. No, this would be hardcore prison for a long, long time. Forever.

He'd been over all of this. He had made his decision. *Right? This or what? Do nothing? Then dance on demand for this woman? Be her puppet the rest of his life to protect the baby, protect Gran, protect Christine?* No, it was too revolting. At least this plan would be an end to hope that never materialized, never resulted in anything lasting. The pain of hope would stop.

Ninety minutes. He had sat at the armory waiting for ninety minutes. His phone vibrated and glowed on the seat. It pulsated against the gun briefly before Jared picked it up and read Tracy's text.

"ur at armory COG again. b at yr place 2 a.m.. must talk."

So Tracy wanted to talk and she was at the bookstore tracking him. And she didn't care that he knew. *No more secrets, Tracy?* But she wasn't in Lebanon and she wasn't coming.

He sighed in relief that his decision had to change, or at least be delayed, then drove the two blocks needed to park on Meridian Street under the warmth of Christine's house. The upstairs lights glowed out onto his car. Feathery snow continued to fall, blanketing Christine's street like a Christmas card—soft and pure.

Tomorrow Tracy would come and he would be here too—he'd finish something. He put the gun in his pocket, closed his eyes and saw himself waiting for Gran behind a heavy pane of prison glass as she hobbled to a heavy metal chair and lifted the phone to talk to him. He saw her place her crooked bony fingers on the glass, her watery eyes stared at him through his dirty reflection. The vision of her was very clear. Very real. *What was he thinking? What an idiot.*

He should have been man enough to stand up to Tracy. Man enough to return the gun to Donavin long ago. Man enough to talk openly to Christine. Man enough to make better choices for Gran, and for Eugene and Claire, for his nephews and bright-eyed niece. Damn it, if Tracy was pregnant, he had to be man enough to get the baby away from her and be a real dad.

His car door suddenly opened and Jared found himself striding across the street and up onto Christine's front porch. Before he could think, he pushed the doorbell—no sound from within. No lights, no movement. Christine and Donavin were probably asleep in each other's arms upstairs. Courage skittered off the porch, habitual fear nipping at Jared's heels. He stood on the wet sidewalk and looked up at the house helplessly. He had to return this stupid gun tonight or he'd do something he'd regret with the thing. Why didn't they answer the damn door?

He'd call them. He pulled his phone out to dial, then stopped. What was he thinking, calling Christine? It was now well after midnight.

He turned suddenly, seeing for the first time the trashcan at the street. It had "O'Garra" neatly written on it. Just like Christine to label her garbage can. Jared lifted the can and its emptiness bounced in his hand. Snow slipped from the top of the lid and plopped onto the sidewalk. Knowing Christine, she'd take the can in first thing in the morning. He opened the lid, tossed the loathsome gun inside, hauled up the hinged lid and let it fall shut with a sharp snap.

He hurried to his car to drive home. Just go home. Call Christine later and tell her where he had put the gun and apologize. Just tell her that he had returned the gun and that he was sorry for being an idiot.

A block down the street, he was shocked to see Christine's green coat walking toward him, but he didn't stop. Too late. Too panicky. Too much of an idiot. Except she was obviously awake at this late hour. He pulled over just short of the interstate and typed a text letting her know the gun was in the trashcan. She'd see it as she walked down the sidewalk, or in the morning. She'd finally have the damn thing and would give it back to Donavin. He'd have to call her and explain that he'd been an idiot. He watched his shaky finger push "send."

Friday, December 4
Tracy: Going Off Plan

Tracy didn't need the computer in the Bookworm Bookstore to know where Jared was. She made a few stops on the way to Lebanon and leisurely picked up a little late night fast food south of town. It was snowing and the wintery whiteness reflected off the street lights. Nothing stuck to the roads, only to the grass and trees. She planned to park at the armory as always and enjoy a stroll in the velvety darkness. If, on rare chance he wasn't at Christine's, she'd text him to let him know she'd be stopping by his apartment.

Fortunately, she saw the back of his parked car as she approached the armory. She pulled down an alley to circle the block behind him. This was new. Jared always parked on Meridian Street in front of Christine's house. Tracy crept her car slowly down the alley and settled onto a side street near Christine's to text Jared. Moments later, he pulled up into his regular spot. Tracy could barely see the back of his fuzzy little head, as she watched and waited. Jared did what he always did—nothing. Evidently a house call was needed to her little cinnamon stick later tonight. She sat a few minutes and watched him restlessly squirm in his car. Just when she decided to leave, he opened his car door. She cracked her own door as he slammed his. He hurriedly crossed the street toward Christine's house. This too was new. Tracy made her way in the dark behind her car then raced through two dimly lit backyards, the light snow crunching softly under her feet. She slipped quietly along the shadowy sidewalk of the house that stood directly across from Christine's.

Although Tracy could barely see him, Jared was standing on his pointy toes at the front door peering into the dark house. She gingerly moved away from the sidewalk and took concealed shelter against the neighbor's house. Jared left the porch and stopped briefly at a trashcan, then suddenly dropped something in. It clattered loudly. He closed the lid and hurried back to his car—tore off like a frightened bat.

Now this was fun. Tracy watched Jared speed toward town. He braked once far down the street, his tail lights glowed out red and round before he turned toward the interstate.

Tracy quickly raced across the street and opened the lid of the trashcan, then held her phone down into the can and poked a button to get light. There was a gun at the bottom of the empty can. Tracy couldn't suppress a giggle. *Jared, Jared, Jared. Tossing guns into people's garbage in the middle of the night.* She lifted the gun and hastily crossed the street into the safety of the darkness to lean against a lone, large tree that waited for her there.

The small revolver felt comfortable in her hand. She lifted it to her cheek and enjoyed its harsh coldness, its oily smell. She caressed her pretty new gun with her gloved hand, appreciating its dainty size.

Tracy heard the soft sound of shuffling steps and slowly circled her dark form around the side of the large maple tree. A person was approaching on the sidewalk. A neighboring yard light reflected off the familiar hooded green coat of Jared's beloved. Tracy felt the familiar rage swell in her as she watched Christine climb the steps to her dark porch. Tracy didn't try to push her fury down, not this time. Christine's shadowy form stopped at the door and bent down. Although it was very dark,

Tracy could see her set the bright white bag onto the porch before she stood again at the door, likely digging for keys. Jared just couldn't stay away from this damn woman—this woman had a strange power over him.

So get rid of her, Tracy. She stepped from behind the tree, raised the gun, and fired toward the dark green silhouette on the distant porch. Christine's body jerked, did not fall. Tracy ran toward the house and fired once more. Christine's dark form slumped onto the porch as Tracy flipped the gun back into the trashcan and ran to her car. She forced herself to breathe steady deep breaths as she pulled away slowly, calmly. Lightheaded, she drove at a safe legal speed toward the interstate and headed to the big city where night life was much quieter, safer. She couldn't stop laughing. Too sweet really, getting rid of Christine, and teaching Jared once and for all that she wasn't to be trifled with.

Friday, December 4
Jared: Just Once, Don't Be an Idiot

A man doesn't return a loaded gun to its owner by throwing it into a trashcan and texting. Only a cowardly fool does that. An idiot. And Jared was finally tired of being one of those.

As he pulled up to her house again, a light in the house across the street flicked on, then another next door. The frantic barking of a dog energized the entire street as he scrambled around his car. Strangely, the lid was off Christine's trashcan, so the relief was nearly overwhelming when he discovered the gun was still at the bottom. He fished it out and briefly considered going back to the dark porch. He had seen Christine walking on the sidewalk only minutes ago. She'd certainly still be awake in the house. Only, the house was still dark and quiet. Very, very quiet.

A second dog began barking as he hopped back into his car and headed home. He'd already sent the stupid text about the gun being in the trashcan, so he pulled over and sent a second text to tell Christine he would personally return the gun. He would call and set a time to meet her and Donavin first thing in the morning. He'd make it right in the morning.

Saturday, December 5
Christine: Opening Doors at 1:00 a.m.

Whack! A sharp metallic crack ricocheted among the naked trees as Daddy hammered the syrup tap into a large maple tree. Babe neighed, lifted her thick head and shook at her jangling bridle and reins. Christine could hear the kitten's pitiful muffled mews. *Hush, Daddy will hear you.* He had told her not to bring the kitten, the one hidden deep inside the soft safety of her coat. She hugged herself tightly to soften the mewing, to calm herself.

Whack! A second piercing burst cracked at her ears, startling her enough to let loose of the coat and reach for the tied-off reins as Babe stomped nervously. The soft slippery kitten suddenly scratched up Christine's chest, clawed at her neck. It tumbled off the wagon and bounced like a fuzzy orange ball before disappearing into the heavy blanket of leaves and dark undergrowth.

"Whoa, girl. Easy," Daddy steadied the horse. He slipped a bit of apple from his pocket, patted Babe's huge munching nose and cradled a nuzzle to his chest. The metal bucket and lid he took from the wagon clanked as he hung them on the tree's oozing spout. Christine's chest and neck were stinging from the kitten's needle-like claws. She stared helplessly into the brushy darkness where she had last seen her kitten. A full-grown cat with honey-colored eyes crouched among the leaves instead. It tilted its head, Jared-like, then turned and slipped away.

Try as she would to stop them, tears rolled down her cold cheeks and her nose bled with salty slime that couldn't be sniffed back. She wiped at her weeping nose with the sleeve of her itchy coat. Her kitten was lost in the woods far from home. It would die. She was an evil little girl. Her scratchy wool mittens desperately raked at her face to stop the crying, hide her shame.

"Why are you crying?" Daddy had seen. He pulled himself up onto the wagon beside her then lifted her onto his lap as if she were an oversized doll. He quietly held her. His huge callused hands gently wiped at her swollen red cheeks. He kissed her small cold nose, and listened to her sob out her confession as he held her close.

"The kitten will struggle, but it has a good chance of getting home. It will have an adventure and adventures always mean having to struggle to get back home…"

Knocking, knocking, knocking, and she was alone in her freshman dorm room groggily stumbling to the door yet again. It was always 1:00 a.m. when she flung open the door. Why did she always open the door? Someone wanted in. There was a black man, holding her bath towel, part of the flowered set Mother had selected. Ugly burgundy and green flowers. She reached for the towel, thanking him for bringing it to her. Very kind of him. She was reaching for the towel; she always reached for the towel. Don't reach for it this time, Christine. Just this once, don't. Christine reached for the towel yet again just before it was shoved in her mouth, and she was thrown onto the polished linoleum floor. The panic. The pain. The shame.

Hello, Lieutenant Patterson of the university police department, what part of the rape do you need me to explain again? Do you need me to remove the bandage on my neck so you can study his bite mark once more? You took photos, didn't you? Do you want to see it yet again? Lieutenant Patterson let her crochet during the questioning sessions. Always be productive, Christine. Time is life; make your life count. The lieutenant watched her hands with his head at a slight tilt as the hands hooked and looped, hooked and looped in rhythmic motion. He had eyes the color of dark honey, like a lost cat.

It wouldn't make sense for Seth to love her. Not now. There would be no wedding night. She didn't deserve to be his bride, couldn't wear white. A tear fell on the yarn looped on the hook. Christine never slowed. It would dry. No one would notice. No one ever sees dried tears. Hook and loop. Hook and loop.

"Do you know that you're the first black man I've ever

spoken to, Lieutenant Patterson? I don't think the rapist counts, do you? I did thank him for returning my bath towel, though."

"Why did you open the door? Why didn't you fight back, Miss Steiner? Scream?" he asked. Hook and loop. Hook and loop. Hook and loop. He watched her hands, waiting for an answer. Must she share, yet again? He had asked her these questions many times. Why couldn't he understand that she was not allowed to fight? Retribution was the Lord's work.

She watched his mouth move, his unheard words replaced by harsh clipping footsteps as his face faded. The steps were coming closer, down the gleaming courthouse hallway yet again, Jared-like, clip-stepping noisy feet clacking across the dark granite floor. They walked past her as she sat alone on the oak bench waiting for Lieutenant Patterson after the sentencing.

The rapist's sisters whispered as their footstep's turned and clacked back toward her with steady, strong taps. They silently stood over her, watching her hook and loop, hook and loop. Christine smiled up at them, not knowing who they were. The taller sister smiled back, leaned over, and spat on Christine's lap. A foamy mound of whiteness puddled on her lap and soaked a heavy navy stain on her blue skirt. When she didn't move, the second sister spat on her yarn. Christine sat quietly and hooked and looped. It had to be a mistake. No one spits on someone on purpose. It didn't matter, it was only spit. Even so, hot tears fell onto her wet yarn. They would dry. The spit would dry. Her yarn would dry and no one would ever know. Little bits of feathers floated across the glistening courthouse hallway and swirled around her feet. One caught on her shoe and shivered up at her as the sisters laughed and strutted their ugliness around the corner.

Again the knocking, except there was never knocking in the courthouse hallway. Christine forced her eyelids to move, open. The slow, painful dreams resentfully drifted off leaving dark, pouting shadows. Red numbers glowed 12:56 a.m. from the nightstand. Christine lay very still, wanting to crochet again. Shaking away the absurd thought, she wondered why she had dreamt of losing her childhood kitten. She could still see it rolling from her arms and running away, lost. Clover was missing, that's why. He hadn't come when called. Clover worries were interrupted by noises outside her house, from the backyard. From the front, too? Was there really knocking? Yes, there it was again under her bed, at the back door.

More knocking, then voices. She wasn't dreaming, not now. She had foolishly fallen asleep in her bathrobe and her bare feet were ice cold and numb. She pulled herself up and sat, her head reeled in the pale softness of the throbbing red room. Always a heavy sleeper, she scooted slowly, groggy and senseless to the edge of the bed.

Hadn't Donavin decided to stay the night? Why didn't he see who was at the door? Maybe it was Donavin knocking to get back inside with his late night takeout. Her feet stung prickled pain when she stood, stumbled to the window and pulled the curtain aside. Yes, his car was in the back drive, but he wasn't answering the door. There were voices. Harsh red lights pulsed under the trees in the backyard and a siren somewhere echoed a retreat. Lieutenant Patterson was walking around the corner of the garage. Perhaps she was still dreaming. The roof of the back porch blocked her view of the door where there was yet more knocking. She smoothed her hair in the dark, and groped her way out into the lit hallway. The wooden stairs creaked as she made her way down to the front living room.

"Donavin," she hissed into the darkness. "Donavin, are you deaf? Someone's at the back door." No sound from the room. She flipped on the light; there was only an empty couch, a pillow, a blanket, but no Donavin. How could he have lost the front door key? It was in the pocket of the ridiculous old green coat he had worn out the door when she went upstairs to bed. Her mother's coat. It was missing from its hook at the front door.

Christine padded back to the kitchen. *It's one o'clock in the morning, Christine. Don't just open the door like a naïve college freshman.* She flipped on the back porch light and yes, there was a man who looked like Lieutenant Patterson holding his shiny badge out for her to see through the window in the door.

The short female officer with him said loudly, "Christine O'Garra? I'm Deputy Olinsky and this is Deputy Gregory. We need to come in and talk to you. We got a call to respond to this address." Christine unlocked and opened the door. She stared at the black uniformed man with dark golden brown eyes.

The officers introduced themselves again: Detective Reba Olinsky and Deputy Eugene Gregory. They sat at the kitchen table and Christine moved the tissues and April's perfume aside for them. Her hands trembled as she pulled her robe closer around her neck to hide the claw marks of a kitten and the brand of a rapist.

The deputy with Jared-like eyes said, "Mrs. O'Garra, we found a man lying on your front porch. He'd been shot and he's being transported to the hospital. ID on him indicates he's

Donavin Bayer. Do you know a man named Donavin Bayer?"

Donavin had been found lying on her front porch? Donavin had been shot? On her porch! Shot? The room spun suddenly and the voices from the officers became feathery drifts, only swirling sounds. Christine sat very still and tried to make sense of what they were saying. They were speaking too softly to be heard clearly. She sat and watched their muffled mouths moving for what seemed like a long time. Even though she struggled to put their small sounds back into words, and their words back into sentences, their soft humming bounced in her head like fuzzy lost kittens. She felt the hardness of the chair she sat in, the cold draft that flowed past her bare feet. She reached across the table for her yarn and crochet hook. She moved the perfume looking for her yarn. She moved the tissues looking for her hook.

The cold air at the floor warmed slightly and breathed across her toes. The draft exhaled into a wind that blew hot across her feet. Christine pulled herself into a ball on the rung of the chair and watched, numbly, as searing white wind rushed across the floor under her chair. It flew up the wall and across the tall ceiling. The thick whiteness there swirled into a large tight cloud and settled with a hush on the lone chair against the kitchen wall. Liberty's visible essence formed there, larger than she had ever seen him. Liberty watched the people at the table move their mouths, then turned to Christine. He rose slowly and stood over her. He lifted the points of his mighty wings to the high ceiling and stretched them out gradually until they pushed at the ceiling and the towering walls above her. The silvery expanse covered the space over the room and each feather glowed with such brightness that she had to hold her hand to her eyes and squint up at him. Christine's gasp wasn't noticed by her frozen guests. Their statue faces had slowed to a stop—their mouths open, their eyes closed.

Liberty lifted her off her chair and took her in his arms as if she were a rag doll. He sat again and held her on his lap. She settled there like a small child and stared up at his white molten face, a face that was stern, but strangely comforting. She had never before seen the small wings above his ears, and she reached out and touched one. It was warm and vibrated under her fingertips.

She startled at the hush of Liberty's breath on her small face. Angels don't breathe. Nevertheless, he blew softly, smelling of rich maple syrup, feeling like tenderness and peace. Its heat flowed through her nose and into her lungs and poked through to her heart leaving a warm burning. She felt her heart pounding as it sucked at his peace.

The angel opened his mouth wide and she could see words without letters floating there, God's words, quietly waiting until she was ready. They weren't Liberty's words, they were God's words and they came at her in a rush, unspoken, delivered fully and complete:

There is nothing to be afraid of here and it is here you will do your work. In time I will bring you home to a place that has no crying, no pain, and no evil.

Liberty closed his mouth and his hands wiped the fear from her face. She felt the warmth of his smile burn into her like the hot summer sun. He rose with her still in his arms, yet she felt at peace as her body elevated to the center of the room. He smiled at her once more before he turned and lowered her gently back onto her chair. His glow slowed, and his huge wispy form paled and gradually, slowly, he disappeared. The small wings on his head were the last to fade away.

The uniformed voices began sighing out into the room at her. Only small parts of sounds came from their sluggish puffing mouths. They spoke unheard as feather dust floated in the air like a light fog around them. They breathed in the soft whiteness and returned it to the room much less beautiful.

Christine touched her mouth and gently bit at her lower lip. She pulled a quick gasp at the sight of her robe that was now brilliant white, fluffy and warm and new. Had it always been white? She didn't think so, she didn't remember. There was a small feather on her sleeve and she picked it off and held it between her thumb and forefinger. She twisted it slowly and it danced from side-to-side. She could hear Deputy Gregory's low steady voice clearly now. Christine turned to look at him as the feather danced.

He was studying her, pulling details from her face that would lead him. Even though he had placed a recorder on the table when they started, he held a little notepad, his pen was ready. He tilted his head slightly and watched her. He asked questions and watched her fingers twirl the dancing feather. She answered his questions calmly, directly, respectfully. Deputy Gregory's dark hands scribbled her soft honest answers across the pages of his notebook.

And when he asked her if she could think of anyone else they should question regarding the shooting, the first of her morning tears dropped onto her lap, but she answered that question honestly, too.

Saturday, December 5
Jared: Brother to Brother

Jared lay sleeplessly waiting—still waiting. The soft glow of dawn wouldn't arrive for another hour or more. Maybe Tracy wouldn't come. Maybe she would. A couple hours and he could think in the light, the real light, not the buzzing harshness from the lamps. Decide once and for all what to do about Tracy and how to get the gun back to Donavin. *They know I have it. Just call Christine and set up a time to meet, idiot.*

He started at the sudden rapid knock at his apartment door, held his breath and waited for her. Waited for the soft tapping to start again, for it to get softer then louder and never stop. *Tracy wanted to talk.* She had finally come to talk about where he had been last night and the night before.

"Jaden, open up. Your sorry-ass car's in the lot. You're in there, now open the damn door," his brother's voice pounded out.

Eugene here? At this hour? All the lights in the apartment bravely glowed at him as he struggled out of bed and plodded out to the living room. Jared steadied his eye at the peephole. Sure enough, his brother, in full sheriff's uniform, was peering anxiously down the hallway. His head made a nervous jerk and he knocked again, harshly this time. The beaten door bounced rudely on Jared's nose.

Jared unchained and twisted back the bolt, "All right already."

Eugene exploded through the door, shoving Jared into the room. His fist delivered a harsh blow to the side of Jared's face, sending him reeling backward across the coffee table. Jared's frantic arm reached to soften the landing, but his flailing knocked the lamp off the end table with a clatter instead. It rolled helplessly to the floor, shade cockeyed and dented. Jared landed in an awkward heap on both the couch and the coffee table. He struggled to sit up.

Eugene made two strides back to the open door, slammed it shut then thumped his struggling brother back down across the coffee table onto the couch. The veins in his forehead bulged as he stood over him. Eugene thrust his face down to Jared's and hissed, "You stupid nigga. You stupid, stupid nigga. You outta your head? Steal a gun and shoot the guy outside your lover's house?"

Eugene gripped Jared's T-shirt in his fist. "How's that, Jaden? How's somebody get that to make sense?" The brass on Eugene's uniform jacket glistened as he let loose of Jared's shirt with a sudden toss of his hand. "You done fucked up big this time." A small dot of bright red blood grew through Jared's shirt at the battered scab. The stunned and aching Jared remained strangely silent. The inside of his mouth started bleeding again. Jared swallowed it down.

Keep swallowing, Jared.

"Get my attention, Jaden. Say something that makes sense."

Jared blinked stupidly as he struggled to understand any of what had happened in his apartment over the past minute. His head throbbed, the wounds from last week were making a painful return, and his brother was a crazy man.

"What the hell are you talking about?" he dared ask as he gingerly tested his face for signs of moisture. He wiped the drool from his mouth and studied the pink glossiness on his fingertips. His tongue once again began probing the hidden wound now reopened.

Eugene hissed, "What - am - I - talking about?" He stood upright, continuing to tower over him.

Jared pushed himself upright, his legs still sprawled across the coffee table. Eugene harshly shoved him back down, deep into the cushions. His thumb again found the curved wound on his chest. Jared stared up at his brother's fury.

"Stop messin' with me," Eugene demanded then hurried on. "Your lady friend got a body at her front door last night— her boyfriend. You know, your dance student, the guy you stole the gun from at the shooting range. Donavin Bayer."

Jared's head swirled in a feeble attempt to comprehend. "What? Are you saying Donavin was shot last night at Christine's house? Is he okay?"

"Why you get me started?" Eugene popped out. He paused and pulled in a deep breath. Another pause, then the anger in his voice came out more controlled, "The man's in critical condition. Transported here to Indy for surgery. Searching his house now for his guns, but they're not gonna find what they're lookin' for there, are they? You dumbass." The toppled lampshade was emitting a foul scorching stench from the heat of the lightbulb. Eugene quickly bent and yanked the cord savagely from the wall. The cord whipped into the room and fell at his feet.

"I told brass I'd get to hospital and question the man, only he's not outta surgery yet, and I needed to have a chat with you first. So, where's the gun?"

Jared eyed his brother cautiously, considering his few options. "Look, Euggie. You come slam-fisting your way in here yelling, and you want me to talk to you? Just back off, let me sit up and say something. You're actin' crazy." Jared dared to finally struggle his way upright and unfold his legs off the cockeyed coffee table. "And don't touch me. Don't shove at me," Jared said as he pushed the table back where it belonged.

"Okay, Jaden. Let's hear from you. I'll just sit over here and you can tell me all about how stupid you were last night. Go ahead." Eugene sank heavily onto a side chair and fixed his eyes on Jared. "But look, before you start, you understand I have to report everything you say. If I don't, and they find out I talked to you this morning, I'll be in deep shit. I'm goin' have to remove myself from this case and I won't be able to talk to you about the investigation after right now." Eugene poked a finger at Jared as he talked.

Jared worked to absorb this and thought better of sharing anything. Eugene waited; Jared remained silent. Eugene finally picked up a men's health magazine with a ripped weight trainer emblazoned on the cover. He thumbed through the pages too quickly to see anything.

"I'll tell you what I've gathered so far—make it all clear for you. Talked to Gran on Thursday night at supper before you finally showed up. She said you've been sick but you didn't look too sick to me. Just late like always." Eugene eyed his younger brother. "Mrs. O'Garra said you've been sick too. Said she and her boyfriend have been trying to call you at your work. Except you've been calling in sick there, too. All week. Are you sick? Your work is telling people you're out sick."

Eugene flipped to the back of the magazine and studied a shaving cream ad.

"And here's something else interesting. Gran tells me

you've been driving on Meridian Street. You got Gran in your car drivin' by Mrs. O'Garra's house twice every Sunday, some on weekdays. Funny thing though, Meridian's not on the way to the grocery, not on the way to doctor's…bro, it's outta the way no matter where you're going." The magazine pages nervously rustled. "And you wanna hear what Gran tells me she read outta your notebook? The one you leave in your car?"

Jared scooted himself to the far corner of the couch, gripped a defenseless pillow. He patted at it. He smoothed the soft tufts of fuzzy nap so it lay smooth and shiny. It became wet velvet under his hand.

"The way Gran tells it, you're pretty gone over some woman. She says you writing about ways to get hold of some gal named Cog and ways to get rid of some D. guy. Cog. Cog's a pretty funny name for a girl. I just laughed about it on Thursday thinking it was pretty funny you finally went sloppy over a girl. A girl named Cog. Gran wasn't laughing, though. She's saying Cog is somebody else's woman." Eugene paused and glared at his brother. "We're all talkin' about Christine O'Garra, right? Right, Jaden?"

Eugene jabbed the pointed corner of the magazine in the thick air toward Jared. "Guess what? I'm not laughing anymore." Eugene stared at the ceiling thoughtfully and sighed, "Can't see it myself. That's one sorry lookin' white woman. Not sure she's even right in the head. Moved things all over the table and played with a feather the whole time I'm talking to her." Eugene extracted a small notepad from his shirt pocket and flipped it open.

"Just came from questioning your Mrs. O'Garra about the man bleeding out on her porch. Questioned her over two hours—just now left a squad finishing up a search of her house. Didn't realize she was the woman in your notebook till I put the street name and the initials together." He flipped through the pocket notebook. "Christine O'Garra and Donavin Bayer. C.O'G. and D. The clincher was at the end though, when your lady tells us that she and Mr. Bayer took up dance lessons at a place north of Indy. She thinks we should question a guy named Jared Garrison who works at a dance studio. Thinks this Jared character might have it in for Mr. Bayer, mighta stole Mr. Bayer's gun."

Jared pulled the pillow to his pounding chest and allowed his tongue to explore the inside of his throbbing cheek. Blood mixed with pleading fear—it tasted like warm melted metal. He willed himself to breathe slowly through the cold tension and looked at his brother. Just looked, tried to listen.

Eugene carefully returned the notebook to his shirt pocket and lifted the rumpled magazine from his lap. Each page was now forcefully turned with a sharp ripping sound. Jared said nothing. He rolled past Sundays and weekdays with Gran through his mind and relived the times he had left her in his car. *The drugstore plenty of times. The florist.* She had read his notebook. He had recorded his ugly jealousy there and Donavin had been shot. Christine told the police that he had stolen Donavin's gun. This couldn't be happening.

What was the point of staying silent? Eugene was his brother—his brother wanted to protect him, help him, yes? Jared felt his face again. *But I haven't done anything wrong. I haven't done anything, and I'm the one who's getting beat on.*

When Jared turned toward his brother with the intent to tell him to go to hell, Eugene interrupted, "Look, Jaden. I could be suspended for even being here talking to you. Probably fired. I'm supposed to be at the hospital waiting to talk to this Bayer guy. Had to park the cruiser there and walk the mile. Had to leave my cell phone there so I wouldn't be tracked as ever being here. Got myself all tuned up on the way over here for this chat. Can't believe you did this shit." Jared waited and watched his brother slump back and study the ceiling again before he continued, "But I'm your brother…first. First…" There was a long pause as Eugene twisted his neck and gazed intently at the ceiling. He pulled his soft shiny eyes toward Jared. "First, I'm your brother then I'm a deputy sheriff." Eugene's arms sagged under the weight of the magazine and it dropped to the floor with a shudder.

"I had to get over here before they come and they will, Jaden. It's not gonna take them long to figure out that their Jared Garrison is really Jaden Gregory at this address. They might not get a search warrant today, but they'll come soon enough to search your apartment, your car, your workplace." Eugene's face softened and he tilted his head slightly as he studied Jared.

Eugene had a distant, tender look—one Jared hadn't seen for a long, long time. They were kids again and he was sitting on the cold floor under Euggie's skinny arm. They were alone. They were always alone sitting on the floor. Just him and Euggie. His stomach ached and he could feel Euggie rubbing his head, hear him singing softly at his ear. A hush hush song. Jared's wet eyes blinked away the rare, haunting memory that lay between them like an embrace of unspoken pain. Eugene's face was normal again, still staring at him. Jared wanted to talk about it, wanted to stop everything and talk to his brother about the cold floor, the pain in his five-year-old tummy, Euggie's bruised arms and face. But he didn't know how, or why, now, after so many years. Jared slowly lowered his hand from the brittle scab on the top of his head and felt his face with his fingertips.

Eugene softly said, "Sorry I rapped on your face. Hope you don't turn me in to the cops or anything."

Jared smiled weakly and shook his head. The pain spoke sharply to him, throbbing up and down the side of his face. "I deserved it."

Eugene nodded in agreement. "You wanna tell me how much you deserved it or do you want me to leave so you can think some things over? Maybe you want to take a little drive over to the lake to let a gun go swimming. Go to the park and burn a notebook or something." Eugene paused then hurried on, "Don't you dare even think about doing those things, Jaden. Don't you dare." They sat together listening to the hum of the heating register. Eugene's words were rolling in Jared's head over the noise, his disjointed thoughts and fears fighting and flapping.

"You have to share everything I tell you, right?" Jared asked. His teeth hurt. The aching teeth leaned against the coppery ooze.

"That's right," Eugene said.

"Okay, yeah. Yeah, I stole a gun from Donavin when we were at the shooting range. That was a month ago, and I never shot it, not once. Didn't shoot anybody, that's for sure."

"So where is it?" Eugene waited then added, "Look. Right now Christine O'Garra is our number one suspect. Lover's quarrel with the boyfriend gets outta hand. She shoots him in a moment of passion. It happens. Except her registered guns are accounted for and they're clean. Clean and oiled up like they'll be going to church. Bullet tests won't match any of her guns, right? What do you think? You think Mrs. O'Garra cracked, snuck across the street in front of her house, and shot her man? Plugged him at her front door?"

"Donavin was shot from across the street?"

"Looks that way. Not a close range wound. Got boot prints under the tree there. Kinda' big for a lady, certainly too big for your lady. Taking plasters and photos about now, I'd guess."

"Christine wouldn't shoot Donavin from across the street. He wouldn't be close enough to hurt her and she'd be afraid of damaging her windows, blood staining the porch floor or something." One glance at Eugene and Jared immediately regretting sharing. Even though he couldn't explain, it was true, and it was something Christine would probably have thought, and said, if she were here now. Eugene glared at his younger brother.

"What's your plan? Say stupid things till you convince me you're nuts or guilty?"

"No. No, but it doesn't make sense. That's just not Christine. She might shoot someone if they came at her, trying to hurt her, but she wouldn't shoot anybody from across the street."

"Pretty sure I agree with you on that. But if your lady didn't shoot him then we're kinda back to the dumbass who stole the gun. That would be you. You stole his gun, wanted him dead, and you was there last night. Right?" Jared remained quiet as Eugene waited.

"The neighbor described a black car in front of his house on Thursday night and again last night. He says that car is there a lot for no reason he can figure. He finally called the Lebanon

Police about a black man sitting there in the same kinda car. Said the car's got perfectly round tail lights. Round, like your Nissan."

Jared regretted not being able to curl up under the pillows. Eugene was right; it would all come back around to him. Raw, fragile fear finally penetrated through his swirling thoughts.

"I gotta go." Eugene stood and turned away from Jared. "Look. I love…" He picked up the rumpled magazine and set it carefully back onto the end table with others, tapped the stack into a neat pile.

"By the time I get back to the station they'll know they're really lookin' for Jaden Gregory. I've got to come up with some excuse for not telling that up front. Could be lots of Jared Garrisons out there teaching dance. Maybe I forgot your fake name. And I'll be pulled off the case and have to agree not to talk with you about the investigation." Eugene paused and watched his kid brother. He finally moved to the unoccupied corner of the couch, settled in and looked at Jared for a long time.

"We'll get you a lawyer and all, but you sure you don't want to tell me what your side of this story sounds like right now? I can help move the investigation in the right direction if I know."

Jared sat up and edged himself off the couch. The room swayed. Jared commanded it to stop. "I need to tell you." He made his way to the bedroom and returned with Donavin's gun. It clattered to a halt on the abused coffee table. They both stared at it silently.

"Is it loaded?"

"Yeah. I bought ammo and loaded it myself."

"How many bullets you put in?"

"I don't know. Six, eight? I loaded it is all."

"You loaded a bullet into each of the holes in the cylinder, right?"

"Well, yeah. All the holes. Like I said, I loaded it."

"Have you fired it since you loaded it?"

"No. No, I loaded it and stored it in the bedroom. Threw it in the glove compartment, but never shot it."

"Okay. Open it and lay it back down on the table."

Jared picked up the gun and fumbled with it awkwardly.

"Geez, Jaden. Keep your fat stubs away from the trigger."

Jared pressed the release button forward and unlocked the cylinder with a click. It fell open and he laid the open gun down. Eugene removed a pen from his shirt pocket and thrust the pen into the muzzle to turn it and lift it slightly from the table. Eugene peered into the business end of the cylinder. Six coppery heads glimmered, two chambers were dark. He leaned over and sniffed at the gun.

"Two rounds spent, and recently. You didn't shoot this gun last night, you swear on those ashes of Granddad's? You swear you didn't?"

"I swear." Jared stared at the gun as if it were a snake.

"If you lying to me, I swear I'll make you eat those ashes. I swear I will." The thought made Jared sink back onto the couch.

"Was the gun out of your sight? Off your person? Outta this apartment last night? Ever?"

Jared nodded. "Yeah, I threw it in Christine's trashcan and left, then went back and got it again so I could return it to them in person."

Eugene rolled his eyes and settled them back on Jared

with a shake of his head.

"We both know this gun was used to shoot Mr. Bayer, and you're ready to tell me what you know, I see that. Only not here, and not now and not with me. I'll call this in and explain best I can and the sheriff's deputies will be here in thirty minutes, likely less. You let them in, and let them find that gun right there. You don't touch it again. You let them search everything too. Your apartment, your car, everything." Eugene suddenly stopped his litany.

"You don't have drugs in here, do you?"

"Of course not. I don't use any more. You know that," Jared's frustration sputtered out.

"Well, thank God for that at least. Now look, you only answer the questions they ask; don't run your mouth. They'll be recording everything you say. I'll call in and they'll be here, okay?" Eugene stood and paced the length of the room then quickly returned and thrust his finger toward Jared.

"And don't you leave here. You don't need to be getting yourself into any more trouble, so don't you go anywhere, ya hear? And don't touch that gun. There just might still be DNA or prints on it from whoever shot it last night, so don't touch it."

Eugene studied Jared who still sat swallowed up on the couch. "God, you beat all. Just when I thought you'd cleaned yourself up and now this. I can already hear Claire with her 'I told you so's'…and what are we gonna tell Gran?"

Eugene fumbled for his cell phone but found an empty pocket. "I got to get over to the hospital. I'll make the call and they'll be here, okay? And I'll work on getting you a lawyer." He turned without waiting for a response.

Even though Jared nodded painfully as the door slammed,

his thoughts were not reviewing the words Eugene left hanging in the room. He hadn't heard many of them; his thoughts were, as always, with Christine. Christine was alone, and afraid, and she thought he had shot Donavin.

Saturday, December 5
Christine: Burning Anger

The last of the sheriff's detectives and the lone Lebanon police officer had finally left, and their search had been thorough, very thorough. Although they had made an attempt to put things back as originally stored, Christine walked from room to room and saw a great deal of work was needed to make things right. Her clothing needed to be refolded, her canned goods realigned, the books shelved in proper order, the area rugs centered. Every room had been inspected, every closet unpacked, the contents of every drawer and container examined. And so it was that Christine's small suitcase had been pulled out and pawed through by a stranger. She had sat on Seth's leather couch watching the detective. His questioning eyes darted at her as he examined the battered candle, the tattered washcloth, Seth's sad ripped letter. He had lain each item cautiously aside, as she herself had done so many times. Trash—carefully stored garbage.

Christine had asked the detective to leave the suitcase out so there it sat, lid open against the closed closet door. Christine could see the burgundy and green flowered washcloth peeking out from the top. It had always been ugly, even when new. Christine had never felt so weary, not tired—weary. She sank on Seth's couch and stared at the suitcase.

I love you, Christine.

Christine's first response was to push the voice away—God's voice, God's message. Only, she couldn't ignore the overwhelming feeling of being loved, even in the middle of yet another heartbreak. She reflected on the arms of His servant, the rushing wind, the heat of Liberty's face, his wings, his breath and the words in his mouth.

You know I love you.

"Yes, Lord, I know. But…now Donavin…and Jared… Jared is lost too. I've accomplished nothing by loving people, by caring. Why should I keep trying?" Christine dropped her fist to the armrest and pounded it softly as she begged out her request, "I just want to come home now. I want to live forever but not here, not like this."

Everyone lives forever. You will do so in peace, because you have accepted My Gift and there is no sin here. Every person's cry, every moan, every sigh, through history has been paid for and taken away. You will be here in time. Get rid of the anger. Give yourself freedom, Christine.

"But if I had been more honest with Jared, more clear, he might not have done this. Now he's going to spend his life in prison. And Donavin. He and I should be having coffee right now. Instead, he's lying in the hospital. If he dies, it's because of me."

No, not even I would prevent this hurt. People are not My puppets, not My toys—they are children who make choic-

es. Hurtful, ugly choices. I want you to make a choice toward peace because I love you.

Christine approached the suitcase and knelt beside it. She twisted against the urge to shove it back into the darkness. Finally, she made her way to the kitchen where she found a book of matches. She slipped on a coat from the kitchen closet, wishing she had her mother's coat, the one now at the hospital, or more likely stuffed into a clear plastic bag at the sheriff's office.

It had been a very busy morning, yet it was still very early, and crisp cold. Christine shoved several folds of newspaper under her arm and carried her burden to the snow-covered backyard. The stars shone brightly against the dark morning sky. It didn't take long for the dancing flames to melt the candle. The dripping wax helped the rest of the process along. The flames quickly consumed Seth's letter and journal. Moments later, April's school and medical records became ash. The washcloth, however, coughed out billows of angry smoke before finally yielding to the blaze and curling into a brittle mass of nothingness. Christine sat on an upside down bucket and watched the collection withdraw, gasp, and collapse. She poked at the final flicks of red. Grey ashes puffed out from under her boot as the hurt yielded with soft hushed whispers. A corrosive smell rose as she poured a bucket of ice cold water on the remains and returned to the cheerful light coming from her home.

No more bitterness, no more holding onto hurt. Christine felt a fresh resolve—a new energy that she would nourish and allow to grow and use. A calmness. A peace.

Saturday, December 5
Tracy: Looking for Death

Although the bookstore wouldn't be open for hours, Tracy had work to do. She tossed a bloated trash bag, catapult-like, into the dumpster on the way through the back parking lot. She sighed heavily at the thought of losing her pink coat. A lot of memories had been made in that coat. Tracy was cheered, though, knowing that new, exciting memories would begin today—the date of her first murder. The darkness enfolded the fast shadow of a retreating cat as her desk light flickered on. She was looking forward to reading all about the shooting in sleepy little Lebanon, Indiana. Not finding what she expected in the live broadcast headlines, Tracy hurriedly scrolled through the newsfeed, frustrated that the shooting of Christine O'Garra wasn't easily found. She finally returned to the top of the front page to start again more slowly. Surely the shooting of a prominent member of the small town of Lebanon would make the news. There was a story on a shooting in Lebanon—the victim was some guy named Bayer, transported to the hospital in serious condition. It was the address that finally jumped out at her: Meridian Street in Lebanon. *Damn.*

She pulled at her long brown hair and several strands of it floated down onto her naked black keyboard. She had shot some guy named Donavin Bayer. This is the kind of thing that happened when she didn't follow the plan—stupid things. She trembled with rage. The glow of her cigarette rested briefly on her arm. She closed her eyes and breathed in deeply. *Okay, calm down and so what? So what.* No one could tie it to her. No prints. No motive even. Less so now than if it had been Christine. Who was this guy? He had been outside Christine's house, on her porch trying to get inside. Tracy Googled "Donavin Bayer" and several photos of the thin man who had hugged on Christine at the gala popped up. He was probably Christine's new dance lesson partner, the man she had seen driving off in the flashy silver Lexus. A late night lover running around in a woman's coat. Geez. People are so weird.

Jared had motive. Christine could have done it, too. Sweet Christine could be convicted of murder. Tracy was suddenly smiling. Sweet possibilities rolled through her mind on the ways this unusual mess could play out. She reread the article carefully, slowly absorbing each detail. There was a very remote chance that the police would interview her and ask her what she knew about the lovers and about Jared. It was doubtful the police would be able to link her to the shooting. Nevertheless, it was best to be prepared.

Jared would certainly be questioned. Poor lamb. Poor little black lamb. Tracy envisioned him anguishing over the news this morning—likely right now. That emotionally-driven brain of his was a little slow, but he wasn't stupid. Jared would be able to see to the end. He'd be charged with the shooting, perhaps murder, and he wouldn't have an alibi. The only prints on the gun left in the trash would be his, smudged perhaps, but his. He had been dancing with Christine, stalking Christine, writing about Christine. Jared had been seen many times kissing on his precious Christine. Tracy pulled on her cigarette and tapped it at her forearm again. Damn, why hadn't it been Christine in that coat? Tracy shook the regret away. The police will think Jared shot Donavin. Jared shooting Christine's lover seemed reasonable, a bit cliché, but reasonable.

They'd search his apartment. Who knows what goofy lovesick evidence they'd find there to strengthen their case of a young man's jealous fit of rage pulling a trigger on Meridian Street. Tracy hated the thought of losing Jared to prison after carefully developing her plans for him. He would have been an excellent escort for paying customers. Sometimes plans must change. Besides, Jared was being far too difficult. Unpredictable. And there was always Kyle. Inferior product, but easy. Most importantly, she had won in the end; she controlled Jared, sent him off to prison for being bad, for leaving her. She had told him; she had warned him.

The police might search the dance studio. Tracy cringed as she looked up at the wire that slithered up the wall and into the dance studio's instructors' lounge. They probably wouldn't see the microphone in the ceiling tile of the lounge. Regardless, she needed to get rid of it. Be smart and certain. She removed her shoes and shoved a chair against the wall. Just yanking at it wouldn't work—it was wired tight. She'd have to borrow the pool supply store's ladder later, then work quickly to get rid of the wire and recorder.

Next, Tracy did what she did every morning; she checked the GPS tracker for Jared's whereabouts. The clacking fingers suddenly stopped. They'd search his car. They'd search his glove compartment. Tracy leaned back in her chair; she had gotten very, very sloppy. The beeping signal was in Lebanon. He had run to Christine. She had probably called her sweet Jared for hugs and kisses and he had complied. Jared always did what women told him to do—always. Jared had run up there to comfort her. Maybe confide in her. Damn, leave it to Jared to make life difficult. She grabbed her keys and headed out the door.

Saturday, December 5
Jared: First House Visit

"God whispers in our pleasures and shouts in our pain."

— C.S. Lewis, *The Problem of Pain*

Jared's headlights couldn't shove the predawn darkness aside fast enough. Christine was alone in that big house wondering why he tried to kill someone she cared about. *Christine thought that. Yes?* He was certain Christine wouldn't have gone to the hospital. Not yet, not if Donavin was still in surgery, or just getting into the recovery room. It wouldn't be a good use of time. That's how Christine would think. Even so, he couldn't keep from looking across the median to examine the cars in the southbound lane, watching for her car heading toward Indianapolis. He did notice two Boone County Sheriff Deputy cruisers heading south just as he slid behind a semi-truck. They'd be at his unlocked apartment in fifteen minutes.

Jared pulled into Christine's backyard driveway behind Donavin's Lexus. He popped from the car and ran through the dim morning light to her back door. The cold, still air smelled caustic. His pounding quickly produced a bleary-eyed Christine who stared at him through the window in the door.

"Why are you here?" Her muffled voice vibrated through the glass.

"I heard about Donavin. I just need to talk to you. Let me in, Christine, please. Just let me in so I can talk to you." His pleading voice cracked against his reflection. He saw the fear in his swollen face, the face Christine was studying through the door. She pulled the door open slowly, it wasn't locked. And for the first time in his pathetic life, Jared stepped into Christine's house. She backed into the room as he entered. He leaned against the heavy wooden door and watched as she reached, without looking, to grab the back of a chair. He had imagined this moment so many times—being invited into her home to talk with her, to talk about questions, and answers, and purpose. But instead, he was here to convince her that he was not a want-to-be murderer, not of Donavin anyway. She sat, slid her unzipped purse from the table and placed it on her lap. The sight of her like this tore at him. He futilely sought for some normalcy. He had to look away from this precious person. The woman he loved.

He surveyed the long narrow kitchen. The room had the feeling of orderly expanse, everything in its place, everything as it should be. There was an open Bible on the table and the bottle of perfume he had failed to find for her. Her eyes never left his as she reached over and pulled a chair out for him. He sat. He sat, and they simply looked at one another. Jared didn't know how to start, where to start, what to share. So he simply sat and looked at her, silently suffering under her cold distant eyes. Blue-grey and hard.

"I just called the hospital. Donavin's out of surgery." Christine's words were strong and calm.

"That's good," Jared said. *Idiot. That's all you can say?*

"Why are you here, Jared?"

Words finally came. "They'll be here any minute. I left a note on my apartment door to tell them where to find me."

"And who would that be, Jared? Who will be here any minute?" Christine tucked the purse a bit tighter on her lap. Her eyes, like stony blue pebbles, were strangely detached. Her voice was crisp and steady, her body held in composed silent dignity.

He blinked at her. He had expected to find her here crumpled up sobbing, helpless, and miserable. He wanted her to need him, to reach out to him. He wanted her to collapse into tears. He was here to comfort her, and yet she was calm, cautious, and controlled. And she had her hand inside that purse. She lowered her chin, narrowed her eyes at him, and waited. None of the words he recited during his panicked drive here made any sense. No sense at all. He had no idea where to start, or what to say to the quiet power that sat beside him. He couldn't get the right words to form in his head, words he had to share. Share quickly. *Talk to her, idiot. Talk.*

A burst of emotion rushed up from his gut. It rolled over him, and try as he might, he couldn't suck the sounds back into himself. He cried. He cried like he had never cried before: not like his grandfather's funeral, or after his arrests, not even like when Tanisha left him—left him and stole his son from him. He leaned over the table and sobbed, shook uncontrollably.

Her chair scuttled closer and he felt her hand on his rounded back. She was making the same hush hush sounds Euggie used to make. Sounds that once came from Gran late at night.

"Stop...Stop now," Christine calmly whispered. "You're going to turn yourself inside out if you're not careful," she said as a mother would to comfort a child.

He was embarrassed that she should see him this way. Broken and weak. Pitiful.

Then he started talking, talking through the pain that curled him over the table as he snatched short breaths through his mouth. He couldn't look at her as he stammered out how special she was and how much he wanted to be with her, all the while knowing he sounded foolish. She sat quietly.

He told her about stealing the gun and how stupid it was. He glanced at her—she took a tissue from a box and wiped slow silent tears from her face. Ignoring the one she offered, he continued to wipe his face with the back of his hand.

And finally he told her about Tracy. He pushed himself back in his chair, stared angrily at his hands that lay open and limp on the table, and told her about the Friday assault and Tracy's plans for him. When he told her how Tracy had sucked his lip and bit him, Christine's hand flashed to her mouth to cover a soft cry. She rested her hand on her neck as he shared the threats Tracy had made. The dead cat.

"I can't believe it. Trying to get me to do what she wants by doing all that and killing your cat."

Christine pulled gently on his arm and put her hand on his wet face. He turned away from her and abruptly stood. "She's sick. She liked doing it and she's not gonna stop." He stood there with his back to Christine, angrily flashing through the things Tracy had done—had gotten away with.

"Come here, Jared," she said. Jared slowly turned and stepped toward her, refused to look at her face. Couldn't look at that pale controlled face. Couldn't look into those disappointed grey-blue eyes.

She took his hand and lifted it to her neck. Jared watched his wet, shiny hand, as she placed his fingers on her neck beside the scar he had so often studied and wondered about. The tiny raised dots stayed white as she pulled his fingers across her pink skin.

"Lots of people are assaulted. Raped. Scarred," Christine

said softly. "It's nothing to be ashamed of. You can't allow her to hurt you anymore." A moment ticked by before he understood. He jerked his hand from her neck as if the scar had burnt his fingers.

Good people, like Christine, hurt by ugly, evil people, people like Tracy. His stomach lurched. He plopped back onto his chair with a thud and stared at this woman he knew so little about. He wanted to hold her, except he wasn't finished talking and he couldn't stop now. He wasn't going to stop. She was silently crying and he thought he should pull her to him. There wasn't time.

"I sat outside the armory last night waiting for her. I wanted to kill her, and I think I would have if she'd come. Nobody knows how much I want her dead. I would have killed her and maybe even gotten away with it. I would have killed her and the baby inside her, if there is a baby. I waited, but she didn't come. So I tossed Donavin's gun in your trashcan and left like a coward, but then I came back for it so I could give it back to you and Donavin. I never used it, Christine. I didn't shoot Donavin. I didn't shoot anybody." Jared hadn't stopped shaking and he fought to control his pleading voice. He curled his arms over his head, and finally looked at her face.

"You gotta believe me. She said she'd hurt Gran and hurt you, too. She's real bad messed up, and I wanted to kill her, but I didn't, and I didn't shoot Donavin. You gotta believe me," his tiny words pleaded.

Christine put her hand back into the purse suddenly and her wrist turned slightly. Jared stopped breathing as he watched and waited. She smiled, and the hand emerged empty from the purse. "I forgot they took all of my guns. I just wanted to

show it to you and let you know that I could never shoot someone who deserves it, either. Don't know why I ever thought I
could." She leaned toward him with those blue eyes of hers.
"Can't live under the power of fear, Jared. We're all in the process of dying, so there's no time for that. Life is all about preparing for eternity, day by day, and there are so few days. Can't
let anger or fear take control." Christine rubbed at his arm and
Jared looked up at her face. He listened carefully. "Best life to
live is one of tenderness and love and it's never too late to bow
to that power. It's the most powerful thing there is."

Christine was studying him. "You look miserable." She
smiled and a gentle single laugh escaped. "It's going to be
okay. God doesn't want you to be miserable. Sobs, and sighs,
and sorrow—it's all sad, but sweet to God because that's when
we finally talk to Him, really talk to Him. That's when we're
ready to hear Him talking back. It will be hard, but it's gonna
be a lot better than where you were headed."

Suddenly, harsh red lights throbbed on the naked backyard trees. Loud harsh voices approached and the rapping at the
back door sounded out the arrival of sheriff deputies.

"I believe we have guests," Christine said. She smiled at
him. "It will be okay. You just tell them everything you told me.
Just tell them the truth, Jared."

"It's Jaden. My name is Jaden," he said firmly. He stood
and held out his hand for her. Christine looked at him strangely
as she took his hand and allowed him to help her to her feet so
she could open the door.

Monday, December 14
Tracy: For Old Times' Sake

The non-descript grey car blended into the sparse traffic driving toward the near evening sun on Interstate 40 just west of Oklahoma City. Tracy's thumb and ring finger were unknowingly pulling on her short blonde hair as she mulled her options. She squirmed and patted the kilo of cocaine stashed inside the passenger car seat. Funny to think how it had traveled east a couple weeks earlier—probably on this same road. Even though the bundle of cash stowed with it would last a long time, she needed to settle soon, just for her own sanity.

She had kept only two of her fake identification cards. One was April O'Garra just for old times' sake. Dead people are easy to steal from. The other was for her new self, her new name: Heather Gregory. Names are important. The baby deserved to have his father's last name. Maybe the baby would be a girl. Shit, girls are a pain. Stubborn and cunning.

Tracy cursed at the half-smoked cigarette in her hand and flipped it out the car window. No sense ending up with a sickly stupid kid because of smokes. "The baby will love me and never leave," she said aloud—an attempt to convince herself. She would never let the kid leave. She wouldn't allow it, ever. She fumed again with thoughts of Jared. Couldn't understand it, how he went back to that woman even after she had told him about the baby. That was what he wanted, wasn't it, dammit? Doesn't matter now—forget the little black bastard.

She glanced in the rearview mirror then beeped gaily as an older model Nissan Altima zipped past her. It had to be going at least eighty-five miles an hour. Heather Gregory smiled and tilted her head as the round tail lights flashed out a brake signal suddenly then sped around a slow semi-truck and into the approaching sunset. There were other Jareds, other opportunities.

Sunday, January 3
Christine: Pulling in Pieces

"Whenever we're afraid, it's because we don't know enough. If we understood enough, we would never be afraid."

— Earl Nightingale

"Yes, I thought that, too…well, this is great news. I was able to visit him last week, except he didn't know about this early release then…well, thank you…I know you're not supposed to let us in on all these details, but you know how important it is to Donavin and me that Jaden be cleared in this matter." Christine glanced over at Donavin who lay on her huge couch like a comfortable lizard. He had his fingers under his shirt playing mouse with the two kittens on his belly. Donavin peered at her briefly then made inappropriate kissy sounds at her as she talked, and she thrust a middle finger toward the ceiling at him. Donavin rounded in a snicker, then winced in pain. Christine stifled a giggle and mouthed "serves you right" at him as she listened to Gran Gregory's parting words, "Uh-huh.…us, too…okay then, thanks for calling, Mrs. Gregory.

Keep in touch. Bye-bye."

"That sweet old lady sure can talk," Donavin said. "Glad she calls, though. We can't get the timely details she can ferret out of Eugene."

Christine pushed Donavin's legs aside on the cushions and sat herself down beside him. Her Christmas kittens launched themselves across her lap and onto the floor in a furious game of fuzz-ball tag. She and Donavin began once again reviewing their separate lists of the growing evidence that was mounting against Tracy, who had disappeared the day of the shooting and had yet to be located.

"Okay, so the long brown hairs found in my trashcan, snagged in the bark of Mr. Zachman's tree across the street, and the little bitty hair caught in the gun trigger all match Tracy's DNA. Her boots match the prints in the snow behind the tree and across the backyards of my neighbors, and her phone was used within a few feet of this house only minutes before the shooting," Christine read from her list.

"And the lab found gun residue on the clothing pulled from the dumpster behind the bookstore—Tracy's bright pink coat, and her gloves, pants, and sweater. People don't throw away perfectly good clothing without a reason," Donavin said.

"A detective called me yesterday to tell me they found Tracy's car in Saint Louis and there's a lot of black and white cat hair on the back seat, probably from Clover." Christine sighed and bit at her lip.

"Well, for me this is more about building evidence that will dismiss the charges against Jaden, not convict Tracy," Donavin said. "I saw Jaden two blocks from your house just minutes before I was shot. He was driving away, Christy. There's no way he could have driven back, parked, positioned himself behind that tree, and shot at me. There wasn't time for all that. No way…" Donavin's voice trailed off. They had talked about this fact many times.

"Well, the judge lowered bail to ten thousand dollars and will be releasing him. Mrs. Gregory said it looks like the attempted murder charge will be dropped. Not certain about the minor charges though, like obstruction of justice. Maybe the judge will decide he's suffered enough, especially in light of what they're uncovering about Tracy." Christine slowed her pace and noticed that Donavin looked tired, his eyes heavy.

"Hey, how 'bout you just lay here like a slug and take a nap," Christine said. It didn't take much convincing—Donavin was asleep before Christine located a notecard and fully settled at her desk.

Dear Jaden,

Jaden, meaning "God has heard." An appropriate name for an honorable young man.

I have prayed for you every day for many months, long before we spoke at my kitchen table. There is no doubt you will experience a full and rich life, one of sorrows, one of joy. Remember, however, that God gives people more than they can handle all the time in order to draw His children toward Him. I trust you will be open to God's leading and His comfort. Take in His strength.

Blessings as you move forward in your life's purpose,
Christine O'Garra

Christine intentionally addressed the envelope upside down as Jaden had done in a note she had received from him. She quietly slipped on her new green coat and skipped down the back steps with a light quickness. She sang as she walked down the sidewalk toward town, "Gott ist die Liebe, lässt mich erlösen; Gott ist die Liebe, er liebt auch mich. Drum sag' ich noch einmal: Gott ist die Liebe. Gott ist die Liebe, er liebt auch mich."

Wednesday, January 20
Jared: She Wore Blue

"Kyle told me she was tracking your car. Is that right? I just can't believe you didn't tell me. Just unbelievable, really." Mavis's anxious words tumbled from his phone into his ear. "Seriously, I was just horrified to hear what the police found on that woman's computer. The video, recordings from our lounge, records of her drug deals and her plans for you—and right here beside my dance studio. Unbelievable. I heard human trafficking charges are being considered. Ghastly woman, simply ghastly." She was still rambling as Jaden pulled his car into the church parking lot for the early evening Wednesday service.

"Look, Mavis, it's great to hear from you, and I appreciate you offering me my job back and all, but I just need a little time to think it over. I'm considering a few other career options. Besides, I'm not sure your students will want to dance with someone who's served time in prison." Jaden laughed as Mavis sputtered in his ear. "Hey, I'll get back with you soon about that, okay. Yeah. Bye."

"Don't you even think about goin' back to that woman's dancin' studio. Nothin' but trouble waitin' for you there," Gran said. Jaden simply smiled as he pulled into a parking spot close to the entrance.

"Oh...there's Miss Hawkins now," she said and pointed her gnarly finger at an elderly woman who was shuffling slowly toward the front steps. "And there's Miss Sharon comin' to walk with her."

Jaden had already noticed Miss Sharon, hadn't looked at Miss Hawkins for a quick second, but he certainly took a long look at Miss Sharon. He kept his eyes on the young woman in a blue coat as he got out of the car to help Gran. The girl's little hat tilted ever so slightly, hiding one of her enormous brown eyes. Jaden slowly rounded the back of the car as he watched Miss Sharon provide her arm to the stooped Miss Hawkins. The delicate pair carefully made their way up the steps to the landing. Jaden finally found the handle to the passenger car door and planted himself firmly on the pavement, leaning into the car slightly to ready himself for his duty. He pulled on both of Gran's arms to lift her up and to her feet. She rocked a bit before she steadied. The process brought a light giggle to both of them and they celebrated their victory in a quick hug. Jaden turned toward the church again. Miss Sharon's blue coat was just disappearing into the church. Gran tilted her head at him and grinned.

"Looks like you'll be comin' to church with me a lot."

Jaden brought his eyes back to his grandmother with a smile. "I think I will, Gran. Yes, I think I'd like that a great deal." He kissed the soft cheek of the most beautiful woman in the world and added, "But not just because your church has girls as pretty as Miss Sharon. Girl lookin' like a blushing bride."

Gran swatted his arm playfully as they made their way toward the steps.

Discussion Questions

1. Christine resurrects an angel from her childhood as a reminder that she should enjoy the freedom of making her own God-guided choices. Is Liberty simply Christine's self-made coping tool or could there be a real angel in her life?

2. In part, the women in *Let Me Lead* take ballroom dance lessons to recapture a feeling of being desirable and valued—and to be touched. How important is it to simply experience the caring touch of another human being? What happens when we don't get that human contact?

3. Each of the three main characters describes the gala from their own perspective. What did you enjoy about experiencing the gala from three different points of view?

4. Christine is twenty-four years older than Jared. What attracted Jared to Christine? Was he really in love with her? Why didn't Christine realize that Jared was experiencing these feelings?

5. Was it realistic that Jared became Tracy's victim in an attack? Why didn't he fight her off, report what really happened, and then press charges against Tracy? How did the reversal of gender roles impact your reaction to the attack and to Tracy's attempt at human trafficking?

6. Did you feel even a little bit sorry for Tracy, or are sociopaths undeserving of our compassion?

7. Jared is extremely caring toward his grandmother and is largely dependent on her for friendship and support. What could have contributed to the fact that he has no strong friendships with people his own age? Where will Jared get support when Gran passes?

8. If Jared had stayed home the night of the shooting and kept quiet and submissive, would Tracy have allowed him to be a loving, protective father to their child? What's likely to happen to the child now that Tracy has fled?

9. Jared's past haunts his current relationships—with his employer, co-workers, girlfriends, his brother and sister-in-law. How can Jared gain the trust and respect of others? Or can he?

10. Christine finally burns the contents of her little suitcase. She'll never again "review the tangible justification for her bitterness." Forgiving and forgetting are not the same, but how are they related?

Bonus Questions
For brave readers who want to dig deeper

1. From Christine's perspective, "April stopped her pain Friday morning." Typically, the term "committed suicide" is used to describe this type of death. Does word choice here matter? Why is discussing and understanding suicide so difficult?

2. Tired of being pitied and defined by loss, Christine moves to a new community to "start over." If you were Christine, would you have done the same? Have you ever "started over?" If so, when and why? How did it work out?

3. Christine experienced a mix of grief-related emotions including anger and depression, but she also developed fresh resolve to use her time wisely by mentoring and encouraging others—especially young people. How does grief reframe a person's priorities and their perspective on life?

CPSIA information can be obtained
at www.ICGtesting.com
Printed in the USA
FFOW04n1312200316
22430FF